D1166679

THE WITCHES OF ST. PETERSBURG

IMOGEN EDWARDS-JONES

HARPER

NEW YORK · LONDON · TORONTO · SYDNEY

THE
WITCHES
OF
ST. PETERSBURG

a novel

HARPER

P.S.™ is a trademark of HarperCollins Publishers.

THE WITCHES OF ST. PETERSBURG. Copyright © 2019 by Imogen Edwards-Jones. All rights reserved. Printed in the United States of America. No part of this book may be used or reproduced in any manner whatsoever without written permission except in the case of brief quotations embodied in critical articles and reviews. For information, address HarperCollins Publishers, 195 Broadway, New York, NY 10007.

HarperCollins books may be purchased for educational, business, or sales promotional use. For information, please email the Special Markets Department at SPsales@harpercollins.com.

FIRST EDITION

Designed by Jamie Lynn Kerner
Title page photograph by Corrado Baratta/Shutterstock

Library of Congress Cataloging-in-Publication Data has been applied for.

ISBN 978-0-06-284851-2

19 20 21 22 23 LSC 10 9 8 7 6 5 4 3 2 1

FOR KATYA GALITZINE
I could not have done this without you.

AND NIKOLAI ANTONOV
(In Memoriam)

Rasputin is a vessel like Pandora's Box, which contains all the vices, crimes and filth of the Russian people. Should the vessel be broken we will see its dreadful contents spill themselves across Russia.

PAPUS, OCCULTIST AND FOUNDER OF THE MARTINIST ORDER, 1905

I will set my face against anyone who turns to mediums and spiritists to prostitute themselves by following them, and I will cut them off from their people.

LEVITICUS 20:6

THE WITCHES OF ST. PETERSBURG

CAST OF CHARACTERS

Grand Duchess Militza Nikolayevna—second eldest daughter of King Nikola of Montenegro; she was one of twelve children, only nine of whom survived into adulthood.

Grand Duke Peter Nikolayevich—cousin to Tsar Nicholas II of Russia, married to Militza.

Grand Duchess Anastasia (Stana)—third eldest daughter of King Nikola of Montenegro.

George Maximilianovich, 6th Duke of Leuchtenberg—Stana's first husband.

Grand Duke Nikolai Nikolayevich (Nikolasha)—brother of Grand Duke Peter Nikolayevich, commander in chief of the Russian army, viceroy of the Caucasus, and cousin to Tsar Nicholas II; second husband to Stana.

Tsar Nicholas II (also called Nicky)—reigned as emperor of Russia from 1894 to 1917.

Tsarina Alexandra Fyodorovna (née Princess Alexandra of Hesse-Darmstadt, also called Alix)—empress of Russia.

Their children:
Olga
Tatiana
Maria
Anastasia
Alexei, the Tsarevich

Grand Duke George Alexandrovich (Georgie)—younger brother to Tsar Nicholas II; he died of TB by the side of the road in Georgia when he was twenty-eight years old.

Dowager Empress Maria Fyodorovna (née Princess Dagmar of Denmark, also known as Minny)—widow of Alexander III, mother to Tsar Nicholas II.

Grand Duchess Elizabeth Fyodorovna (Ella)—elder sister of the tsarina; married to Grand Duke Sergei Alexandrovich, uncle to Tsar Nicolas II.

Grand Duchess Vladimir, Maria Pavlovna (also known as Miechen)—one of the richest women in all Russia.

Grand Duke Vladimir Alexandrovich—husband to Maria Pavlovna and uncle to Tsar Nicolas II.

Count Felix Sumarokov-Elston (also known as Count Yusupov)—married to Princess Zinaida Yusupova, the richest woman in all Russia; father of Prince Nikolai Felixovich and Prince Felix Felixovich.

Prince Felix Yusupov—married to Princess Irina Alexandronva, daughter of Xenia (Tsar Nicholas II's sister) and Alexander Mikhailovich (Sandro); one of the murderers of Rasputin.

Anna Vyrubova (née Taneyeva)—the tsarina's best friend.

Dr. Shamzaran Badmaev (otherwise known as Dr. Peter Badmaev)—apothecary, philosopher, and purveyor of fine drugs; born in Tibet.

Countess Sophia Ignatiev—hostess of the Black Salons.

Philippe Nizier-Vachot (Maître Philippe)—guru and Martinist from Lyon, France.

Grigory Yefimovich Rasputin (Grisha)—man of God, hierophant, and holy satyr from Siberia.

PROLOGUE

FEBRUARY 10, 1911, ZNAMENKA, PETERHOF

THEY HAMMERED ON THE ENTRANCE TO THE PALACE, pounding with their fists. The heavy wooden doors shook on their hinges, and cries of bloodlust rang out into the night.

"Open up! Police! Open up in the name of the tsar!"

Militza stood in the hall. She could hear him panting with fear from behind the heavy silk curtain. She glanced across. His pale eyes stared at her from the darkness. The most powerful man in Russia was finally asking her for help. He'd arrived drenched in sweat, his clothes sodden, his bare feet crimson with cold. He'd come careering through the woods like a deer chased by a pack of hungry wolves, had begged her for protection, implored her, promised her anything, everything—and she could hardly contain her pleasure.

They hammered again. The glass in the windows at the front of the palace rattled. A few of the domestic household, some sixty souls, were now gathered on the stairs, some shocked, some quizzical, some clasping their hands together in terror. All were staring at the doors.

These were dangerous times; there was more than a whiff of revolution in the air and anything could happen. The burgundy-liveried footman went to open the door.

"Wait!" commanded Militza, taking a step forward and raising her hand. She pulled a diamond comb from the back of her head, shook her long dark hair over her shoulders, and partially opened the front of her red velvet robe. "Now," she said and nodded.

The footman pulled back the brass lock and opened the great doors. An icy blast tore into the hall. In front of her stood a seething gang of some twenty or so policemen. Dressed in navy tunics with lambskin helmets, they surged towards her, their breath white and their eyes wild with the chase. The young officer in charge lunged forward.

"It has gone midnight! What in God's name," Militza demanded, dramatically crossing herself, "are you doing waking my household at this hour?"

"Where is he?" barked the officer, leaning in, glancing around the hall.

"How dare you!" Militza stood her ground.

"I am sorry, Your Imperial Highness." The young man withdrew slightly, cheeks tinged with contrition, clutching a piece of paper. "We are searching for Rasputin. Grigory Yefimovich Rasputin—"

"The devil!" someone shouted.

The young officer swung around. "Quiet!" he snarled. He turned slowly back and, wiping his mouth on his coat sleeve, he smiled. "We believe he came this way."

"Well, I am sorry to disappoint," Militza replied, returning his smile, "but I have been here, alone, all evening, and as you can see . . ." She looked down at her smooth, white, carefully exposed skin. "I am about to retire."

The young man immediately averted his gaze. She had managed to disconcert him, but it was only momentary. "I would like permission to search the palace."

"You doubt my word?" Militza glared.

"Witch!" came a shout from the back of the pack.

"He is not here," she said, ignoring the accusation. She stood aside, calling his bluff. "You are very welcome to search the palace of Grand Duke Peter Nikolayevich, cousin of the tsar, should you so wish, but you will not find the dog."

The mere mention of her husband's name called them to a halt. At least some titles still managed to instill a scintilla of respect, fear even, despite the ever-shifting sands.

"That will not be necessary, Your Imperial Highness." He paused, fixing her with a stare. Militza's face was impassive, her body completely still. She had always been an excellent liar. His men's feet pawed the ground, itching for a fight, but the officer was not quite brave enough to enter. "We know for certain Rasputin came this way." Militza stared, a gentle half smile curling her lips. "So . . ." The officer cleared his throat. "We'll stand guard on the entrance to your estate. It is, after all, our job to protect you."

"Protect me, indeed." She nodded, taking in his young face, the blond mustache struggling to cover his top lip. "How kind of you. I shall send out warm refreshments for your men."

"No need, Your Imperial Highness. My men will be quite warm enough."

The wooden doors slammed shut, and Militza slowly closed her eyes in relief, then turned and dismissed her servants. Rasputin waited for the household to disperse before he drew back the curtain. Stepping out of the shadow, he walked towards her, arms outstretched. He pulled her towards him, enveloping her firmly in his embrace. She could feel her stomach tighten.

"Thank you," he whispered in her ear. His hot breath sent a shiver down her spine. "May the Lord bless you." He kissed the backs of her hands with his dry lips, his coarse beard tickling her skin and the acrid smell of his fetid hair filling her nostrils. He looked up. "I shall exit by a basement entrance and head towards the sea. I will trouble you no more." He brushed his rough lips once more across the back of her hand. "I am forever in your debt."

It was now or never, she thought. He had come to her of his own free will. It would only work if he was compliant. And here he was. This was it.

"Stay!" she replied, a little too swiftly. He looked puzzled. "You are cold," she added. He hesitated. "And you must be hungry, starving. We have sweet cakes, Madeira. All your favorite things. Let me warm you and get you something to eat."

"But the soldiers?"

"Many things might have changed, but no one would doubt the word of a grand duchess." She smiled encouragingly. "They will soon disappear to find vodka in the village."

Half an hour later a servant delivered a tray of small cakes and Madeira wine to Militza's private drawing room, which was intimate, filled with many of her most precious philosophical and religious texts; it was rare she entertained here. The fire was well stoked, and Rasputin was lying on her peach velvet button-backed divan, his damp clothes steaming, his small leather bag of possessions lying next to him on the floor.

Militza was at his gnarled feet, gently washing them in a bowl of hot, scented water.

"Relax," she soothed.

"Are they still out there?" He sat up, nervously glancing towards the window. "I can feel their presence and smell their sweat; their blood is up, the night is cold and getting colder still—their master shall not keep his hounds at bay for much longer."

"They wouldn't dare. You are safe here."

"Safe?" He snorted. "None of us is safe, my dear, not anymore."

"What happened to your shoes?" she asked, wringing out the cloth and letting the warm water trickle between his toes. The sweet smell of Indian sandalwood rose up in the vapors and began to fill the air.

"I lost them somewhere in the forest. I took my boots off on the train and didn't have time to get them on again before I saw them at the station. I had to leap from a moving train to get away from those bastards! They mean to banish me from the city. Me? From the city. My city!" He laughed. "Little do they know who they are dealing with!"

He sat in silence while Militza continued her washing. The severity of his situation had stunned him. He had been utterly unprepared. He would not make the same mistake again. Who had sent them? Who had betrayed him? Didn't they know who his friends were? How powerful he was?

The heat of the room, the noise of the crackling fire, the wine, the cakes, and the gently dripping water wove their soporific charm. Slowly, he sat back into the divan, closing his eyes; his head relaxed; his mouth fell slightly ajar as he lightly licked his lips. He was enjoying the warmth of the water and the softness of her touch. She picked up the bottle of oil again. She had chosen it carefully. Sandalwood: the realizer of dreams. And this was her moment. She could not believe it had arrived so soon after asking. The Fates had indeed been kind. She dried his feet with a towel and then, pouring a few drops of the oil just above his toes, began to massage the liquid into his chapped skin. Her nimble fingers moved adeptly up the arch of his foot, her sensuous touch causing him to moan unconsciously. Suddenly he opened his eyes.

"What are you doing to me, woman?" he barked, retracting his feet. "What wicked enchantment are you up to now?"

"Don't be ridiculous. Sit back and let me tend to you."

"Why?" he asked warily, trying to read the expression on her face. "What are you planning—witch?"

"You, of all people, know better than to call me that!" She laughed as lightly as she could, trying to control the rising flush in her cheeks.

Rasputin leaned forward. Militza's heart was pounding. She could feel the cold metal of his golden crucifix as it swung against the warm flesh of her breasts. His breathing was heavy.

"I've had enough of your tricks," he mumbled, slowly running his coarse fingertip down the side of her throat. Militza shivered again in an intoxicating combination of mounting fear and desire.

"Let me be Magdalene to your Christ," she whispered, staring into his eyes. She could see his pupils were dilated. Was it natural? Or had he willed them to, as she knew he could?

There was a pause. Militza didn't dare to move or breathe—and then Rasputin roared with laughter. He threw back his bearded chin and his large frame shook as his crucifix danced on his belly.

"As you wish," he chuckled, leaning back and returning his feet to the towel. "As you wish, my little . . . bitch."

Militza echoed his laugh with as much enthusiasm as she could muster, and somehow she managed to control her shaking hands enough to continue the massage. She worked hard and deep, moving up his strong ankles and down between his thick, splayed toes. Clearly this wasn't the first time he'd run through the forest unshod. She poured on more oil; her hands were beginning to hurt, but she forced herself to continue, humming gently under her breath. Not long now, she thought. Not long. It would take an iron will not to succumb to slumber. And sure enough, Rasputin's chest began slowly to rise and fall. After a while he started to snore.

At last! Militza sat back on her haunches for a second, allowing herself a moment's rest. She could kill him now, as he lay there, snoring and slack-jawed, exhaling through the blackened gaps in his filthy teeth. She could slit his throat, plunge a dagger into his rotten, duplicitous heart: it would be quick and easy, and no one would need know, least of all the tsarina. She could even feed him to the dogs outside. But he was her creation, her creature, her thick-shafted lover—and she had not finished with him yet.

Quickly, silently, she crossed her boudoir to find the sewing sampler she'd left on the arm of the sofa earlier that afternoon. She lifted it up, and from underneath, she rescued a small pair of ornately carved golden scissors. Quickly, she knelt back down at Rasputin's *feet, and slowly, surely, she got to work. The toenails were thick and difficult to cut, but one by one, she very carefully snipped them off, keeping them as whole as possible, curved as new moons. Only when she had collected all ten did she place them very carefully in a beautiful wooden box.*

CHAPTER I

AUGUST 28, 1889,
PETERHOF, ST. PETERSBURG

RIGHT FROM THE VERY BEGINNING, MILITZA KNEW IT was not going to work. She was like that. She knew things, saw things, sensed things . . . Second sight was what they called it. She saw the omens were bad . . . and the omens never lied.

She'd lit a candle the night before, something she and her mother had always done—a little bit of apotropaic magic to ward off evil. You placed a lit candle in the window to dispel the dark, welcoming in the light and good fortune. But it kept going out. There was a breeze, an ill wind, which meant that no matter how many times she lit the flame, it flickered, guttered, and died.

Naturally, she didn't tell her sister. Anastasia was two years younger and upset enough already, so much so she'd woken up in tears. What sort of bride wakes up in tears on her wedding day?

"I can't," she sobbed, propped up by a pile of soft white pillows. "I just can't."

At the time, Militza didn't know what to do. Anastasia was weeping copiously; her black hair, loose around her face, clung in damp curls to her wet cheeks. Her huge black eyes were mournful and completely piteous.

"You've got to help me!"

"He's not so bad," Militza heard herself lying to her sister. "He's a good match."

"How can you say that? He is sixteen years older than me, he has been married before, and—"

"And he's been handpicked by Papa."

"I've only known him for four weeks. Four weeks! His eyes are cold and his heart is even colder. Oh, God! Why didn't Papa choose someone else?"

"He has his reasons—and he expects both of us to do our duty." Militza stroked her sister's damp hair, trying to placate her. But it was no use.

"I want to marry for love!" she exclaimed, collapsing back on her bed and staring up at the ornate ceiling of the Grand Palace.

The floral gilt border shone in the early-morning sun, the crystal chandelier glittering and swinging a little in the breeze. The opulence and splendor of their surroundings was completely overwhelming.

Militza laughed—she couldn't believe what her sister had just said. "Don't be so naive, Stana! Women like us don't marry for *love*."

How typical of Anastasia! Even when the sisters were growing up in their father's court in Cetinje, Montenegro, running along the narrow corridors of their cozy little palace with its russet walls and white shutters, Anastasia had been the romantic, the one who believed the fairy tales their mother told. She'd listen, wide-eyed, sitting on her knee playing with wooden poppets and planning her own wedding. She'd always fantasized, had always thought, always known, that one day her prince would come. Out of all the sisters—and there were nine of them at the last count—Anastasia was the dreamer, the romantic. Even the Montenegrin belief that daughters were a misfortune seemed to pass her by. She ignored her parents' endless conversations about money and about the dearth of suitors, she was impervious to their father building a nunnery on the shores of Lake Skadar in case he needed to house his ever-growing cabal of useless daughters—and she was deaf to her mother's schemes and plans as to how to rid themselves of so many costly women.

So, when the two sisters were invited to St. Petersburg, at the behest of Tsar Alexander III, Stana was the first to be thrilled, the first to be excited, giddy with the idea of the clothes, the parties, the whirl, and unlike Militza, she was the last to realize the plan.

"Women like us marry for money," Militza reminded her sister. "We marry for position, security, and status, and as we have none—"

"But we are princesses!"

"Of a feudal backwater, with barely an army to call its own."

Stana looked shocked.

"We both know that is true," continued Militza, "and so we have to take what we are given, take whom our father chooses, which will always be whomever he deems useful, who can advance him and our country. And our job? Our job is to produce children. Sons. We're a couple of broodmares! That's why the tsar invited us here. We've been told as much."

"A broodmare . . ." She sighed.

"You're almost twenty-one, Stana! You are not young anymore. You can't have little-girl fantasies of a handsome prince rescuing you from your fate."

"So we're to be sold off for thirty pieces of silver!"

"A little more than that, I hope!" Militza laughed. Her sister did not. "We do not have a choice," Militza conceded quietly.

"A life without choice"—Stana stared at her sister and slowly shook her head—"is no life at all."

"It's our duty."

"Duty to whom?"

"Our father, our country." She paused. "Honestly, it is not so bad. And you hope, you pray, that eventually, over time, you can grow to love your husband."

"Do you love your husband?" asked Stana, sitting up.

Militza smiled. "It hasn't been long."

In fact, it was just four weeks since she herself had been a bride. Her marriage had also been arranged by her father and the tsar. She'd even sat next to Alexander III as he toasted the union between her and her husband, his cousin Grand Duke Peter Nikolayevich.

"I drink to the health of the only sincere and faithful friend of Russia," Alexander had said before placing the golden goblet to his lips. There had been no mention of happiness, or joy, or love of any kind. That's not to say that Peter was not charming—he most certainly was—but the real reason behind the union did not go unnoticed by newspapers.

"It would be unwise to ignore the tender feelings which prompted this celebration," said one. "But it would be foolish not to recognize all the great national and political reasons, which have joined together, in friendship and family ties, the mighty Royal House of the Romanovs of Russia and the modest court of Montenegro."

"The modest court of Montenegro . . ." Militza smiled ruefully. That phrase had made her father furious, incandescent. She turned to stare out of the window at the manicured gardens below. It was such a beautiful day. The morning sky was fresh and cloudless, perfect for a wedding; the fountains at Peterhof were sparkling like decadent glasses of fizzing champagne, and a warm wind was blowing off the Gulf of Finland. She and Stana were young and beautiful; they should both be so happy.

So why did she feel the desperate sickness of foreboding in her throat and the tight knot of dread deep in the pit of her stomach?

Militza dared not look Stana in the eye. What could she tell her? She was supposed to be the strong one, the cleverest of all the children, fluent in Persian, Russian, and French, as well as all the languages of her motherland. She was the one who had the sensible head, the clear vision. Zorka, the eldest, might well be able to predict earthquakes, and their mother could tell the sex of unborn babies, but it was she, Militza, who had the real power, the one who could really see things. She was the one who spoke to Spirit, the one who was headstrong, who had an answer for everything. She was known in her family as a reader of runes and oracles, a sibyl who always found it hard to curb her tongue, so why was she so quiet now? What was she to say? That Stana had no choice but to accept this widower duke as her husband? That marriage was lonely? That she herself was struggling to find happiness? That the wedding night was something you just had to get through?

And she knew her husband, Peter, and he also knew where she had come from. He had toured Montenegro with her, witnessed the toasting and fireworks that greeted their engagement. He'd sailed down the Croatian coast in his beautiful white yacht to stay with her family in Cetinje, had seen their unprepossessing palace, its narrow corridors and wooden shutters; he had walked through their scrub of a garden without so much as a fountain, or a manicured lawn, and they'd traveled back to Russia together to be married.

But Stana, poor Stana, had not been so fortunate. She had met her soon-to-be husband just four weeks before, their father selecting him from the shallow pool of eligible suitors at Militza's wedding. Quite what made the widower, with a motherless seven-year-old son, stand out for their father, neither of them knew.

All Militza knew was there was to be no celebratory cannon fire on Stana's wedding day, no party at the tsar's palace. In fact, neither the tsar nor even their father was going to attend. It was as if Nikola could not wait to give Stana away, at any price.

Militza sighed. What were they doing here, two sisters so far from home? How could their father have done this? She couldn't help but think how cruel it was to be born a woman, how cruel it was to be powerless and unable to decide one's own fate. However, she said nothing, did nothing, except continue to stare out the window and try to quell her own misgivings.

IT TOOK STANA HALF AN HOUR TO COMPOSE HERSELF ENOUGH to sip her tea. She had it strong and sweetened with a little cherry jam dipped in on a silver teaspoon. The maid had delivered a plate piled high with warm blini with soured cream and honey, but neither of them could stomach anything.

"You're right," Stana declared flatly as she licked the jam off her spoon. "There is nothing else to be done. I have no choice. It is either George—"

"Or the nunnery on Lake Skadar."

They looked at each other. It should have been a funny joke: it was something they'd laughed about as children, that they'd end up in the nunnery their father was building. Militza had often declared, in lofty tones, that she was looking forward to a life of learning without distraction. But the older they became and the steeper and thicker the convent's walls grew, the more terrifying a reality it was. How could their father truly think this was a good solution to the problem of having so many daughters?

Anything, anywhere, anyone—even George—would be better than the nunnery on Lake Skadar.

Militza leaned over and took the spoon out of her sister's mouth. "Don't do that. We are not at home anymore."

"Don't I know it! I hate this place! The Grand Palace!" She snorted. "It's like a cage!" Stana leapt out of her chair and walked towards the large open windows. "Why does it have to be him?" She turned back towards Militza with her large, imploring eyes. "Why does it have to be now? I know people are talking. I hear them whisper. I feel them stare. What is that stupid saying of theirs? 'An uninvited guest is worse than a Tatar'? Well, that's us. A couple of uninvited Tatars. They don't like us. They disdain us." Her pretty lips curled. "I'm scared. I'm scared of these big, cold palaces. I'm scared of the people who live here—and most of all I'm scared of my husband. He doesn't love me, I know he doesn't. He can barely look me in the eye."

"He proposed to you and that's all that matters."

"How can you say that?"

"I don't know what else to say."

The sisters sat in silence and drank their tea. The only noise was the scraping of Stana's spoon as she stirred more jam around her cup.

"I just wish Mother were here," said Stana, suddenly putting down her cup and pulling her knees up under her chin. "Both Mother and Papa came to your wedding."

"You will be fine." Militza squeezed her hand.

"I miss our little palace."

Militza looked out through the large open window to the beautifully manicured lawns beyond. "So do I." She added swiftly, turning back to her sister, "You *will* be fine. You are not alone. You have me to look after you."

"You?" Stana's eyes filled again with tears. "What can *you* do?"

"I will look after you."

"Please . . . I am not sure I can do it without you. You've always been the strong one, the clever one—the one everyone looked up to." She grabbed hold of her sister's shoulders and gripped them tightly. "Promise you'll make it all right? Promise!"

Her grip was strong, her pain evident. Militza looked deep into her sister's black eyes. Perhaps it was guilt that fate had dealt her the better hand, perhaps it was instinct, the older sibling's duty to look after the other, or perhaps it was just the raw vision of her sister's shattered heart, but Militza did not pause. She did not waver. "I promise," she whispered. "Cross my heart." She hooked a strand of hair behind her sister's ear before cupping her chin. "Together, we can do anything," she said softly, then kissed Stana's cheek.

Years later, Militza remembered, then and there, that with one small kiss, she had sealed both their fates. Forever after she was obliged to help her sister, to come to her rescue. She'd promised. She'd crossed her heart. There was nothing more to discuss.

"Smile," she said. "You're getting married."

THE WEDDING WAS AT 3 P.M. AND STANA HAD MUCH TO DO. As was traditional, her dress was in the style of the court. Made of white silk, it was embroidered with silver thread, pearls, and a scattering of diamonds around the neck that took her over an hour to put on. Her fine lace stockings were difficult to fit in the heat, and her new lady's maid, Natalya, took an age tugging them over Stana's knees. The lace underskirts were fitted next, to give the dress volume, followed by the starched petticoats. A wider dress, made of silver and silk, was layered over the top. The inverted V at the front allowed the other skirt of finer silver tissue to peek through. Due to the late-summer heat and humidity, instead of a more usual heavy velvet train, Stana had opted for a simple mantilla and veil of delicate handmade Chantilly lace. It was attached to a diamond-and-pearl tiara, her wedding present from the tsar. Fortunately, Monsieur Delacroix was on hand to make sure her coiffure was perfect. A corpulent fellow with a florid complexion and a long, waxed mustache, he arrived amid much flamboyant fanfare, accompanied by a phalanx of flunkies and a fug of lavender. Monsieur Delacroix had been court hairdresser for so long he knew more secrets than the police, more gossip than the servants, but most especially he knew about nervous brides and he never traveled anywhere without a chilled bottle of Roederer champagne. His energy, and indeed alcohol, went a little way to lightening the mood.

"So, have you heard the Grand Duchess Vladimir is pregnant?" declared Monsieur Delacroix, combing Stana's hair. "That's number four or five."

"How fortunate," replied Militza, sipping her champagne.

"That's a lot of babies," commented Stana, staring into the mirror.

"All that money and all those children—and still no nearer to the throne!" He laughed into his round chest. "You know when the tsar was in that railway accident at Borki in the Ukraine last year? When twenty-one people died?" He turned the heat up on his curling tongs. "Rumor has it that neither she nor her husband returned to Russia, or even asked about his older brother's health. They were sitting in France with their fingers crossed, spitting at the devil, hoping against hope the tsar and all his children would be wiped out and they'd inherit the throne! Ouch!" he said, burning his index finger on the hot brass as he pulled a set of tongs out of the gas-fired heater. "I don't think the tsar has forgiven him. It'll be you soon," he joked, pausing midcomb and nodding towards Stana's slim belly.

"Me? What?"

"Lots of boys, that's what every wife needs." Stana blushed.

Noticing the bride's evident discomfort, Delacroix continued swiftly, "The Grand Duchess Vladimir is sponsoring Cartier to open up here. She's just ordered another kokoshnik tiara." He rolled his small currant eyes and tweaked the end of his mustache. "Apparently, they are all going crazy trying to source the diamonds, scouring Siberia! Not that anything can rival her Vladimir Tiara, the one she was given when she got married. That's got more pearls than the Indian Ocean. I think she wants more stones than the Yusupovs, but no one can compete with them."

He worked meticulously to smooth Stana's hair into the two traditional fat ringlets that he placed hanging down over each shoulder. After he had brushed each curl, he then sprayed her hair with a mist of violet cologne from Guerlain in Paris. Finally, he picked up the diamond tiara with the flats of his palms and, careful not to dirty it with his sweat, set it gingerly in place.

"There!" he said, deftly wielding a small silver hand mirror. "Perfect."

Stana got out of her seat and turned to look at herself in a full-length mirror. The tiara, the French lace veil, the silver dress, her dark hair all curled and smooth—she barely recognized herself. She looked ethereal, a princess from a different time and place. She looked across at her sister, whose eyes were full of tears.

"You look beautiful," Militza whispered.

There was a knock at the door, and Brana, the elderly nursemaid the sisters had insisted on bringing with them from Montenegro, shuffled in. Hunched, dressed in a loose knitted shawl, with her thick gray hair plaited across the top of her head, she was an unusual sight in these rarefied surroundings. The refined Monsieur Delacroix took a step back; even Natalya, the maid, left her mouth open. From the coastal city of Ulcinj, one of the pirate capitals of the Adriatic, Brana had been with the girls since their birth and had looked after their mother, Milena, before them.

"Since your mama is not here . . . roses," she said, holding out the tightly bound bridal bouquet. She spoke in Albanian. The hairdresser and the maid were at a loss to understand. "And myrtle," she added, with wide, toothless smile. "The height of fashion since Queen Victoria's wedding, or so I am told."

"Oh, Brana! Thank you!" Stana bent down to hug and kiss her fleshless cheek. "You always think of everything!"

Stana returned to the mirror. The bouquet was the finishing touch. Her heart stopped. The wedding was suddenly real, and she felt sick to the pit of her stomach.

"It'll be all right." She spoke softly to her own reflection, her mouth dry with nerves.

"Be a brave girl now," said Brana, smiling at Stana. "Your mother," she continued, rooting around in a pocket in her skirts, "was engaged at six, married at thirteen, when she was not yet a woman. It took her a full four years to produce. And look at her now . . ." She smiled. "Eleven children." She handed a small blue bottle to Militza. "And another one on the way."

"Open your mouth," demanded Militza, taking a step towards her sister.

"What is it?" asked Stana, doing just as she was told.

"Laudanum." Militza squeezed the top of the glass pipette. "A few drops of bitterness and then you won't feel a thing."

It was around two thirty when they set off from Peterhof towards the Sergeyevsko Estate in an open carriage pulled by six bay horses and festooned with white roses. Militza traveled with her sister, as did a substantial guard of honor all dressed in their immaculate scarlet uniforms. Arriving at the white marble church at exactly 3 p.m., they were met by throngs of newsmen and the official court photographer, as well as crowds of excited onlookers who had gathered from all the nearby estates.

"God help me," mumbled Stana, turning her glazed eyes on the crowds and then back towards her sister. "God help us."

The carriage drew to a halt and the crowd fell silent. In attendance were some six grand dukes dressed in full-plumed military splendor, their golden buttons and epaulets glinting in the strong afternoon sun. At six feet, seven inches, Nikolai Nikolayevich, Militza's recently acquired brother-in-law, certainly stood out from the crowd. His straight nose, intelligent, sharp blue eyes, and elegantly waxed mustache made him a welcome sight in the sea of unfamiliar faces. He smiled encouragingly at the approaching bride.

"Papa would be so proud," Militza whispered in her sister's ear.

"Help me," Stana muttered listlessly in reply.

Stana stood up in the carriage and swooned slightly—the drugs, the weight of the dress, the heat of summer. Militza gasped, as did some members of the crowd. Stana gripped the side of the carriage to balance herself, her white hands shaking as she fumbled. Fortunately, Nikolai Nikolayevich was swift enough to catch Stana before she fell. He rushed forward, pushing aside a footman, slipping his hands firmly around her waist as her legs went from under her. He pulled her close to his chest, and her head fell against his shoulder; she shivered as she tried to control herself. Breathing in deeply, she could smell only the lemon sharpness of his cologne.

"Thank you." Her lips parted in a dry smile. The smallest bead of sweat slithered down her temple.

"Your Highness," he replied, holding her firmly at the elbows. "Do you need a glass of water?"

"No need."

"A little air?"

Stana shook her head.

"Don't worry," he added, turning to address the anxious-looking Militza. "She just needs a moment. You go inside. I will look after her, I promise."

Militza hesitated—she was late, she should go inside the church—but . . . She looked at him again.

"I promise," he said again, holding Stana a little more closely to his chest. "Go."

Militza nodded and turned. As soon as she walked through the open doors, the sweet, sickly odor of incense and lilies filled the air. It smelled more like a funeral than a wedding. Lit by the glow of a thousand candles, the cream of St. Petersburg society were lined up, decked out in their finery, and as they jockeyed for the best position, their diamonds, emeralds, rubies, pearls, gold, and silver silks all coruscated like a basket of wet vipers writhing in the sun. Militza was momentarily blinded by the opulence and gripped her fan all the more tightly as she walked through the church. She heard the conversation dip and felt the glare of a hundred pairs of eyes. Dressed in a yellow silk dress, with a yellow diamond necklace and the small diamond tiara her husband had recently presented to her, she nervously scanned the church.

The first to approach her was the tsar's sister, the Grand Duchess Maria Alexandrovna, who was married to Prince Alfred, Duke of Edinburgh, second son of Queen Victoria. Her diamond and Burmese ruby parure was impressive, yet her little round face was impassive and sagging with boredom.

She yawned gently. "So here we all are, again. Twice in four weeks." She managed a pinched smile as she thrice kissed the air next to Militza's cheeks. "What a horribly hot day." She flapped her huge mother-of-pearl fan by way of a demonstration. "And my brother is not coming. He is in Denmark. Copenhagen. With Minny's family," she added with a little shake of her coronet. "A previous engagement."

"Shame," added Prince Alfred, who looked as weary as his

wife as he surveyed the scene. "It makes it so much less of an occasion without the tsar."

"And your father, the king of . . . ?" Maria Alexandrovna paused very pointedly, fiddling with her large ruby ring.

"The crown prince of Montenegro." Militza could feel her cheeks beginning to flush with irritation. This was not the first time someone had pretended not to remember the name of her country. "He is unable to attend."

"Your dear mother is not here either?" she remarked, her lips pursed, already knowing the answer.

"Sadly, my mother is confined."

"What is it now—ten?" The grand duchess giggled. "Not even the old serfs had that many children!"

"Twelve," replied Militza, her eyes finally alighting on the tall, slender frame of her husband. "Will you excuse me?"

She fled, weaving her way through the rustle of silk and glimmer of diamonds straight to his side.

"There you are!" He leaned over to kiss her. "Everything all right?" he whispered in her ear.

"I've given her a little something for her nerves."

He stood and smiled at her. Dressed in an immaculately fitting red hussar's uniform, with large gold epaulets that highlighted his broad shoulders, Peter had a glint in his gray eyes and a generous curl on his mustachioed lips; he was a charming, ebullient sort who always looked if he were about to tell the most excellent story.

"Good girl," he replied, tapping the back of her hand. "I wish you'd spared a little for me!" he added, with a small sigh as he gazed across the church. "It's quite a turnout. Difficult for a young girl. Well done, you." He nodded, squeezing her hand. "I remember our wedding day," he added.

"I should hope so!" Militza smiled. "It wasn't that long ago."

"Four weeks and five days." He smiled. "That tiara suits you."

"You chose well," she replied.

"Thank you, my lady." He bowed in jest. "I have an eye for beautiful things," he declared, before turning to talk to the guests standing on his right.

"For the love of Christ!" hissed a rather beautiful woman as she bustled in front of Militza. Wearing an overly embroidered court dress trimmed with pearls, she had two heavy diamonds swinging from her earlobes and a substantial diamond-and-pearl tiara on her head. She exuded the ennui of entitlement. "I don't know why we are here!"

"I agree," mumbled her husband, stroking his thick mustache. "Who's heard of a court wedding without the tsar?"

"Can you blame him? I only wish I too had managed to slip away to Denmark. It's embarrassing. Such a dark little shrew of a girl. With no money! And from some god-awful backwater no one has ever heard of. What on earth is George doing? Couldn't he get anything better? Montenegro, of all places. The streets are full of goats!"

"Have you heard they've even brought a crone with them?" added her husband. "A crone! I suppose they can't afford a proper lady-in-waiting."

Militza dug her sharp fingernails into the palms of her hands. How she wished her father had not forced both her and Stana to come here. Even the nunnery on Lake Skadar was preferable to this.

"Ah, Felix! Zinaida! Lovely to see you!" declared Peter, turning towards his wife and noticing the couple in front of her. "Militza, my darling," he added, "have you met the Yusupovs? The most glamorous couple in all of Russia!"

Militza's voice died in her throat as a hush came over the crowd and all eyes turned towards the entrance. Stana and Nikolai Nikolayevich stood in the doorway, the bright afternoon sunshine pouring in behind them. Thank goodness her sister had a little more color in her pale cheeks, but still Militza felt her chest tighten with nerves. Everyone stared. She looked back across the church towards the groom.

George Maximilianovich, 6th Duke of Leuchtenberg, stood dressed in his immaculate scarlet military uniform, complete with rows of gleaming medals and a bright turquoise sash, his back set firmly towards the door. Why doesn't he turn around? she thought. Don't all men turn around to watch their future wives enter the church? Militza looked back at her sister, who was holding so tightly to Nikolai Nikolayevich's hand that her knuckles had turned white. Not that he appeared to notice, he was so intent on helping her down the aisle.

Just as Stana raised her head high to walk towards the priest, there was a commotion behind her. Everyone turned to witness the late arrival of the Grand Duchess Vladimir, Maria Pavlovna, and her portly husband, the heavily mustachioed Grand Duke Vladimir Alexandrovich, younger brother of the tsar. Amid much huffing, puffing, and fan waving, they followed the bride into the church and took up their place just inside the entrance. Militza stared. Loaded down with jewels, a necklace, a *collier de chien*, a *devant de corsage*, a tiara, brooches, and a sash, all made of sapphires and diamonds, the grand duchess sparkled with self-importance as her every facet caught the sun. Seemingly oblivious to the sensitivity of the moment, Maria Pavlovna smiled and nodded to the assembled company, overshadowing the arrival of the bride. She was not a woman known for her tact—that much Militza knew. She filled her enormous palace with gamblers and ne'er-do-wells and was the epicenter of St. Petersburg society. No one could eat, dance, or entertain in the city without her say-so. However, even for the Grand Duchess Vladimir, such an entrance was more than a little vulgar.

"That woman just has to be the center of attention all the time," Peter whispered into his wife's ear. "Dreadful."

More interestingly, thought Militza, watching Maria Pavlovna smile and nod and mouth little words, flapping her fan, Monsieur Delacroix's gossip appeared to be well sourced. Maria Pavlovna's normally angular face had filled out slightly, and her dress was not as tightly fitted as high fashion dictated. She was definitely with child.

The priest, Father Anthony, valiantly ignored the attempted interruption and continued to bless the rings. George and Stana exchanged their vows, he with significantly more volume than she. Yet Stana looked serene holding her candle and barely faltered as she leaned forward to kiss the icon. Even the tight-lipped Maria Alexandrovna managed to muster a small smile on her otherwise sour little face.

When the ceremony was over, George's son, little Alexander Romonovsky, led the procession out of the church, holding the icon firmly in his young hands. He was clearly taking his responsibilities very seriously, for he bit his bottom lip all the way out of the church to Villa Sergievka and the reception itself.

And what a reception it was. One that few, if any, would ever forget.

CHAPTER 2

LATER THAT EVENING,
VILLA SERGIEVKA, PETERHOF

MILITZA WAS SITTING OPPOSITE HER WHEN IT HAP-pened. Why didn't she notice? she asked herself all those years later. She of all people. She might have been able to do something. To have prevented what happened. Or, at the very least, made it better.

The party was in full swing; the feast—turtle soup, pirozhki, veal, turkey, duck in aspic, and ice cream, all served on heavy silver platters—had been cleared away, and a gypsy band was playing. Regulars at the hugely fashionable Cubat restaurant in St. Petersburg, they'd just "kidnapped" Stana, and the singers were going from table to table, their caps out, collecting money to pay her "ransom," otherwise known as their fee for the night. The guitarists were working themselves up into a frenzy, and most of the guests were laughing, throwing rubles into the boys' caps, clapping along in time to the music.

But Grand Duchess Vladimir was not. In fact, Maria Pavlovna

was barely moving. She'd not spoken for a while, which was quite unlike her. Militza noticed she was turning pale despite the yellow candlelight and her mouth looked dry. Suddenly Maria Pavlovna turned, looked across the table, and let out a low, loud, bellowing moan. It sounded primal, as if it came from the very depths of her soul. She stood up with a lurch, gripping the table with both her hands, and the heavy diamond ropes on her *devant de corsage* swung forward and smashed two glasses. The red wine poured everywhere, a crimson stain seeping into the white linen cloth and trickling onto the parquet floor. She leaned forward against the table, using it for support, as she tried to breathe. She stared at Militza, panting through the silver candelabra, her eyes glassy, blind with pain. One of the servants, standing behind the grand duchess, covered his mouth in alarm. Peter, who was sitting next to her, stood up and pulled back her chair. The silk cushion on which she'd been sitting was sodden and black with blood. Those close to her recoiled. The gypsy band, however, carried on playing, and the guests farther up the table continued clapping, as the full magnitude of the situation took a while to sink in.

It was the Grand Duchess Elizabeth Fyodorovna, the tsar's sister-in-law, not Militza, who was the first to react. Renowned for both her kindness and her beauty, she rushed over, pushing various guests and servants to one side, and grabbed hold of Maria Pavlovna by the shoulders.

"We need a doctor," she declared, looking down at the floor. Her pretty face winced. "Right now!"

Finally, Militza forced her way through the crowd of guests, most of whom were rooted to the spot with shock. The amount of blood on the floor was distressing, and with every bellow and moan, more poured out from below Maria's skirts. Elizabeth Fyodorovna snatched napkins and started to wet them in the silver water jug on the table to cool Maria's brow. Maria's face was now completely drained of color and covered in a film of sweat.

Militza took hold of her hand. It felt cold. Maria looked up at her but didn't appear to know who she was.

"You need to lie down."

Elizabeth and Militza each took an arm. Holding Maria firmly by the elbow, they helped her through the party. The guests looked away as they passed. Only when they neared the band did the music finally stop.

The women reached the door in silence. Maria collapsed, and as Militza struggled to pull her upright, she turned back to see the horror-struck faces of the guests. Maria's drenched skirts had dragged across the parquet floor, leaving a thick, wide trail of blood in their wake.

Just then Stana came racing back into her own party, her "ransom" having been paid, shouting, "I am back! I'm free!"

But where was the applause? Where were the rapturous cheers? Everyone in the room should be on their feet! The "ransom" had been paid; the band could play all night long.

But Stana had run into a room in shock, a room steeped in tragedy and covered in blood. It brought her up sharp, like being slapped in the face. Militza saw the terrified look in her sister's eyes. Her wedding day would be forever marred by Maria Pavlovna's terrible loss. Stana and Militza's arrival in St. Petersburg society would be marked in blood. The fetal blood of an unborn baby.

"For God's sake," shouted Peter, stepping forward. "Someone call for a doctor!" He looked around the inert crowd and rushed out himself.

Elizabeth and Militza managed to escort Maria into the yellow drawing room. Within minutes there were servants with towels and jugs of warm water, but there was little that could be done.

The dead baby came about forty minutes after her exit from the party. Fortunately, a sturdy woman from the village with strong forearms was there to help. One of the servants had raised her from her bed and brought her to the palace while they waited for the doctor Peter had sent for to arrive. She'd helped deliver something like thirty babies in the village, and her experience proved invaluable. She dosed Maria with a strong liquor of brandy and herbs to dull the pain, which made the passing of the baby much easier. It was less than four months old—almost formed but red raw. The village woman immediately wrapped it up in a towel and took it away.

The second fetus was, of course, rather a shock for everyone in the room. They had all concluded the worst was over, so when Maria began panting again and arched her back before delivering a dreadful scream, they were completely taken off guard. They had no towel ready, and no one was prepared. The clot slapped noisily onto the parquet floor, spattering the village woman's skirts and some of the silk chintz furniture. Fortunately, Maria herself was completely feverish, so she was spared the true realization of what was happening to her. She was moaning and rolling on the divan, and though her dress had been loosened, she was still fully clothed, for they had not had the time, or indeed the presence of mind, to remove it. She was propped up on some cushions, delirious with pain, covered in blood, but still wearing her magnificent tiara.

After the second child was delivered, the blood did not stop. They used sheets, rags, towels—anything they could find—to stem the flow, but the situation was becoming critical. When Dr. Sergei Andreyevich finally arrived, the Grand Duchess Vladimir was unconscious, her temperature high, and her condition very grave indeed. The loss of blood, the doctor concluded, was most definitely life-threatening. They just had to wait and see.

By the time Militza left the yellow drawing room, the reception was over and most of the guests had disappeared into the night. However, some were still seated in small groups in the grand dining hall, waiting for news. As she walked in, Stana leapt out of her chair and George stopped pacing the room. She could see a few other members of the court turn towards her.

"You're covered in blood!" said Stana as she rushed towards her exhausted sister. Somehow her glorious coiffure, tiara, and silver dress looked completely incongruous after what Militza had just witnessed. "Is she all right? Will she live? Has she lost the baby?" Her questions came thick and fast. The rest of the room was quiet, dozens of pairs of eyes trained on Militza's face.

"I don't know," she said, shaking her head slowly, wiping her bloodied hands down the front of her pale silk dress. "There were two babies. Twins."

There was a small but audible gasp. Out of the corner of her eye a man collapsed into one of the dining chairs, head in his hands. It was Maria Pavlovna's husband.

"Twins?" Stana repeated.

Grand Duke Vladimir Alexandrovich made a small whimpering noise, like a dog that's been kicked by its master. He appeared to bite the back of his hand. No one moved. No one wanted to appear vulgar, crashing in on his private moment of grief. Eventually, Peter picked up a delicate crystal decanter of Armenian cognac and a small glass and walked slowly towards Vladimir Alexandrovich. He squeezed the man's heavily brocaded shoulder, poured a drink, put down the decanter, and pushed the glass slowly towards him. Vladimir took the glass and, without saying a word, knocked the amber liquid back in one. He put the glass back down on the table. Peter refilled it and Vladimir drained it once more. Then, in one swift movement, Vladimir stood up from the table, sniffed deeply, smoothed down his thick, lengthy mustache, cleared his throat, and clicked his heels together.

"Gentlemen," he said quietly before he nodded and left the room.

The remainder of the party took this as their cue to leave.

With the husband gone, the idea of loitering in the hope of hearing any more news suddenly appeared a little unseemly. The two sisters, one dressed in silver, the other covered in blood, stood next to the door as the guests began to walk out into the warm, pale night and their carriages beyond. Some muttered "Thank you" under their breath as they left. But for others the recriminations had already begun. "It's all their fault," mumbled someone from behind their fan. "They shouldn't have come here," declared another. "It's not a good omen for the wedding," added another as she drifted past. "Did you notice they both smelled of goat?"

The doors closed behind them, leaving only Stana, Peter, George, and Militza in the room.

"Do something!" implored Stana. Her face was white. Her eyes were burning as bright as the candles. "Her babies may be dead, but we cannot let her die. Not her! Not the grandest of all grand duchesses. If she dies at my wedding—our wedding—what will they say?"

"I'm not sure," whispered Militza.

"I *know* you can do something."

"What can you do?" sneered George, taking a goblet of wine off the table and draining it. "You're just a couple of peasants from the mountains!"

"I am a princess in my own right!" retorted Stana, turning to face her husband.

"Really!" he scoffed. "Princess of where? Your father's not even a king! The real king was assassinated! Your father dresses like a peasant, your palace is made of wood, and you've barely got a silk dress between you! I have seen your trousseaux; it would be amusing if it weren't so pathetic. If the tsar had not paid out for your dowries, to the tune of one hundred thousand rubles a year, you'd still be rotting away in that one-street town you call a capital!"

"It is a capital." Stana's voice was quiet. "And it is a beautiful capital, with wide streets and pretty houses. In the spring it smells of juniper and you can hear the waterfalls splashing through the gorges of the Black Mountains. The Monte Negro that fell as rocks from Satan's sack . . ."

George slowly put his glass down on the table and stared at his wife. Small, lean, and lithe, he wore his brown hair swept back off his forehead, and his neat beard and mustache covered the lower half of his face. He was certainly handsome and yet at the same time unattractive. His cruel eyes were narrow with disdain.

"'Satan's sack'! I have never heard anything so ridiculous in all my life! Satan doesn't exist, any more than there's a god." George snorted with derision as he picked up a half-empty bottle of Burgundy. "Your father thinks he's moving up in the world, consorting with kings. But you two are nothing! And you'll always be nothing. You're not even pawns! You're two out of nine sisters. Nine! You were going cheap, my dear. A few thousand rubles each! Broodmares! Fresh blood, brought here to replenish St. Petersburg's stock. Just what the tsar ordered! Everyone knows that!" His head wobbled as he smirked.

"You're drunk," whispered Stana, her hands beginning to shake as she sank slowly into a chair.

"Of course I'm drunk!" he replied, pouring himself another glass of wine. "It's my wedding day. Every man gets drunk on his wedding day! It's the only way to drown the bitter taste."

"You don't know what you're saying," said Peter, striding towards George. "You're upsetting everyone."

"Leave me alone!"

"Listen, my friend, I think you should leave."

"Leave!" George sneered. "It's my wedding!"

"Indeed it is. But your bride is very distressed. Let me get you to bed." Peter moved to take George by the arm.

"Get your hands off me!" shouted George as he staggered towards the door. "I'm more than capable of taking myself off to bed! In fact, I can drink more than this and still rut like a ram!"

Stana looked horrified. The color rose in her cheeks, and her black eyes shone with tears. This was not how she and her little wooden poppets had imagined her wedding day; this was not how she'd imagined it at all. Militza rushed over to hold her hand.

"Don't worry. He doesn't mean it."

"Go on!" George goaded, turning around. "Everyone says you're a couple of witches. Gossip says you can call up the devil himself, that you're his daughters! The devil's daughters! With your black hair and your black eyes from the Black Mountains. Well, get out your cauldron, witches! Give it a stir!"

"You underestimate us at your peril!" Militza hissed.

George simply laughed in her face. Militza stared back at him, the blood pumping through her veins. "Now I am scared!" he scoffed as he left the room. "Very scared!"

"Please!" said Stana, tugging at her sister's arm, tears now tumbling uncontrollably down her cheeks. "Forget him. Do it for me. Don't let her die. You promised me. You did. Today . . ."

Militza hesitated.

"You crossed your heart and you kissed me."

"There will be a price," declared Militza, slowly turning to her sister.

"There is always a price." Stana nodded in agreement. "We both know that."

"What price?" asked Peter.

"Don't ask questions," Stana shot back. She turned once more to face her sister. "You heard them as they left. Our life isn't going to be worth living if she dies—"

"Very well then," Militza replied. "Call Brana and tell her to get my things."

THAT LONG, HOT AUGUST NIGHT, THE COURT HELD ITS COL-lective breath. And the fact that the Grand Duchess Vladimir survived to see the pale light of dawn was, according to Dr. Sergei Andreyevich, nothing short of a miracle.

All the next day, snippets of gossip flew back and forth, recounting how the doctor had apparently prepared the grand duke for his wife's imminent death. They'd been spotted taking a late-night walk through the gardens at Peterhof, where the grand duke had nodded repeatedly, tugged anxiously at his mustache, and looked very grave indeed. Come daybreak, when the good doctor returned to the yellow salon to find the grand duchess sitting up, awake, he could not believe his eyes. He never questioned Militza as to her methods—and she never offered up any explanation.

The Vladimirs went on to hold a discreet burial for one of the babies just outside the grounds of the family church on their estate at Peterhof. It was quiet and quick, the spot unconsecrated but peaceful; a young silver birch tree was planted, and the priest kindly said some prayers. But as to what happened to the second baby, the other clot, and who exactly the shuffling old woman who tidied up the yellow salon was, no one ever knew.

And just as Stana had predicted, the result of the grand duchess's double miscarriage was a rigid, intractable frostiness that was colder and more impenetrable than the frozen taiga itself.

For in lieu of any concrete details that she could recall, the Grand Duchess Vladimir simply created her own story, her own narrative, which, rather than placing the sisters at the heart of her recovery, blamed them for her terrible plight in the first place.

"They are the sort of women who could sour milk with one glance," she would say, taking a sip of champagne. "All I can really remember was the distinct smell of goat," she'd declare, laughing uproariously. "Goat!"

"Goat!" they'd laugh. "The Goat Princesses!"

Truth be told, what Maria Pavlovna could remember of that long, white night perturbed her so much she preferred not to think about it at all. It haunted her in the early hours and whispered to her from the quiet shadows. So, like most things unpleasant or taxing, she simply decided not to engage with it. She liked to flap anything disagreeable and unlikable away with a little waft of her fan. It was far better to tell a different tale, much easier to sow different seeds.

And the court of St. Petersburg proved to be the most excellent and fertile of grounds; it wasn't long before the sweet, heady, lemon musk of goat could be smelled in the most unlikely of places.

CHAPTER 3

NOVEMBER 1, 1894, ST. PETERSBURG

IT HAPPENED AGAIN!" DECLARED STANA AS SHE MARCHED into Militza's cavernous red salon on the second floor of the Nikolayevsky Palace on Annunciation Square. Dressed in a dark green skirt with a matching fitted jacket, she flounced towards the crimson velvet divan, plucking her black gloves off one finger at a time. "I was just coming out of the dressmaker's on Moika, and I heard two women giggling, whispering, always whispering, about the terrible smell of goat. Again!" Her black eyes narrowed as she flopped onto the divan and, slapping her gloves down on the marble-topped table, crossed her arms firmly across her chest.

"Who were they?" asked Militza, sitting up. She closed her copy of *Isis Unveiled*, by Helena Blavatsky, and rearranged her navy silk kimono. Despite the late hour, approaching three, she had not yet dressed for the day. While other society ladies had already donned their diamonds, muffled themselves in furs, and called a troika with a bespoke, livery-clad postilion to the door to pay their daily calls, Militza had spent the morning going through a package of esoteric books that had arrived from Watkins, Cecil Court, London.

"I didn't know who they were, and neither did George."

"George was there?"

"He told me I was hearing things, being hysterical, foolish. He said I was making it up. You know what he's like. If it doesn't please him, he doesn't hear it." She sighed, hugging her arms more tightly around herself. "Honestly, Militza, it has been five years—and I thought it would be better after the children. That's what Mother said, didn't she?" Stana's voice cracked a little. "'Have children as soon as possible, they respect you more.' Didn't she say that?"

"Children are power." Militza nodded. "She used to say it all the time."

"All the time," agreed Stana, picking up her gloves and throwing them back down on the table in frustration. "Well, it's made no difference to me. Pregnant within three months of marriage, and with a son at that!"

"Surely George is delighted with Sergei and little Elena? Two children in two years, and one a son—it's more than I have managed." She laughed a little. "Any husband would be satisfied by that!"

"One would have hoped," declared Stana, tugging at the covered buttons on her left sleeve and then her right. "One might have thought so." She sighed and looked out towards the window.

It was beginning to snow outside. Large, fat white flakes were falling swiftly, swirling in the wind, like the flurries of blossoms buffeted by the breeze that the sisters had run through as children in the orchards of Cetinje. Except here the sky was not a bright, clear cobalt blue but a flat, yellow, impenetrable gray.

"It really is truly miserable here. Don't you think?" Stana

asked, looking back at her sister. Her dark eyes were clouded with melancholy. "Miserable," she repeated. She slowly shook her head. "And now winter is coming, again." She gestured towards the window. "And George will be frustrated and angry, again. For no matter how many elegant court dresses he buys me, I'll still not be embraced by the *beau monde*. It frustrates him, you know, our lack of invitations. And as the season approaches, it galls him even more."

"But—" began Militza.

"We are, of course, invited to the *official* events. To the balls. Those numerous, endless balls. But to the dinners, the luncheons, the soirées—no."

"We are not very much either," said Militza, gesticulating to her dark silk kimono. "The rest of the city might be looking forward to not seeing the light of day for three months of parties, but I shall be very well rested!" She laughed dryly. "And now I have little Marina as well . . ."

"How is Marina?" inquired Stana, with a brief smile.

"Growing up fast, she's over two and a half, can you believe it?" Militza smiled, stroking her flat belly.

"Good." Stana nodded slowly, as if thinking about something else. "But the difference is that Peter has his position," she said suddenly, "his money, his status. He has his estates to manage, his paints, his drawings, his books on architecture. George has nothing. He has no real title, no land because his family home was sold to clear their debts . . ."

"But he was brought up in the court."

"With a mother in exile and a marriage no one could speak of."

"The grandson of Nicholas I. His mother was the tsar's favorite child." Militza paused and shivered a little. "Imagine being so close to power you can taste it, only for it to suddenly slip away, it's enough to send you mad. Don't you think? It would corrupt the soul."

"Well . . ." Stana shrugged her shoulders. "I barely see the man, hardly talk to him. I'm like a window to him—I honestly think he actually sees through me." She laughed dryly. "He tries hard not to acknowledge my presence. All he really wanted was a mother for his son. He'd run out of governesses and I was a cheaper alternative!"

"That's not true."

"Then what deal did our father make? Drinking brandy round that dinner table at your wedding?"

Militza shook her head. A heavy silence came between them. It was difficult not to feel that they were both pawns in a game they had yet to comprehend.

There was a knock at the door.

"Excuse me, Your Imperial Highness," announced a butler, dressed in burgundy livery, his head bowed. "Everything is prepared for you downstairs."

Stana looked across at Militza and smiled. Despite everything, an afternoon in her sister's company always made her feel a little better.

They followed the butler's padding footsteps along the marble corridors that led from one ornate salon to another, past high-arched windows with views out onto the square. They walked alongside Corinthian half columns and on towards the immense U-shaped staircase with its sixteen gray granite columns and elaborate vaulted ceiling, with ornate black iron-worked balustrades featuring doubled-headed eagles. Their entire palace at Cetinje could fit into the staircase alone. Still they continued on, through one great hall after another, each more elaborate than the last. The most beautiful was the Moorish room, with its star-tiled floor and carved walls painted in red, blue, and gold.

"Down here," said Militza, lifting the hem of her kimono.

"I remember." Stana nodded.

Both of them had trodden this route before.

"One second . . ." Militza paused as she turned back towards the butler, who was poised at the top of the stairs, his buckled shoe slightly recoiling; he was not a servant who ever ventured below. "When is my husband due home?"

"The grand duke will be home this afternoon," replied the butler, his tone not entirely courteous.

"Any particular time?"

"This afternoon." He bowed.

"Then we must be quick," said Militza. "Come."

DOWN THEY WENT, CLINGING TO THE THIN METAL HANDRAIL to steady themselves, their silk leather-soled shoes slipping a little on the well-worn staircase. As the smell of cabbage and boiled meats increased, so the light began to fade. A few minutes past three in the afternoon, after just over six hours of daylight, it was already dusk below stairs. Oh, how Militza found those long, dark days depressing! How she hated the weak sun, barely able to raise its head above the city skyline for months at a time. She was born of the south, of the land of apricots and almonds, and such a protracted twilight made her listless and melancholy. And with few afternoon calls to make, the sisters could play only so many games of cards, enjoy so many massages at the banya, before those long afternoons really began to pall and they found other ways to amuse themselves.

"Do you have it?" asked Militza, walking into the crepuscular kitchen. Brana stood up. Her pinched face was bound in a tight gray handkerchief, and she reached into the pockets of her long black cotton skirt to retrieve a perfect white egg. She proffered it.

"Freshly stolen?" asked Militza.

"From right underneath her feathered belly," came Brana's grinning reply.

"Shall I do it?" asked Militza, deftly picking up the warm

egg between her thumb and forefinger. Her long fingernails curled around the edge of its shell as she held it expertly up to the candlelight.

"Go on." Stana shrugged. "I am a little out of practice and you were always so much better at it than me."

"Are you ready?" asked Militza, looking at the round-faced lady's maid.

Sitting at the end of a lengthy wooden table in the center of the room, its walls festooned with copper cooking pots and pans, were the elderly housekeeper, two younger housemaids, and Natalya, Stana's lady's maid, who was nervously clasping her hands and licking her plump lips, a round bulge protruding out from under her skirts. She must be six months gone, at least.

"Oh, I'm more than ready, I'm excited, Your Imperial Highness," she said, fluttering her sandy eyelashes. "Honestly, I don't mind either way."

"But you'd like a boy?" suggested Militza, sitting down.

"Just so long as it's healthy," said Natalya, giggling anxiously. "I have heard your mother doesn't need eggs—she can tell what sex a child is just by looking at your belly!"

Militza fixed her with a dark stare. "Who told you that?"

"I did," interrupted Stana. "But my sister is just as talented." She patted her maid's pink hand to reassure her. "She predicted my Sergei and Elena perfectly."

Militza could feel a wave of irritation. Why was Stana always so indiscreet? The maid didn't need to know about their family, their business. Ever since the wedding the sisters had deliberately decided to keep their "customs" to themselves. And although there was an embryonic interest among the more enlightened at the fringes of St. Petersburg society, it was not so long ago that witches were being hounded, ducked, and burnt. Women still had to make cakes and hold "phantom" tea parties if they were going do something so rudimentarily primitive as tasseomancy—

reading tea leaves. So both she and Stana had to be careful to protect themselves. They had not survived, along with generations of other wise women, without the use of their substantial wits. In fact, they had both so overtly and wholeheartedly converted to the Russian Orthodox faith on the eve of their marriages that no one could possibly question their piety or probity.

Militza would have admonished her sister then and there had she not been so anxious to get on. She was worried that Peter might return, and she'd been warned by him before not to get involved with the servants. Quite apart from the fact that it was unseemly for a woman of her position ever to venture below stairs, it was dangerous to tell the servants too much of anything, he insisted. That way gossiping lies.

"Well, let's see, then, shall we?" asked Militza, cracking the egg swiftly down on the edge of the white plate. Everyone stared as she forced her sharply filed thumbnails through the fissure in the shell and pulled them apart. The egg broke and spilled its bloody contents all over the plate. In silence, the maids watched the writhing gasps of the premature chick as it slithered around on the cold plate in its own womb sac. Unable to breathe, its unformed eyes still firmly glued shut, it frantically opened and closed its pale beak as it panicked and snatched at the air. Its puny legs and soft-boned feet skidded back and forth on the smooth porcelain until, eventually, its brief life and struggle was over and, as its beak shuddered open one last time, it died.

Natalya glanced across at the shocked faces of her friends, covering her own mouth with her hand to prevent herself from vomiting. The wave of nausea was immediate. She had not really thought through what she had asked. It was supposed to be a bit of fun, something to while away the boredom of a cold gray afternoon, finding out the sex of her unborn child, but she certainly had not expected anything quite so visceral.

"Poor chick," she whispered.

But neither Stana nor Militza appeared to notice the servants' reactions. Accustomed to such sights since early childhood, they were more intent on finding out the sex of the bird. Militza picked up the flaccid chick and, turning over its soft body, she pressed her thumb hard between its legs.

"Boy," she announced. She nodded down at Natalya's stomach. "Congratulations." She smiled before dropping the dead bird back down on the plate.

"Well done! A son!" added Stana, giving Natalya's broad shoulders a small squeeze.

Natalya promptly burst into tears.

"I really must go," declared Militza, anxiously glancing up at the wooden clock above the large open fireplace. "The grand duke will be home soon."

In fact, he was sitting in the red salon, smoking a cigarette, leafing through a copy of *What Is to Be Done?* by Leo Tolstoy, having just returned from a luncheon. His face lit up as she walked into the room.

"Where have you been?" he asked, getting out of his chair to embrace her. His question was not accusatory, but his eyes were inquiring.

"Just been upstairs to check on Marina," said Militza, with a little wave of her hand.

"But the nurse said she's been out in her perambulator all afternoon."

"Did she?" Militza frowned. "She's mistaken. We have just been up to see Marina." Militza turned and smiled at Stana.

"And what a sweet fat thing she is too," replied Stana.

"Elegant fat thing," corrected Peter, flicking his ash into a small silver tray. "Soon to be just elegant—oh, and extremely intelligent; fortunately, she has her mother's attributes." He smiled. "Are you well, Stana?" he asked.

Peter was extremely fond of his sister-in-law, only he wished she'd spend a little more time in that rented mansion of theirs on Sergievskaya Street, for it was rare for him to find his wife alone.

"Just as well as I was yesterday," she said, smiling.

"Is George still angry about not being invited to Minny's birthday at the end of the month?" he asked.

"What do you think?" replied Stana, helping herself to a small sugared almond from a silver bowl on the gilt table in front of her. "He's known the tsar ever since he was a child, and now the tsarina won't invite him to her birthday party."

"It is supposed to be a small event."

"Since when has the Empress Maria Fyodorovna ever done anything small? She and the Grand Duchess Vladimir rule this city." Stana crunched the almond and stared out of the window.

"I think it's smaller this year. The tsar's not well; he's traveling south at the moment to recuperate," said Peter.

"He hasn't been well for a while," agreed Militza.

"It's his kidneys. Ever since that accident at Borki, when he held the train roof aloft to save Minny and the children," agreed Peter. "I think that must have broken something in him."

"Anyway, George is still furious at not being invited and blames me, naturally," said Stana. "Much as he blames me for all his ills." She sighed. "I'm quite sure I don't know why he married me in the first place. Are you invited?"

"If we are, I shan't go," declared Militza. "I am not sure I want another evening of being stared at, giggled at, whispered about, or almost entirely ignored. I don't know what to tell Father. All those letters and requests badgering me to ask the tsar for help or a bit more money—it's not as if Maria Fyodorovna allows us anywhere near him!"

"Anything to help shoe that barefooted army of his!" added Peter, stubbing out his cigarette. "What?" he said, looking up and catching his wife's eye. "We all know your country is perfectly charming, but the roads are impassable, the peasants don't want to work—frankly, its only use is its warm-water ports. Am I not speaking the truth?"

"Sometimes the truth is not necessary," replied Militza.

"Well, personally, I think you need to make more of an effort," he said, glancing from one sister to the other. "Get out of the palace. When was the last time you went skating, for example?"

"My darling, we are not children." Militza smiled.

"All the ladies skate on the Neva in the morning," he said. "It's excellent exercise. And Minny's in the Crimea!"

So the next day, November 1, 1894, Militza packed the elderly skates she hadn't used since her days at the Smolny Institute and met Stana, just in front of the house, on the English Embankment.

In contrast to the dull, moribund afternoon before, that day was bright and crisp. The snow was dazzling, and the ice crystals that hung in the air sparkled more brightly than the Grand Duchess Vladimir's latest tiara. And the air was cold, so cold it cut like a knife as Militza inhaled. But it was, at the same time, so delightfully pleasurable. After days spent cooped up in her palace with only her sister and the servants for company, there was something incredibly liberating about filling her lungs with little sharp daggers of cold and feeling her eyes water in the brightness.

"Glorious, don't you think?" she said as she found her sister waiting for her by the river. Sporting a white mink hat with a matching muff, trimmed with little white mink tails, Stana looked particularly beautiful in the surprisingly warm sunshine. "Do you have your skates?" asked Militza, shielding her eyes with her black-gloved hands. She too had made an effort with her attire. Dressed in a bitter-chocolate-colored suit, trimmed with sable, with a matching hat and muff, she felt excited and braced for any eventuality.

"I couldn't find mine," said Stana. "I looked through all the pairs we had at home and I couldn't find any to fit. I shall hire some when we get there."

"Perfect. Shall we take a troika to the Winter Palace?"

"I think I'd rather walk."

So they walked alongside the river, up the English Embankment towards the Admiralty, in the bright blue sunshine. After days of gray blizzards, the streets were surprisingly busy. The roast-chestnut sellers were out, their smoking stalls sending curls of toasted deliciousness into the air. The postcard painters had taken up their spots, trying to catch the beauty of the frozen Neva in the glorious winter sunlight. Others were wrapped up against the cold, their heads determinedly looking at the ground as they marched along, focused on the day's business. Occasionally a child would pass by, pulled along on a sledge, bundled up tightly against the cold, arms and legs rigid; the only thing exposed to the elements were their bright pink cheeks.

On past the Bronze Horseman rearing at the river and the giant golden dome of St. Isaac's Cathedral they walked, towards the Winter Palace, eventually stopping at the two giant bronze lions on either side of the Palace Pier.

Below, at the bottom of the granite steps, the Neva was frozen as solid as steel, and all the recently fallen snow had been swept aside into large mounds, clearing the way for skating on the smooth, shiny ice underneath. To the left of the steps were simple wooden chairs and tables and rugs thrown across the ice, creating what appeared to be the most commodious of salons in the open air. The tables were laid with glasses and a giant silver bowl of punch, while servants in scarlet livery, with black leather gloves and boots, were handing around small shots of fruit-flavored brandies and vodkas on the gleaming silver salvers. To the right was a brass band, complete with accordion, playing the sort of jovial, upbeat, oompah music one might hear at a country fair.

Militza stood next to her sister, clasping her hands under her muff, searching the crowd of spinning skaters for anyone familiar. It was difficult to tell under the fur hats in the bright sunshine, but she thought she saw Zinaida Yusupova in a floor-length sable cloak, and next to her was the distinctive figure of the Grand Duchess Vladimir.

"I see simply *tout le monde* is here," said Militza, watching the two women on the other side of the crowd notice their arrival.

"Oh, really," exhaled Stana, following her gaze. "I suppose it was too much to ask just to be able to enjoy oneself a little, for once."

"Let's ignore them." Militza smiled, looking around the rest of the crowd. "Over here," she said, indicating a small hut. "He looks as though he rents skates."

They walked over to a small wooden hut erected on the ice. Inside, an elderly man with cheeks the color of beetroot was leaning on the diminutive counter, gazing at the skaters.

"Excuse me," said Militza. "We were looking for some skates?"

He turned slowly and looked them both up and down. "I do skates for gentlemen," he sniffed. "Ladies have their own."

"Well, this lady has lost hers." Militza pointed down at Stana's feet.

"Well." He wiped his nose on his large black mitten and looked over the counter at Stana's feet. "I'm not sure what I can do about that."

"Do you have anything, sir?" asked Stana, placing her white-tailed muff on the counter.

"Well . . ." He turned and looked under the counter before grabbing hold of a pair of skates and slamming them down on it. "These?"

They all looked at the skates. They were black, old, and well used, the blunt blades in need of grinding. They looked like a pair of workman's boots with metal rods attached. Stana took a small step back and hesitated. Militza glanced over her shoulder; they had an audience. The Grand Duchess Vladimir and her small entourage of ladies were all watching; their smiles were tight, and the sisters could hear the whispering over the noise of the band.

"Perfect!" Militza declared loudly. "How much are they?"

"Three kopeks," he replied.

IT TOOK STANA ABOUT FIFTEEN MINUTES OF HUFFING AND pulling to get the skates on, and even then they were distinctly too big.

"They're enormous," she hissed. "I can't possibly skate in these."

"Of course you can," said Militza, her head high, pretending to take in the view. "Everyone's watching."

So the band played, the silver salvers circulated, and Militza and Stana took to the ice. Within seconds, as they skated side by side, Militza rather more successfully than Stana in her rented skates, the ice began to clear. First some rather indignant ladies left; then a few children were dragged out of their way. By the time the sisters had been around the small circuit five or six times, they more or less had the rink to themselves.

"What's happening?" asked Stana over the slicing sound of her skates as she glided left and right.

"It looks as if everyone is having a break," replied Militza.

"Of course," said Stana. "Nothing to do with our arriving."

"Nothing at all," said Militza as they continued to skate around and around the empty rink. "If we keep going, they'll soon get bored."

"I'm sure they will," agreed Stana. "Although I have to say my feet are killing me!"

"So are mine!" Militza replied, and they both laughed.

Neither of the sisters had ever skated so long and so determinedly in their lives. Their feet were freezing, their breath was landing in small crystals of hoarfrost all over their furs, but still they carried on.

"I am not sure how much longer I can do this," muttered Stana, her ankles beginning to burn.

"I shall skate until the aurora borealis comes dancing up the river," declared Militza, clasping her hands a little firmer in her muff.

It was the children who returned to the ice first. Unable to hold them back any longer, reluctant mothers and governesses released them, scrambling and skidding, back onto the ice. They were rapidly followed by the young couples and giggling groups of girls. The day was too beautiful and too rare not to be taken advantage of. In fact, it was only the old guard, sitting on their benches, stiffening in the breeze, who seemed able to smell the heady lemon musk at all.

At just after 3 P.M., the ice began to empty. The Grand Duchess Vladimir was one of the first to disappear, along with her silver salvers and gloved servants.

"I am not sure I have ever seen skates like those!" she declared as she walked past the sisters. Stana and Militza simply smiled in reply.

AFTER THE GRAND DUCHESS, THE OTHER SKATERS DISSIPATED quickly, leaving the sisters among the last out on the ice. They sat on a wooden bench, untying their skates as the sun slipped behind a cloud.

Suddenly, it was deeply cold, and the drop in temperature was accompanied by a sudden rush of wind. Militza looked up. Flying towards them, at low level, was a flock of starlings, some two to three thousand strong. They swarmed past her and up in the air over the spires of the Peter and Paul Fortress on the opposite bank, beating their wings, swooping overhead, sounding like the smacking of waves or the gentle clapping of applause. They curled up like smoke, spun like a top, flowed like a great river. Militza had never seen a murmuration like this before. They dispersed; they came back together. They seemed to disappear completely and then gather like a large, dark, ominous cloud over the golden spires, snaking around the spires like a giant serpent. They ebbed and flowed, morphing from the shadow of a great black beast into a disparate cloud of nothing, only suddenly to reappear, racing across the river like a swarm of locusts. Once, they flew so low and fast over the ice, Militza could feel the wind of their wings on her face. She closed her eyes and inhaled slowly. She could feel their energy. It made the hairs on her arms stand up. She felt a sudden rush of adrenaline.

"The tsar is dead," she muttered under her breath. "He's dead," she said, turning to look at her sister sitting next to her on the bench.

"Who?"

"The tsar is dead."

"Long live the tsar," replied Stana, staring across the frozen river at the heaving black swarm. "Long live the tsar."

CHAPTER 4

JANUARY 10, 1896, ST. PETERSBURG

IT WAS ON A NIGHT IN EARLY JANUARY 1896 THAT THINGS began to change. There was a significant shift in power. The moment, Militza later remembered, that she and Stana slowly and determinedly, like a couple of well-rehearsed chess pieces, made their opening move.

The Nicholas Ball was the first and the largest of the season. Just after Orthodox Christmas, it was the precursor to almost three months of solid parties and dancing. The balls themselves decreased in size and increased in importance as the season wore on. The final Palm Ball, just before Lent, was therefore the most exclusive, most intimate evening. For a mere five hundred guests, it was the most sought-after soirée in town. However, since the death of Alexander III, there had been no parties, there had been no soirées, no balls, and very few had managed to make the acquaintance of the new tsarina, Alexandra, fresh from her little provincial town of Hesse. No one outside a very select circle had managed to meet her face-to-face.

But tonight was her social debut. Expensive court dresses had been ordered from Madame Olga Bulbenkova's workshop on Yekaterinsky Canal. Bolin and Fabergé kokoshnik tiaras had been unpacked and dusted down, and now troops of hairdressers and manicurists were speeding from palace to palace, trying to keep warm between appointments.

With as many as eight thousand guests attending the Nicholas Ball, with carriages and drivers to accommodate, an early arrival in Palace Square was essential. Not only was the carriage jam unbearable, sometimes lasting up to three hours, but also the flaming braziers closest to the Winter Palace were at a premium for the thousands of coachmen who had to wait around for hours in the stamping cold, braving the arctic winds gusting up the Neva.

"The streets are full tonight," remarked Militza, pulling her white ermine stole a little tighter around her shoulders, gazing out of the window of the carriage as they drove along the embankment. Through the falling snow she could see gangs of shadowy figures trudging along the pavements, bent against the wind.

"Haven't they got homes to go to?" asked Peter, lighting a cigarette and flicking the dust off his sharply tailored black trousers. "Ever since the famine they've been pouring into town. It's desperate. I heard the slums around Sennaya Ploshchad are full to groaning."

"Who is going tonight?" asked Stana, her large diamond earrings catching in the light.

"Anyone who is anyone," replied Peter, exhaling. "Half of Moscow is here, calling on their old friends, begging long-lost cousins for introductions and invitations. Poor old Count Vladimir Freedericksz has never been so popular in his entire life as head of the court! He's had endless provincial souls begging him to put them down on his list. I think he is finding the whole thing terribly amusing."

"Are the Yusupovs in town?" asked Stana.

"*Everyone* is in town, my dear. And besides, Zinaida and Minny are very dear friends. Everyone's saying that it's Minny who's actually done the list, anyway. She and Freedericksz."

"I am amazed we're on it," muttered Militza.

"Why didn't the new tsarina do the list?" asked Stana.

"She doesn't know anyone, does she?" replied Peter. "And she hasn't made any effort to meet anyone. No one has seen much of her since the tsar's funeral, and that was over a year ago." He paused. "That's no way to enter the city, is it? Next to a coffin pulled by eight horses caparisoned in black. It's no wonder thousands of mourners crossed themselves as she passed. It's a bad omen, everyone says so."

"'She has come to us behind a coffin. She brings misfortune with her.'" Stana laughed. "Listen to you, Peter! Talking omens! You've been married to my sister far too long!"

"And the wedding a week after the funeral, with no banquet, no ball, and Minny weeping copiously throughout," Peter continued.

"Was she weeping for the loss of her husband or the loss of her son? That really is the question," declared Militza.

"Your guess is as good as mine," replied Peter, taking another drag on his cigarette. "And then they've been shut away in those six little rooms at the Anichkov ever since, so it is hardly surprising that the Dowager Empress put herself in charge of the list. Alexandra doesn't know a soul. And she never will if she remains locked away."

"My goodness, the square is nearly full," interrupted Militza.

Peter looked out. "I told you. Half of Moscow is here." He paused. "Oh, look! How delightful to see the Vladimirs ahead of us. I'd know that dear discreet little carriage anywhere!"

With their coachmen dressed in their distinctive scarlet livery and their coat of arms emblazoned in gold across the side of their carriage, the Grand Duke and Duchess Vladimir were not a couple who chose to blend in with the crowd.

"I presume she is wearing that tiara?" mused Militza, looking at three freezing coachmen huddled around a brazier. Their red faces were barely visible through their hats, wraps, and the haze of frozen breath. She watched as they passed around a small bottle of samogon between them.

"Of course, she's wearing *that* tiara!" replied Stana, her face pressed closer against the glass. "I can see those enormous swinging pearls from here."

"They can see them in Vladivostok," observed Peter, taking another drag on his cigarette. "What is it with that woman and her jewelry? Why does she have to be so completely vulgar?"

"Monsieur Delacroix told me she's ordered a gondola from Venice to moor on the embankment," giggled Stana.

"Lord!" exclaimed Peter, rolling his eyes.

"You'd think that woman had never seen a ruble in her life!" added Stana.

"Well, she hasn't really, not where she's from." Peter grimaced. "Tell me, where is George tonight? Doesn't he know what he's missing! He can't still be in Biarritz?"

"Isn't he always?" replied Stana, digging deeper into her sable muff and hunching her fur-clad shoulders.

"When is he coming back?"

"I am the last person who's privy to his plans," Stana replied, looking firmly out of the window.

"I can't think what keeps him there," mused Peter. "It's such a dreary little town. Especially out of season."

"Good evening!" announced a footman as he opened the carriage door. His frost-blasted nose poked over the top of his gray coat. "Your Imperial Highnesses . . ." He bowed low, holding on to the top of his heavy astrakhan hat. He held out a sturdy black-gloved hand to help Stana out of the carriage first, followed by Militza and finally Peter.

In front of them the dark red walls of the Winter Palace were illuminated from every window like an overblown Christmas tree. Outside, the thick snow and the cold air swallowed the noise of the arriving carriages, yet as they approached the door, the excitement was palpable, the entrance hall abuzz. Who was here? Who was not? Who had made the cut?

The guests entered the palace according to rank, and the grand dukes used the Saltykov Entrance. Once inside, Peter, Stana, and Militza deposited their coats and furs with the white-stockinged footmen and changed into their silk party shoes.

"Right." Stana braced herself as she handed over her fur. The two sisters faced each other. "How do I look?"

"Beautiful," declared Militza, taking in her younger sister's pale skin, fine nose, and deep black eyes. Even at twenty-eight years old, Stana still drew admiring glances with her fresh face and unusual coloring. "So, we try to make her acquaintance tonight."

"Two or three words?" asked Stana, reaching into her bag, thinking to add a little more rouge.

"More. She may not make friends easily, but every queen needs a confidante."

"Or two!" added Stana with a wry laugh.

After briefly pausing to rearrange their jewelry in the large gilt-framed mirror on the wall, they left the cloakroom to rejoin Peter, and all three proceeded towards the grand Jordan Staircase. Flanked by crimson-coated footmen in velvet breeches, their hair powdered white and stiff with a thick paste, they slowly made their way towards the Malachite Hall.

"I wonder who the tsar will favor with a few words tonight?" Militza mused to her husband, plucking a glass of champagne off a silver tray.

"I imagine it will be impossible to engage in any sort of conversation with dear Cousin Nicky. Every aristocrat in the country will be buzzing around him like flies," replied Peter with a vague indifference as he began to scan the crowd.

"Are we not to be introduced?" quizzed Stana nervously.

"Hush!" Militza shot her a frosty look. "Oh, Maria Pavlovna! How very lovely to see you," Militza said and nodded charmingly.

"Militza Nikolayevna." The Grand Duchess Vladimir nodded briefly in reply, and the three women looked at each other in silence.

Despite her fine fashions and exquisite jewels, the parties, the late nights, and the years were beginning to take their toll on Maria Pavlovna. Her waist had thickened, and her skin no longer glowed, yet her lust for power and position remained undiminished. In fact, rumor had it that she was contemplating converting from the Lutheran to the Russian Orthodox faith to advance her eldest son, Kirill, closer to the crown. It amused Militza to watch the grand duchess's irritation at bumping into them. Her keenness not to be delayed by two women so low down in the pecking order at court was obvious. Maria Pavlovna actively twitched as she desperately surveyed the crowd, searching for her exit.

"Looking forward to meeting the new tsarina?" ventured Stana.

"Meet her? I have known little Alix since she was a child at Hesse-Darmstadt," replied Maria, looking over Stana's shoulder. "Such a quiet, mousy little thing. She speaks practically no Russian at all."

"I suppose it's all happened so quickly, what with the tsar's sudden death. I don't suppose she thought she'd be on the throne that soon," replied Militza, her eyes fixed on the grand duchess.

"Yes," she said, glancing around the room.

"I hear her English is good," added Stana brightly.

"She is virtually English," Maria replied, her eyes closing with a jaded boredom that verged on disdain. "She's Queen Victoria's favorite grandchild and spent many summers with her English cousins."

There was another pause.

"I do think your new tiara is quite delightful," enthused Stana.

"The pearls and diamonds are fashionably large," agreed Militza.

"Thank you." Maria's head swung contentedly. "It was very expensive. *Ma chère . . . !*" she declared loudly at a passing guest. "*Comment ça va?*"

"Sometimes I wish you'd left that appalling woman to die," Stana whispered to her sister, taking a sip of champagne as she watched Maria disappear into the crowd.

They walked along the high-ceilinged corridors, the air redolent with the smell of pine from the festive evergreen boughs overhead, plus the sweet scent of a thousand perfumed candles. Huge floral displays of exotic blooms shipped in from the Crimea filled the alcoves, along with potted palms and fragrant orange and lemon trees. Music, played by string quartets and roaming gypsy bands, competed with the loud noise of conversation. The farther they walked through the marble, jasper, and russet porphyry columns, the denser the crowd became and the greater the heat. Princes, princesses, dukes, barons, diplomats, and government ministers, all dressed in their brightly colored military uniforms, their chests sagging with medals, traded nods and greetings, mingling among the haze of pale blue cigarette smoke.

In the bottleneck at the doors to the Nicholas Hall, Peter bumped into his favorite relative, Grand Duke Nikolai Mikhailovich, fondly known as Uncle Bimbo, sipping iced vodka and talking to the French military attaché; they immediately engaged in conversation.

"Make way for the Yusupovs," whispered Stana as Zinaida

and her husband, Count Felix Yusupov, barged through in a rustle of silk and a shimmer of expensive stones. "Honestly, Militza,
I give up sometimes! These people . . ."

"Don't you feel it?" declared Militza, suddenly taking hold of
her sister's wrist. A powerful pulse coursed through her body and
her nostrils flared. "Can't you sense it?" She inhaled as if smelling
the sweetest, headiest scent, her eyelids fluttering with intoxication.

"What?"

"Look around you." Militza's black eyes darted left and right.
"Don't you see? The old guard are in retreat. The hierarchy is
changing. An era is over. Nicholas is very different from his father.
He is new. He is young. He never expected to come to the throne
this soon. The wind . . . Listen!" Militza pushed her sister gently
up against a pillar. "Father managed to use his friendship with
the last tsar to the benefit of our country, and now that the old
tsar is gone, it is up to us."

"But how?"

"I don't know yet, but I can feel it. Look." Militza proffered
up her right arm. All the thin black hairs were standing on end.

The sisters chose two more flutes of champagne from a footman's heavy silver tray and passed a group of Cossacks dressed in
scarlet coats and dark breeches with a red stripe down the side.
They approached three of the tsarina's ladies-in-waiting who,
wearing their special encrusted diamond-framed brooches with
the tsarina's portrait, were standing near a table of chilled beluga
caviar. The ladies looked across and, flapping out their fans, immediately began to whisper.

Stana took a step forward.

"Don't!" hissed Militza. The women recoiled slightly. One of
them stepped behind a plant as protection. It was clearly amusing
to gawp and giggle at the Goat Princesses from afar, but saying
anything straight to Stana's determined face was obviously something else.

"Oh, at last! I was hoping to bump into you," began a large bustling woman. Her elderly-looking court dress was slightly faded and yellowed around the neck. "I have been searching the halls, looking for you both. I am dying to invite you to my salon!" She beamed, flapping a substantial ostrich-feather-and-mother-of-pearl fan in front of her flushed face. "I'm Sophia Ignatiev!"

Militza and Stana smiled. Everyone knew about the Countess Ignatiev and her thrice-weekly salons, where the enlightened, the mysterious, and the divorced would meet and exchange ideas. It was a veritable crossroads for mystics and healers, a place to discuss radical theories, exchange ideas, and indulge in a little table tipping and some coffee-ground reading. The Countess Sophia Ignatiev's reputation did indeed precede her.

"*Enchanté*," said Stana, holding out a white-gloved hand to the countess. "We know exactly who you are."

"Oh, do say you'll come!" said the countess, enthusiastically taking hold of Stana's hand. "I know you'd enjoy it."

"You do?" asked Militza.

"Oh, yes." She smiled, encouragingly. "There are so many people I want to introduce you to."

"We shall be sure to attend," replied Stana.

"As soon as you can!"

"Of course." Stana smiled.

"You two would be such an exciting addition!" exclaimed the countess, silently clapping her gloved hands together. "I shall send over my card. I am at 26 Kutuzov Embankment."

"We should hurry," said Militza, glancing towards a large gilt clock in a nearby alcove. "It is nearly nine, time for the procession."

THE SISTERS WOVE THEIR WAY THROUGH THE MASS OF EMBROI-dered dresses and brocaded uniforms towards the Malachite Hall, where the atmosphere of anticipation was growing as courtiers, counts and countesses, princes and princesses all maneuvered themselves into better positions. Large palms were pushed out of the way as everyone readied themselves for the arrival of the tsar and his new wife.

"Ah!" said Peter, taking his wife's hand. "I have been looking for you."

"As soon as the tsar passes, we follow on behind," whispered Militza to Stana.

"Are you sure? I think we should hold back," she replied, looking nervous. Not only was Militza asking her to push to the front, which was neither their place nor their position to do, but she was also suggesting Stana parade through the halls on her own, advertising the absence of her husband.

"Nonsense," hissed Militza. "We need to assert our affiliation early. We need to start as we mean to go on."

"But—" Stana's heart was racing. She could not walk behind the tsar and tsarina alone. People would talk. They'd ask questions.

"My brother is here to hold your hand for the polonaise should you so wish?" suggested Peter, reading her mind.

"Grand Duke Nikolai?" Her face lit up.

"At your service," replied Nikolai, clicking his heels together and bowing his head slightly. Dressed in a red hussar's uniform, he looked even more attractive than the day he'd escorted her down the aisle. Elegant, a little bronzed by the sun, and so very tall, he exuded the clean health of a man fond of fresh air. "No George tonight?"

"He's in Biarritz." She smiled.

"Biarritz?" he replied. "I can't think what keeps him there. It's such a dreary little town."

"So they say," said Stana, her voice a little clipped.

"Nikolasha has just come back from a hunting trip outside Moscow. He's got some of the most beautiful borzois you have ever seen. He breeds them," enthused Peter, looking up at his elder brother. "You should go and see them, Stana."

"I'd like that." Stana smiled, offering up her hand.

"It would be my pleasure," replied Nikolasha, gently kissing it.

It was odd, thought Militza as she watched his lips press against her sister's white glove, that a man of his standing should not yet be married.

"Are you looking forward to this evening, my darling?" asked Peter, looking his wife up and down.

"I am a little nervous," whispered Militza.

"I'll look after you," he said, smiling.

The grand marshal of the Imperial Court, Count Benckendorff, appeared and thumped his ten-foot ebony staff, embossed in gold, on the wooden floor three times. The hall fell silent.

"Their Imperial Majesties—the tsar and tsarina!"

The two six-foot-four Abyssinians, wearing exquisite twisted golden turbans, heaved open the great mahogany doors inlaid with gold, and the tsar and tsarina slowly appeared. She shimmered with silver thread and the light of a thousand diamonds and pearls, while he was dressed in a red hussar's uniform, covered in the thick golden ropes and tassels of various orders and honors.

Militza stared at them. The tsarina was indeed beautiful, with her exquisite pale eyes, her delicate features, and her red-gold hair, but she had not expected the young tsar to be so attractive. She had made his acquaintance on several occasions before, where she'd always found him a little frivolous and perhaps a little short, but now, standing within a few feet of her, dressed in his uniform, in his new role of tsar—ruler of the largest and richest country on earth—she felt the unmistakable allure of power. She held her breath as his pale eyes scanned the room and then rested on her for a moment. She smiled and slowly curtsied, careful to lower her thick, dark lashes last of all.

"Your Imperial Majesty," she breathed.

The tsar and tsarina stepped forward. A deferential wave of bowing and curtsying swept through the hall and out into the corridors beyond. The orchestra struck up the lugubrious "God Save the Tsar" as the imperial couple began to walk through the hall.

Behind them, there was a mad scramble among the most well connected in the land as each couple vied for position, prestige, and proximity to the royal couple. The Vladimirs were in first, the Yusupovs not far behind. Momentarily, a gap opened up. Militza saw it and seized her chance. She grabbed hold of a deeply reluctant Peter, dragging him in her wake.

"What do you think you are doing?" he hissed, his face flushed with embarrassment. "This is not the way it is done!"

"Trust me!" she replied. "Come on, Stana!" She pulled on her sister's arm. And she and Grand Duke Nikolai had little choice but to follow.

"There they go," muttered someone. "Scylla and Charybdis, pushing their way to the front."

"Ignore them," said Militza, holding her chin aloft as she stepped forward in time to the music.

THE PROCESSION BEGAN TO WEAVE ITS WAY THROUGH THE Winter Palace. Led by the tsar and tsarina, it graced every room with its magnificence as the lengthy column danced three times around the building. Only several steps behind the empress, Militza could feel her heart pounding with adrenaline as she gripped her husband's hand. It was the tsarina's first outing, and here she was, so very near to her! Yet her moment of triumph was somewhat dissipated by the tsarina's evident discomfort.

The expectation, the anticipation, the examination, the scrutiny of thousands of pairs of eyes were all proving too much for her. A virulent rash started to spread up the back of Alexandra's neck and across her shoulders, and her ears began to throb a bright scarlet. The bowing crowds began to mutter and whisper their disapproval as she passed. And the more they muttered, the brighter the rash became. As the tsarina turned a corner, Militza could see the bright pink blotches all over the empress's face. She did not look like a proud, glamorous Imperial Majesty, parading in front of her adoring public, but more like a nervous young woman on the verge of tears.

Finally, they came to a halt back in the Nicholas Hall. The procession broke up and the dancing began. The tsar was first to choose a partner, the middle-aged wife of a member of the diplomatic corps. Meanwhile Alexandra was forced to dance the quadrille with the woman's rotund husband. Peter took hold of his wife, placing his hand around her waist as the orchestras at each end of the enormous hall began to play.

"I am not sure your little move has been much appreciated," muttered Peter. "Half the eyes of the room are upon you."

"Really?" replied Militza, pretending not to care. "And the other half are on my sister." They both looked across at Stana, who, dressed in pale pink, was surrounded by a small troop of young officers waiting to take her hand.

"I am not sure the other ladies look too pleased," suggested Peter.

"Nor indeed does your brother," retorted Militza, noticing the tall figure of Nikolasha brooding slightly by an orange tree.

"I don't know what you are talking about," declared Peter. "Your sister is a married woman."

AFTER THE FOURTH QUADRILLE, THE ORCHESTRAS STRUCK UP A mazurka and Peter immediately took his leave. Not the most coordinated of dancers, he had ripped his wife's expensive Worth dress with his spurs at the last party, and she had vowed never to dance the mazurka with him again. Relieved to be spared, Militza leaned against a marble pillar and searched for the tsar among the swirl of dancers. Instead, she spotted her sister on the other side of the hall, dancing with the tsar's younger brother. Militza smiled; if only her father were here to witness this, Stana in the arms of the tsarevich, Grand Duke Georgie, who looked so very handsome as he swooped up and down on one knee. Papa would surely toast Stana with a glass of the sweet apricot rakia that he was so fond of.

"May I?" came a voice from behind her that made Militza jump slightly. She turned to see the unmistakable thick mustache of Count Felix Yusupov.

"May you what?" asked Militza, somewhat confused.

The count did not reply, but merely gripped her hand a little too fiercely as he led her to the dance floor. Militza wanted to resist, but she feared causing a scene—something Count Yusupov knew perfectly well, of course. He said not one word to her as he spun and swirled her this way and that, maneuvering her into the middle of the room. The more Militza tried to pull away, the tighter his grip became.

"You probably think you are very clever," he whispered as he held her firmly against his chest. He smelled of vodka and tobacco. "Getting so close in the line behind the tsar and tsarina."

"Not at all," she replied, her mouth a little dry.

"I saw you pushing in." Militza attempted to say something, but he pulled her in tighter. "I don't know what pushy little ideas you have, trying to befriend the new tsar, but let me be the first to warn you: we don't like trespassers here." He held her so tightly against him now and whispered so forcefully in her ear that she could feel the brush of his lips against her skin.

"No," she whispered in agreement.

"Some of us belong to families that have been here for hundreds of years—we have earned our places, our titles, and the tsar's patronage." His fingertips were boring into her waist and her shoulders. She could feel her own skin bruising.

"Doesn't *your* family have more riches than the imperial family? You own lands the size of France!" Militza attempted to laugh lightly, trying to flatter the man.

"It's not about money, you foolish Goat Girl!" His mouth was now so close to hers, their lips were almost touching and she could taste his acrid breath. "It's about power! Influence is power and power is influence. You pull a trick like that again, and you will understand what real power is."

Finally, the music stopped and the old count released her; he clicked his heels, bowed his head, and walked away. Militza could hardly breathe, her chest and throat were so tight. It took her a few moments to gather herself together enough to walk through the crowd. The music started up again, and the couples in the packed ballroom began to dance once more. Militza was left to weave her way through them like a street drunk who's imbibed too much.

"I saw you dancing with Count Yusupov," commented Peter when she approached her husband.

"Yes," replied Militza, her hands shaking.

"An odd person." Peter sucked on the end of his cigarette. "I'm not sure I like him much. She's the one with the title and all the money. He's from nowhere—and that's never good for a man. Poor chap, I think that's what makes him so charmless. Are you all right, darling?" Peter looked at her suddenly. "You look a little pale."

"I think I just need some air."

It was all Militza could do to stop herself from running towards the open side door. But once through, she let out a loud sob as she fell against a window. Tears of anger, fear, and indignation poured down her cheeks. She had been so stupid! Overcome with ambition and giddy at the sight of the tsar, she had made a foolish mistake. What she had done was reckless. And she was not the reckless type. It was Stana who rushed in regardless. Not her. What had she been thinking? Had Yusupov seen the ambition in her eyes? She must be more careful next time, must play a longer, smarter game. She was too clever, too talented, to be caught out that easily.

The windowpane felt cool against her hot forehead. Militza dried her tears and then suddenly caught a glimpse of herself in the glass. Her white skin, her black hair, and her ruby necklace and tiara were reflected back at her. She was not a woman to be defeated. She would use all that her mother had given her to make her father proud. If Count Yusupov wanted an easy victory, then he had picked on the wrong woman. She looked at herself again, and this time her deep black eyes shone back at her, brooding and burning. Her pupils quivered as they began to dilate, and the fine hairs on her arms stood on end. What? She desperately needed a second chance. But so soon?

A pitter-patter of tiny feet came running up the corridor. Militza turned around. And there she was: a little girl with pretty blond curls and a pale blue bow in her hair.

"My goodness!" said Militza, bending down, a smile on her face. "You should be in bed!" The little girl giggled and fluffed up her white party dress. "What's your name?"

"May," said the little girl, dancing from one foot to the other.

"How old are you, May?"

"Four," laughed the little girl, holding up four fingers on her chubby little hand; then she turned and started to skip along the moonlit corridor, singing.

"Where is your mummy, May?" called Militza.

"My mummy's dead," came her reply.

"Who are you talking to?" asked a voice.

Militza looked up to see the young tsarina as she stepped out of the shadows and shimmered in the moonlight. Militza quickly swooped into a deep and graceful curtsy.

"Your Imperial Majesty," she said. "I am Grand Duchess Militza Nikolayevna."

"Good evening," replied Alexandra with a small smile. In the half-light and away from the intense heat and scrutiny of the ball, the empress appeared calm, controlled—and certainly more beautiful. "Who were you talking to?"

"Oh, it was just a little girl. A little girl who very definitely should be in bed!"

"What was her name?" The tsarina fiddled with her fan as Militza stared into her blue eyes.

"She said her name was May."

"May?"

The sound of a child's running footsteps echoed farther down the long dark corridor.

"May! Is that you?" the empress turned and shouted, her hollow voice reverberating against the walls. "Little Marie? Are you there?"

"Wherever she is, she should be asleep." Militza laughed gently, looking up the corridor towards the noise. "It is long past her bedtime."

"She is asleep," replied the empress starkly. "Fast asleep. She has been lying in the ground for a long while now." She turned to look at Militza. "May has been dead for eighteen years."

CHAPTER 5

FEBRUARY 1896,
ZNAMENKA, PETERHOF

SO SHE SENT WORD, JUST AS MILITZA HAD ALWAYS KNOWN she would, and now the tsar and tsarina were on their way to Znamenka. Their carriage, complete with an entourage of police and Cossack bodyguards, had been spotted on the road from the nearby Lower Dacha. It would not be long before they'd be turning into the long, tree-lined drive, and Militza felt her heart beat a little faster.

The idea of having the young tsar and his wife visit her country palace, newly refurbished in the Russian Baroque style by the architect G. A. Bosse, was all she could think about. What would the Yusupovs say when they found out? How would Maria Pavlovna react? How contorted would her furious face become now? But what Militza did not think of, what she did not pause to consider, was quite what events would be put into motion, how a vortex, once opened up, would be hard to shut.

Instead, she stood naked but for a red velvet robe and admired the sweep of her black hair in the mirror. Her maid's coiffure skills were improving by the day, she thought as she ran her hand over her flat stomach. That would change in the coming months. And this time, she knew, it would be the son Peter longed for, a boy he could dote on and spoil and, most importantly, to whom he could pass on his esteemed title and somewhat diminished estates. She smiled. Sweet Marina, now almost four years old, was asleep upstairs, and she had not yet told Peter that he was to be a father again.

She looked down. Next to her dressing table stood the large chest she'd brought with her from Cetinje. She opened the heavy lid; how rough and coarse the material felt, she thought, as she leafed through a pile of her old clothes. How simple the patterns, and how poor the cut! She held up an old pair of lace-trimmed underclothes—they looked so terribly old-fashioned. How quickly one becomes accustomed to luxury, she thought, smiling, remembering the last time she'd worn them, the night she and Stana had packed to leave for her marriage to Peter. She remembered curling up with her sister in their bed, remembered her mother, Milena, telling them not to be afraid, how they would be looked after—and she had given them her cast-iron pot, just in case. It was ancient and had belonged to her and her mother before that. "Use it wisely," Milena had warned. "And use it with care. You both have a gift that must not be squandered. Call upon your guides; ask Spirit, and Spirit will watch over you." And now here it was, at the bottom of the chest. Simple, solid, effective. The stories it could tell. She'd get Brana to fill it, light it, and place it in the room for later. But first Militza took off the heavy lid, and inside she found some drops.

"Belladonna," she whispered, extract of deadly nightshade. She rolled the dark brown bottle between the palms of her hands.

Turning to look in the mirror, she pinned back her eyelids and expertly squeezed a drop of liquid into each eye. She inhaled sharply. The acid sting was painful, but the effect was almost immediate: her pupils dilating, her black eyes becoming even more luminous and glassy. The result was bewitching and completely unnerving.

Militza smiled and, leaning forward, she clipped two drop-pendant topaz earrings to her lobes and turned to look through a gap in the curtains at the falling flakes of snow outside. She opened the window and inhaled the cold salt air from the sea beyond before closing her eyes. She held her palms out in front of her and began to chant:

> *Sabba pāpassa akaranan,*
> *Kusalassa upasampadā,*
> *Sacitta pariyō dapanan,*
> *Etan Buddhānasāsanan*

Her lips moved in a well-practiced rhythm as she rocked back and forth, repeating her sutta three times. "Cease to do evil," she said in Tibetan as she undid the rope to her robe. "Learn to do well. Cleanse your own heart, this is the religion of the Buddhas." Deeper and deeper she went into herself, climbing further and further down inside herself, right into her soul. She called upon her spirit guide to help her. A breeze swirled around the room, and the glass chandelier tinkled, the curtains fluttered and ballooned. She could feel his presence. A small shiver rippled through her body; her chest puffed forward, and her mouth fell open with a small, ecstatic sigh. The robe cord hung limply at her side, revealing her naked form framed by the folds of the dark material. She began to caress her own bare breasts, running her hands over her smooth flesh, watching her nipples swell and harden in the mirror. Her skin felt so warm, so soft to her touch as she ran her fingers over her flat belly. She inhaled again, her mouth wide, her lips engorged. Her whole body was tingling with life and energy.

She loved it when he possessed her. It made her feel dizzy, powerful, completely sensuous . . . There was pressure on the top of her arms. They felt tight, as if someone were holding on, gripping hard, burning, although no one appeared to be standing next to her. She looked at herself once more in the mirror; her huge black eyes stared back at her. She looked ecstatic. Her heart was beating hard; her blood was pulsing. He'd come. She was ready.

DINNER IN THE CHINESE DINING ROOM WAS POLITE AND PERhaps a little rushed. It was obvious that most of the assembled were trying to get through it as quickly as possible to move on to the main event. The poor chefs, downstairs in the subterranean kitchen, had sliced their best salted cucumbers and laid out their most sublime smoked salmon, only for them to be returned almost untouched. Their hot stuffed mushrooms and borscht were a little more successful, as were the roast venison and spatchcock partridge followed by pineapples and preserved cherries from the Crimea.

Even the conversation was stilted, and the surprise arrival of George, back from Biarritz, had not helped matters. Stana was laughing a little too enthusiastically, constantly touching his knee, whispering in his ear, trying to engage him with conversation. The poor girl was trying, but George simply looked uncomfortable and complained of a terrible headache. Even when the tsar inquired as to what he had been doing in Biarritz for all that time, he was not at all forthcoming.

Meanwhile Militza, finding it difficult to keep calm, sipped glass after glass of sweet red wine. Her appetites were not normally this voracious, but her guide always made her more lustful; her white skin became more luminous, her lips rosier, and her touch altogether more sensitive. But it was her deep black eyes that held the tsar transfixed.

"You look particularly enchanting tonight, Militza Nikola-yevna," he opined as he sipped his wine.

"'Enchanting'?" Militza smiled. "It is the good company, Your Majesty."

Thankfully, once the dinner was over, the party could move upstairs to the paneled library. Peter requested the servants leave the liqueurs and sweetmeats on a small table in the red hall so the guests could help themselves.

The library was thick with a heavy smoke emanating from the cast-iron pot that stood in the middle of the table. The smoldering cocktail of henbane and hashish had been burning all through dinner, filling the room with its intoxicating fumes.

"I can't believe we are about to do this," Stana whispered into her sister's ear as she followed her into the room. "Are you sure you're going to be all right?"

"I will be fine," she replied tersely. "We have come this far."

"But when was the last time you did this properly?" asked her sister.

"Can you light the six candles for me?" Militza simply replied.

Stana lit the candelabra while Militza covered the pot with a cloth. There was certainly enough smoke in the room now; as the guests sat down, it mixed with the fine wines from dinner, and it did not take long before the sedative and mildly aphrodisiac qualities of the drugs took effect. The tsar's posture relaxed and he positively flopped down into his chair. As the most important guests, the tsar and tsarina sat on either side of Militza, while Peter was opposite, with Stana to his right and George to his left.

Before commencing, Militza laid a square cloth on the table, on which were written a series of numbers around the edge. In the middle there were the letters of the alphabet and four squares, on which were marked "Yes" and "No," as well as the words "Hello" and "Good-Bye." She produced a well-worn glass from a small table in the corner of the library.

"This," she said, holding it up to show everyone, "is the planchette. I shall try and contact those who have passed over without using the Ouija board. But sometimes, if things are proving difficult, we can rely on the board. You will all need to place your fingers lightly on top of the glass, which will move around—but Spirit will be the one who moves the glass. We are just there to make sure that it doesn't fly off the table." She smiled and then breathed in deeply, flaring her nostrils as she inhaled the heady smoke and spread her arms out. "Does anyone have any questions before we start?"

"Will anything bad happen?" asked the tsarina.

"No. I have my spirit guide here to help. He should prevent too much interference from the lower astral."

"All right." Alexandra nodded, not quite understanding what Militza was saying, but the mixture of the hashish, the wine, and the henbane made her so delightfully relaxed she didn't mind.

"Shall we start?" requested Nicholas.

"Let's all hold hands, then we close our eyes and wait," said Militza. The tsar slipped his hand into hers. She felt his soft skin. She glanced across at him, but his eyes were already closed.

Within a few seconds the atmosphere changed. The air went cold and the six candles began to flicker. It was as if a fresh breath had entered the room. Alexandra kept her eyes firmly shut and squeezed Militza's hand all the more tightly. She had waited so long for this, she could not believe it was about to happen. She turned her head, her eyes still closed, towards the ceiling and began to pray under her breath.

"Our Father, who art in Heaven, hallowed be thy name; thy kingdom come; thy will be done . . . Oh, please, God, dear God, please let me speak to May . . ."

Suddenly, the gentle pitter-patter of feet was heard in the room. Militza sat quite still, her hands clasping those of the tsar and tsarina. Stana did not move a muscle. The little footsteps circled the table at a gentle trot, and then the rhythm changed and they began to skip. Hop skip, hop skip.

"She's here," announced Militza. "You can open your eyes." As the group opened their eyes, two candles blew out, leaving the room in a more profound darkness.

The four remaining candles lit up Militza's face. Her eyes shone, her topaz earrings glittered, and her bosom rose and fell with increasing heaviness. It was as if she were in some sort of trance. She nodded as if in response to a question and then laughed silently at a joke that only she could hear.

"All right, May," she said and smiled and nodded again. "I understand the joke. Four candles because you are four. Don't blow them all out—otherwise we won't be able to see anything." Militza chuckled. Peter glanced across at his wife. It was not a laugh he recognized. "Your sister is here, May," she said.

The sound of skipping increased dramatically, and the whole group felt a wind on their backs as if a small child were running around behind them. The silver servant's bell on the mantelpiece rang three times, and random books flew off the library shelves while the smell of spring flowers filled the air. A May bough. Alexandra looked around the room, trying to see where the heady scent was coming from.

"May, stop showing off," said Militza, shaking her head from side to side. Her tone was kind but firm. "Your big sister wants to speak to you." She turned to look at the tsarina, her eyebrows raised in expectation. The empress looked blank. Eighteen years of sorrow and sadness, and she did not know what to say. Her mouth went dry. She looked across at her husband for support. His pale blue eyes stared back.

"Um," said Alexandra, clearing her throat. She looked around the room, as if hoping to catch a glimpse of her. "May? Is it really you?" Three more books fell off the shelves as the patter of feet continued to run around the room. George shifted in his seat, more than slightly uncomfortable; he was not enjoying himself. In fact, if the tsar had not been expected, George would sure as hell not have been there either.

"May?" the tsarina continued, glancing around. "How are you? I miss you so very much."

Militza nodded. "Are you sure that is what you want to say?"

"How do we know you're actually talking to her?" asked George, rubbing his eyes with the back of his hand.

"I am fine," continued Militza in a sweet singsong voice that bore little resemblance to her own. She turned to face Alexandra, completely ignoring George. "May is fine. She is happy. Lots of people are looking after her. How is Mrs. Orchard? Is she still looking after you?"

"Mrs. Orchard!" Alexandra held her hands up to cover her mouth. Her face softened slightly as a wave of sadness rolled over it. "Dear Mrs. Orchard . . . our English nurse," she announced to the table and then shook her head in disbelief. "Marie was always her favorite. How extraordinary! She is well, May. She is looking after my little Olga now. Just like she looked after you." Alexandra's voice was high and strained, cracking slightly with emotion. "I have a little girl, just three months old. But then, you probably know that already."

Militza smiled suddenly, a playful smile. She raised her shoulders with the sort of exaggerated exuberant delight that adults use towards small children. "Oh, that sounds delicious. Lucky you!" Alexandra looked at her expectantly. "Sorry." Militza shook her head. "She said that she loves baked apples and rice pudding."

"Really . . . ?" said Alexandra quietly. She bowed her head and took a lace hankie out of her evening purse. Her tears were almost entirely silent, and she barely moved. Finally, she looked up. "She always asked for them . . ."

"It's almost every child's favorite," declared George, pushing his chair back slightly and stretching his arms above his head.

"Does anyone mind if I get a little brandy?" As he stood up to make his way to the library door, two more candles suddenly blew out and a tray of small crystal glasses crashed to the floor. The noise was shocking and the whole table recoiled.

"May!" shouted Militza, holding up her right hand. "Calm down!"

"Calm down, Marie," Alexandra joined in.

"Darling! George! Please sit down," hissed Stana. "Spirits don't like being ignored, especially four-year-old girls."

George walked very slowly back to his seat, and as he sat down, the two candles ignited once more.

"Good." Militza nodded. "She is happy," she declared. "OK." She nodded. "And she wants to say she is sorry about all your toys."

"My toys?" asked Alexandra.

"Yes," confirmed Militza. "The ones they burnt. What a terrible smell!" She shook her head. "My nostrils are filling with the smell of soot and burning." She stared at the tsarina. "They burnt your toys after she died?"

"All of them." Alexandra shook her head again. "All my lovely toys. Gosh," she sighed, as the memories came flooding back, "they burnt everything to prevent the spread of diphtheria."

"How terrible," Stana sympathized.

"My favorite toys were gone, as well as Mother and my sister . . . I remember weeping in the playroom, not being able to find my teddy bear, not being able to find anything . . ."

The tsar leaned across the table and took hold of his wife's hand. "But you are all right now, darling," he said, gently patting her hand. "You have me and little Olga."

"Your mother gives you her blessing," Militza interrupted suddenly, sitting up. "Right, of course." She looked at Alexandra. "She says not to mourn her, that she is happy. She is with . . . Frittie?"

"Frederick," whispered Alexandra, looking down at her hankie as she picked at the lace edge with her fingers. "He died at the age of two and a half. A hemorrhage."

"A hemorrhage?" asked Stana.

"He fell; he had weak blood," said Alexandra. "He wouldn't stop bleeding."

"She says she wants you to be happy," Militza declared very formally. "She urges you to be happy. Be happy, my love, that is all she is saying, over and over . . . Try and be happy."

"Excellent," said George, rubbing his hands together and pushing his chair away from the table. "That's all good advice. Now . . ."

Suddenly Militza slumped forward on the table and three candles blew out. A whistling wind rushed through the room, and a lamp fell off the table by the door; the temperature in the room dropped dramatically and Stana reached out and grabbed Peter's hand.

"This isn't good," she mumbled.

"What's wrong with Militza?" demanded Peter, standing up.

"Sit down!" said Stana, her dark eyes rounded with fear, and she grabbed hold of his hand again. "Everyone has to keep sitting down! Sit down and don't break the circle!"

Militza dragged herself up off the table, slowly raising her head. In the light of one candle her face looked dramatically different; the flesh was hanging, the muscles flaccid, her mouth drooping at the corners, her shoulders hunched, and her eyes heavily lidded. She looked remarkably like an old man. Peter gasped. He was horrified. He had never seen anything like it. Even George sat back and stared. The tsar let go of Militza's hand.

"She's transfiguring," said Stana, staring at her sister.

"How extraordinary," mumbled Peter.

"How unpleasant," said George.

"Your . . . father . . . is . . . here," Militza announced very slowly in a deep voice that seemed not to come from her own body at all.

"Whose father?" whispered Peter.

"Your . . . father!" she said, raising a finger and pointing to Nicholas.

"The tsar!" said Nicholas, looking shocked.

"You're the tsar," said George.

Nicholas turned and looked at Militza; not only did she look terrifying, with her flaccid gray skin and half-closed eyes, but she also looked vaguely familiar. Nicholas's already pale face blanched further as the blood drained. His large watery blue eyes shone in the candlelight as he remembered the last time he'd seen his father: the thick fog that surrounded the Maly Palace in Livadia, the horrific sound of blood being coughed up, the oxygen tanks, the nosebleeds, the vomiting, the emperor awaiting death while the holy man John of Kronstadt held him in his arms, whispering words of religious comfort as the last rays of the sun disappeared from the sky. The noise of the holy man's mutterings, his hooded black cloak, his long dark beard—Nicholas would never forget it. His mother, Maria Fyodorovna, weeping, plus the sweet smell of death and the constant religious chanting, still haunted him in the early hours.

"Should I ask him some questions?" he stammered. He had always been slightly afraid of his father, and he knew that the emperor had never really had a high opinion of him.

"No," replied Militza, inhaling and exhaling heavily, her palms flat on the table as she fought the powerful waves of the spirit. The whole experience was obviously exhausting her. "He wants to tell you something." She looked up again at Nicholas. Her black eyes were blank as if she were blind. "And he wants you to listen!"

"Right." He looked across the table at his wife. She smiled weakly in support.

"Fear not," began Militza, "I am well. The illness is past and

I am well." Nicholas nodded, thankful. "The coronation will pass well. Many thousands will come. Many thousands will want to come and pay tribute. But beware the advice of others. My brothers."

"Absolutely." Nicholas looked puzzled.

Militza shook her head. Her eyes were rolling backwards in her skull as she gripped the table again. Her fingernails dug deep into the cloth. "Beware the advice of others," she repeated, rocking in her chair, her head moving from side to side. "And Khodynka Field."

"What field?" asked Alexandra.

"This is ridiculous!" declared George, getting up from the table.

"Sit down!" said Peter, tugging at the sleeve of his brother-in-law's dinner jacket, forcing him back into his seat.

"I am not sure I understand what you mean, Father?" ventured Nicholas tentatively, as if he were talking to a cankerous old man, his eyes shifting nervously from his wife to Militza and back again.

"My brothers," Militza whispered deeply and quietly. Her whole body hunched and twisted over itself in exasperation. Her hands clawed at the tablecloth, pulling it towards her.

Nicholas stared at his wife for guidance. She nodded at him with encouragement. "Um, thank you . . . Father . . . I shall listen to your advice. I shall listen to it and act upon it faithfully."

And then, suddenly, the heavy, tense atmosphere dissipated. Militza hung her head at the table for a few more minutes, catching her breath; then she slowly raised her chin. Levity had returned to her. Her hands released the tablecloth and her shoulders visibly relaxed. She puffed her cheeks, exhaling the last vestiges of what appeared to be the old tsar. A shiny, youthful luminosity graced her skin, and she once more began to resemble a charming young wife in her twenties. Her cheeks plumped, a smile played across her pretty lips, and her dark eyes glittered again in the candlelight.

"Who would like some wine?" suggested Peter, his hands shaking. "I am suddenly extremely thirsty."

AS EVERYONE WALKED BACK INTO THE RED SALON, THE ATMO-sphere was subdued. Neither the tsar nor the tsarina had expected quite such an evening, and the tsarina was overcome. The combination of wine, henbane, and hashish only exacerbated her reaction, causing her to collapse onto the nearest sofa, weeping and talking rapidly.

"I remember hearing my mother scream when she arrived too late to save May," she said, looking across at both Militza and Stana. "It was awful. But what I also remember are the lies and the secrets after May's death, the way they pretended she was still alive and the way they hid her in the family mausoleum."

"Diphtheria is a terrible disease," agreed Stana.

"It swept through that house, choosing its victims irrespective of age. Even the physician sent by Queen Victoria could not save my sister. Or my mother." The tears flowed freely down her face as Alexandra smiled ruefully. "She was thirty-five and buried alongside her two little children." She sighed and then looked up at Militza. "I can't thank you enough. Really, I can't. I am so very grateful. Don't you agree, Nicky?"

"Indeed." The tsar nodded, looking haunted, his hand gripping his glass; he did not know what to make of the whole damn thing at all.

"Well, I thought it was all very jolly," declared Peter brightly, opening up a large silver cigarette box and offering them around. "Fascinating stuff, don't you think?"

"If you say so," muttered George, taking a cigarette and lighting it. He looked from one sister to the other. "A rum business."

"Who knew my wife was so talented!" declared Peter.

"A very good show indeed," said George, staring at Militza as he exhaled. "Where did you learn such tricks?"

"Indeed!" laughed Peter, walking over to his wife's side. "Indeed . . . So," he said, turning his back on the room, his face etched with nerves, "are you all right?" he whispered, holding on to Militza's arm. "That was quite something. I have never seen anything like it."

"I'm perfectly fine." She smiled. "It could not have gone better."

"Oh, good, because you know I would hate . . ."

"Don't worry." She smiled again, patting him on the arm. "You worry too much."

IT WAS ANOTHER HALF AN HOUR OR SO BEFORE THE TSAR FELT suitably recovered enough to leave.

"An extraordinary evening," he said, embracing her, caressing Militza's cheek with his soft mustache. "Thank you, we shall most certainly return to do that again," he murmured into her ear, before walking rather slowly towards the waiting carriage.

"Thank you," agreed Alexandra, holding Militza's hand in hers, her eyes still full of tears. "I can't tell you what it means to me to know my sister is safe and well and being looked after." She smiled, still holding on to Militza's hand. "Eating baked apples! You have made me so happy tonight. For the first time in this sad and lonely city."

CHAPTER 6

AUGUST 1899,
TSARSKOYE SELO, ST. PETERSBURG

AFTER THAT SEMINAL DINNER, THE TSARINA CONTINUED
to visit Znamenka with increasing regularity—each time
revealing a little more about herself, each time shedding
another layer. However, it wasn't until the morning of August 10,
1899, when Militza received that fateful telephone call, that all re-
sistance crumbled.

Militza could hear the sound of the tsarina weeping as she
ran across the bridge. The agony and the raw emotion were all too
obvious as her cries floated across the lake. Not since the death
of Militza's own stillborn daughter a year and a half ago had she
heard a cry so painful. And how she remembered that agony. It
was visceral; it stopped her heart and tore through her like a bur-
nished sword. Dear Sofia. Poor, sweet Sofia, born to die so her
twin sister, Nadezhda, should live. Born to never draw breath . . .

Militza picked up her skirts and ran faster.

"Wait for me!" begged Stana as she tried desperately to keep up. George was abroad, again, and so she had her hands full with her two children, seven-year-old Elena and nine-year-old Sergei, neither of whom were inclined to run on such a hot and humid day. Their clothes were uncomfortable, the sun was beating down, and they were desperate to get into one of the rowboats lying up-turned on the grassy bank.

Militza didn't look back. Ignoring her sister and hitching her white chiffon dress even higher, she held tightly to her picture hat and the rope of pearls around her neck and ran faster. She could see Alix now through the leaves, under the shade of a large oak tree, reclined on a long wicker chaise surrounded by cushions. Her two daughters were playing on a rug in front of her, and the prim and tight-lipped nanny, Miss Margaretta Eagar, and the more elderly yet robust nurse, Mrs. Mary Anne Orchard, were also in atten-dance, entertaining Grand Duchess Olga and Grand Duchess Tatiana so they did not disturb their grief-stricken mother.

"Oh, Milly!" wailed Alix on seeing Militza approach. She half rose from the chaise, her tiny six-week-old daughter, Maria, still suckling at her partially exposed breast. "I am so glad you are here. Thank you for coming."

"I came as soon as I heard," said Militza, trying to catch her breath as she wiped the glow of sweat off her forehead with the back of her hand.

"Isn't it awful?" Alix wailed. She began to shake, her red-rimmed eyes streaming with tears. She held her newborn to her bosom and tried, unsuccessfully, to stifle a cry. The sound was so miserable that her other children stopped playing with their dolls and stared. "When I think about it," she whispered, fighting her own emotions for air. "Him lying there on the road, blood trick-ling out of his mouth, his motorbike lying next to him. He should never have gone for a drive. He was told not to go out on his own. I can't bear it." She struggled to inhale through her sobs. "No one should die like that, Milly. No one should die alone."

Militza sat down on the end of the chaise and took hold of Alix's hot hand, still gripping her handkerchief.

"He didn't die alone," she soothed. "A peasant woman held him in her arms until he passed."

"He may as well have been on his own," the tsarina replied, flapping away the suggestion. "He was only twenty-eight." Her eyes filled again with tears.

"Not many people live for ten years with tuberculosis—he did well. How is the tsar?"

"He is so upset, so sad." Alix shook her head as more tears tumbled silently down her face. "I know the agony of losing a brother, but I don't think even I can help him. Georgie was not only Nicky's younger brother, but also his best friend, he was so brilliant—"

"And so handsome," interrupted Militza. She looked across towards the lake at her approaching sister. "I remember him dancing with Stana at the Nicholas Ball. He was so dashing and fun. I will never forget how his eyes lit up when he smiled."

"Nicky's been in his rooms, sitting at his desk, the door closed since yesterday. He keeps taking little jokes out of his box and reading them." Militza looked confused. "Nicky used to write down Georgie's best jokes and put them in a box. He has been reading them constantly since we got the news, laughing and crying to himself."

"Maybe I can help him?" offered Militza.

"Oh, I am so sorry!" declared Stana, rushing over to Alix and kissing her on the backs of her hands. "It is such a shock." She sighed loudly. "I feel as if I have been struck by lightning. How is the tsar?"

"I haven't seen him this way since . . . the tragedy," replied Alix, sniffling into her handkerchief.

"Khodynka Field?" blurted Stana before immediately covering her mouth with her hand.

Regretful, she looked quickly from the two nannies to the tall Cossack bodyguard who was standing in the shadow of the tree. Everyone shifted uncomfortably. The tragedy of Khodynka Field, where nearly fifteen hundred peasants were trampled to death in the sudden rush for the free beer, gingerbread, and enameled cups, all presents from the tsar to celebrate his and Alix's coronation, was not something ever mentioned in polite company, let alone in front of the tsarina.

"That was slightly different," suggested Militza, glancing around.

"Trampled running for free beer and a cup. It would be pathetic if it weren't so awful." Alix looked up, with an air of slight defiance. "And I know you warned us—or at least the ghost of Nicky's father did. And I know that Nicky should never have gone to the French ambassador's ball that night. You warned us about that too. I know. But his uncles were so very insistent that we show the monarchy was undiminished. It was such a terrible mess. But what's done is done. It's all so very silly."

"No one blames you." Stana smiled at the weakness of her lie.

The three women fell silent; the stiff atmosphere was broken by the cries of Maria as she rooted at the breast for more milk.

"You see!" declared Alix, looking down at the tiny red-faced baby, her short legs rigid with indignation as she inhaled deeply before letting out a loud wail. "I can't even get this right. Orchie dearest . . ." she said, turning towards the rug.

"Your Imperial Majesty," replied the rotund Mrs. Orchard.

"Please could you take her to one of the wet nurses? All this grief has made me run out of milk!"

Mrs. Orchard gathered the crying baby from Alix's breast and disappeared off towards the Alexander Palace.

"Mama, it is so hot!" yawned Elena, flopping down on the rug.

Elena's likeness to her father irritated Stana. "Have some iced lemonade," she suggested, indicating to the small picnic table and chairs to the right of the rug.

"Isn't there anything else?" complained the girl. "I'm not fond of lemonade."

"Miss Eagar?" said Alix, sounding slightly exasperated. "Can you take the children boating on the lake?"

"Oh, yes please!" squealed Sergei, jumping up and down and tugging at the woman's skirts. "Please, Miss Eagar."

"Calm down, Sergei!" she ordered, her long thin finger in the air. "Follow me, quietly now, down to the lake." She smiled stiffly before nodding at the tsarina.

"Take Ivan," added Alix, gesturing towards the bodyguard. "He can row the boat for you."

As the children, Ivan, and Miss Eagar made their way towards the lake, Alix turned to look at Militza and Stana, her eyes wide, her expression fearful. She looked terrified.

"Now that we are all alone!" She looked from one sister to the other, her pale eyes darting from side to side, her breath short. She appeared almost feverish. "You have to help me! You both have to help."

Militza took her hands again. "Whatever you want."

"Now that poor Georgie is dead, I have to have a son!" Alix sobbed. Her golden hair fell down in wisps across her face, making her look like a young child. Her hands were shaking, her bottom lip quivering. "The whole question of the succession has come up again, now that he—the tsarevich—has gone."

"There's Michael," interrupted Stana.

"Michael can't be tsar, he is far too irresponsible. Everyone knows that. I need a son. You can almost hear the Vladimirs pawing at the ground, their eyes hungry for the fight, and there are rumblings in the Duma . . . Everyone keeps asking *when?* When am I going to have a son? When am I going to produce an heir? When? When? It is all down to me." Alix's eyes were hollow. "I have to have a son." Her hands were turning over and over in her lap.

"But you've just had a baby," said Stana, looking up towards the palace.

"If you could have seen Nicky's face when Professor Ott told him Maria was a girl. Another girl! Nicky managed to smile when Tatiana was born, but this time I saw him try—and he couldn't. He pretended, but it never reached his eyes. He didn't even touch the baby. He went for a walk. He walked for an hour. More. When he came back, only then did he take Maria in his arms." She turned and looked at the two sisters. "Is it too much to want to lie in my bed and hear the three-hundred-gun salute ringing out over the city announcing the birth of my son to the world? Three times I have heard the guns stop after one hundred and one rounds, and three times I have seen the dismay on the servants' faces, three times I have seen my husband have to overcome his terrible disappointment . . . I just want him to be happy . . ."

"I am sure he is not disappointed," insisted Stana. "You have three healthy, beautiful daughters."

"What use are daughters? Especially now," replied Alix, staring out at the gang of children playing on the lake, more particularly at the thriving and boisterous Sergei, with the sun in his blond hair as he laughed and rocked the rowboat back and forth on the water. "It is easy for you to say. You both have sons," she said, turning back towards the sisters. Her face was haunted with longing. "You have Sergei, Stana, and you have your beautiful Roman, Milly. Please, you have to help me. I will do anything, absolutely anything. I cannot rest, Russia cannot rest, until we have a son."

Stana softly patted the back of Alix's hand, but the tsarina snatched it away with irritation and glared. "You don't understand! You have no idea of the pressure to produce a son while a nation of millions holds its breath! It is suffocating me! And every confinement is worse: the headaches, the fainting, the endless, endless sickness. D'you know Nicky's mother even suggested I eat cold ham lying in bed in the morning to stop the sickness? Cold ham with thick white fat! Can you imagine? I can barely stomach a slice when I am well, let alone five months pregnant with a mouth as dry as a desert. And I know what they whisper. They whisper that I am cold and aloof, that I don't like their parties, their balls, their wretched games of cards. They say that I am a prude, that I tell women off for showing too much flesh at court, that I want to stop my husband going out. But it's not true. I just feel so unwell. The room is spinning, my head is turning—and I feel sick all the time! And my back . . ." She looked from one sister to the other and then burst into tears. "It is the whispering I hate most," she sobbed into her handkerchief. "I just wish it would all stop!"

She looked up, and through the mist of her tears, she could see Militza and Stana completely understood.

What she didn't know was that they more than understood; they themselves had heard those whispers; they'd felt the same loneliness. And they also knew what it was like to have a mother who was desperate for a son. They had seen the potions, the lotions; they had smelled the smoke, seen the fires, and heard the incantations. Their palace in Cetinje had been full of it— the freaks, the fools, the endless spells. And they knew exactly what to do.

"Don't worry," said Militza, nodding fiercely, her lips pursed with determination. "You will have your son."

"I promise," added Stana.

"Cross your heart?" whispered Alix before lying back, exhausted, into her chair.

CHAPTER 7

DECEMBER 17, 1899, ST. PETERSBURG

MONDAY WAS THE MOST PRESTIGIOUS NIGHT TO BE INvited to perch on the Countess Ignatiev's elegant, raspberry-colored velvet upholstery and enjoy the sweet wines, the cakes, and the latest and most glamorous guru in town. And as she collected her pack of Marseilles cards from her dressing table drawer and wrapped them carefully in their peach silk scarf, Militza felt a shiver of excitement. The thrice-weekly Black Salons were always exciting, but this Monday was going to be different. Tonight, Countess Ignatiev had promised her someone special, someone very special indeed.

Walking into the large dimly lit drawing room, packed with the usual princes, diplomats, and divorcées, Militza was met by a rather overexcited Countess Ignatiev.

"There you are!" she exclaimed loudly, clapping her hands together and then clutching at her ample bosom. "At last! You're late!" Sophia Ignatiev was nothing if not dramatic. "Darling, there are so many people waiting for you to read for them. We almost have a queue! Here, here," she repeated, bustling Militza through the party to a corner where she had placed a marble-and-gilt card table, covered with a fringed gypsy scarf, and two heavy armchairs. "Is this all right?" She smiled, holding her arm out. "I was trying to make it as mystical as possible."

"It's perfect!" agreed Militza, for she was very fond of the countess.

Sitting down at her table, Militza carefully took out her peach scarf and unwrapped her cards.

"May I?" came a familiar voice as a bronzed hand placed a small clay hash pipe on the table.

"Dr. Badmaev!" Militza immediately leapt out of her chair to embrace him.

A Buryat by birth, Shamzaran Badmaev (also known as Peter) had grown up on the steppes of Siberia and trained with the monks of Tibet. He was a master of Asiatic medicine and Tibetan apothecary, with a worldwide reputation. Along with his brother, Zaltin, he owned the most auspicious "chemist" in St. Petersburg, capable of curing the most stubborn and pernicious of maladies. There wasn't an infusion, herb, or tincture he did not know. His laboratory behind his shop off the Fontanka was a veritable Aladdin's cave of delights. Militza had once been very privileged to pay him a visit, and even to her expert eye, many of the bottles and bags and powders were completely incomprehensible.

"How are you?" He smiled, kissing her three times, his narrow eyes fizzing with an extraordinary energy. There were many in St. Petersburg who thought Dr. Badmaev was a spiritual master, and Militza was one of them.

"Well," she replied as they both sat down.

"You look well." He nodded and then patted his pocket. "I have what you asked for."

"You have?" Militza's eyes sparkled with excitement. "My friend will be so pleased."

He pulled a small envelope out of his loose-fitting trousers and handed it over to her. "There is ashoka flower for sadness and grief, black lotus essence for rebirth, and mandrake—"

"Mandrake?"

"I have a hermit woman who's collected it for me for years. She lives in the forests outside Irkutsk, at the crossroads where they used to hang men for stealing horses. There is an abundance of hanged men's seed in the ground around there and the mandrakes are plentiful."

"How does she harvest it without hearing it scream?" asked Militza, handing him over the pack of cards to shuffle.

"She was born deaf."

Militza nodded and smiled appreciatively. "Do you have a question for the cards?"

"Only the question that is on everyone's lips." Militza looked at him quizzically as he expertly mixed up the pack. "The succession?"

Militza's heart leapt; she glanced quickly around the room to check that no one else had heard. The succession was, of course, the question on everyone's lips: three pregnancies and the tsarina had yet to produce anything but daughters. People were beginning to say that she was cursed. Her poor Russian language skills didn't help, and neither did her inability to understand the importance of the court, but to hear it voiced out loud was not only shocking; it was dangerous.

"Hush," she said, taking back the cards and clutching them close to her breast.

"Don't tell me you aren't curious? And haven't you asked the same question yourself several times over in the comfort of your peach boudoir?" He smiled, nodding for her to continue. "Go on . . ."

She watched him cut the cards with his left hand before she

laid them out in formation. She turned over the first card. "Ah. The High Priestess . . . of course," she said, moving the card dexterously through her fingers. "Wisdom, sound judgment, foresight, and intuition."

"I have also added some black henbane, so tell our friend that if she has hallucinations or sensations of flying, she's not a witch but should decrease the dose immediately." He chuckled to himself.

Militza turned over the next card. "The Star . . . Hope. Effort. Faith. Inspiration . . ."

"Otherwise she should have a teaspoon in warm water every day," continued the doctor. "And her husband should always mount her from the right. If he mounts from the left, she will have another girl. Is that understood?"

Militza nodded, slowly turning over a new card. "So, a teaspoon?"

"Every day."

They both looked down at the card. "The Wheel of Fortune . . . Destiny. Fate."

"The cards are very accurate tonight," concluded Badmaev.

"They always are. No matter how many times you ask them the same question, they will always come out the same." She picked another and turned it over.

"The Ace of Cups," he said, staring. "Look! There you go—fertility and joy!"

"Yes." She nodded. "Fertility and joy." She placed the small envelope very carefully into her silver-thread evening bag and looked back down at the card. "But upside down."

"Upside down," he repeated. They both stared disappointedly at the card. "So, the antithesis is true?"

"Yes." Picking the card up, she turned it round in her slim fingers. She sat back in her chair and sighed.

"But for how long?" asked Badmaev. "How long exactly will the antithesis be true?"

"Time is not something that Spirit understands," said Militza. "You know that."

"But the wait . . ."

"The wait is unbearable," she whispered. "It is agony. And it eats away at her soul."

"Do you mind if I take my turn?" came a familiar, unpleasant voice.

"Count Yusupov!" declared Dr. Badmaev, leaping out of his seat, swiftly picking up the cards. "Of course! We were just finishing . . ."

Before Militza could say a word of protest, Dr. Badmaev had vacated his seat for the count. "My dear," he said, leaning forward and firmly gripping Militza's wrist with his sweaty hand. "How very charming to see you again."

"Count Yusupov," she replied, staring at his painful, plump fingers. "I didn't think this was your sort of salon. A little beneath you?"

"Needs must, my dear. And anyway, I have heard the tsar likes this sort of thing. Apparently, it is all the rage!"

Militza looked down. "If you continue to grip me so fiercely, I will not be able to deal the cards." Her black eyes shone with fury.

"I have no interest in your frivolities," he replied, leaning closer and licking his lips.

"People are beginning to stare," she hissed. He loosened his grip but leaned farther across the table.

"A small bird tells me that you and your sister have penetrated right to the heart of the palace," he began, raising a large eyebrow.

"Which palace?" Militza smiled, shuffling the cards. "There are so many in this city."

"Don't play coy with me, Goat Girl!" he spat; a small splash of saliva landed on Militza's cheek. She slowly closed her eyes and wiped it away with her finger.

"Shuffle," she said, handing him the cards.

He looked at the cards suspiciously, but he inhaled and began to shuffle. "People don't like you. They don't like you, and they don't like your sinister little sister; most of all, they don't like your little-girl games."

"My little-girl games?" repeated Militza, furiously taking the cards back and snapping down three of them.

"Games," he repeated. "This rubbish!" He gestured dismissively towards the card table. "They want you to desist."

"Or what?" asked Militza, turning the three cards over.

"Or—"

"*Death!*" she said, looking down at the table. "Ten of Swords!" She paused, taking in the image of a hunched young man with ten daggers firmly planted in his back. "The King of Swords." Militza stared down at the cards. She pushed her chair away slightly. She had never seen anything quite like this before.

"What?" demanded the count, staring at the cards. "What? Tell me!" His face was growing darker, his heart beating faster. What was the witch hiding?

"It's just little girls' games," she whispered.

"Girls' games," he repeated. "I have nothing to fear."

She sighed and looked down at the table, avoiding his gaze. Uncontrollably one tear ran swiftly down her cheek, and she deftly swept it aside with her index finger. It was unlike her to feel so emotional, but she had seen something—something terribly sad indeed.

"Your son," she said quickly, not looking up.

"I have two sons," he replied, slowly getting out of his chair.

"Two?" she asked, sounding puzzled. She looked at the cards and then across at the count. "Well, look after them," she bluffed, hurriedly clearing the cards away. "Both of them . . ."

"And this is Grand Duchess Militza Nikolayevna!" interrupted the Countess Ignatiev. "I am sorry, Count." She smiled at Yusupov.

"I was just leaving," he replied, getting to his feet hurriedly.

"Here's the someone I am dying for you to meet," continued the countess, bubbling with excitement.

Militza turned and caught her breath. Before her stood a young, heavily bearded priest, swathed from head to foot in a long black hooded cape. Under the cape, his floor-length black robes were emblazoned with a large golden Orthodox cross. His hooded black silhouette was an arresting sight among the gold and raspberry velvet of the salon. He looked like the grim reaper himself. Militza stood up.

"This is Father Egorov!" announced Sophia. "He has come all the way from the Optina Pustyn monastery to be with us."

"Optina Pustyn," repeated Militza; its highly devout and austere practices were well-known.

"Where Dostoyevsky went before writing *The Brothers Karamazov*." Sophia smiled encouragingly.

"I know it," replied Militza, staring intently at the monk, waiting for him to speak, trying to work out what his intentions were.

"My friend Prince Obolensky has an estate not far from the monastery, near Kozelsk. Dreadful place," continued Sophia, taking a swig from her glass of champagne. "Nothing to do but hunt in the miserable forest. But he heard this amazing story about a holy fool called Mitya Koliaba who makes prophecies. Only recently he predicted that a local countess would have a baby. And Father Egorov is the only person who understands Mitya and his predictions." She smiled. "Mitya is a mute epileptic."

"What baby did the barren woman have?" asked Militza, wondering why the Fates had brought this man before her.

"A son."

"And you can understand the epileptic?"

"I prayed before the icon of St. Nicholas, and the voice of the saint came to me and revealed to me the secret of Mitya's sounds," Father Egorov mumbled into his lengthy beard.

"You understand every word?" she asked. The monk bowed again. "And his prophecies are reliable?"

"As God is my witness," he replied.

CHAPTER 8

JANUARY 1900,
ZNAMENKA, PETERHOF

IT WAS ONLY A FEW WEEKS LATER, AND MILITZA, STANA, and Alix were sitting in silence, drinking tea in the red salon at Znamenka, their eyes trained on the door. Such was the anticipation of Mitya and Father Egorov's imminent arrival that none of them could concentrate on their embroidery.

Six months had gone by since the birth of baby Maria, and the court was growing restless. The season was in full swing; the gilded and the well connected had all left their country estates or Moscow palaces and descended upon St. Petersburg for the annual three-month merry-go-round of feasting, dancing, and, most important of all, gossiping. Two of Alix's ladies-in-waiting had recently announced their own confinements, and the pressure on the tsarina was growing.

"Have you seen the Yusupovs recently?" asked Militza, to break the monotony of the crackling fire.

"No." Alix shook her head. "The only people I see are you.

Everyone else has abandoned me!" She laughed wryly. "They exhaust me with their questions and their looks. I don't know how anyone lasts more than a few hours at these wretched balls."

"I agree," Militza sympathized.

"And then I am afraid I have to go. Nicky often stays on well after me. He says that it keeps him in touch, that he can discuss politics, that sort of thing. How else, he says, is he to know what is going on in and outside the court?"

"Well, that is important," added Militza.

"I don't see why. Nicky rules by divine right and his people love him. You can see it on their faces when we ride by. One smile from him, one glance in their direction, and their souls are full, their life is complete. It is better than a basket of bread." She sighed. "And besides, the Yusupovs spend much of their time at Arkhangelskoye these days; Zinaida is far more interested in my sister and the Dowager Empress. She, Elizabeth, and Maria spend hours taking carriage rides and endlessly discussing Elizabeth's new Orthodox faith." She smiled. "I have enough worries of my own without listening to lengthy tales of my sister's Damascene conversion from the Lutheran church."

"How is the tsar getting on with his herbs?" inquired Stana.

"Nicky is smoking hashish every night," confirmed Alix. "And not only does he sleep so much better than before, but his stomach cramps have completely disappeared."

"That is good news," said Stana, taking another sip of her tea.

"At least Dr. Badmaev's cures work for someone," sighed Alix. "I have been taking them every night and nothing . . ."

"Give yourself some time," suggested Stana.

"Time is the one thing I don't have!" snapped Alix, jabbing her needle into her sampler. "Can't you hear them all? Squawking like starlings? Saying that the tsar should have married a nice Russian girl? That I am barren? Sent by the Germans to bring down the house of Romanov?"

"You just must have faith," replied Militza. "And it will happen."

"It must." She sighed. "Otherwise I am lost."

Suddenly there was a terrible shrieking from the corridor outside. All three women put down their teacups and sat up rigidly in their chairs.

"Is that them?" asked Stana, turning her head.

The shrieking was replaced by a low growling and then a deep moaning. There were sounds of a struggle and then some banging and crashing from the other side of the double doors. Mitya sounded extremely reluctant to enter the room. The doors finally opened, and the screaming intensified as the hooded monk dragged in the poor iurodivye, or holy fool, by a chain tied around his neck. The man was half blind, with short handless stumps for arms, his festering hair, stinking rags, and raw bare feet only adding to his woeful appearance. With one hefty tug of the chain, he at last arrived in the center of the room and cowered in front of the three women. He appeared to be completely overawed and confused by the bright lights and the opulence of his surroundings. He started to rock his head from side to side, screaming and hopping about.

"Shush!" ordered Egorov, tugging at the chain. "Quieten yourself!"

Militza had known a little of what to expect, so was only mildly upset by the sight of Mitya, but Stana was appalled. It was all she could do to prevent herself from crying out in horror as she swiftly retreated, moving behind a chair. Alix, on the other hand, was completely enthralled. She got out of her seat and walked slowly over to the monk and his charge, her arms outstretched as though she were trying to calm a skittish colt.

"Hello," she said calmly. "I am Alexandra Fyodorovna—and I promise I am not going to hurt you."

Mitya tugged on his chain as he tried to move away. Alix took another two steps towards him.

"I would not come any closer," said Egorov, raising his hand in the air. "Mitya doesn't like it when people are too close."

"I promise you no harm," said Alix, ignoring the monk and taking another step forward.

Mitya stopped in his tracks and turned back towards the empress. Walking slowly up to her, he raised his two stumps in the air and, placing his nose close to hers, screamed loudly in her face. The sound was piercing; the sight of his open mouth, his six fetid brown teeth and the shower of spittle that emanated from it, made Stana cover her mouth with her lace handkerchief. The tsarina was, however, unmoved. She turned and looked at the monk.

"What is he saying?"

"I can only understand when he is having a fit," explained the monk. "It is only when he has one of his attacks that he becomes clairvoyant."

"And how often does he have one of those?"

"When God decides."

IT WAS A FULL TWO WEEKS AFTER MITYA AND EGOROV MOVED into the Alexander Palace at Tsarskoye Selo that Militza finally witnessed one of the holy fool's crises in action. She, Stana, and Alix were sitting in the Mauve Boudoir when it happened. Militza was playing Schubert's "Serenade" on the piano, while Stana was telling Alix about who and what she had seen at luncheon the day before at the Imperial Yacht Club on Morskaya. Then one of the servants came running. Mitya was having a fit. He had collapsed outside in the snow and they should come quickly; otherwise they would miss their opportunity. Grabbing the nearest coats and hats they could find, the three ladies ran, still wearing their silk slippers, through the snow.

It was early afternoon and almost dark. The air was freezing, and each inhalation sliced their lungs like a knife. Fortunately, the monk and the fool had not strayed far from the palace.

As the women arrived, Mitya was rolling around on his back in the snow. Egorov had apparently let go of the chain and, still swathed in his black hooded cape, he was on his knees, his eyes closed, his hands together, fervently praying.

"Mitya!" demanded Militza, raising her arms in the air as she looked down at the flailing creature, now growling and foaming copiously at the mouth. "Will the empress have a boy?"

They held their breath. The fool yelped and writhed and kicked in the snow. He emitted some high-pitched squeals and moans, which the monk began to interpret.

"It is still early days," said the monk, his eyes shining from underneath his hood. "It is still long before the birth, and Mitya cannot say whether it will be a girl or a boy. But he is praying unceasingly and in the course of time will give exact information."

Alix looked at Militza, confused, panicked even. She had waited on tenterhooks for over two weeks for this? She'd believed, had given the monk and his charge her complete trust; she had done exactly what Stana and Militza had told her to do!

"Mitya! Mitya!" barked Militza. "How long? How long before you can give the exact information?"

The fool arched his back, threw back his head, and let out an enormous groan.

"Mitya cannot say," repeated the monk. "It is still long before the birth. But he is praying unceasingly and in the course of time will give exact information."

"But when she does get pregnant, will it be a boy?" Militza glared hotly at the fool and then at the monk for some sort of hope, some sort of inspiration.

"Mitya cannot say—"

"He must know!" Stana shrieked, stepping forward. "We've been waiting! The empress has been waiting. For two whole weeks she has sat and waited. Come on, Mitya, tell us something!" She was beginning to sound hysterical. "Give us a sign! Something—anything!"

Mitya suddenly sat up in the snow and looked blindly at the empress. His stump arms outstretched, he let out one last roar before being violently, biliously sick at her feet. He then flopped back into the snow, rolled over on his side, and curled up like a child, whimpering quietly.

"Mitya says you should cleanse yourself," said the monk, looking at the puddle of vomit on the ground.

Alix looked from Militza to the monk, and neither of them moved. She hesitated.

"Cleanse yourself and be free," the monk repeated, still staring at the bilious liquid in front of him. "Cleanse yourself!" he barked.

Alix dropped to her knees and began frantically scooping the yellow vomit out of the snow with her bare hands. She ate it, desperately forcing fistfuls of the foul, freezing mixture into her mouth, silent tears of deep humiliation coursing down her cheeks. Stana covered her mouth in horror. Militza slowly closed her eyes and began to pray. The monk crossed himself, and the iurodivye emitted a final pathetic yelp before falling asleep.

MITYA AND FATHER EGOROV STAYED FOR ANOTHER THREE months at the palace. Although Alix was never asked to "cleanse" herself again, she could no longer bear the screaming and the wailing. Her nerves were frayed at the anxious anticipation and the constant running to his side when the moments of clairvoyant clarity were announced. Eventually she was driven to fits of hysterical weeping whenever Mitya went into one of his episodes. For not only did she not conceive, but also, most disappointingly, neither the fool nor the monk ever changed his prediction for the tsarina's future. It was always "early days" and Mitya was always "praying unceasingly" for her situation to change. In the end, it was the tsar himself who asked Egorov and his charge to leave.

But Militza and Stana would not give up. They could not. Now they had the ear of the tsarina, now they knew her every worry and wish, they were not about to let that position slip. They were the inner circle—and there was no one else. Through her they could influence the tsar, and their father was delighted because the old alliances between Russia and Montenegro were back in place. And as one of Russia's closest allies, he could expect the perks of this honored status: financial assistance and greater diplomatic weight on the world stage.

And besides, the sisters had promised the tsarina they would help.

So they enlisted the help of the tenacious Brana and the trusted members of the Countess Ignatiev's Black Salon, and together they trawled the streets of the city and its outlying churches in search of miracle workers, mystics, and the latest iurodivye. They found a young woman, Matryona, from nearby Peterhof, who arrived barefoot, dressed in rags, and carrying an icon. She stayed at the court for a month, shouting prophecies like Delphic oracles that Militza was called upon to translate. Although she was not prone to fits and could speak, the noise and her filthy clothes eventually made Alix ask Matryona to leave.

In the sinking traktirs, or communal dining rooms, near the crowded, desperate slums around Sennaya Ploshchad, Brana found an old woman who swore that if you collected the menstrual blood off the tsarina's sheets you could predict the sex of the next child. The sheets were duly collected and rinsed, and the menstrual water was used to fertilize a small pot of earth. Should a blue flower grow, the tsarina would have a son. Unfortunately, after a month of waiting, only a tiny pink flower pushed its head up through the well-tended soil.

Militza was also in regular correspondence with her mother, who sent her a collection of ancient chants and tinctures. A follower of the Zoroastrian religion, she also sent a small bronze statue of Anahita, the fertility goddess, which the tsarina was instructed to bathe with, as well as a collection of poppets to be placed under the tsarina's bed. The first, with its wooden crone face and its cotton scarf pinned tightly around its cheeks, looked like the old kitchen witch that used to hang by the fire in Cetinje and was supposed to prevent the roasts from burning and the milk from boiling over, but this one came accompanied by a small cloth baby-boy doll filled with yarrow, the love plant. The tsarina was instructed to rock the doll to sleep at night and sing it a sweet lullaby. Which she duly did. Every night.

All the while the three women prayed for a miracle, and all the more Alix cleaved to the sisters, and all the more the pressure mounted. Then suddenly, out of the blue, the Countess Ignatiev called.

CHAPTER 9

MAY 18, 1900, TSARSKOYE SELO

IT WAS THE MIDDLE OF MAY, AND A BLANKET OF PURPLE crocus carpeted the woodland surrounding Tsarskoye Selo. Militza and Stana had been invited to an intimate luncheon to celebrate the tsar's thirty-second birthday.

By the time Militza and Peter arrived, most of the guests were already assembled in the Rosewood Drawing Room. Felix and Zinaida Yusupov were just back from Moscow and talking to Baroness Sophie Buxhoeveden, the tsar's old friend and the tsarina's new lady-in-waiting. Grand Duke Sergei Mikhailovich and his eldest brother, Uncle Bimbo, were ensconced in the corner with the Countess Marie Kleinmichel and, on the right, wearing a brand-new couture dress of spring-yellow silk teamed with a diamond-and-pearl *collier du chien*, the Grand Duchess Vladimir. Standing next to her portly husband, she was sipping champagne and admiring the view over the park when Militza and her husband approached.

"How are you, Militza, darling?" she said, looking Militza up and down and kissing the air beside her cheeks.

"Very well, Maria Pavlovna," replied Militza, slightly taken aback by her apparent friendliness. "Um," she floundered. "What a nice dress."

"From that little place on Moika, Madame Auguste Brissac. You must go." Maria smiled, raising her eyebrows. "She always says she drops her prices for me because I wear her clothes so well, but then I hear she says that to all the ladies! Oh!" she continued, turning to talk to Stana, who had entered behind her sister. "Still no George?"

"Sadly, no," replied Stana, with a formal smile.

"Not still in Biarritz, surely? No one can possibly fathom quite what keeps him there!"

The portly Grand Duke Vladimir chortled into his vodka shot as he exchanged a knowing glance with his wife and whispered loudly in her ear, "I hear the prince is washing his filthy body in the waves of the ocean!"

Stana flushed. It was becoming abundantly clear the nature of George's "business" in France was something that could not be contained *en famille* any longer.

"Isn't the new decoration looking wonderful?" suggested Militza as she looked around the room with a deliberate fascination.

"Haven't you been here since Roman Meltzer supervised the renovations?" asked Maria, her top lip curling slightly as she eyed the endless watercolors of Hesse palaces. "Very homely, don't you think?"

"I have been here a few times since," replied Militza, unable to control herself.

A butler announced luncheon was served. Peter finished up the joke he was sharing with Uncle Bimbo, while Militza and Stana walked through to the Corner Salon, where Monsieur Cubat's famous suckling pig with horseradish sauce would be served.

"Here come the Black Pearls," mumbled Zinaida Yusupova as the girls walked past her.

"Don't you mean the Black Peril?" added the Grand Duchess Vladimir.

Count Yusupov remained silent and sipped his drink. He had not spoken to Militza since his visit to the Monday salon. In fact, he rather avoided her. Her dark hair, her large oblong black eyes and unusually pale skin, gave him the creeps. As for her pleading with him to look after his sons, it was obviously all nonsense— but there was something about her tone that still haunted his dreams.

"The knives are still out for us, Milly, let me tell you," Stana hissed.

"Jealousy is the weakest of emotions," whispered Militza as she took hold of her sister's arm. "Don't worry."

"But I do worry."

"Our position is secure."

"How can you say that?" Stana pulled her sister aside into the Small Library opposite the Corner Salon. "We are not at all secure. Quite apart from my marriage becoming the laughingstock of the whole city, they are waiting for us to slip up. And we're just about to. We have trawled town and country and found nothing. The tsarina is not even remotely pregnant, let alone carrying a son. The people are watching her belly like a hawk. Where's the heir? Where's the son? Where's the tsarevich? And just as long as that is the case, our position is perilously weak—we could be dismissed at a moment's notice." She looked intensely at her sister, before adding in a soft voice, "We could use the price—the one we extracted from Maria Pavlovna. It wouldn't take much and you could do it."

"You panic too easily, little sister. You always overreact. You're not thinking clearly."

"I'm thinking perfectly clearly."

"Don't be ridiculous!" Militza looked affronted. "We're not going anywhere near the price."

"Why not?"

"Because we are not desperate!"

"But we *are*."

"Not after today," whispered Militza.

"What do you mean?"

"Have faith."

"I have plenty of faith," replied Stana, more than a little irritated. "I say my prayers every night. In the absence of my errant husband, that is all I have! Faith and a loveless future."

"Someone very powerful has just arrived in the city."

"How do you know?"

"I have been waiting for him." She smiled contentedly. "And what is more, he will be much more to the tsarina's liking."

"He had better be," snapped Stana, staring fiercely at her sister. "Because you and I are rapidly running out of time. We need a son! And we need him soon!"

"Everything all right in here?" The tsar was standing in the doorway, looking curiously at the two sisters. They both had their hands on their hips, and the atmosphere was as frosty and frigid as the steppes in winter.

"Fine," they both replied rather too quickly.

"Shall we go through?" he suggested.

"Of course." They nodded.

"Militza?" he said. "May I have a word?"

"Of course, Imperial Majesty," she replied.

"I need to see you. Alone." Militza blushed, while Stana obligingly left the room. "It is urgent—I need to speak to my father. I need to talk to him about Japan, Manchuria, about foreign policy. This evening?"

"Absolutely, Imperial Majesty."

"Nicky. Please. It's my birthday," he said, smiling, taking hold of her hand.

"And what a wonderful day for a birthday," replied Militza, gesturing to the pale spring sunshine in the park outside.

"The day of Job. The long-suffering Job." He laughed a little. "Only the unluckiest man alive is born on the day of Job. I can't help but think my life is predestined to be unhappy. I have a deep certainty I am doomed to terrible ordeals."

"We can all change our fate," she replied. "No one's life is predestined."

Although, as she looked at his pale eyes and his troubled face, she couldn't help thinking how truly plagued by misfortune he was. To have married through his mother's tears, to have a wife who entered the city behind a coffin, and to have his coronation tainted by the tragedy of Khodynka Field, when nearly fourteen hundred people died in the stampede—and yet to have gone to a party afterwards, while the field still flowed with the blood of his trampled subjects, as if he didn't care, showed foolish judgment in the extreme. Maybe his misery was preordained, written in the stars before he was even born . . . or just maybe he was weak, poorly advised, and too powerless to do anything about it.

"I wish I could believe you," he replied.

MOST OF THE GUESTS WERE SEATED WHEN THEY ENTERED THE Corner Salon. The Yusupovs were at one end of the table and the Vladimirs at the other. In the middle were the tsar and tsarina's high-backed gilt carved seats, and on either side of them were three empty places. A hush went over the room as Militza entered on the tsar's arm. They all watched as he escorted her to sit next to him. As Militza sat down, Maria Pavlovna could not stop herself from kicking her husband under the table.

The luncheon was not protracted. The tsar only ever drank two glasses of wine at lunchtime, even on his birthday, and the tsarina was almost entirely teetotal. The conversation was mainly dominated by the presents the tsar had received—a cage of songbirds from the Yusupovs and a delightful Fabergé box from Alix. There was much made of the recent Peasants' Ball held at the Vladimirs', where the ballroom had been redecorated to resemble a cottage, real cows had wandered around, and the servants had been dressed in tunics and loose-fitting breeches as they had handed out the drinks. It had been hailed as one of the top five parties they had ever held—and they'd held many. The tsarina expressed great regret that she had been unable to attend what had obviously been such a marvelous and much-lauded event.

The three courses started off with hors d'oeuvres of caviar, smoked goose, and pickled herring, followed by the famous suckling pig and horseradish and then fruit and cheese. The waiters, with their soft-soled shoes, were discreet and efficient, and as soon as the last plates were removed, the tsar lit a cigarette, indicating that the rest of the party were allowed to follow.

Coffee and birthday cake, with port wine and Allasch kümmel, were taken standing up in the Maple Drawing Room, which, although full of Fabergé-framed photographs and trinkets, was still awaiting renovation.

"How long are you here for? Is Felix enjoying his new posting in Moscow? We must come and see you now that you are here?" Peter suggested to Zinaida Yusupova as she sipped a cup of strong coffee.

Her delicate features formed a small smile. "Yes, that would be nice," she lied. "Be sure to bring your charming wife."

"She is so busy these days—I hardly see much of her myself," joked Peter. "She is always here!"

"So I gather," laughed Zinaida. "It's quite the little group!"

"If you will excuse me?" said Militza as she walked across the room towards the empress, who was engaged in conversation with Sophie Buxhoeveden. With a sure-footed directness, she went straight to the tsarina's side. "I have some good news." Her voice was hushed so that only Alix could hear. Alix's face lit up.

"Meet me in the Mauve Boudoir in five minutes," she whispered, before turning back towards the baroness and looking out of the window. "Aren't the flowers so beautiful at this time of year?"

MILITZA FOUND HERSELF WAITING FOR A FULL FIFTEEN MINUTES for Alix to extricate herself from the party. She sat on the chaise longue in the corner of the room, furnished entirely by Maple & Co. of London in the empress's favorite color, pale purple. From the Chinese bowls to the furniture to the striped Parisian silk wallpaper, it was all mauve. The only exception was the cream-colored enameled upright Becker piano.

"I am sorry," declared Alix as she burst through the door. "Felix Yusupov would not let me go. He kept fingering that giant mustache of his, talking about some dull military parade he saw in Moscow."

"I have found someone!" Militza declared immediately, leaping off the chaise. "Someone so powerful, so clever, so brilliant. He lives between two worlds, and he has power, real power . . ."

"Does he believe in God?"

"He was *sent* from God. He is the answer to your prayers, all our prayers . . . to all Russia's prayers!"

"When?" asked Alix.

"Now. He is here."

"In St. Petersburg?"

Militza nodded. Alix fell upon her, enthusiastically kissing her cheeks. "Thank you!" she said, kissing her hands, her forehead. "Thank you, thank you. I knew you'd find him. I knew you'd find the One. I knew you would not let me down." The tsarina pulled Militza closer and embraced her tightly.

"Don't worry, my darling," soothed Militza, her soft cheek caressing the tsarina's. "Help is on its way."

CHAPTER 10

JUNE 16, 1900,

ZNAMENKA, PETERHOF

MILITZA RECALLED HOW SHE SPENT ALL THAT MORNING briefing Philippe. Not that the tsarina's desire for a son was a secret anymore. There had been mutterings in the foreign press, even the *New York Times*, and it was by now, frankly, all the salons of St. Petersburg could gossip about—that and her persistent bouts of back pain, her reclusiveness, plus her inability to attend any event at court without looking visibly bored or withdrawn or leaving early.

So both Militza and Stana, who sat side by side on the buttoned sofa in her red salon, felt no discomfiture in enthusiastically sharing Alexandra's innermost secrets.

To say that Militza wanted to believe all of Philippe's glittering recommendations was an understatement.

She remembered feeling this man had been sent to her by Spirit. She had seen his face at night as she stared between two mirrors, chanting her mantras and burning her herbs; he'd appeared to her with his beatific smile and his healing hands, crossing himself and assuring her that all would be well. He was exactly who she had been waiting for: a mystic from Lyon who had been feted in the fashionable drawing rooms of Paris. What higher recommendation was there?

And here he was. Just as she'd hoped, he was finely dressed, with clean, manicured fingers, and he neither screeched, nor vomited, nor stank of the slums of St. Petersburg. He was shorter and more rotund than she'd anticipated; however, he could mix easily at court and, naturally, spoke excellent French and was far more palatable to the tsarina's refined sensibilities. In short, he wasn't Russian, and frankly, that was a relief.

So Militza was not only relieved as they retired to the salon after their light luncheon; she was bristling with optimism. And her sister? Well, Stana already appeared to be in his thrall. Her dark eyes were shining, and her lips could not help but smile.

The footman just managed to announce the arrival of the tsarina before she burst into the room, her white chiffon skirts rustling.

"You're here!" she declared, directly addressing Maître Philippe, who was so shocked at the speed of her arrival, he didn't know whether to leap out of his seat, or bow, or both.

"Your Imperial Majesty," he said, standing to attention before bending deferentially low.

"Your Imperial Majesty, please may I present Monsieur Philippe Nizier-Vachot?" said Militza. "A truly holy man."

"*Impératrice . . .*" He bowed again. His southern French accent grated slightly.

"How was your journey? How long have you been here? Tell me . . ." Alix paused, looking a little wistful. "How is Paris? Cannes? Didn't you meet in Cannes?"

"Not meet exactly, but when I was there Count Muravyov-Amursky could talk of nothing else," Militza acknowledged. "We were having luncheon on La Croisette when he told me so many stories about Maître Philippe's abundant gifts, his ability to cure so many varied ailments, it was imperative he come here to St. Petersburg. Countess Ignatiev invited him."

The tsarina sat down, her white skirts spread out over the divan, her back straight, her pale eyes catching the afternoon sun; Militza had not seen Alix this engaged or this excited in months. It was clear that she too felt the power of Philippe; he was most certainly the man to answer both her prayers and the nation's.

"Dear lady," began Philippe, smoothing down his thick lengthy mustache, "tell me your problems, for I am here to help."

THE POT OF TEA HAD LONG SINCE TURNED COLD BY THE TIME the tsarina had finished talking. Philippe was now more intimate with her thoughts and fears than perhaps even the tsar himself. As Alix left, Militza could not believe quite how wonderfully well the first meeting had gone. Maybe she and her sister had been a little indiscreet in telling him so many of the tsarina's secrets? Maybe they had revealed rather too much? But the result was so marvelously above their expectations. What did it matter they might have betrayed a few too many confidences? Everything was going to be fine from now on.

IT TURNED OUT TO BE A GLORIOUS SUMMER. EVERYONE DE-camped for the long warm evenings of the Crimea, Nicky and Alix moving with their three little grand duchesses to the imperial summer palace, Livadia, along with the head nursery nurse, Mrs. Orchard, and their Irish nanny, Margaretta Eagar, while Militza and Peter with Marina, Roman, and Nadezhda, as well as Stana, George, and their children, Sergei and Elena, moved nearby into their new summerhouse, Dulber.

An homage to Peter's obsession with fifteenth-century Egyptian architecture and inspired by his travels in Syria, Dulber (meaning "splendid" in Persian) was a grand and glamorous project that had taken him two years to oversee. With silver domes and more than one hundred rooms, it was stocked with delicious wines and had beautifully planted exotic gardens full of palms and fountains. It was like a vision from one of Scheherazade's tales and their little slice of paradise. And, of course, Philippe came too.

The families were inseparable. These were relaxed, languid, happy days, away from the prying eyes of the court, where the hours were whiled away playing cards and highly competitive games of tennis, at which Nicky particularly excelled. In the afternoons the gentlemen swam off the Sapphire Coast, while the ladies took afternoon carriage rides and long walks in the fragrant rose gardens. Luncheons, spent together at Livadia, were long and included all the staff, as well as any visiting dignitaries who'd traveled the five days from St. Petersburg with important court papers for the tsar to sign. Afternoon tea *à l'anglaise* was taken promptly at four, also at Livadia, while the evenings were spent in either of the palaces, discussing the day's events, plus the goings-on at the numerous nearby country estates, before finally, after dinner, withdrawing to gather around the card table in the salon, where Philippe or Militza would host séances long into the night, while the smell of henbane and hashish drifted out onto the verandas beyond.

Mostly Nicky wanted to converse with his father, discussing complex affairs of state, constantly asking, "What would Father have done?" which bored his wife but intrigued both Peter and George, who couldn't help but question the veracity of such a discourse. It took all Peter's willpower to hold his tongue.

On one memorable night the party spent the evening in the old emperor's bedroom in the Maly Palace, where the armchair in which Alexander III had died remained untouched and unmoved, still turned to face the window and the view out over the Black Sea. The tsar wept so uncontrollably while sitting in his father's old armchair that everyone, save Alix, was forced to withdraw due to acute embarrassment.

However, the majority of the time Alix would try and control events, steering conversations away from dull foreign policy, the unrest in Manchuria, and the dreary politics of government and back to family matters, summoning either her dear departed mother or her little sister, May. Mostly, these sessions passed without incident. There were the occasional breakages; little cut glass goblets would tumble and shatter on the parquet floors at moments of particular excitement, and once a Venetian lamp was upset during a vigorous bout of table tipping.

But there was one night in Livadia towards the end of August when the group was visited by something very uncomfortable indeed.

It was a particularly dark night, for the summer was on the move and the moon had long since disappeared behind thick clouds. The party had been drinking kümmel, some of them smoking small amounts of hashish out of little clay pipes. The mood was relaxed and a little merry. Even Militza had filled her small bowl full of aromatics and was feeling the pulsing force of her belladonna drops as her heart raced and her vision grew a little blurred. Despite the autumnal chill in the air, her hands, as she held on to the tsar, were damp with sweat. She had been channeling for a while, her spirit guide leading the way through the miasma of souls and visitors who wanted to communicate with the illustrious company.

"Wait!" said Militza, her eyes half closed, her elbows on the table as she held on to Nicky and Philippe. Her pale green silk evening dress shimmered in the candlelight. "There is someone else here . . ." She opened her eyes and glanced around the room.

"There!" She spotted something in the corner. The rest of the assembled followed her gaze.

"Where?" asked Peter, trying to see into the darkness.

"Behind Stana," whispered George, who was transfixed, his mouth slightly ajar; his pupils, dilated through hash and alcohol, shone in the half-light. This was more than the usual trickery he'd been witness to.

Alix gasped as a young girl dressed in a white nightdress walked slowly out of the shadows. She must have been about six years old; her feet were bare, her hair hung long and loose over her shoulders, and her hands were covering her eyes.

"May?" asked Alix, a little confused, for the girl was small enough to be her sister, but so far, in all their conversations, May had never actually manifested, and anyway, this child was thin and dark, whereas May had had blond hair and deliciously fat cheeks.

"Happy . . . birthday . . . to . . . you . . ." Philippe started to sing in a quiet, low voice. For the child looked as if she were covering her eyes, waiting for her birthday surprise. A cake with candles? "Happy birthday . . . to . . . you . . ." continued Philippe, conducting along with his short fingers.

". . . to you . . ." Stana joined in, nodding and smiling at Philippe across the table, matching him note for note.

"Happy birthday . . ." sang Alix, also copying Philippe, her head nodding in time to the song.

". . . dear . . ." added the tsar, a little tentatively.

They all turned to stare as the girl flung her arms into the air. Alix screamed, Stana gasped, and Militza covered her mouth in horror. The small, white-faced child stood there, her face expressionless, her mouth impassive—but instead of eyes she had two deep black holes. It was as though they had been gouged out, leaving two dark, soulless pits. They all stared, terrified, not daring to breathe. And then she spoke. It was not the singsong voice of a child but a deep and low demonic growl that seemed to come from the very depths of hell.

"The man who turns his back on God," she snarled, facing each one of the assembled in turn with her empty black sockets, "looks the devil in the face!"

She then turned and walked back into the shadows. Alix started to whimper and weep with fear, while Stana looked across at her sister, who in turn stared at Philippe, looking for some sort of explanation.

"Well," he began, rubbing his smooth hands together as he blinked rapidly behind his round, wire-rimmed spectacles, "the advice of a fallen angel, um, a very fallen angel, should not . . . not be taken too seriously. And as no one here has turned their back on the Lord, not one of us. No one has turned their back on God," he repeated. "No one at all." He paused and cleared his throat. "So . . . so I think we should simply ignore this."

Alix nodded in agreement and mumbled, "Yes. Ignore it."

"For the Lord moves in mysterious ways," went on Philippe, growing in the confidence of his diagnosis.

"Of course," confirmed Peter.

"And we all have faith," agreed Stana.

"Yes," confirmed Nicholas. "All of us."

The only person to remain silent was Militza herself, who, as she picked up her small glass of claret, found it difficult to stop her hand from shaking. She glanced over at Peter; his gray eyes were fixed on her, his expression questioning. Militza looked at him and slowly and almost imperceptibly shook her head.

THE INCIDENT WAS NOT MENTIONED AGAIN. HOWEVER, Philippe decided to avail the tsar of a small golden bell that would magically ring if an evil person were ever to approach him. Its sound was only audible to Maître Philippe himself, but the tsar insisted on taking it with him wherever he went, and with the political situation as it was, with increasing unrest in the countryside, one could never be too careful.

The other thing Militza recalled from that period was Maître Philippe's magic hat, which, when he wore it, would make not only him invisible but also those who traveled with him. She could not personally vouch for the efficacy of the cap, though, for the only time she bore witness to it was when she spotted her sister out in a carriage with the Monsieur, his hat firmly in place.

"I saw you out driving with Maître Philippe this afternoon," she mentioned to her sister later that evening over a glass of tea on the veranda.

Stana looked rather puzzled. "But that is impossible!"

"It is?"

"Maître Philippe was wearing his magic hat, so neither of us was visible at all." Militza raised her eyebrows. "He told me so himself."

"How strange," said Militza.

"Impossible," confirmed Stana.

"I must have been mistaken," her sister replied.

However, not one of Militza's growing concerns about Philippe and his practices mattered much because one afternoon in October, as they were playing bezique in the tsarina's Mauve Boudoir at Tsarskoye Selo, listening to little Olga learning to play the piano, Alix tentatively declared to Militza that she was with child again at last.

Over the next few months, excitement in the court grew as the tsarina disappeared from view, removing her corset and putting on her customary dark velvet, loose-fitting gowns, declining all dinner invitations and refusing even to go to Grand Duchess

Vladimir's pre-Christmas bazaar. The tsar himself was abuzz with energy, and the news spread at speed across the empire. Letters of congratulations arrived from some of the farthest estates, and Militza's mother sent a short telegram welcoming the good news. The sisters were delighted—their trust in Philippe had been vindicated—but no one was more delighted than the Countess Ignatiev, whose Black Salon was now so glamorously popular that anyone who had ever been to Dr. Badmaev's apothecary was clamoring for an invitation. For if the tsar and his wife were embracing the black arts with seemingly magical results, then what better way to ingratiate oneself with the increasingly isolated couple than to try and follow suit?

At the Palm Ball the following year, the tsarina's good news was now visible for all her intimate circle to see, and Militza and Stana's position at court was unassailable. When they arrived at the annual intimate gathering for five hundred of the most powerful and connected, resplendent in their couture dresses on the arms of their respective husbands, they caused a parting of the crowds.

The Grand Duchess Vladimir was one of the first to approach. With a flutter of ostrich feathers and lace, she was at her friendliest and most beguiling best. She picked up a Sobranie cigarette from a crystal case, removed the band stamped with a doubled-headed eagle, and waited for a footman to light it.

"Wonderful evening, don't you think?" She smiled, exhaling a plume of gray-blue smoke and waving her fan in a futile attempt to ward off the claustrophobic heat of the ballroom. "Your friend from Lyon not here?"

"Alas, no. He has more important things to do than attend parties," declared Stana, with a tilt of her chin as she surveyed the Malachite Hall.

"How foolish of me! A man of his talents, he must be off

healing the sick somewhere . . ." She cleared her throat. "Tell me, will you be in Moscow this Easter?"

"I am not sure," replied Militza, acknowledging the half-bowed head of Baroness Buxhoeveden.

"It depends on the empress," added Stana, doing the same.

"Of course," concurred Maria Pavlovna.

"Being so heavy with child, she may not want to travel," continued Stana.

"Indeed," agreed Maria Pavlovna swiftly. "We all know how difficult it is for her to carry."

"Do we?" asked Militza, turning back and fixing her with a dark stare.

"Some of us, obviously, are privy to much more than others, but her discomfort is well-known." The grand duchess continued, hesitating a little, "Well-known in general, but to her exclusive intimates, I am sure there are many other secrets."

The woman began to blush, much to Militza's pleasure. "Yes," she confirmed with a small, self-satisfied smile. "There are many other secrets."

"May I?" interrupted the tall elegant figure of Nikolai Nikolayevich as he bowed his head and clicked his heels together, offering his hand to Stana. "I know how well you dance the polonaise."

She glanced briefly across towards George, who seemed to be engaging the attentions of a young tittering female over a glass of champagne. She exhaled furiously. Why not? Imperiously she took Nikolai Nikolayevich's hand—and along with it the attention of the room. Why was she, a married woman, dancing so intimately with her brother-in-law? And as they danced through the hall, holding hands and bending their knees, the younger girls in their fresh white frocks, out at a dance for the very first time, could do little but stand to one side and stare, letting the more glamorous, powerful, and distinctly more fascinating couple through. In fact, the only person to turn their face away in a moment of overt irritation was the Dowager Empress, Maria Fyodorovna, who had long since given up being remotely cordial to either sister. Ever since she'd heard of the séances and the table-tipping evenings at Znamenka, she had ceased to accept their visit cards or invitations to afternoon tea at Annunciation Square.

"Congratulations," came the whispered, tobacco-tinged tones of Count Yusupov in Militza's ear. The hatred in his voice was as cold and hard as the deepest Siberian winter, but Militza stood her ground, sipped her champagne, and instead of turning to face him, she continued to look ahead and smile rigidly at the glittering swirl of dancers. "I hear you have made it into the bedchamber itself," the count continued. "Collecting the morning pot, or so I am told." He paused. "How very befitting."

"Believe what you wish," she replied curtly, maintaining her gaze on the dance floor.

"And your friend—or 'Our Friend,' as I gather he is now known—remains in the bedchamber all night, I hear? I suspect that special invisible hat of his must come in useful during the *moment critique*!" He chuckled.

"Well, the tsarina *is* with child," she hissed, turning at last to face him.

"I didn't think pregnancy was the problem. Just the lack of heir."

"This time I know it will be a boy."

He smiled. "You know? Or you pray? Or, more accurately, chant and dance with your devil, burning your herbs, crossing your little fingers, and hoping to triumph? Because if it is not a boy, if you and your friend fail, then what? Where will your little Black Circle of mystics, miracle workers, and gurus be then? If we have to welcome yet another girl? A tsar with four daughters? How useless is that? But then, one only needs to ask your father, he'd know all about it."

"It's a fool who underestimates the power of a woman." Militza turned back to face the dancers and took another sip of her champagne. She was determined not to let this puffed-up, florid dog of a man ruin her triumphant evening.

"Perhaps," he replied. "But it is also a fool who puts all her trust in a hairdresser from Lyon."

"He's a doctor."

"He's been arrested five times in France for practicing without a license."

"He can cure syphilis."

"With what?"

"Psychic fluids and astral forces."

Count Yusupov laughed. "Those trifles may work in your salons and in the drawing rooms of your hysterical ladies, but in the real world, syphilis kills—and kills you very slowly. Your friend is no doctor, my lady. No doctor at all."

"I don't see any of your doctors making a difference," she replied. "I don't see any of *your* doctors doing anything at all."

What was it about this man that he managed to get under her skin? What was it about this family that made them think their influence was superior and they were somehow above it all? After all, she was the one who had access to the tsar. Total, unadulterated access. No one could get to him without her approval. She and Stana were the gateway—they'd made sure of that. And their father could not have been more delighted. There was money for his barefoot soldiers in Montenegro, money for his roads, and Militza herself had paid for a shiny new water system in the capital, Cetinje. The Yusupovs would be forgotten when it came to write this chapter of history.

She withdrew from his company and walked behind a porphyry column before searching in her silk bag for a small green bottle. It contained a cocaine-laced liquor that Dr. Badmaev had recently given to her to combat lethargy and nerves. She took a small swig and felt immediately rejuvenated. The consommé will soon be served, she thought, and the Yusupovs will soon be defeated. Everything shall be as it should be. All she needed was a boy.

CHAPTER 11

JUNE 19, 1901, ST. PETERSBURG

MILITZA NEVER FORGOT THE MORNING SHE WOKE UP to the 101-gun salute. For the last two weeks of Alix's confinement, both she and Stana had been almost continuously by the empress's side. The increasingly hot and humid days under the long summer sun had been spent in a state of heightened and yet contented alert; they'd drunk tea, sewed samplers, and quietly waited for Alix's waters to break. The confident assurances of Maître Philippe had meant the usual anxiety that surrounded the final days of the tsarina's pregnancy had dissipated into a sort of balmy blissfulness. She was to have a boy, and hers and Russia's problems would soon be over.

So when Militza lay in bed that morning and heard the resounding silence following the 101st firing of the cannon over the Neva, her head began to swim, her heart began to race—and it was all she could do to reach the nearby pot in her bedroom before she vomited. Despite the bright sunshine outside, her teeth began to chatter. She could not understand how this could have happened. Philippe had been so sure, so confident. She had trusted him completely. So had Alix, and so, indeed, had the tsar. How could she and Stana ever come back from this? What would happen to their friendship with the tsarina? Their influence? Their power?

She had to think—and she had to think at great speed before all that she had worked for, all that she had achieved, disappeared like sand through her quivering fingers. She pulled on her dressing gown and began to pace her bedroom. She caught a glimpse of herself in her gilt triple-paned dressing table mirror: she looked haunted, ashen-faced, and her long dark hair tumbled, unbrushed, over her white lace chemise. She was shocked by what she saw. She had been so *certain*. Tears welled in her black eyes. What could she do? There were no incantations to change the sex of a baby who had already been born, no spells to alter what had already come to pass. Where was her magic now? How could it have gone so wrong?

There was a knock at her door, and Brana walked in holding a tray.

"Oh, Brana!" she cried, rushing across her bedroom and throwing herself at the aged crone, collapsing onto her small hunched shoulders and inhaling the acidic smell of old sweat and garlic. "I can't believe it! Where's Peter?"

"He left for his club early this morning," replied the crone.

"The tsarina has had another daughter!"

"A fourth!"

"What are we to do?" The old woman could offer little advice, but instead she stroked Militza's hair, as she had done a thousand times before, muttering simple platitudes in her ear. Slowly, as Militza sat back on the bed, tears of frustration and humiliation trickling down her face, Brana poured her a cup of chamomile tea laced with laudanum and wild strawberry jam.

"This will make you feel better."

"I am not sure if even one of your special drinks can make a difference," she replied as she watched her old nursemaid replace the lid on her familiar blue glass bottle. "I am not sure how we can ever come back from this."

"You will come back from this," said the crone. "You always have a plan."

IT WASN'T LONG BEFORE A SWEET LAUDANUM SLEEP CAME OVER her. Cradled in its soft opium embrace, Militza lay back and loosened her gown, relaxing in a seminaked state on the bed, feeling the gentle summer breezes flow over her exposed skin. Down she went, deep down into her disturbed subconscious, and the voices began: whispering, chastising, teasing, the faces, the tears, the cries, the longing, the desperation, Count Yusupov's laughing eyes, the sneers of Grand Duchess Vladimir, the words "Goat Girl," "Goat King," all finally dissolving into the loud, painful screams of labor. She woke dramatically from her slumber to find her sister violently shaking her by the shoulders. Stana was fully dressed, and sunlight was streaming through the open window.

"Wake up, wake up!"

"What time is it?" mumbled Militza, gathering her white shift around her.

"It has gone two o'clock in the afternoon!" declared Stana, her eyes wide with panic. "It's the most appalling day of our lives, and you take one of Brana's cocktails? What is wrong with you? We need to think! We need to act! We need to come up with a plan!"

"I am sorry, I am sorry . . ." Militza roused herself as fast as she could. Clearly, Brana's tea was stronger than she had thought. "Give me a minute, I shall be fine."

"Fine! I am not sure we shall ever be fine. It was all anyone was talking about on the English Embankment as I came over here. You can hear the whispering all the way along the park. You can almost hear the Vladimirs sniggering from here. We are lost. Our country is lost. Papa will never forgive us. Montenegro was relying on us for grain, for arms. The tsar promised Father forty thousand rifles—do you think he will give them to him now?"

"The tsar will give Papa his rifles," Militza stated quietly, buttoning up her shift. "You have my word on that."

"Your word? What use is your word when Alix has had another daughter? We should have cracked an egg, done the test, then at least we would have known."

"Don't be ridiculous! That's a parlor game, not something you can play with a tsarina!"

"Have you spoken to Philippe? Philippe will know what to do," declared Stana, pacing around the room. "Philippe always knows what to do."

HALF AN HOUR LATER, A SURPRISINGLY CALM-LOOKING PHILIPPE strode into the red salon at the Nikolayevsky Palace. The two sisters were sitting side by side on the button-backed divan, their backs straight, their hands on their laps as they awaited his explanation. But instead of any browbeating or hand-wringing, the diminutive guru from Lyon stood by the fireplace, placed his hand on the marble mantelpiece, and slowly shook his head.

"She did not believe."

"But she did," corrected Stana. "We all did."

"She did not believe . . . enough," replied Philippe with a shrug. "Maybe she had doubts? Maybe she did not listen enough, maybe she didn't believe with her heart? Monsieur Philippe never fails. Monsieur Philippe always succeeds."

The two sisters stared at him in silence. Was this the best he could do? Was that all he had to say? Stana had been expecting more. An idea, at the very least. Something to give them all hope, a scintilla of a chance against the growing clouds of jealous animosity that were gathering on the horizon.

"Yes!" Militza agreed suddenly, standing up and starting to pace the room. Her sister looked at her a little surprised. "Monsieur Philippe never fails." She nodded. "He always succeeds. He never fails. We never fail." It was as if she were trying to convince herself. "The tsarina simply did not believe enough. It is that simple. One should always keep it very simple. She needs to try harder; she needs to submit entirely to Philippe's will. To the will of God."

"I am glad you understand." Philippe smiled, smoothing down his fecund mustache. "I have done nothing wrong. I am a man of my word. I have cured all my patients from many terrible diseases—and those I haven't cured simply didn't believe enough. Remember the other day when I calmed a storm while we were sailing on the *Standart*?"

"Yes," enthused Stana. "We were so lucky you were there, otherwise who knows what would have happened!"

"Yes," agreed Militza, remembering the dark gathering clouds and the subsequent lashing rains and the hands of Philippe raised at the bow of the *Standart* as he shouted incantations into the roaring wind. It took a while for the storm to abate, but abate it did, and everyone who'd been cowering belowdecks, holding on for dear life, gave him the credit. "You *did* calm the storm. You absolutely did calm the storm."

"As God is my witness, you did," added Stana.

"So, as you can see, I am a man of my word." Maître Philippe smiled confidently, his argument won.

IT WAS FOUR DAYS LATER AND THE MIDNIGHT SUN WAS LOW IN the sky when Militza and Stana left Znamenka carrying two small wicker baskets and a couple of sharp knives. It was St. John's Eve's night—midsummer's eve—and the most auspicious night of the year for gathering herbs. This was a childhood hobby that had, over the years, gained in importance, but that night, Militza remembered, was perhaps the most significant of all. They had been invited to see the newborn, Anastasia, at Tsarskoye Selo the following day, which, given that she was only a few days old, was a great honor indeed. It suggested to Militza that all was not lost with the tsar and the tsarina; it appeared they were to be given a second chance. However, to arrive without a persuasive plan would be foolish, possibly terminal. Like losing one's footing on a steep cliff, it would leave their hard-won position entirely vacant, ready for someone else to step into, as they themselves fell, bruised and lacerated, all the way down.

"So, we reiterate Philippe's suggestion," began Militza as she walked through the woods, hitching up her white skirts, already damp with dew.

Being alone in the forest with her sister brought her no fear. In fact, she loved the feeling of solitude, loved listening to the wind as it rustled through the leaves of the silver birch; it was as if the trees themselves were talking to her, muttering and mumbling their secrets, telling them exactly where to find the woodland treasures that they were seeking. She loved the light at that hour of night this far north, when the weak sun never waned and the sky was a pale, clean, clear blue; it was as if everything was crisp and new, about to be reborn.

"Alix simply didn't believe enough," she continued, picking her way along the path. "She may have thought she had, but she did not."

"Maître Philippe doesn't fail," agreed Stana, sounding equally determined. "We just have to make her realize her mistake. It's all her own fault; if only she'd trusted Philippe, trusted *us* a little more."

"It's not just her we need to convince. There!" Militza said, pointing to a small patch of blue flowers nestled at the foot of a tree. "Knapweed. Adam's head, the tsar of herbs, for the tsar of Russia." She smiled. "Just what we were looking for."

Stana rushed over with all the enthusiasm of a child, knelt down, and cradled the small blue flower in her hand. "What a perfect specimen—and gathering morning dew just as it should be. We couldn't wish for better."

"Lord, bless me." Militza took a small wooden crucifix out from deep in her dress pocket and, waving it over the flowers, started to chant. "And you, Mother Fresh Earth, bless me to cull this plant." She made the sign of the cross over the front of her breast. "You have brought it forth for man's use, and thus I take it. From the earth a plant. From God a medicine. Amen."

"Amen," repeated her sister.

Militza took out the short, sharp-bladed knife and knelt down before the plant. A curl of loose birch leaves blew off the ground and spun and danced before them like a wisp.

Militza smiled. "Here come the woodland spirits," she said, looking up at her sister. "Are you ready? Turn around, otherwise the herbs will lose their power."

Stana turned her back and prayed. "Holy Adam plowed, Jesus Christ gave seed, the Lord sowed it, the Mother of God watered it and gave it to the Orthodox people as an aid." She crossed herself and spat three times on the ground. "Amen."

"Amen," repeated Militza, and plunged the point of the knife into the palm of her hand. A searing agony ripped through her and she cried out. Her eyes watered, but as she exhaled through her half-open mouth, she began to feel the rush, the high, giddy joy of the pain. She sucked on the wound, drawing the blood closer to the surface. Eventually two scarlet drips appeared and snaked down her wrist, staining the white cuff of her dress. She knelt over the flower, squeezing her left hand harder and harder until finally another three large drops fell, splattering the small blue petals.

"Adam's head, the dew of midsummer morn, and the blood of a witch," declared Stana, and she swiftly sliced the stem close to the root. "It does not get more powerful than that."

"Mix with holy water, and even the most barren will conceive a son."

LATER THAT MORNING THEY OPENED THE DOOR TO THE TSARI-na's bedchamber. Crepuscular and devoid of oxygen, with the curtains tightly drawn, the room was hot and crammed with photographs, icons, and endless painted images. Between the two brass beds swathed in pink bows and a fussy English floral-wreath-patterned chintz, every nook, cranny, surface, and space hosting pots, plants, bronze statues, or little knickknacks from Alix's travels, the effect was not only an assault on the eyes but also overpoweringly claustrophobic.

Through the half-light they could see Alix propped up on her pillows, the mewling infant by her side. The tsarina's hair was loose, her face covered in a cold, dank sheen, and she looked weak and lost. Such was the shock and the disappointment of a fourth daughter that she had, apparently, been driven mad by insomnia. She had not slept for three days, stalked by the twin demons of guilt and fear. On closer inspection the sisters saw that her eyes were rubbed red raw, her mouth was dry, and her parted lips were barely capable of speech.

"You are here. At last," she said.

She spoke so softly the sisters had to strain to hear her. She closed her eyes as a tear slipped out of the corner of one eye and slithered down her cheek. "Tell me all is not lost." She turned her head towards the closed window and tried to stifle a small cry. "Tell me I am not lost."

"All is not lost," replied Militza, sitting on the bed and taking Alix's thin hand in hers. "You are not lost."

"We're here now," added Stana, sitting down on the end of the bed. "And we have something for you."

While Alix stared listlessly, Militza placed twelve little wooden dolls, one by one, in a circle on the bed. Made from laundry pegs carved from rowan wood, they wore hand-snipped head scarves of various hues tightly pinned around their smooth, faceless heads. The last time she'd used her Herod's daughters, Militza had managed to quell the worryingly high fever that had gripped the son of Stana's lady's maid, Natalya. For two nights he had tossed and turned, pale and pouring sweat, but eventually the dolls had performed their magic, and the fever had calmed. This morning, as they sat in the dark, stuffy bedchamber, Militza was hoping they might cool Alix's fever and help her overcome the terrible disappointment of Anastasia's birth.

"What lovely little dolls," she whispered, stroking the smooth, featureless face of the one closest to her with a quivering hand. "Rock-a-bye, baby . . ." she began singing in a thin, quiet voice, gently under her breath. "On the treetop . . ." She slowly swayed the poppet back and forth. "When the wind blows, the cradle will rock, and when the bough breaks . . ." She paused and turned to stare at Militza. "The cradle will fall . . ." Her eyes were so haunted and pale, and although she was looking at Militza, Militza wasn't sure if she could see her at all. "And down will come baby . . . cradle . . . and . . . all." She suddenly looked at the wooden poppet and threw it across the room. It smashed into a small mirror, sitting on one of the many cluttered shelves, which fell to the floor and immediately shattered into a thousand little pieces. The shocked silence that followed was only broken by the gurgling noises from the tightly swaddled baby lying on the bed.

"Philippe says you will have a son," declared Militza. Alix did not reply. She simply stared into the darkness, her face devoid of expression. "Philippe promises you will have a son—and Philippe is never wrong."

"Really?" she responded eventually, sounding so very hopeless and so very unconvinced.

"Yes! You just have to believe."

"Yes," added Stana joining in. "You just have to believe."

"Believe in what Philippe said. He's been sent from God. Believe in God and the will of God. Believe with all your heart," confirmed Militza, taking hold of both of her thin white hands and squeezing them.

"Just believe . . ." Alix sighed and closed her eyes, all her fight gone.

"Just believe, my darling, open up your heart and it will happen," whispered Militza, gently stroking the back of her hand.

"Believe," hushed Stana.

They carried on whispering, caressing her hand, stroking her hair, until it almost became some sort of mantra; they rearranged the small wooden poppets, moving around the bed in the half-light, like shadows in the night, their footsteps light, their movements slow. It was like a dance. They lit the heavy rose-oil incense burner in the private oratory just off the bedroom, and the sweet, sickly smell wafted into the room, its odor overpowering. The more the girls moved, the more the airless atmosphere was rendered claustrophobic. The chanting, the cloying perfume, the whispering around the bed—the effect was hypnotic. Alix was slowly drawn into their vortex so that when they came to administer the drops, she was powerless to resist. She opened her mouth like a compliant child as they slipped the pipette between her gently parted lips.

"Adam's head," Militza whispered in her ear. "The tsar of herbs for the tsarina." Alix managed a small smile. Militza leaned in closely, and her lips brushed against Alix's cheek; then slowly, tenderly, she moved lower, gently kissing Alix on the mouth. The tsarina inhaled sharply, her eyes suddenly wide-open, her face questioning. Undeterred, Militza continued. "Two drops a day, every day, my darling," she whispered, kissing her again. "Then, when your menstrual blood flows again, four drops every day after that until you conceive again. Which you will . . . I promise."

"I will," repeated Alix, smiling slowly at her friend as her pale cheeks flushed pink. She stared into Militza's deep black eyes, her own burning more brightly than before. She caressed her cheek before she turned her head and, with a relaxed and heavy sigh, let her lids slowly close. Finally, a few minutes later, her chest began to rise and fall. At last she'd fallen asleep.

OUTSIDE THE ROOM, THE ANXIOUS TSAR WAS PACING UP AND down the corridor, his polished boots tapping on the wooden floor. He looked gaunt, his eyes emanating a deep sadness; it was as if he had aged a dozen years overnight.

"How is she?" he asked, taking hold of Militza's shoulder as the two sisters exited the room, chased by a heavy cloud of incense. His grip was urgent. "Dr. Ott wants to prescribe aspirin."

"He always wants to prescribe aspirin, that's his answer to everything," said Militza. "She is asleep now and she needs to rest. Let the wet nurse take the child."

"You know Alix doesn't like that."

"Alix needs to sleep—desperately needs to sleep. She can feed her child later," asserted Militza.

There was a noise at the end of the corridor, and Nicholas turned to stare as his two eldest girls, Olga, aged five, and Tatiana, who had just turned four, appeared. Dressed in identical white frilled dresses, their long hair tied back with large pale blue ribbons, they rushed towards him.

"Papa!" exclaimed Olga as she fell against his legs and embraced him.

"Papa!" cried Tatiana, doing exactly the same.

"How is Mummy? Is it a one or a two today?" Olga asked, her pretty face upturned towards her father. "I hate it when her back pain is a two because I know we are not allowed to see her."

"It is not her back that is hurting today," said Nicholas, kneeling down and stroking the top of his daughter's head. "It is the new baby, she's making Mama tired."

"When will she be awake? When will she be better?" continued Olga.

"I want to see Mama," Tatiana announced, trying to push her father to one side to get into the room.

"No, no, no," said the tsar, taking both his daughters gently by the hand. "Mama needs some rest, she needs to sleep. Why don't you come outside with me? It is a beautiful day; let's go for a walk. A walk always makes everything much better."

CHAPTER 12

AUGUST 1901, ZNAMENKA, PETERHOF

MILITZA REMEMBERED THE SUMMER OF 1901 AS A BLISS-ful few months. She and Peter were happy. She knew he loved her, for he told her often, not in so many words but by his deeds. He was kind, protective, and he adored his children, was forever trying to engage them in his favorite subject of architecture. Marina, Roman, and little Nadezhda were not the most willing of students, Militza recalled, but they were well and thriving nonetheless. Even Stana was content. George was in Biarritz, of course, but she and her children had become so used to his absence that no one questioned where he was anymore.

Perhaps it was the calm before the storm? Although, truthfully, no one really knew then that there was a storm brewing, or what a terrible storm it would be. Granted, the spark of unrest was being heartily fanned in the countryside, and the city was increasingly crowded and fractious, but out in Peterhof, blissful Peterhof, surrounded by the gentle, lush forests, rocked by the cool breeze off the gulf, there appeared to be few concerns. The weather was not unduly hot, and the afternoons were bathed in a glorious golden glow, the evenings light and languid—and the tsarina was an almost daily visitor.

Her morning telephone call from the Lower Dacha was generally followed by the loud sound of her carriage wheels as they came rattling up the drive, usually in time for tea. She was very fond of tea, as were her girls. English tea with milk and sugar, not the usual Russian jam. Sometimes she would bring all of the girls with her, including the baby, Anastasia, so that they might amuse themselves with Marina, Roman, and Nadezhda as well as Stana's Sergei and Elena. (George's son Alex was thankfully away serving with the hussars.) Sometimes the tsarina would bring along just the "bigs," Olga and Tatiana; sometimes she would come on her own. And if she didn't manage to come—if her back was hurting her or, more recently, her heart, or if one of the children was unwell—then she would always make another telephone call in the afternoon. A lengthy telephone call, where all manner of intimate minutiae was discussed. It was as if the sisters had become her daily fix and, like a laudanum addict, she could not manage without them.

The Dowager Empress reacted to their relationship with consternation. Her previously frosty behavior towards the "Black Spiders," as she now called the sisters, became increasingly hostile. Minny could not stand to be in the mere presence of either Stana or Militza and would quite often refuse to attend any function she knew they might attend. Militza was fascinated by the withdrawal of the Dowager Empress. How unlike Maria not to have put up more of a fight, she thought at the time. The Dowager Empress, along with the Grand Duchess Vladimir, might still control the pockets of St. Petersburg, but she had totally lost control over her son. The tsar and tsarina's circle was now so small and the influence that the two sisters exerted so strong that no one dared cross them. Helped in part by Dr. Badmaev and his regular supply of hashish and cocaine elixir—of which Militza was growing increasingly fond—the sisters' grip around the couple became very tight indeed. Along with that, the gossip became increasingly vicious and slanderous.

"You will enjoy what I heard yesterday at the Yacht Club," pronounced Peter as he lit a cigarette at the breakfast table one morning and slowly stirred his coffee. "You and Alix are having an affair. Or was it Stana? I am not quite sure." He chuckled and twisted the ends of his mustache. "And Philippe is in the bedroom with you both! Or was it all three of you? I had rather too much claret to remember. But it was jolly amusing nonetheless!"

"Fascinating," replied Militza, dressed in a pale blue silk morning dress, as she slowly punctured two raw egg yolks with a silver fork and whipped them into a light froth at the bottom of her glass. "One should never underestimate the creative power of jealousy."

She put her lips to the rim of the glass, opened her throat, and swiftly swallowed the medicinal cocktail. She was not overly keen on her early-morning egg potion, but since the Grand Duchess Vladimir had been overheard extolling its health-giving properties, all the ladies of the court, including Alix, were drinking raw egg for breakfast.

Militza slowly pressed the corners of her mouth with her napkin as she tried to calm herself. The mere mention of her closeness with Alix made her heart beat faster. She had not kissed her again since that hot, heady afternoon in her bedchamber, but she had thought about it, relentlessly, as she lay in bed, the images churning around in her head, the smell of Alix's flesh, the touch of her bosom, the taste of her. Militza had become so intimately familiar with Alix, her moon cycle, and her desperate desire to have a son that she now knew of every occasion she was penetrated by the tsar and how and for how long, and whether he mounted from the left or the right or from behind, that there were times when she felt herself flushed with a hot, fiery emotion that was hard to explain.

All she knew was that it was a dangerous emotion, for it clouded her judgment. She'd made that mistake once before, and she was not going to let it happen a second time.

A footman bringing a letter on a silver salver disturbed her thoughts. She plucked it from the tray and turned it over and over in her hands. She'd recognize that script and seal anywhere.

"Who's that from?" asked Peter with vague interest, looking over the top of his newspaper. Sporting his navy silk dressing gown and monogrammed maroon velvet slippers, he had yet to dress for the day.

"Father."

"What does he want now? Not more guns? I am intrigued to know what he did with the last forty thousand. And quite how you managed to procure those, I have no idea."

"They were a present from a grateful emperor on the birth of his fourth daughter." Militza smiled at her husband as she opened the letter.

"No one is grateful for four daughters," replied Peter, taking a sip of coffee.

"Queen Victoria had five," retorted Militza. "God rest her soul."

Peter coughed. "What does your father want?"

"Money . . . Grain . . . More money." Militza skimmed the letter, turning over the pages. "He wants to build more roads." She put the letter down before adding with a small shrug, "He is trying to drag Montenegro into this new twentieth century."

"A lofty ambition, I am sure," agreed Peter, twisting the corners of his dark brown mustache. "But a little hard to do with one hand tied behind your back financially."

"That's why he has daughters in high places." Militza smiled, breaking off a small piece of black bread. "I heard someone call him the father-in-law of Europe the other day!"

Peter looked less amused. "Why can't he ask your sister? Why is it always us Russians who end up paying?"

"Well, Zorka is dead, so I am not sure she is of any use." Militza held the piece of bread to her lips and stared defiantly down the length of the highly polished rosewood table at her husband.

"There is no need to be sarcastic. I am well aware your sister died . . ."

"Along with her son."

"Along with her son," repeated Peter.

"Andrei was his name. And she was twenty-five!" Militza's laugh was a little hysterical. "But such is the lot of us women. You either burn us at the stake or drown us along with all our healing properties and our worldly powers. Or you try and kill us with children. And if we don't die having them, then we kill ourselves trying to have them."

Peter ignored his wife. He'd heard this little speech quite often, especially late at night when the two sisters got together with their tarot de Marseilles, reading palms or runes, always returning to the land of witches, mavens, and wanderers where women were once revered for their intuition and powers and not burnt at the stake for witchcraft.

"Actually, I was thinking more of Elena, now that she is queen of Italy," he eventually replied.

"She's only been queen for just over twelve months!"

"Even so," continued Peter, slowly squeezing the white tip of his cigarette between his thumb and forefinger before extinguishing it in the malachite ashtray in front of him, "it isn't good to ask too often, for too much. People start to begrudge you. It's annoying. Especially when your position is so precarious."

"*Our* position," corrected Militza as she fixed her husband with a dark stare. "Ours, my darling, for you and I are linked. Our position is linked. Our privilege is linked, as is our access. We ride high together."

She reached across to a small scarlet bottle sitting next to her empty glass. She picked it up, removed the lid, and carefully squeezed the rubber-topped pipette, drawing up some liquid from the bottle before swiftly delivering a river of droplets onto the surface of her own protruding, curled tongue. She sucked the tincture back, with a relishing hissing sound, half closing her eyes.

"High? But for how long?" Peter put down his newspaper. "Your friend—"

"'Our Friend,' that's what Alix calls him now. And I rather like it."

"Our Friend is not terribly popular, you know. There are mumblings, there's talk."

"There is always talk. That's all there is—talk."

Militza's pulse was beginning to race. It was difficult to ascertain whether it was her growing irritation with her husband or merely the powerful effects of Dr. Badmaev's cocaine elixir.

"There is no need to be so bad-tempered," continued Peter. "I was just passing on what I had heard."

"What? Snippets you picked up at the banya while chewing gherkins and drinking vodka? I am not sure those sources could possibly compare to the tsar himself—to my source, the apex of power!"

"Well, you probably know the other rumors then?"

"Probably." Militza shook her head. She inhaled, expanding her chest, preparing to enjoy whatever her husband said.

"That Maria Fyodorovna has sent a team of spies to France to find out about Our Friend. The tsar's mother doesn't like the way Philippe is with her son, doesn't like the way he has managed to get such a position at court, doesn't like the secretive meetings, the furtiveness of it all, and she doesn't trust him."

"The Dowager Empress has sent spies?"

"Secret agents. They'll report back to her."

"When?"

"Soon. And the problem is, we both know what they'll come back with . . ."

Militza was shocked. This was news indeed. She reached forward to pick up the red bottle again. More elixir. She needed to think and she needed to think fast.

"I think you should stop taking so much of Mr. Badmaev's bloody potion." Peter nodded towards the bottle. "I hear he's prescribing half of Countess Ignatiev's salon these days. It's ridiculous. The man doesn't seem to be able to cure anything except stubborn nervous diseases, mental maladies, and disturbances of the female physiology."

"Tell that to the tsar and all those patients he's put forward for ministerial posts. And anyway, he's a doctor," she replied, raising her fine, large black brows. "Dr. Badmaev, if you please. Not 'Mister.' He knows what he is doing."

"Well, everyone trusts a doctor! Don't they?"

Militza nodded, staring out of the window towards the large fountain in the garden and the calm sea beyond. "Yes, they do," she said slowly. "I think I have an idea."

AND AS WITH ALL IDEAS, MILITZA FOUND IT MUCH BETTER FOR the person to "come up with it" themselves. So it was a few days later that Alix announced, while taking a small walk through the fragrant rose garden just to the left of the long terrace at Znamenka, that she'd thought of something simply splendid. The fact that Stana had planted this suggestion in her head when she'd visited for luncheon the day before was neither here nor there.

"I think," Alix declared, as she spun her parasol, "I think that Nicky should make Our Friend an honorary doctor."

"Oh!" Militza stopped in her tracks and clutched her heart in ostentatious excitement. "How clever of you! That is such a good idea."

"It just came to me," continued Alix, with a small shrug and a curl of a smile. "He has been so incredibly helpful and loyal, he deserves something. Don't you think? It seems such a shame that he has not been recognized."

"Absolutely."

"I suggested it to Nicky at breakfast this morning and he wasn't completely sure, but I explained it would help with Dr. Ott and the others . . . It would be nice for him to have a position. An official role. I feel they look down on him sometimes. I see their faces when he speaks. I know he has an appalling southern accent, but then I speak Russian with such a terrible thick accent too! And no one thinks any the less of me for that!"

"No," agreed Militza, fighting the smile on her face, "I think most people find your accent . . . charming."

"Yes." Alix nodded. "Charming."

How could she not hear the sniggers and the titters when she opened her mouth to speak Russian? Militza wondered. Had she become inured to the antipathy at court? So used to the frosty reception she received that she no longer felt it? Is it possible to have one's feelings so hurt that one ceases to feel at all anymore?

As they continued their walk, arm in arm, down the gently sloping lawn, through the thick line of cedar trees, towards the sea, Militza remembered a story that Alix had once told her about her early days in Russia and about how she'd always felt "quite alone and in despair." She'd described an afternoon's drive that she and one of the more unpleasant ladies of the court, Countess Vorontsov, had taken along Nevsky Prospekt, when they'd come across a beggar asking for alms. He'd approached the carriage with his hands outstretched, and she, Alix, had been so touched by his plight and his kind eyes, she'd given him a few coins from her purse. The beggar had smiled gratefully at her. "That was the first smile," she'd told Militza, "I'd received in Russia." And she had been there for over a year.

Now even the beggars don't bother, thought Militza as they paused on the brow of a hill to catch their breath, staring out to sea. Perhaps it is preferable, then, that she no longer notices.

"Perhaps we could ask the French?" suggested Alix. Militza stared at her blankly. "To give Our Friend a doctorate?"

"I don't think that is a good idea," Militza said hurriedly.

"Oh?" Alix looked a little surprised. She was not a woman used to being contradicted.

"The French . . ." Militza's mind was whirring. How could she tell her that Our Friend had in fact been arrested five times in France for practicing without a license? Not that there was any doubt that Monsieur Philippe had special powers. Of course he did. It was, Militza reasoned, just a great shame that the French authorities were the last to realize them. "I think a Russian doctorate, a Russian medical diploma, would be much more fitting for services in Russia, to the Russian court, to the Russian tsar himself," she declared. "Rather than anything Our Friend achieved in Paris. Although he has clearly achieved a lot in Paris, and in France, the whole of France, of course," she swiftly added.

"Yes," sighed Alix. Her voice suddenly sounded a little weak. "You know best."

"Let's ask him tonight," suggested Militza.

She turned away from the sea and looked up the hill towards Znamenka. Its huge neoclassical facade stretched expansively before her. Three stories high with a large domed roof tower, plus endless bedrooms, ballrooms, salons, dining rooms, servants' quarters, its own greenhouses, stables for one hundred horses, cellar, and kitchen gardens, it was an impressive and imposing sight. The weak afternoon sunset made its yellow and white frosted pillars glow a pale orange, and if she squinted slightly, she could see several white dots, the children, playing on the terrace. Militza smiled to herself and sighed with a gentle contentment.

She turned back. Alix was looking pale in the wind. Over her shoulder, the sun dipped behind a thick cloud gathering on the horizon. She shivered; her white chiffon ensemble rippled against her.

"I am cold," she said, closing her flighty parasol and wrapping her arms around herself. "And tired." She looked up at Militza. Her pale blue eyes appeared to be fighting back tears.

"Are you all right?" Militza moved swiftly, placing her hands on Alix's shoulders.

"Yes, yes," she replied breezily, avoiding looking Militza in the eyes as the wind whipped loose strands of hair around her face. "Just tell me," she stammered, fighting to get the words out as her lips shook and her nose started to run. Try as she might she could not stop her tears. "Tell me . . ." She was inhaling and exhaling, shivering and stammering, trying to keep in check the bubbling brook of emotion that was desperately busting out of her. "Tell me it will be all right. Tell me it will." At last she sobbed and at last she cried, but instead of cleaving to Militza, she stood there on the clifftop, rigid, her fists clenching, her pale golden hair flying around her face, biting her bottom lip as the tears streamed down her face.

"Yes, it will," Militza said, moving towards her and wrapping her in a tight embrace. "It will all be fine." She slowly kissed Alix on the cheek and then on her soft, sensitive mouth.

"Goodness gracious!" announced Alix, pulling away swiftly and rapidly searching in her pocket for her handkerchief. "Look at me." She stared down her damp, milk-soaked shirt. "Even my breast is weeping."

CHAPTER 13

DECEMBER 1901, ST. PETERSBURG

MILITZA WAS SITTING IN THE BACK OF THE COVERED carriage, swathed in silver fox, watching her sister. From low in her seat, her stole covering half of her face, she stared through the gaps in the fur. She wasn't sure if Stana could see her staring; perhaps she didn't care. Either way her behavior was verging on the flirtatious. In fact, it was not *verging* on the flirtatious, concluded Militza; it was completely flirtatious. Stana was sitting close to Peter's elder brother, Nikolasha, very close, a large diamond necklace glinting around her neck, laughing at his every word, touching the back of his gloved hand, letting her sable fur hang loosely around her shoulders, exposing her pale white throat to his gaze.

"I promise you, you will enjoy it," she said, stroking the sleeve of Nikolasha's greatcoat. "The Black Salon is among the highlights of St. Petersburg nightlife."

"Better than the gypsies in the Islands?" Nikolasha had

certainly been drinking; otherwise it was unlikely he'd be so candid about his choice of after-dinner activity.

Stana sat upright, opening her pretty mouth with faux prudishness. "I didn't think you were the sort of man to frequent the gypsies?"

"Well . . ." Nikolasha blushed a little, unable to tell whether she was joking or not. "Don't all men?" he stammered. "After too much Madeira at the Cubat or the Donon? They say there is nothing more beautiful, more full of soul and melancholy, than to hear Varya Panina sing? There's many a man in St. Petersburg whose huge debt and frequent visits to the moneylender are due to nights of carousing in the Villa Rhode. Or so they say." He hesitated. "Some would spend their last thousand just to spend the night, hypnotized by wine and song, till dawn in Novaya Derevnaya."

"Personally, I am not overly fond of gypsies," replied Stana, biting her bottom lip as she leaned in closer, slowly turning the button on his coat with her white gloved fingers.

"Really? I would have thought their bright clothes—the red, the violet, the purple—would appeal to you. Surely their dark exoticness must remind you of home?"

"No, just her wedding party," Militza muttered through the tail of her silver fox. What was her sister doing, flirting so heavily with Nikolasha? "Look," she said, as she glanced out of the frosted window, "we are here."

IT WAS GONE MIDNIGHT BY THE TIME THE THREE ARRIVED AT 26 Kutuzov Embankment, and the Countess Ignatiev's salon soirée was in full swing. Having tired of a rather boring dinner at Grand Duchess Vladimir's, where the young actors and singers who were supposed to arrive from the Mariinsky Theatre had failed to materialize, they had agreed to continue the evening at the Ignatievs'—it had been Stana's suggestion, as she was loath to let the handsome Nikolasha disappear off into the night. She had spent most of the summer in the company of her children, had seen her sister obviously and the tsarina, but with George in Biarritz, she'd been deprived of male company. Not that she ever enjoyed her husband's company: his wits were too slow and his conversation too dull for her liking. Nikolasha, however, was bright and sharp and rather attentive.

"My darlings!" declared the countess as the butler showed them into the raspberry drawing room. "Grand Duke," she added, looking up at the imposingly tall and immaculately presented Nikolai Nikolayevich, "you are very welcome." She smiled. Dressed in a House of Worth evening gown of black velvet, embroidered with silver leaves and with a large frill across the shoulders, the countess looked extremely glamorous. Gone was the yellowed court dress; popularity was clearly suiting her. "What an evening! What an evening. *Tout le monde* is here. How wonderful that you are here also! Your friend Philippe is next door!"

Weaving her way through the crowd of guests and the dense, sweet-smelling smoke, Militza spotted Dr. Badmaev in the corner.

"My dear," he said, putting down his clay pipe and getting out of his chair. His eyes were smiling as he came over to kiss her. "I didn't know you were coming this evening."

"No, neither did we," replied Militza. "We were having such a very boring dinner at the Vladimirs', discussing the Christmas bazaar and the problems in Manchuria, waiting for some actors to jolly things up, but when they didn't arrive, we made our excuses."

"Manchuria? How interesting."

"You would think."

"Was anything said?"

"I am not sure many in the room knew where it was!"

He leaned forward and muttered into her ear, "His Imperial Majesty and I have been discussing the very subject recently. He thinks I should travel there myself. He says I might be able to help, opening up some diplomatic channels, handing out some small change, lining a few pockets."

"I could think of no one better to calm troubled water than you," replied Militza.

"Or you!" Dr. Badmaev smiled.

"Now you flatter me."

"I don't believe so." He smiled again. "I hear the tsar is giving your father thousands more rifles, mountains more grain, and more rubles than he's spent on any of his palaces."

"You are remarkably well-informed."

"Isn't he arriving in St. Petersburg next month?"

"Once again, may I remark on the reliability of your sources?"

"It is amazing what you pick up at my simple little apothecary," he laughed.

"Or, indeed, during your little personal consultations."

"I hear also that your Friend, next door, is going to be made a doctor."

"Such a lovely idea. The tsarina came up with it herself!" It was Militza's turn to smile.

"I didn't know the German had any ideas of her own."

"Oh," replied Militza. "I take it you don't approve?"

"Approve of him? Or the doctorate?"

"Both."

"Of neither, I am afraid."

"But he is a man of God!" Militza's response was reflex.

"Really?"

"He works between two worlds."

"The question is, which two?"

"He can cure syphilis." Militza could feel her pulse rising.

Dr. Badmaev had been her friend and ally ever since she and her sister had arrived in the city. He leaned in very close and whispered carefully in her ear.

"Let me give a word of advice. Rifles? Grain? Money? Your

father arriving next month? All eyes are on you. Your time is running out. The knives are out. You need the boy, Militza, and you need him now."

"Oh, there you are!" declared Stana, taking her sister by the arm. "We're all waiting for you next door. Philippe says he won't start without you."

"Me?"

Militza was confused. Dr. Badmaev's words had upset her. He had never spoken to her like that before, and he was a man who knew much, everything perhaps. He had more direct access to power than anyone, even the Yusupovs or the Vladimirs. And moreover, unlike the Yusupovs and the Vladimirs, he was trusted. He was a doctor, after all.

STANA DIRECTED HER SISTER INTO THE DARKENED ADJACENT room, where an expectant crowd clustered around a large, highly polished dining table. Countess Ignatiev was sitting across from the door, rubbing her hands with excitement. Next to her was a buxom woman in a defiantly low-cut dinner dress whose husband, so it was rumored, had recently run off with a dancer who was great friends of the ballet-dancing courtesan Mathilde Kschessinskaya. To her right was a French diplomat whose legendary fondness for wine often resulted in him slithering down the walls at parties. Tonight, observed Militza, he looked more sober than usual, and opposite him was a heavily mustachioed general whose well-known fondness for paying for "conversation" had seen him visit Philippe's late-night clinic on more than one occasion. Next to him was a British journalist whom Militza always tried to avoid due to his irritating habit of pinning one into a corner and talking at one like the captive audience one was.

And so it went on around the table, old faces, old acquaintances—

and yet, on closer inspection, the circle was decidedly more peppered by a new crowd. It looked a little more louche, a little more decadent, a little more fashionable. Militza was a little taken aback. Perhaps the closest confidantes of the tsarina and her physician should not be here? Clearly the countess's little Black Salon was no longer the best-kept secret in town. In fact, she'd go so far as to say it was not a secret at all.

"*Ma chère*," said Philippe, patting the seat next to him. "How very delighted I am to see you."

Militza smiled tightly. She smoothed down her dark green silk dress and took her seat, inhaling a large curl of sickly, heavy incense as she did so.

"I was just about to begin," he said, wrapping his long, sharply filed fingernails around the planchette in the middle of the green felt Ouija board. "This . . ." he began, explaining to the crowd in his heavily accented French, "is the planchette . . ." There were murmurs of acknowledgment. They were clearly used to the vagaries of the occult. "One keeps one's fingers lightly in contact with the planchette, but one makes no attempt to move it oneself," he continued, fanning his short fingers at his audience. His buffed nails shone in the candlelight. "And my close friend the Grand Duchess Militza Nikolayevna will assist me."

"Right," replied Militza, a little taken aback. She was not prepared for a séance; she had not contacted her spirit guide, nor had she opened her chakras or even administered her belladonna drops. She'd had a few large goblets of claret at dinner, and she was more than a little tired, which was not the ideal preparation. Then again, she thought, as she looked around the crowded, increasingly hot and airless room, this was not the sort of atmosphere conducive to contacting a passed-over soul, no matter how far down the lower astral they were. This was surely an occasion when only drunkards or the murdered would be likely to appear, and even then, she thought, they probably would not bother. They'd be lucky if any old soul could make it through.

Philippe brought out a small ceramic bowl and began to light a selection of herbs, adding to the already heady and thick smoke. Militza blinked as her eyes watered and turned to look at her sister. But Stana was looking at Nikolai, who was standing behind her, his hands resting on the back of her chair. He smiled at her and twisted up the corners of his mustache.

Philippe began to chant, at first in French, then moving on to a rather poorly pronounced version of Sanskrit.

"Please," he said finally, indicating for Militza to manage the planchette. "I know you are good at channeling." She looked at him and didn't move. She had no desire to take it up. "There are a lot of people here," he hissed. "Show them how it is done."

Reluctantly, she placed her fingers on the upturned glass and closed her eyes. Almost immediately she felt some movement, a force tugging at her fingers, pushing her hand this way. Militza tried to resist. Personally, she didn't like using a planchette. When she made contact with the spirit world, this was her last method, and she was not hugely familiar with the technique. But whoever this was was determined to be heard. A terrible shiver came over her body, and she could feel a biliousness that made her want to be sick. She felt the color drain from her cheeks as she rocked in her chair.

"Someone is here!" declared Philippe, stretching his arms out dramatically across the table. "See! Spirit makes a wind. Look how the candles move!" He flapped his hand in front of the silver candelabra on the table. "It is someone important!" he added. "I feel it. Terribly important! I feel the weight of state . . . or perhaps . . . of legacy."

"How exciting!" Countess Ignatiev couldn't contain a small squeal of delight.

"Let's hope it is not bloody Pushkin," drawled the British

journalist. "I remember he came through the other day and was awfully full of himself."

"Shh!" said the buxom woman in the low-cut dress.

Militza felt the planchette move swiftly across the felt, dancing from letter to letter at slick and accurate speed.

"P . . ." said Philippe as he watched Militza's hands move across the board. "A . . ." he continued. "U . . . L . . . Paul," he pronounced. "Spirit? Is your name Paul?" Militza felt the planchette move quickly across to "Yes." But as she did so, she gasped.

"Oh," she exhaled as she doubled up over the table.

"Are you all right?" asked Stana, immediately taking her arm.

"I feel . . . I feel . . ." Militza was breathless and panting, gasping for air. "I feel as if I have been stabbed in the stomach. The pain! The agony!" She began to sway listlessly in the chair, and yet her fingers firmly gripped the planchette. "I was murdered," she mumbled under her breath. "I am unshriven . . ."

"Paul?" continued Philippe, leaning forward, looking keenly at the board, clearly delighted that such a communicative spirit had come through with such a large audience to witness it. "Were you murdered?" Militza practically punched the "Yes" square with the glass. "Yes! Yes! Yes!" Three times the planchette struck the square; three times Militza's arms shot forward. Her eyes were closed, and her head was on one side as her tongue began to loll out of her mouth. Yet her back and arms were rigid, alert, attentive, waiting to respond to the next question. It was as if her body had been completely taken over by something—or someone—else and she was no longer capable of controlling it.

"Is she all right?" Nikolasha asked Stana. His concern was touching.

"I think so," replied Stana. "She has done this many times before."

"My neck," wheezed Militza. "I can't breathe . . ."

"Spirit? Paul?" continued Philippe, staring at Militza, trying to read the expression on her face as she appeared to fight for breath. "Where you throttled? Strangled?"

Militza's body went limp, but once again her arms shot across the board, hammering the planchette up and down on the "Yes" square.

"Oh!" declared the countess, leaning back, away from the table. "How ghastly."

Standing behind Stana, Nikolasha gripped the back of her chair. His impassive face, with its straight nose, fine brows, and elegantly upturned mustache, began to sweat. His normally erect back hunched forward. Stana sensed his discomfort and, turning around, touched his right hand; it felt cold.

"Ask Paul if he was trampled?" he whispered quietly into Stana's ear. She looked at him, frowning. "Just ask," he said, shaking his head. "Please."

"Spirit?" The whole table turned to look at Stana. "Were you trampled?"

"Yes. Yes. *Yes.*" Militza hammered the glass down repeatedly as if she were in some sort of frenzy.

"Oh, my God, save us!" exclaimed Nikolasha, staggering back from the table, covering his mouth and breathing heavily. "It can't be! It can't be!"

"What?" Stana leapt out of her chair and went immediately to his side.

"I thought this was supposed to be frivolous? Entertaining?" He was speaking in a low whisper in a dark corner of the room, had grabbed hold of Stana's shoulders and was spitting as he spoke, clearly fighting some very deep-rooted emotion. "Instead you bring me here and raise the hideous specter of Paul I's unshriven soul! The very ghost that has haunted Gatchina since he was strangled and trampled to death at Mikhailovsky Castle by his own soldiers. Nicky, me, Peter—we have always been terrified of him."

"I'm sorry," said Stana.

"None of us could ever sleep at that hideous palace." He shivered a little at its memory. "The irony! Sent there for our own safety after the murder of my uncle only to have our nights turned white with the noise of Paul's screaming, wailing soul. And now," he said, pulling her extremely close, so that his nose was almost touching her, "you have brought him here! For fun?"

"Time to grow up. Go and rule!"

Nikolasha froze and looked over Stana's shoulder in the direction of the voice. Militza was standing by the table, facing him. Backlit by candles, she appeared in silhouette, the index finger of her right hand pointing at him.

"Time to grow up. Go and rule!" Her tone was hateful, hard, and completely heartless. It did not sound like her at all.

"Lord Jesus," whispered Nikolasha, crossing himself as he looked across at her in the darkness. "How does she know?"

"Know what?" asked Stana.

"What the murderers said after they pulled the young Alexander I from his bed, having just killed his father? 'Time to grow up. Go and rule.'" He shook his head. "No wonder my family are haunted by death, no wonder they hide in their palaces, fearful of assassination. No wonder they cower when they've been hunted and shot like dogs over and over again, for centuries."

"Sergei!" Militza declared.

Nikolasha left the corner of the room and approached her. Militza was standing next to her chair, her hands by her sides, her eyes glazed, repeating the same word, "Sergei," over and over.

"Sergei? What? Sergei? Who?" Nikolasha quizzed her ever more intensely. "None of the assassins were called Sergei."

"Spirit?" Philippe now stood up, his voice sounding a little panicked. "Spirit. Paul. Who is Sergei?"

"Sergei!" Militza crashed her fist on the table. Everyone gasped as glasses shattered and a goblet of red wine splashed across the table.

"Oh, dear!" Countess Ignatiev leapt out of her seat. "Someone call a servant!"

Then suddenly there was shouting and a loud hammering of rifle butts on the paneled wooden doors. A man burst through, accompanied by the sound of rattling sabres.

"Grand Duchess Militza Nikolayevna?" he bellowed, his cheeks crimsoned above the great gray bushiness of his mustache. "Grand Duchess Anastasia Nikolayevna?" His eyes narrowed. "Philippe Nizier-Vachot?"

Everyone stood still, some with drinks in hand, as if paused midconversation. A small group of soldiers entered the room and surveyed it, taking in the Ouija board, the planchette, the smell of incense, and the heady aroma of hashish and herbs. It was obvious this was no ordinary gathering. The dark arts were most certainly being practiced here.

"Nizier-Vachot?" the red-faced officer barked again.

"*Oui?*" came Philippe's tentative reply.

"Outside!" the soldier ordered, pointing towards the next room.

There was a pause as Philippe, his faced blanching rapidly, walked slowly out of the room.

"Grand Duchess Anastasia Nikolayevna?"

His eyes darted from face to face. Stana said nothing. She silently picked up her small evening reticule and walked in a slow and dignified manner towards the door.

"But this is a private party—" began Countess Ignatiev, starting towards the door.

"Sit down!" he shouted. "This is not a matter that concerns you."

"But it is my house," she insisted.

"Then do as you are told!" he replied, indicating a chair.

"I am not sure this is correct," announced Nikolasha, stepping forward.

"Grand Duke," replied the officer, bowing his head. "I have my orders if you would like to see them?"

"Yes, I would," he stated, stepping forward. "What is your business with Monsieur Philippe and their Imperial Highnesses?"

"Nikolasha, there is no need. Let us not make a scene and ruin everyone's evening. I am sure it is nothing. I am sure we shall be fine; just let my husband know what has happened. Let's go," declared Militza, gathering herself up off her chair. Spirit apparently having left her almost as quickly as he had arrived, she appeared alert and focused. "And let us accept whatever the Fates have in store for us."

OUTSIDE ON THE STREET IT SHOULD HAVE BEEN TOO COLD TO snow, but somehow flakes were falling. Beneath a streetlight, their white breath bellowing, a small unit of waiting soldiers were covered, their shoulders and bearskin hats frosted white. They had been outside for quite some time.

"In here." The crimson-faced major indicated a large carriage.

"Who? Me? Just me?" asked Philippe, skittish with panic, looking left and right, slipping and dancing about in the snow. His round face was growing red as he tugged repeatedly at the large corners of his mustache. "I am a French citizen, you know; I need to contact the embassy. I have done nothing wrong. I know lots of people, very important people—I know the tsar!"

"All of you"—the officer hit the side of the door with the butt of his rifle—"in here."

"All of us?" Philippe's relief was palpable. He had no idea where he was going, but at least he was not going on his own. "After you, ladies!" he said, laughing a little wildly as he opened the carriage door and offered his hand.

Wrapped in her sable fur, Stana was the first inside, sitting down on the poorly padded seat. Militza followed, her silver fox in hand.

"It's all right," she said sitting down next to her sister. "Look," she said, nodding towards the bench opposite. "We have traveling rugs. They don't give prisoners traveling rugs."

"They might do," replied Philippe, sitting down and immediately covering his legs in the thick rug. "You never know what is going to happen. Especially not in this godforsaken country. I wish I had never set foot in the place. It's freezing and dark and so are the people. This is not going to end well."

"That is neither charming nor helpful," snapped Stana. "Just because you have been arrested before."

"Not for anything serious," insisted Philippe.

"I call impersonating a doctor serious." Stana grabbed hold of the blanket.

"Not if you are curing people," he replied.

"It's against the law."

"So is witchcraft."

"Not if you are curing people," retorted Stana, shivering with cold. She pulled back the short black curtain and peeked through the frosted glass of the carriage window. The streets of St. Petersburg were almost entirely deserted, the few people braving the cold at such a late hour wrapped up tightly, their footsteps silent and their shoulders hunched. "I wonder where they are taking us?" she asked suddenly, inhaling and biting her bottom lip as she tried to control the wave of rising panic. She looked across at her sister. "Where do you think? Why didn't you let Nikolasha stop them?"

"I didn't think there was much he could do," she replied sanguinely.

"But where are they taking us?"

Militza shrugged. "We shall know soon enough."

THEY TRAVELED IN SILENCE THROUGH THE NIGHT. THE ONLY noise was that of the carriage wheels slicing through the snow, and the longer the journey continued, the tighter the knot became in

Stana's stomach. Philippe somehow managed to doze, occasionally erupting into loud snores as his large nose tipped backwards towards the ceiling of the carriage. Militza, on the other hand, never moved. She sat stock-still, staring ahead as if in some sort of trance.

Finally, towards the early hours of the morning, they arrived. The carriage pulled up outside a large building and they were released, hearts racing, back into the night. Standing in the snow, still dressed in their evening wear, fine diamonds around their necks, the two sisters held hands for comfort. They blinked as they took in their surroundings.

"Tsarskoye Selo!" exclaimed Militza, looking at her sister.

"What are we doing here?" asked Stana, with increasing confusion.

"Follow me," barked the major.

Still surrounded by guards, the three of them were escorted into the back of the palace, past the sentries and up the back stairs into the tsar's private quarters and the bedchamber. As one of the guards raised his hand to knock on the door, Alix burst out. Dressed in her nightclothes, her hair loose around her shoulders, her eyes were wide with panic.

"You're here! You're here!" She embraced first Militza and then Stana, covering them with kisses, as if she were a lost child found in the woods. "Philippe!" She embraced him too. The three prisoners stood there, their arms by their sides, too shocked to understand what was going on. "They have searched St. Petersburg for you. Or so I hear. From the Vladimirs' to the Yacht Club and finally the Ignatievs'—you have been hard to find! But I was desperate, you see, desperate, so Nicky sent for you."

"Nicky?" Stana frowned.

"Sent for us?" asked Philippe.

"Yes, you see I had a terrible dream!" declared Alix.

"A dream?" Stana was bewildered.

"Arrested? In front of all those people? For a dream?" asked

Philippe, looking from Stana to Militza. He didn't know whether to be relieved or furious.

"You weren't arrested," Alix said, laughing. She looked from one to the other, appearing feverish, her skin shining with sweat and her lips pale. "Nicky only asked them to fetch you! How silly. Oh, how silly everything is." She laughed again. "But I just had to tell you my dream, it was so terrible and I need your help. So . . ." She clapped her hands together.

"What was your dream?" asked Militza, her dark eyes narrowing.

"Oh, it was terrible!" Alix shook her head.

She walked back into the bedchamber, indicating that they should follow. She climbed back into her bed and, drawing her knees up under her chin, went on to explain she felt as if she had been visited by an evil spirit.

"It stood," she said, "at the end of the bed. It was tall, much taller than a man but was the shape of a man. It was wearing a black hooded cape like Santa Muerte and it carried a baby. But the baby was tiny and red and covered in blood and it was screaming, it wouldn't stop screaming. The man was doing nothing to stop the screaming and all the time the blood dripped out of the baby and landed on the floor there"—she pointed—"at the foot of the bed. And then it laid the baby on the bed, still covered in blood and screaming. I leaned forward to comfort it, to stroke it, to stop it from screaming, and it turned into a snake and slithered away, leaving a trail of blood behind it. By then I was screaming so loudly in my sleep that I woke Nicky and some of the servants, I was shaking and covered in sweat—I couldn't stop shaking and I went to be sick, but there was nothing to throw up, so I retched and retched until eventually I had no strength in me, but still I cried and shook, so Nicky offered to send for you."

Just then Nicky appeared at the doorway. "There is nothing to worry about, is there? It was just a dream?"

"But all dreams have meaning," replied Philippe, sitting on the end of Alix's bed, taking charge. "Just as all illness is the soul's memory from a past life. The soul is much older than the body and, as such, we return to this world to pay our debts, because everything has to be paid for. To heal the sick, you have to ask God to forgive your faults, and at the same time the soul is strengthened and the body is healed."

"I knew you'd understand. I knew you would know," replied Alix, staring at Philippe, a smile curling her lips. "You always understand."

"In the heart is the thought, in the brain is the reflection of that thought. Thought is distinct from reasoning; a thought is a direct penetration into the light." He smiled and patted the back of her hand.

"The light . . ." Alix nodded in agreement.

"But what does it mean?" asked Nicky.

"It means—" Philippe began.

"It means that you are pregnant," interrupted Militza. "The baby is small and not yet full of blood, so it must be nurtured, it must be succored, fed with blood."

"I knew it!" beamed Nicky. "I knew it!"

"A baby . . ." Alix smiled and rubbed her flat stomach. "I do feel pregnant."

"And this time," said Philippe, "you will trust me and trust in God and it will be a boy. The son that all of Russia wants."

"Yes! A son. The son that Russia wants," confirmed Militza.

"And this time," Alix said, smiling broadly, "there will be no Dr. Ott. No doctors at all. Apart from my very own Dr. Philippe and his beautiful Montenegrin nurses."

CHAPTER 14

AUGUST 1902,
LOWER DACHA, PETERHOF

For the next nine months Militza, Stana, and Dr. Philippe rarely left her side. After a short spell at Tsarskoye Selo, the imperial family—including the newly appointed Dr. Philippe, complete with military epaulets indicative of his recently elevated position—moved to the Lower Dacha, Peterhof.

The moderately sized villa, right on the Gulf of Finland, was the most informal of all the palaces. The rooms, recently refurbished by Roman Meltzer, though a veritable temple to the new and highly fashionable art nouveau style, were pokey and cluttered and, frankly, just as Alix liked them. With her newly engaged Montenegrin nurses and her French doctor living very nearby at Znamenka, she spent her days quietly reading, walking, paddling, dozing, or attempting to feed the free-flying hummingbirds that darted around the glassed-in tropical winter garden. While Stana's and Militza's children traveled back and forth between their palace and the Lower Dacha, filling their days with lessons and exercise, the little grand duchesses did the same. Olga, under the instruction of her music tutor, could occasionally be heard practicing on the cream-colored piano in the tsar's reception room, while Tatiana was engaged in lessons with her nanny, Margaretta Eagar, and the "littles" were left to play in the expansive gardens with Orchie or sometimes escorted, parasols in hand, across the rocks and onto the nearby beach.

This was not a palace where Alix and Nicky received. The dining room, with its blue walls and cream-colored curtains embroidered with blue poppies, was far too small for official dinners, and the reception room, despite the piano and the tall vases replete with white flowers, was not formal enough for any but the most intimate guests. So they lived there, without interruption, social obligation, or indeed ceremony, much like members of the petite bourgeoisie in a comfortable but not particularly ostentatious dacha.

Alix was never happier than she was at the Lower Dacha. She had given birth to both Maria and Anastasia in the upstairs bedroom there, surrounded by family photographs. And given the importance of this confinement—the fact that she was most certainly carrying the heir, the future of all Russia—she had little more to do now than wait, sew, read, talk, lie on the veranda, relax on the wicker chaise, drink morning coffee, and listen to the waves and the children playing downstairs.

These were halcyon days, and slowly but surely, as Alix's waistline increased, so did her sense of contented satisfaction. She and Militza had never felt so close. She blamed it on her hormones, but the more Militza was there to rub oil into her tired calves and thighs, the more Alix enjoyed the way the Montenegrin's hands moved inside her legs. How delightful their secret afternoons were, spent in soft, tender caresses and furtive coupling. Militza's determined fingers were as magic as her swift, loving tongue, and the rosacea, the awkwardness, her social nervousness, her inability to understand the comings and goings at court, all faded into the background. She had her close friends and husband by her side, and Alix cared little for anything else. Nicky rarely ventured away from the palace; invitations were refused, parties were eschewed, and visitors were few and far between.

By day they relaxed, taking luncheon at one and afternoon tea at four, after which they would always dine with Dr. Philippe and either Stana or Militza or both and talk long into the night about spiritualism, or indulge in palmistry and tarot, while Dr. Philippe would tell them stories of his close friend Papus, otherwise known as Gérard Encausse, who had founded a new Martinist Order, which he, Philippe, was particularly interested in.

"It is so exciting and enlightening," he said over dinner, taking a large sip of wine. "The light we all carry within ourselves drives the shadows of the night away, and the inner sun rises from the darkness." He paused to look out at the moonlit sea beyond the dining room window. "You are Man," he enthused, turning to stare into Nicky's pale blue eyes. "Never forget that you are the manifestation of human dignity. Respect this noble heritage, for that is your first and foremost task upon the earth."

"I have spent my whole life respecting my noble heritage," replied Nicky. "Have you any idea how suffocating that is? To be forced to rule, torn away from the bosom of your family?"

"It is your human dignity you should be thinking about," declared Philippe, with an ebullient wave of his hand.

"But what if the heritage gets in the way of the dignity?" Nicky lit a cigarette and looked at Philippe.

"All journeys are personal, that's what the Martinists believe. And Jesus is the Repairer. Through Jesus all things can be achieved."

"So Martinism *is* a part of Christianity?" asked Alix, sounding a little relieved.

"Most certainly," assured Philippe. "We are esoteric Christians."

Nicky nodded and smoked. "I think it sounds very interesting, you must introduce me to your Papus if he comes to St. Petersburg."

"Like the Golden Dawn, I am presuming it is theurgy based? Using rituals? Seeing magic in nature?" asked Militza.

"Honestly, Militza," Alix said, laughing, "sometimes I don't understand where you learn all these things!"

"They are both equally tolerant of woman," concluded Philippe.

"I have been reading the works of Hermes Trismegistus," said Militza.

"And learning to read the stars as a way to oneness—*henosis*," added Stana.

"As you know, I am also a follower! Hermetic medicine, astrology, alchemy, magic. Are you hoping to open a lodge in St. Petersburg?" asked Philippe.

"All in good time. As Hermes Trismegistus said: 'The punishment of desire is the agony of unfulfillment,'" Militza said, laughing, as she looked across at Alix, whose lips twitched briefly into a smile.

"Indeed," agreed Nicky, picking up a small clay pipe and filling it with some of Dr. Badmaev's hashish. "And we've all had our fair share of that."

IT WAS TOWARDS THE MIDDLE OF AUGUST—ON THE sixteenth—while Philippe was out taking some air on the beach, when Nicky called both Militza and Stana to his office. Despite the good weather and his wife's advanced confinement, he looked pale. Sitting at his expansive desk, surrounded by walnut paneling, he drummed his fingers lightly atop a large cream-colored folder as he looked out to sea. He was clearly deep in thought.

"Sit," he said, not bothering to look at either of them, indicating two Moroccan leather chairs. Militza glanced across at her sister. This did not look good. Did he know about the afternoons she spent with his wife? "So," he said, slowly turning around, "it seems my mother, or rather the Okhrana, has been to Paris."

"What are the secret police doing in Paris?" asked Stana, her back straight, her hands clasped anxiously on her lap. Militza touched her arm, indicating she should be quiet.

"And it seems that they—or, indeed, she—have compiled a little report."

"A report?" asked Militza.

"It seems," he continued, "that Our Friend is a little bit of a fraud."

"No!" replied Militza, shaking her head, her heart pounding.

"Absolutely not!" added Stana. "He cured Roman last summer."

"Yes," agreed Militza. "My son had whooping cough and he came and it went away."

"He can cure syphilis," asserted Stana.

"I know," he agreed, wearily. "I am not sure what I find more disappointing, my mother's duplicitousness or the fact the Okhrana actually carried out her instructions over my head."

"It is terrible," said Militza.

"Not as bad as the things written in here. That he's lied, cheated, that he's a charlatan, that he's impersonated a doctor and practiced without a license."

"But he was highly recommended! He was introduced by a dear friend of mine," insisted Militza.

"I know, I know." Nicky nodded. "And he calmed the storm when we were on the *Standart*."

"Yes!" agreed Stana. "I remember feeling how lucky we felt to have him on board."

Nicky smiled. "So very lucky."

"And he's been such a good friend to us, he is 'Our Good Friend,'" said Militza. "And also, you are about to have your son."

"Yes." He nodded, exhaling slowly, as he pondered. "I am forced to believe—but it is not me I worry for. It is Alix."

"Why?" asked Stana. "She is soon to produce an heir and all her problems will be over."

"Her problems are immense," said Nicky, as if talking to himself. "There are rumors at court that I am to divorce her. Much like Napoleon did Josephine when she failed to produce an heir after fourteen years of trying. And we are only in our eighth year."

"Eight long years," agreed Stana, a little too enthusiastically.

"So this report," Nicky said, suddenly steeling himself, "I shall dismiss it. I shall dismiss it out of hand, and just to make sure my mother realizes I don't believe a word of it, I shall dismiss the agent, or agents, who prepared it. That way, there is no misunderstanding as to how I feel."

"Yes," agreed Militza, with a firm nod of the head.

"And Alix shall be told nothing," added Stana.

"My wife will not hear a thing."

"What shall I not hear?" asked Alix as she wandered into the office, dressed in a white floating robe, her fecund pregnant belly protruding before her. "I came to see if you wanted fresh lemonade, but now I am intrigued! What secrets?"

"No secrets, my love," replied Nicky as he got out of his chair.

"I do so hate it when you lie," replied Alix. "I can always tell, you know I can." She began to walk towards the desk. "What little secrets?" she teased, smiling.

"Nothing," Nicky replied.

"Oh, come on."

"Honestly. Nothing. Leave it alone."

"Don't be so mean," she said childishly as she swayed towards the desk.

"GET AWAY!" Nicky shouted, pulling her back from his desk, but as he did so, her sleeve caught the corner of the Okhrana files, sending leaves of paper and photographs floating to the floor.

The tsar was the first on his knees, scrabbling about on the rug, picking up the documents as quickly as he could.

"Oh, look, that's Philippe?" said Alix, more than a little curious. "Is that a police report? Has he been arrested?"

It was too late. Despite her size and condition, Alix sank slowly to the floor. Surrounded by paper, she slowly picked each one up and examined it, if only briefly, before letting it drop from her limp hand.

"Oh, my darling," she said eventually, her huge blue eyes looking up from the floor, "say it is not true."

"It is not true," repeated Nicky, with the brightest of smiles. "How can it be? Look at you! You are pregnant. Pregnant with our son!"

"Yes," she sobbed, "I am."

"I am getting rid of the file, I am getting rid of the man who wrote the file," he said, bending down towards her and offering her his hand.

"Yes," she nodded, sniffing. "Let's get rid of them." She took his hand. "Let's get rid of them all, including the person who commissioned the investigation."

"Yes," agreed Nicky. "Let's get rid of them all."

It was only when he pulled her up off the floor that they all saw what had happened.

"Blood!" stated Stana.

"A pool," whispered Militza.

"Someone get Dr. Philippe," said Alix as she swooned into her husband's arms.

It took several minutes to carry Alix upstairs and place her in the blue-and-white bedroom. Militza propped up her listless marble-white face with pillows while Stana went to find Dr. Philippe, commanding the servants to fetch water, towels, and Brana. There was chaos and shouting and the sound of running feet as panic spread through the palace; everyone had been caught completely off guard.

The first to arrive was Dr. Philippe. Flushed and fresh from the beach, his face was bright pink, and he was sweating and short of breath.

"How is the patient?" he huffed as he arrived at the top of the stairs, running his thumbs around his tight, damp trouser waistband. "Has her time come?"

"There's blood," replied Militza, whispering with concern. "Quite a lot of it."

"Oh! Blood is like vomit," he replied boldly. "There always looks like more than there actually is."

"She'll be all right, won't she?" asked Nicky.

"She has done it a few times before," declared Philippe. "I am sure she'll be fine. God is looking after her."

"I know, but it is always such a dangerous time. What it is to be a woman." Nicky sighed, his brow furrowed with anxiety. "And I do love her so very much."

Dr. Philippe patted the back of Nicky's hand and then entered the brightly lit room. The afternoon sun was pouring in through the open curtains, and the seagulls were screaming outside.

"There, there," said Philippe as he sat himself down on the edge of her bed. He took hold of Alix's cold, damp hand. "How are you feeling?"

Alix opened her eyes; her mouth was dry, and she was clearly in some pain. "Well," she said quietly, "all will be well now that you are here."

"Do you feel that it is time?" asked Philippe, his hands on the edge of the sheets, preparing to pull them back.

"Not yet," replied Alix, wincing slightly.

Suddenly there was a loud bustle and commotion down in the hall and the sound of footsteps bounding up the stairs.

"Dr. Ott? Dr. Girsh?" said Militza, standing between the two agitated middle-aged gentlemen and the bedchamber. "Why on earth are you here?"

"We were called," Dr. Ott replied smartly. "As the court physician I am expected to attend every imperial birth."

"We have been standing by for the last ten days at Peterhof, waiting to be summoned," added Dr. Girsh, the slimmer of the two, with significantly more hair.

"And who summoned you?" asked Militza.

"I did," came a voice from the bottom of the stairs.

They all turned to see the nanny Margaretta Eagar standing somewhat stiffly at the bottom of the stairs. Dressed in a simple gray frock and a white frilled apron, her reddish-blond hair piled high on the top of her head, she had a defiantly determined look in her small piercing blue eyes. Militza looked down on her from the landing. She had never liked this bossy former matron of an orphanage in Belfast, whose Limerick accent was so thick, even a fluent English speaker like Militza struggled to understand her.

"You?"

"Yes, Imperial Highness." Margaretta might have curtsied, but Militza sensed her seething anger even from this distance. Militza said nothing. "As a former trained medical nurse," Margaretta began, "I thought Her Imperial Majesty might require her physician." Her head shuddered from side to side as she tried to control her emotions.

"I'm not sure if washing bandages and changing bedpans in Ireland qualifies you for much, my dear, but seeing as you are here"—Militza turned to the two gentlemen on the landing—"I shall inform the empress."

BACK IN THE BEDROOM, PHILIPPE HAD CLOSED THE CURTAINS and the atmosphere was a little calmer.

"I have been chanting and using a little hypnosis and she seems a little more settled," said Philippe as Militza approached the bed.

"Alix?" she said. "Dr. Ott and Dr. Girsh are outside." She spoke slowly. "They said they'd like to examine you?"

"No!" Alix replied, shifting in the bed. "Tell them no. Tell them to go away. I don't want them to examine me. Those two buffoons only deliver daughters."

THE BLEEDING STEMMED, AND IT WAS FOUR DAYS LATER THAT full labor began. Initially, Alix took the pains and moans in her stride. During the hours of the early evening she held on to the bedpost, with both hands, moaning and lowing as she rode the waves of each of the contractions, while Philippe, Militza, and Stana stood by, occasionally mopping her brow and murmuring words of encouragement. But by midnight she was growing weak and was laid to rest in her bed, with Brana offering little sips of Madeira laced with laudanum to help her through. By now the bedsheets were sodden with blood, and her cries echoed around the palace. Militza had her hands between Alix's legs, her fingertips slipped inside, as she desperately tried to free the baby's head. As she pushed and kneaded, Alix moaned plaintively and pathetically with pain. It was patently clear there was not much time left.

"We need chloroform and forceps—this baby appears to be coming out neck first," pronounced Militza.

"Here," said Philippe. He rattled around in a box and handed over a small glass bottle and handkerchief. "But we have no forceps."

THE STRUGGLE WAS IMMENSE AND THE LOSS OF BLOOD OBSCENE as Militza fought, up to her forearms, desperately trying to ease the baby out. Alix battled against the pain and the chloroform, slipping in and out of consciousness. And then finally, at around 4 A.M., just as the sun was coming up over the sea, an exhausted, small, rather skinny baby was born.

Stana stared at the red, wriggling creature on the bed.

"It's a girl."

Such was the shock that no one bothered to swaddle it; they all simply stood there, unable to believe their eyes. A girl. Another girl. How could this be? The tsarina had believed Philippe wholeheartedly. They all had. And now there was a girl. A fifth daughter.

"We could kill it?" suggested Brana, looking at the baby with utter contempt. "A little bit of chloroform?"

"No," said Militza.

"Get rid of it," proposed Stana. "It has to go. She can't have a fifth daughter." She shook her head. "But how?"

They all turned to Philippe, who was so traumatized by what he had seen and what had just happened, he was unable to respond. He stood, motionless and emotionless, staring at the child on the bed, still attached to its mother by a pulsating cord, his whole life clearly flashing before him, for he knew, here and now, that his work in Russia was done. Not even he, the cat with nine lives, the master who could calm storms and hypnotize almost anyone, not even he was capable of coming back from this. A fifth daughter? His life was ruined.

"I could take her with me when I leave," he said simply. "Find her a nice home, a loving family. No one need know."

There was silence as the four of them digested this plan.

"Yes," agreed Militza. "Take her! Take her away and no one need know."

"But what do we say? We will need to say something, something by way of explanation?" said Stana.

"A miscarriage? A stillbirth?" Brana shrugged. "It happens all the time."

"Yes." Philippe nodded, warming to the idea. "Nature is so wasteful, so cruel, the poor tsarina, the nation will mourn with her, all the mothers of Russia will mourn; their Mother Russia suffers like they do, they will take to the streets in sympathy, they will fill the churches and weep for her . . . But a fifth daughter . . ." He shook his head. "No one rejoices for a fifth daughter. No one fires a cannon or rings a church bell for another girl." He shuddered. "That doesn't bear thinking about."

"It's agreed," said Militza.

"But what do we say to Ott and Girsh?" asked Stana. "They will want to see something?"

They all looked at each other, each hoping the other would say something, do something to make the situation better. The baby on the bed began to cry, and Alix moaned slightly in response; the effects of the chloroform were beginning to wear off. Whatever decision they came to, they would have to act quickly.

"Right," said Militza, briskly drying her bloodied hands on a towel. "You"—she pointed to Brana—"cut the cord. You"—she nodded to her sister—"stay here and look after Alix. I will go and inform the tsar, and you and Brana had better keep that baby quiet and sort something out."

Militza left the room and, smoothing down her crimson-stained apron, walked slowly downstairs to the tsar's office. On her way she passed several members of the household hanging around in the hall, awaiting the news. As they raised their eyes expectantly, Militza dropped her gaze as if preparing them for bad news. She knocked on the office door and Nicky opened it. She could tell by the expression on his face he knew something was wrong. Had the child been a healthy boy, the shouts of joy would have reverberated around the house so loudly and wildly, you would have heard them on the beach and in the Gulf of Finland beyond. Instead there'd been silence.

"It's a girl," Militza said softly.

"How?" he asked, collapsing into a chair. "How can it be?" He sniffed as tears of desperate disappointment welled up in his exhausted eyes. "She believed in Philippe this time; we have prayed to God, we have never stopped praying to God; we have begged and pleaded and been on our knees asking for his help and forgiveness, asking for a son. And now this?"

"I know," soothed Militza, sitting down next to him and taking his hands. "I know, I know." He rested his head on her shoulder as he sobbed. "Listen," said Militza as she comforted him with a gentle embrace. "I think you know what I am going to say, even if you don't want to hear it." She paused and steadied herself. "Russia will not take another daughter. Alix cannot have another daughter. The court won't accept it, St. Petersburg won't; in the provinces, the countryside, they will never forgive her. They already think she is a German spy sent to destroy the house of Romanov. You know I am telling you the truth. I am only sorry you have to hear it from me."

Nicky stopped crying and raised his head, staring at her. He was so close she could taste his warm breath on her lips.

"Philippe will take her away. He will take her to France. He will need money of course, but you can give him that. But he must go and he must take her with him. And he must go as soon as possible."

"But what will Alix say?"

"Alix is not quite conscious. But we will tell her when she is well. And she will be grateful. She will be pleased we have helped her. She will be happy we have saved her from the mob. But it must be a secret. It must all be a secret. Who knows what would happen if it was ever discovered that there was another girl? You'd have to divorce her, and she'd be banished and hounded out of the country. If she even got that far . . ."

Nicky just stared at her. It was all too much to take in. He looked haunted, scared; he was indecisive at the best of times, but Militza was asking him to make a decision right here and now. And it pained him so much to think about it.

"Whatever you think is best," he mumbled finally.

IT WAS PHILIPPE WHO CHRISTENED THE BABY GIRL SUZANNA. It was his idea to give her such a decidedly French-sounding name, so that no one would suspect where she was truly from, and the day they left for Paris was one Militza would never forget.

It was cold and dank, and a miserable, thick fog hung heavy over the dacha. It chilled the bone and made you shiver as if someone were striding over your grave.

Only the tsar, the tsarina, and the two sisters saw them off. No one else except Brana even knew the baby existed. The cleanup had been thorough and organized. Drs. Ott and Girsh were the first to be convinced. By chance, Brana, who had uncharacteristically sharp eyes for a crone, noticed a walnut-sized ovule nestling in the blood and sheets as she cleaned up after the birth. This was hastily retrieved and duly presented to the doctors by way of explaining the "miscarriage." Fortunately, when examined under a microscope it proved to be a dead fertilized egg of around four-week gestation, and so they sadly confirmed the tsarina's terrible news: an appalling miscarriage that had manifested as a phantom pregnancy. There was simply no child at all. The Dowager Empress was informed, and then the court. Rumors, naturally, abounded. Alix was said to have given birth to an animal with horns, a creature so frightful, so hideous, the spawn of the devil himself, that they were forced to execute it at birth. Others saw the premature death of the baby and the lack of the long-awaited son as a form of divine retribution for the appalling tragedy at Khodynka Field. Despite Philippe's prediction, very few were sympathetic. However, all this was preferable to the reality. If the truth ever got out, the birth of a fifth daughter? That would destroy them all.

It was decided that Philippe and Suzanna should travel through Finland and then by train to Paris, where Philippe would be met by a trusted colleague of his: Leendert Johannes Hemmes. Leendert and Philippe had been friends for a long time and were of the same Martinist religion. His loyalty was discussed long into the night, as Militza and Philippe plotted and planned. Leendert also possessed psychic powers, which he used to diagnose sickness in the urine of the unwell. He could be trusted. He had to be trusted. The child could not stay in Russia.

"We shall be fine," Philippe assured Alix as she stood in the cold fog, her gray eyes glazed, her expression blank. "It is not a long journey. And we will write."

"No," Alix replied. "No contact. No news. It is the only way. The secret police are everywhere. And I can't vouch that any news won't send me insane. The wound needs to be cauterized. Suzanna is dead. She is with May, eating baked apples . . ."

Philippe nodded. In his arms, he held the silent, sallow, sickly looking Suzanna, who already seemed to know her fate.

"Would you like to . . ." He held the baby up.

"Be sure to keep her warm," whispered Alix.

She reached out a thin, shaking hand to touch her daughter for the last time. Her trembling fingers hovered over the baby, and she looked as though she were going to bless her child, commend it to God, but she withdrew slowly, clearly thinking better of it.

The tsar had given Philippe a new and very fine Serpollet motorcar as a token for all his hard work. It was parked, freshly polished, in the driveway, waiting to be taken to the station and loaded onto the train to Helsinki. Philippe was also given some five million rubles, in sequential notes, to ensure Hemmes's discreet silence. (The fact that Hemmes was later to build himself a rather fine house in Rotterdam, with no obvious means of support, was neither here nor there.) Alix had gathered together a small selection of trinkets by which her daughter would one day, when it was safe, know herself: a small Fabergé box; a traveling icon on a silver chain, also by Fabergé; and a thick rope of pearls. All things she could sell if she ever needed to. Poor Alix was not capable of putting pen to paper, so it was Militza who wrote Suzanna a long letter in which she explained why her brokenhearted mother had been persuaded to give her beautiful daughter away.

Just as he was leaving, Philippe turned to Militza, reached into his pocket, and took out a small icon, which he placed in her hand.

"Take this," he said, squeezing it into her palm. "It is the rarest and most powerful of icons: St. John the Baptist, the angel of the desert. It will keep you safe, for it protects all who own it. No harm will ever come to you while you have it in your possession. It was given to me by Papus, and now I pass it on to you. I don't need it anymore, my work is done and I have no future." He kissed her gently on the cheek. "Remember, it was St. John who declared the coming of the Messiah. And so too will you. You will call him to Russia, like a siren, and when you need him most, he will come. Thank you. Thank you for believing in me. You have a gift, Militza. Use it wisely."

He then turned to the tsarina. "Your Imperial Majesty . . ." He bowed his head. Alix stared at him. Her strained face was impassive; her thin fingers nervously played with the lengthy rope of pearls around her neck. "You will get your son. I predict if you canonize Seraphim of Sarov and swim at midnight in the holy waters, you will conceive and realize your dreams. Seraphim himself once predicted your reign. He said that one day Russia would be ruled by a Nicholas and Alexandra, and he would be canonized in that reign. Do this and you will conceive your son."

Alexandra simply stared and nodded slowly. "As you command, so I shall do," she replied.

"Don't weep for me—and don't weep for your baby," said Philippe, taking hold of her slim shoulders. "I promise you, someday you will have another friend who, like me, will speak to you of God. Here," he said, reaching into his pocket and pulling out a tiny posy of dried flowers. "These violets were touched by Christ. Touched by his very hand. They have been worshipped and prayed over for centuries. I am giving them to you to keep you safe."

"Thank you," she replied.

"I have no need of them anymore. For in a few years, in 1905, I shall be dead."

"Don't say that!" She placed her shaking fingers on his lips.

"It is true. For I always speak the truth."

"Hush."

"But my spirit will live on."

"It will," she whispered, and a single tear snaked down her cheek. "I bless the day we met you."

Her face turned a raw, dark pink. She was visibly shaking as she walked slowly back into the palace.

THAT NIGHT MILITZA PUT ALIX TO BED. SHE WAS GIVEN ONE of Brana's more potent cocktails of poppy-head tea and warm milk, which she sipped in bed, staring at the wall, unable to say a word. Eventually, she lay down, and while Militza slowly stroked her hair, she quietly wept herself to sleep. Equally exhausted by the schemes and plans of the last few days, Militza herself fell asleep a few minutes later on an adjacent divan, only to be woken later by Alix.

It must have been two or three in the morning, she remembered, and the moon was shining through the open window. Alix was standing, in a thin white nightdress, bathed in a silver light, slowly rocking what looked like a poppet in her arms and singing sweetly under her breath. Militza sat and watched, transfixed. The tsarina was not weeping; she didn't look distressed—in fact, she looked blissfully happy, singing a lullaby and rocking the wooden peg doll in her arms. It was as if all her worries and the agony of the last few days were as nothing. Her voice was sweet and childlike, and her movements were effortless. She looked like a wisp, luminous in the moonlight.

"Alix?" ventured Militza as she slowly crossed the room towards her.

"Oh!" she replied, turning around suddenly. "It's you!" She smiled; her cold hand cupped Militza's chin, and she ran her thumb gently along the length of her lips. Her voice was breathy, her eyes glassy. And the look on her face was one of divine bliss. "Look!" she said offering up the poppet. "Look, my love."

Militza caught a glimpse in the moonlight. "A magic doll from Smolensk."

She recognized its sharp wooden face and crude clothing immediately. She remembered asking Brana to find it, sending her to the nunnery in Smolensk. It had taken the crone days to find the right group of nuns, for they had become increasingly secretive over time. Eventually, it was the queue of the barren, weeping outside a small back door down a narrow back street, that alerted her to them. They were all waiting, desperately waiting, for a little wooden doll to rock to sleep at night in the hope that it might help them conceive.

"Look, Nicky, it's like baby Jesus," replied Alix, softly caressing the top of its hard head.

"A boy," whispered Militza, walking towards her.

"Yes, my love, a boy." She smiled. "We have a son at last."

"Well done," replied Militza, taking Alix by the shoulders and directing her back to bed. The opium tea was playing tricks with her traumatized mind.

"Are you pleased?" Alix cowered. "Have I pleased you at last?"

"Yes, yes, you have done well."

"All I want to do is please you, my love," she continued, standing by the bed, swinging the poppet in one hand. She turned back towards Militza, took a step towards her, and placed her lips on Militza's cheek. "I have only ever wanted to make you happy. A son for you, for Russia."

"I know," Militza whispered, before pushing her slowly away, towards the bed.

"Stay with me?" Alix's voiced sounded panicked. It was hard to tell if she was conscious or unconscious, in this world or another. She suddenly grabbed Militza by the elbows and stared, terrified, into her eyes. "I don't think I will make it through the night on my own."

CHAPTER 15

FEBRUARY 11, 1903, ST. PETERSBURG

THAT NIGHT WAS THE FIRST OF MANY THAT MILITZA spent sleeping on the divan in the tsarina's bedroom. It took a few weeks before she stopped waking and rocking the doll in the middle of the night and a few more for her to stop weeping. Brana's opium cocktails were steadily increased in strength to help dull the pain. It was only when the tsarina found it difficult to rouse herself in the morning that it was decided to reduce the amount of poppy heads in her nightly drink. The tsar himself suggested she should try some of Dr. Badmaev's excellent cocaine as a bit of a pick-me-up; he himself was using it to help him with his persistent toothache as well as the torpor of his day.

Fortunately, during this period the rest of the court had little time to dwell on yet another of the tsarina's failed pregnancies. They had come to expect little more than disappointment from this sour-faced fräu and had other things on their minds: the preparations for the impending Medieval Ball. The invitations had gone out almost a year prior to the event, and the intricacies of one's costume were enough to occupy even the most active of minds. For this was no ordinary fancy dress party; this was the ball to end all balls. It had been Alix's idea to evoke the past glories of the Muscovite court under the first Romanovs, and costumes were to be taken extremely seriously indeed. Alix's dress, which had taken over seven months to make, was a copy of the robes once worn by Tsar Alexei's first wife, Maria, in the 1660s. Embroidered with diamonds, sequins, and pearls using golden and silver thread, it was rumored to have cost over 1 million rubles.

But it wasn't the costumes Militza remembered that night, when 390 of the city's most illustrious guests danced at the Winter Palace as if in a "living dream," although they were extraordinary. Designers and theatrical costume houses had been hard at work for months, and ideas and inspiration had been sought from every quarter. Emirs' robes, Muscovite princes' garb, and even court falconer costumes had been studied and copied in minute detail. Peter and Militza had spent a small fortune on their attire. Peter wore a jacket of black velvet with a golden double-headed eagle embroidered on the front in the finest gold thread; his broad shoulders were edged in gold piping, and he wore loose black baggy trousers and soft black boots, while on his head was a fur-trimmed boyar's hat. Militza wore matching black velvet. Her long wide sarafan was trimmed with jet beads and golden sequins, and her golden kokoshnik headdress quivered with pearls. The Grand Duchess Vladimir was naturally at her extravagant best in a gold velvet sarafan embroidered with jewels, complete with a kokoshnik headdress almost a foot high, studded with enormous precious emeralds, rubies, and diamonds. It dominated proceedings, as indeed did the huge forty-one-carat Polar Star diamond at the center of Princess Zinaida Yusupova's kokoshnik, which was only usurped in splendor by the four-hundred-carat sapphire worn by Alix herself.

"That stone is larger than a matchbox," Peter had remarked, sipping a glass of champagne as they watched the state trumpeters announce the entrance of the tsar and tsarina.

However, despite the fine fashions, the exquisite workmanship, and the ostentation of jewelry on display, Militza recalled that evening for something else entirely.

Stana.

It was just as Anna Pavlova started to dance a few select moments from Tchaikovsky's *Swan Lake* that she noticed them. Standing at the back, hidden—or so they hoped—by a porphyry column, were Stana and Nikolasha. He was dressed as a boyar and she as a boyarina. His arm was around her waist and he was leaning forward, his small black lambskin hat pushed to the back of his head. She held her face close to his as she laughed. He leaned a little closer, and then, as all eyes were on Pavlova's slowly dying swan, he kissed her. Stana did not resist. In fact, she closed her eyes and seemed to kiss him back. It was not a fleeting embrace. It was passionate and public. It was also easily reciprocated, and this was clearly not the first time they had kissed. Militza frantically looked around to see if anyone else had noticed. Peter? The tsar? The tsarina? The Grand Duchess Vladimir? They were thankfully watching the ballet. But then she turned to look the other way, only for her gaze to be met by a man dressed as a seventeenth-century boyar with a white velvet coat with mink trim and a pair of soft cream Moroccan leather boots. His hair was swept back, his mustache had been trimmed, and he wore a dagger at his waist.

"I see the necromancer has found fresh blood," he said, staring across at Stana and Nikolasha as she fell backwards against the column, her mouth straining still higher, hoping for another kiss. "Does she not know that incest is illegal in this country?"

"They are not related!" snapped Militza.

"Oh, but they are," he replied, his eyes slowly closing with satisfaction. "You are married to his brother—and brothers are not allowed to marry sisters in Russia; it is a sin." He smiled. "Quite apart from the blatant adultery, which is, of course, an entirely different matter."

"I am not sure it is any concern of yours." Militza turned to face him. "And frankly, you are not in a position to do very much about it, now, are you?"

She could hear the hanging pearls on her kokoshnik shaking as vigorously as a shaman's rattle as she feigned amusement. Her dislike for this man had in no way abated.

"One can only admire your confidence, Goat Girl." He smirked. "Don't you realize your days are numbered? Your butcher's boy has been sent back to Lyon, and you are still without an heir. How long before she tires of you? How long before she sends you back to the Black Mountains where you belong?"

"You will spend a long time holding your breath."

"Are you still in the bedchamber?" he scoffed. "In charge of the imperial pot?"

"Militza?" came a voice from behind.

"Your Imperial Majesty," he said, his cheeks flushing as he rapidly bowed his head.

"Count Yusupov." The tsarina nodded. "How are your sons?" she asked politely as she linked arms with Militza. "They must be really quite grown-up by now?"

"Nikolai is twenty, and Felix is sixteen—he's been in Italy and now he's off to Paris, thinking about going to university in Oxford."

"England is such a charming country," she replied. "We simply don't go there often enough. I used to love our summers in the Isle of Wight. Osborne House." She smiled.

"Ella has mentioned to me your holidays with your grandmother," he enthused.

"Militza," Alix added hurriedly, gripping her hand. "I need to speak to you."

"Of course." She smiled slowly, her head to one side as she turned her back on Count Yusupov.

ALIX WOVE HER WAY THROUGH THE MELEE OF CIGARETTE smoke, stiff jewel-encrusted costumes, and increasingly inebriated dancing. Grand Duke Konstantin Konstantinovich was dancing an enthusiastic quadrille, attempting to keep hold of a glass of champagne, while declaring at the top of his voice how "astonishingly beautiful" everyone was.

"What is your sister doing?"

Alix spun around as soon as they reached the quiet corridor. There was a fiery, furious look on her already patchy red face. She placed her hands swiftly on her earlobes and winced; her earrings were so heavy the lobes hurt when she moved.

"I don't know what you mean," replied Militza.

"How long has it been going on?" Militza remained silent. "It is common knowledge that her husband has a mistress in Biarritz."

"It is?"

"I can't believe it!" The tsarina was exasperated. "Stana must know that it is not allowed for a woman to conduct herself in this manner. People will talk—I am sure they are already talking. You must put a stop to it. Put a stop to it immediately. She can't behave in this way. It is unseemly the way she is carrying on with Nikolasha. Nikolasha, of all people! The man is so respected, so admired by everyone, particularly in the army. He may not be married, but she is!"

"I am sure it is just a flirtation," soothed Militza. It was impossible to deny it anymore. "High spirits, the champagne!"

"That is no excuse!" Alix clasped her hands in front of her and pursed her lips before whispering in a low, seething voice, "Women do not have lusts; they are not allowed to have lusts, and they should not even entertain them." She paused and rubbed her hands together. "They simply have a duty to their husbands. And that is it. A duty." She stared at the floor and then looked up. "This is also a scandal that this court does not need. That I do not need. That Nicky doesn't need. I am sure that a certain lack of moral rectitude in this court was tolerated in the past, before Nicky became tsar, but I find it unbecoming."

Militza nodded. There was nothing more to be said. The subject was closed. Both sisters were to be denied.

BACK INSIDE THE BALL IT WAS LATE; THE PEACOCK CLOCK WAS creeping towards 3 A.M., and it was clear that a certain amount of moral rectitude was disappearing along with the champagne. The Grand Duchess Vladimir was demanding another glass of Madeira while trying to hold on to her enormous headpiece. Grand Duke Konstantin was opening up small enamel cases, looking for some more Sobranie cigarettes, and Nicky, who'd certainly drunk more wine than usual, was complaining his sable-trimmed hat was making him hot.

Militza was working her way through the crowd just as the orchestra struck up another mazurka, scanning the puce, pinked faces in the Pavilion Hall, looking for her sister. Where was she? What was she doing? Her behavior was going to jeopardize everything that she, Militza, and, indeed, their father had been working for. How could she?

In and out, between the white pillars, Militza searched. The enormous glittering chandeliers above did little to illuminate proceedings, and the whirl, the swirl, the constantly circulating and dancing figures were beginning to disorientate Militza, who was growing more and more confused by the second. In the swirling melee she saw Alix's face, her calves, her thighs . . . she could taste her. She needed air and she needed it quickly. The heat of her incredibly heavy ornate costume was beginning to consume her. Add to that the blind panic that it was all about to come crashing down around her and she broke out in a cold sweat. She tried breathing deeply, panting, but the sweating and her parched mouth were too much. She had to get out of the hall. Anywhere. Immediately. She needed air or she was going to faint. Eventually she found her way to a small, curved French window. The door handles were stiff; it was February, and she didn't suppose they expected anyone to go out into the Hanging Garden. She pushed on the doors and staggered outside.

It was a cold night, and the cloud was winning the battle with the stars. Even so, the Hanging Garden was reasonably warm. Built above the imperial stables, surrounded on all sides by galleries, it was away from the heat and the noise and yet protected against the harsh elements of a winter's night in St. Petersburg.

Relief. Militza breathed deeply and willed herself to calm down. She flapped her skirts and tried to loosen the tight collar of her heavily embroidered black-and-gold caftan. She leaned against a wall for support as she inhaled and exhaled, feeling its cold solidity against her back. As she closed her eyes, she heard a stifled squeal, and she suddenly realized she was not alone on the roof.

Moving rapidly into the shadows, she flattened herself against the wall, behind a climbing evergreen jasmine, and peered through the leaves. There, about four arched windows away, she could see a couple below a statue, bent over each other in the darkness. The woman had her skirts pushed high up over her back, her underwear was gathered in a pool around her ankles, and her pale buttocks were visible in the sudden pale moonlight. He had pulled up his robes and loosened his trousers to the floor. They were quite clearly copulating. She'd squealed as he'd first thrust into her, but now she was moaning. The more he pummeled and pounded, the louder she cried. He was gathering momentum as he gripped on the ankles of the statue for support. She was on the tips of her toes, raising her rump, her back arching with pleasure, her chin thrust forward and her mouth wide-open as she welcomed him, more and more. He moved harder and faster, and her thighs shook with each penetration as the force rippled down her legs. He then slowed and moved more determinedly. Her hands edged out from underneath her as she too grabbed hold of the statue for support. One more. Two more. Three more. A fourth. The woman cried out a shrill yelp, weeping with joy as she shuddered and then collapsed, spent, up against the statue. He folded himself on top of her back.

Militza stood completely still. Then, eventually, she slowly closed her eyes. She would recognize that cry anywhere.

CHAPTER 16

AUGUST 1903,

SAROV, TAMBOV REGION

H E IS SO INTOLERABLY STUPID. HE HAS NO CURIOSITY, no conversation, no idea about anything other than the everyday. He barely reads, he can only speak French and Russian—in short, dear sister, he is a terrible bore."

Militza remembered smiling as she stood in the white heat of the Tambov sun. Her sister's description of her husband had been so apposite that even at the height of their extremely fiery exchange after the Medieval Ball, six months before, it had made her laugh. It was so true. The man was not Stana's intellectual equal: he was boorish—and, worse, he was boring. They were utterly unsuited. The candles on the eve of her wedding were right, as candles and magic always are. It was a poor match. Everyone knew it. But they were married now. And there was little either of them could do about it.

Militza had waited almost a week before discussing the scene she'd witnessed in the Hanging Garden. Perhaps it was out of embarrassment, or perhaps she was hoping the situation might resolve itself; either way, Militza avoided her sister and spent most of that week rearranging her library. She had taken delivery of some particularly rare books from Watkins of London, and she'd locked herself away for the week, taking great pleasure in reading them.

So, when she finally did decide to confront her sister, it was seven days later in St. Petersburg. It was a dark gray February afternoon when she called at the palace, only after much searching to discover her sister in one of the smaller studies on the third floor. The curtains were drawn, the lights were off, and the air was redolent with the stench of incense. Stana and Brana were on their knees, chanting and lighting a series of black votive candles. In front of them was a macabre-looking icon of a dancing skeleton dressed as a saint, complete with golden halo.

"What are you doing?"

Militza was shocked to find her sister performing something so base. Both the women remained motionless, petrified like statues. It was Brana who eventually spoke first.

"Praying to Santa Muerte," she replied, with a shrug.

"Lighting black candles? Black? Whom do you wish vengeance on?"

Militza looked from one to the other. This is what she and Stana used to do as children. This was Catholic magic, Catholic ritual. Not something they'd brought with them to Russia.

"Brana?" she asked.

"I am only doing as I am told," mumbled the crone.

"What do you expect me to do?" Stana spun around. She looked different. Her normally bright clear skin was gray, and her eyes were dulled with depression. "I hate him," she said simply. "I love my children. Of course I love them. They are the only things that make my life worth living. But I am humiliated, Militza. Every time George goes to Biarritz, to his actress, another small part of my soul dies." She sighed. "I am trapped and I don't know what to do. I did as Father told me. I married the man of his choice—and now what? Must I spend the rest of my days being dutiful? Still in service to that wretched country of ours? Sometimes I think the nunnery would have be preferable."

"I am so sorry," said Militza, shaking her head.

"Don't be. The pity's the worst of it. 'Poor Stana and her dreadful husband.'" She laughed dryly. "And now I have found someone who makes me happy. Is it wrong to want to be happy? Nikolasha makes me happy. He is dashing and strong and popular at court, unlike George. And he loves me."

She looked at Militza. Her sister always had a plan. What was to be done?

Stana would keep her distance, demanded Militza. Stana naturally protested. It would be unbearable, impossible. But Militza was adamant. Stana would spend the summer in the Crimea, as far away from her lover as possible. While he occupied himself with his borzois and his estates in Tula, south of Moscow, Stana was going to try and take control of herself, and hopefully, eventually, these ridiculous, lustful feelings would go away. That was the idea, at least.

THE THREE-DAY JOURNEY ON THE IMPERIAL TRAIN WAS STIfling. Traveling due south from St. Petersburg to Sarov, the entire Romanov family except the little grand duchesses, plus their entourages, had packed themselves into the airless carriages to attend the canonization of Seraphim in Tambov. The atmosphere on the train was not that of a joyous excursion to celebrate a saint, but was more like a funeral, redolent with a muttering, mumbling, pious fervor that Alix and her sister Ella were particularly adept at. Metropolitan Anthony, the Moscow head of the Orthodox faith, accompanied the royal party. He spent most of the journey walking the length of the train, a trail of incense and prayer billowing in his black-cloaked wake. Everyone else was more or less confined to quarters, drinking endless cups of weak tea, playing interminable rounds of bezique. Militza and Stana shared a cabin. Needless to say, George had declined to come on the journey, citing some business in France, and sharing a cabin was by far the simplest way, Militza decided, to keep an eye on her sister. Her husband and his brother did the same, and although Peter was not yet privy to Nikolasha's blossoming relationship with his sister-in-law, he had been keen on the sleeping arrangements, delighted to be able to spend some time with his older brother.

Alix had been the driving force behind the canonization. Even if Philippe had failed in his bid to give her an heir, his promise that she should have a son in the event of Seraphim's canonization was something she clung to. She remained determined no matter how many times the members of the church hierarchy tentatively suggested that Seraphim was not a suitable candidate for sainthood. There were rules to making someone a saint, and frankly, Seraphim failed to pass any of the tests. Firstly, despite his being dead for over seventy years there were few miracles directly attributed to him. And secondly—and most importantly—they did not find a perfectly preserved body upon opening his coffin, as was expected of a future saint. What remained of Seraphim was only a pile of bones and the remnants of his leather lestovka. But Alix was steadfast, as she always was. And once Alix decided on something, it was almost impossible to dissuade her. As for the emperor, he just wanted to keep her happy. So, against the advice of all concerned, the service was to go ahead. The knowledge of Seraphim's prediction that Nicholas and Alexandra would rule over Russia and he would be canonized during their reign only strengthened Alix's resolve. His other prediction, that "terrible future insurrections that will exceed all imagination and . . . rivers of blood would flow during their reign," was quietly overlooked.

But as they stepped off the train that searing-hot afternoon, nothing could have prepared them for the spectacle before them. The station, the platforms, and the road leading towards the white cupola cathedral and the walled monastery, where the imperial entourage was to collect the disinterred body of Seraphim and rebury him as a saint, were awash with people. They were everywhere—four or five deep along the road, hanging out of windows, up in the trees, every balcony and wall crammed to jostling room only. They were chattering, excited, but as the royal party approached, they all simply fell silent and stared. Through the heat and the dust, all that was visible was row upon row of faces.

Militza was exhilarated, but Stana was overwhelmed. Three days spent locked in the claustrophobic confines of the imperial train, so close to her lover, unable to make true physical contact or properly converse, permitted only polite conversation about religious relics, Old Believers, and the fascinating lot of the Russian peasant whom they viewed, fleetingly, out the carriage window, had taken their toll. Desperate for shade and respite from the constant cloying smell of incense and the low murmur of prayer, she felt herself swoon.

"Milly," she whispered from under her white, broad-brimmed hat. "Help me!"

Militza's grip was swift and strong. "Here," she said as she riffled in the folds of her white chiffon skirt. "Have some of my elixir—it will help."

She slipped the red glass pipette between her sister's parched lips.

"Cocaine. Everyone should take a little of that every day," whispered Nicky as he stood next to her, holding her up by the elbows. "It will make everything appear much brighter."

However, Alix didn't need any such help. The crowds, the heaving multitude, and the magnificent sight of some two hundred or so priests clustered outside the entrance to the church, with their long beards and flowing black robes, their waists encircled with belts of golden rope, assured her of one thing: she had been right all along. No matter what the higher echelons of the church said. No matter what the mealymouthed aristocrats of St. Petersburg spluttered and spat about in their gilded drawing rooms. She, Alix, spoke for Russia. *She* was Little Mother Russia. And here she was with the people. And the people loved her.

Forgotten was the sciatica that had been plaguing her on the train; forgotten too was her rosacea, and her overwhelming shyness in front of an inquisitive public. Taking up her white skirts, a hand on her hat covered in white silk flowers, Alix started to walk. Despite the heat of the day and the clouds of dust churned up by tens of thousands of pilgrims, she walked from the station to the church. Cossacks lined the route, but interspersed between them were the ill and the infirm. There were men bent over walking sticks, women clutching children, a one-armed man who couldn't see, another horizontal in a wheelbarrow, a laborer with no legs who propelled himself forward using two metal irons in his hands. But Alix was not distracted by the pilgrims. In fact, she felt as if she were walking with them, for along with the thousands of ill, lame, or deformed, she too had come to Sarov hoping to be healed.

IT WAS LATE AFTERNOON BY THE TIME THE DISINTERRED BODY of Seraphim arrived in the church in a new cypress coffin supplied by the tsar. The coffin's procession through the streets, carried by Nicky and other members of the royal family, escorted by some seven hundred priests, all dressed in their golden ceremonial robes, holding aloft golden crucifixes that glittered in the sun, had moved Alix to tears. But inside the church she was inconsolable. The singing, the heat, the constant standing, and the tremendous expectation that all her maladies were about to be cured made her weep continuously for herself, her lost daughter, and most especially the son she did not have. Militza stood next to her. She was conscious of the eyes of the Vladimirs upon them. The trial of being forced to travel to the desolate Tambov steppes, plus the tedium of the day, had not endeared Alix to them. This had been her idea and they were less than delighted at having to attend. The Grand Duchess Vladimir repeatedly flapped her fan and her gloves throughout the service, constantly sighing and checking her watch. The tsar's sisters, the Grand Duchesses Olga and Xenia, also looked visibly bored. Only Ella, standing next to her husband, Sergei, really mirrored the religious ecstasy so felt by her younger sister.

The church bells rang at six o'clock, announcing the beginning of the all-night vigil and the procession of pilgrims inside to view the relics of the new saint. The effect of some three hundred thousand souls, all holding candles and gently singing, was mesmerizing.

"All you can hear is music," whispered Alix, taking hold of Militza with her damp, shaking hand. "It's as if the voices are coming from heaven itself."

As dusk fell, the royal party dined in the town hall with the local mayor dancing attendance. Militza sat in silence, forking her cold mutton stew with little interest while the mayor talked of his plans to build around the cathedral and how long it had taken to build the shrine created in St. Seraphim's honor. He was most probably angling for more money, but Militza was only half listening.

"And of course we must build something near the river," continued the mayor, attempting to fold his arms across his stomach.

"Must you?" inquired Nicky.

"The sick and the crippled keep slipping into the Sarov," he replied. "And it can be almost impossible to get them out. Our saint used to bathe there," continued the mayor, "so the waters have healing properties. Hundreds of pilgrims bathe there every day."

"The river!" Alix's eyes shone brightly, remembering Philippe's words. "We must go."

"I am not sure Your Imperial Majesty, if you will forgive . . ." ventured the mayor. "It is dangerous . . ."

"We must go!" insisted Alix.

"Absolutely, of course, you must, Your Imperial Majesty," he agreed effusively, his round dark eyes flickering around the room. "The waters are said to be most powerful at midnight."

IT WAS A SMALL GROUP THAT SET OFF FROM THE TOWN HALL towards the river. Both Nikolasha and Peter elected to stay behind drinking cognac with the mayor, while Alix, Nicky, Militza, Stana, and three bodyguards dressed in full military regalia stepped out into the warm night under a full moon and walked the mile or so to the riverbank. As they made their way out of the town, the full extent of the number of pilgrims gathered for the canonization became apparent. There were hundreds of small fires all along the side of the road, and the air was heavy with smoke and the smell of sizzling shashlik. It was like an army encampment made up of the sick and frail. Everywhere they walked, they heard the mellifluous sound of singing and the gentle ringing of small bells.

"It is as if the Holy Spirit is moving amongst us," whispered Alix, looking left and right, drinking it all in.

Nicky, in his white uniform, was equally entranced. The two of them moved slowly and quietly, she in a gleaming white dress, like ghosts among their people. In the darkness they walked unrecognized, and those who suspected they might be the "Little

Father" and "Little Mother" of Russia dismissed them as a vision, something else extraordinary in a truly magical day.

Upon reaching the river, they paused while the guards cleared a path. Those clustered around the riverbank, dressed in simple cotton shifts, the women with scarves pulled tightly around their faces, were instructed to pull the infirm, the frail, and the limbless from the waters in order to make way for the royal party. Next to the river was a small wooden structure that was used for bathing. Inside were three naked men whose wet, scrawny frames shone in the moonlight as they left the shed and searched in the bushes for their damp clothes.

Alix was too self-possessed to notice the procession of naked and gnarled flesh in front of her. She had been thinking about this moment for an apparent eternity and was nearly there. All she had to do was bathe in the river and it would come to pass, just as Philippe had promised. Her hands were shaking as she began to unbutton her clothes. Militza and Stana helped her with her clothes as they tried not to stare at the other naked bodies around them. Neither of them had been confronted by such poverty since they had arrived in Russia all those years ago, and it stirred a terrible sense of foreboding in Militza's troubled thoughts.

She, Stana, and Alix finally disrobed in the shed near to the river, and then the three of them walked towards the river. Alix went first, her naked backside glowing a luminous alabaster white against the black shallows of the river. Nicky couldn't believe it! His wife was normally so prudish; even the lavatory at Tsarskoye Selo had a special cover on it, so as not to offend her, and now here she was, walking completely naked into the river. He felt such a joyous rush of exhilaration that he laughed out loud.

"Don't you dare laugh at me!" said Alix as she picked her way through the mud, gingerly cupping her own breasts as she slipped into the water. Quite what had come over her, Nicky didn't understand, but he was delighted. He too stripped naked in the hut, and just as Militza and Stana immersed themselves in the water, he came careering towards the bank and, leaping into the air, jumped right in.

The cool water was pure bliss after the airless heat of the day, the joy of its chilled softness against their bare skin so relaxing and liberating. It felt marvelous, so free. After the oppressive, claustrophobic religiosity of the day, to swim naked in the cool river felt like an incredible release. Militza was immediately reminded of her childhood when she and Stana used to run and swim naked in the streams at the foot of the Black Mountains.

"This is wonderful!" exclaimed Alix, swimming and splashing in the water.

"Glorious!" agreed Nicky, executing a few vigorous strokes before relaxing back on the surface.

Just then the clouds cleared and the full moon shone, its silver light dancing on the surface of the water, making the river shimmer and sparkle around them. Above, the stars covered the sky as if they'd been spilled out of a pot of bright white paint.

"You can feel the magic," said Militza as she looked across at her sister's dark silhouetted face.

"Yes." Stana nodded, and they both turned to watch Alix as she lay, smiling, on her back in the river, her naked body floating on the surface of the water, staring at the sky, and quietly began to pray to St. Seraphim, her saint, her people's saint, to grant her the deepest wish of all.

CHAPTER 17

AUGUST 12, 1904, ST. PETERSBURG

MILITZA WOULD NEVER FORGET HEARING THE BOOM OF the gun salute. She held her breath. Bang! There it was. One hundred and two.

It echoed around the city.

And the city stopped in its tracks.

Militza ran to the window and threw it wide-open. Bang! Another one. She couldn't believe it. Bang! Again. She looked down into the square to see that all the traffic had halted. The trams were not moving. Pedestrians were stationary, rooted to the spot on the pavement, in the road, frozen in an instant. They were all listening. Could it really be true? Were they hearing correctly? Had the cannons at the Peter and Paul Fortress just announced the birth of a male heir to a reigning monarch for the first time since the seventeenth century? Bang! There it was again. It was as if the cannon itself were blowing away all that was miserable, all that was woeful and depressing about the war: the loss of life in

Manchuria, the endless news about the Japanese sinking Russian ships. Great explosions of hope and happiness were being blasted through this troubled city.

Militza's telephone rang urgently. Stana! She couldn't wait for her butler to answer, so she ran down the stairs in her morning dress and picked it up in the hall.

"God be praised!"

"*Philippe* be praised!" Stana replied. "We are saved! The tsarina is saved!"

"Russia is saved," enthused Militza.

"And so is Montenegro!"

The rush of adrenaline was so powerful Militza began to tremble. It had all been worth it! They had done what everyone else had failed to do. They had managed to furnish the barren tsarina with an heir. A son! At last.

"I can't believe it," she said, laughing down the telephone. "We did it!"

"We did," came Stana's reply. "No one can touch us now."

Outside, church bells began to ring. There were ripples of applause and shouts of joy from the street below. The servants began to arrive in the hall, their normally sullen, uncommunicative faces beaming with elation.

"It's a boy!" shouted a footman.

"A boy!" confirmed a lady's maid.

Bang! The cannons carried on firing. Again and again. Three hundred and one times in total. It went on for well over an hour and by the time they had finished and Militza looked out again into the streets below, flags were being hoisted up poles, the double-headed eagle was flapping from every conceivable vantage point, and the national anthem was playing in the park across the street. This was going to be a party, a very large party, and everyone was going to join in. Work was most definitely over for the day, and when the factories opened their gates, hours before schedule, the laborers and machinists poured out into the streets. Instead of closing, most of the restaurants pulled their tables out into the streets, and in the more expensive hostelries, the managers cracked open champagne, serving regulars free of charge.

At about four, Stana arrived, running into her sister's salon. Her face was flushed with excitement, and her dark eyes shone as she hurled herself into her sister's arms.

"A boy! A boy! A boy!" She kissed her sister, hugged her tightly, and started to laugh. "I am giddy!" she exclaimed. "Positively giddy! It really is incredible. I thought it would never happen. Do you think it was Seraphim? Philippe? Dr. Badmaev's herbs? The dolls? The poppets? And have you heard the other news?" she said, smiling even more.

"What other news?"

"Nikolasha told me." Stana looked like she was fit to burst. "The Vladimirs are furious! Incredibly furious because Kirill, Boris, and Andrei are now one step further away from the throne.

"Apparently," she said, grinning, "Vladimir went completely silent at luncheon when he received the telegram. He left and didn't return for an hour; then, when he did return, he continued to sit in silence, all the while being handed fresh cigarette after fresh cigarette by the Cossack standing behind him. You could have cut the atmosphere with a knife, apparently. No one knew what to do or say. And when your host isn't speaking, what are you supposed to do? Nikolasha was told by the American military attaché who was there! It was only when he was leaving to return to St. Petersburg that Colonel Mott found out what was in the telegram and what had made them so annoyed!"

"Oh, the poor Vladimirs, all that plotting, all that money, all those connections, undone by a baby that is not even twenty-four hours old."

"Isn't it wonderful?"

"Are you ready?" asked Peter, marching briskly into the room. He was dressed in a white naval jacket with golden buttons and large gold epaulets, clearly ready to go out.

"For what?" Militza looked confused.

"There's been a telephone call inviting us to come and look at the baby."

"So soon?" asked Stana, her eyes darting from her sister to her brother-in-law. "Are we to be the first?"

"Well, apart from Ella and Sergei, who were there for luncheon today, I suppose we are."

"Really?"

"Yes," confirmed Peter. "Apparently, almost as soon as Alix sat down for luncheon at twelve thirty, she felt pains; she went upstairs immediately and then the baby was born less than half an hour later."

"Just in time to ruin someone else's luncheon." Stana smiled. Peter looked across at her. "Don't worry," she said, shrugging, "I'll explain another time."

"So I have the car ready," continued Peter. "We should go." He looked at the two sisters. "Immediately."

DRIVING THROUGH THE STREETS OF ST. PETERSBURG AND OUT into the countryside beyond was one of the most memorable journeys of Militza's life. The air was warm, the sky was a clear cobalt blue, and the noise of singing and the ringing of bells, plus the strains of the national anthem, serenaded them almost all the way to the Gulf of Finland. Even in the tiniest villages, where the chickens outnumbered the wooden houses that clung to either side of the dirt road, they were celebrating. Royal flags were as ubiquitous as the smiles on the faces.

But no one was smiling quite as much as Nicky. When he met them on the top of the steps of the Lower Dacha, it was as if all the worries of the last few years, all the strains that had etched themselves all over his ashen face, had disappeared. He looked so happy, so light and carefree, he almost danced like a feather in the wind before them.

"What an unforgettable day!" he declared from the threshold, his pale eyes shining. "How blessed we are! How blessed we were the day we met Maître Philippe. Come and see him. Come and see the future Alexei II."

"Alexei?" asked Militza as she walked into the hall.

"Named after the father of Peter the Great! Alexei the Great, that's what they'll call him! My son! My heir!"

"How exciting!" said Stana.

"He is such a big boy!" continued Nicky. "Eleven and a half pounds."

"And the tsarina?" asked Militza.

"In heaven!" he replied. "And he is feeding well already. He suckled the breast almost immediately. What an appetite! He's so perfect and I can't wait for you to see him. He has blue eyes!"

"All babies have blue eyes when they are born," said Militza, handing over her hat and gloves.

"Not as blue as these!" Nicky shot back as he bounded towards the stairs. "They are as blue as the Caspian Sea! As deep as Lake Baikal. Hurry up! Alix is desperate to see you! Desperate to thank you! What a wonderful day! It's a sign, you know; our luck is changing. His birth will bring about a speedy and victorious end to the war in Manchuria. In fact"—he stopped at the top of the stairs—"I am going to make all the soldiers, the entire army fighting at the front, Alexei's godparents!" He stood, grinning, his arms outstretched. "What do you think?"

"I think it's a perfectly capital idea!" replied Peter as he climbed the stairs behind the tsar. "That'll boost morale."

"And I shall send them all icons. Icons of St. Seraphim, Russia's greatest saint!"

"Amen," added Stana.

At the top of the stairs the four grand duchesses, dressed in matching frocks, giggled and jostled with excitement.

"Out of the way, girlies!" said Nicky, sweeping them aside in a rustle of white chiffon. "They've come to see Alexei!"

The party reached the top of the stairs and paused for breath.

"I think," said Peter, "perhaps ladies first?" He gestured towards the closed bedroom door. "And perhaps you and I should have a little brandy?"

"A glass of champagne," corrected Nicky. "I think we have cause for it."

AS THE TWO MEN RETIRED BACK DOWNSTAIRS TO NICKY'S study, Militza and Stana knocked on the door.

Inside the room, the curtains were drawn, and behind a screen of white with blue cornflowers lay Alix. Propped up in bed, on a mountain of soft pillows, surrounded by numerous glittering gold icons and dressed in a white frilled shift, she smiled broadly as they entered, a look of soft joy and elation all over her face.

"Stana! Militza!" She spoke softly, shaking her head in disbelief. "He is here! At last. Can you believe it? My son. How can I ever thank you? How can I ever thank Philippe? I know it was that night, bathing in the waters. I felt it. I felt everything change. I hoped. I prayed. I believed. And now God has, at last, given me a son. A son to rule Russia. I am so happy."

Tears welled up in her eyes, and she did not bother to hold them back or disguise them in any way. She held out her hands. Both Stana and Militza leaned forward and kissed them. "My sisters," she said. "My very beloved sisters. Please tell Philippe how grateful I am. Please let him know what he has done."

"What *you* have done!" enthused Stana, squeezing Alix's hand.

"What we all have done," corrected Militza.

"Yes, all of us," said Alix. "Together."

"Together," repeated Stana.

"But write to Philippe," said Alix, "for I no longer know where to find him."

"I will do," reassured Militza. "He resides in Paris now; his health is not good."

"But this news will cheer him greatly," added Stana.

"Tell him he was right, he was right after all," Alix said, smiling.

"Where is he?" asked Militza. "Where is Alexei? May we see him?"

Alix pulled back the covers slightly, and there, lying tightly swaddled and fast asleep, was Alexei. The tsarevich, the naslednik, the future they had all been waiting for. Here he was. Militza half expected the heavens to sing, the voices of angels to burst suddenly into song at the very sight of him. The sisters leaned in, holding their breath, almost as if, by breathing on him, they might cause him to disappear. This child was so precious, a child of prayers. The hopes and fears of millions of souls rested on his not-yet-day-old shoulders. Alix put her finger to her lips as she pulled back the sheets a little more.

"Isn't he perfect?"

"He's beautiful," replied Militza, for he was. He was plump and pink, and he had wisps of blond hair that were already beginning to curl. "How are you feeling?"

"Me?" Alix smiled. "I think I now know what it is like to die and ascend to heaven. I am floating." She laughed. "And that is nothing that Dr. Ott gave me. In fact, the birth was so easy." She shrugged her shoulders. "I had none of the problems that I had with the girlies, none at all. I had barely finished my luncheon before he arrived. A little early," she said and shrugged, "although we all know not early enough! But I am blessed. I feel blessed. I am so happy."

"May I touch his face?" asked Militza. She too laughed a little, for it was truly a miracle. "I just want to make sure that he is really there and is not some form of sorcery or witchcraft!"

Militza stretched out her hand. It was shaking a little as she curled her index finger and touched his fresh, soft cheek. It felt like warm, smooth silk. She let out an involuntary sigh.

"I know," agreed Alix. "Look at his lips! His ears! And his beautiful neck." She began to undress him, removing the tightly swaddled cloth that wrapped him.

"Oh, don't. Really!" said Militza. "There is no need. Don't disturb him. He's asleep."

"Oh, no, I want you to see him, see quite how perfect he is!" insisted Alix. Now her hands were shaking as she tried to undo the bandages. "He is so beautiful, you have to see him. You simply must." She pulled at the cloth, and the baby began to moan. "Shh, my angel. Shh, my beautiful boy," Alix hushed as she continued to unwrap him. Round and round the bandage went. "Oh, my goodness! What has Gunst done!" she said, laughing a little. "So much cloth!" The more she unwrapped the baby, the more agitated he became. "Hush, hush!"

"Honestly, there is no need!" said Militza, her heart beginning to race.

"Don't carry on," agreed Stana. The two sisters exchanged anxious glances.

"I insist!" replied Alix, her eyes shining. "You simply must see how beautiful he is!"

And as the final bandage came off, the tiny newborn baby screamed in pain. His cry was so shockingly loud, so agonizingly visceral, that both Militza and Stana recoiled in horror. And there, in among the mewling, screaming, kicking baby and the swaddling and the bandages, were clots and blots of blood.

"Oh, my God!" exclaimed Stana, leaping off the bed.

The baby's legs went rigid as he inhaled to scream once more.

He opened his toothless mouth and cried out once more in pain. His whole body shook, and his tiny face crumpled and went bright pink with agony.

"He's bleeding," said Stana.

"It's Gunst," said Alix, swiftly trying to gather up all the bandages. "She's bound him too tightly. Far too tightly. What a stupid woman! Stupid, stupid woman. Hush, little one. Hush." But Alix's fingers fumbled; she was shaking too much to pick up the bloody cloth scattered all over the bed.

"Shh," said Militza, taking hold of Alix's hand. "Calm down. If you panic, the baby will too. Let me help you."

"What's going on?" A heavyset nurse, smelling of soap, ran into the bedroom, her head covered in a tightly wrapped scarf. "Why is he crying? Why is he undressed?" She looked from one sister to the other, her small accusatory eyes darting back and forth. "Who undressed him? He must be bound. It is the only way to stem the flow. Who did this?"

She gently gathered up the screaming, naked baby and snuggled him into her large bosom, and without saying another word, she took him straight out of the room, leaving Alix sitting helpless in bed. Militza looked at the bloodied bandages lying on the top of the bed. Some of the stains were crimson fresh, others a dried dark brown. Despite the airless warmth of the room, she suddenly felt cold. She had seen this before. She turned to look at Alix. Her eyes were wide and terrified, and yet her jaw was rigid and strangely defiant.

"Gunst must have swaddled him too tightly," stated Militza, picking up the cloth.

Alix stared at her, and her gaze did not flicker. "I am sure she will not make the same mistake again."

CHAPTER 18

OCTOBER 31, 1905,
ZNAMENKA, PETERHOF

That's it!" declared Militza to her sister as she entered the red salon in Znamenka.

Stana looked up from her sewing. She was embroidering handkerchiefs for injured soldiers returned from the front. It was not something she enjoyed doing, in fact it bored her tremendously, but after the terrible traumas of the last year, one had to be seen to be doing one's bit.

And what traumas they were. There was the mistake of Bloody Sunday, when lines of Cossacks and hussars opened fire on a peaceful demonstration of workers, led by Father Gapon, all marching towards the Winter Palace in the hope of meeting the tsar.

Poor Nicky, it broke his heart. Not least because no one told him about the workers' rally and the terrible overreaction of his troops. The stories of death and blood on the streets of St. Petersburg were appalling, the tales of the bullet holes that riddled the workers' icons and their portraits of the tsar made worse by their cries: "The tsar has abandoned us," "The tsar will not help us," and, worst of all, "We have no tsar anymore." These traumatized and haunted Nicky as he sat drinking his tea and reading the reports in his study at Tsarskoye Selo.

Father Gapon wrote Nicky a letter.

> *The innocent blood of workers, their wives and children lies forever between you and the Russian people . . . May all the blood which must be spilled fall upon you, you Hangman!*

And it wasn't long before the first blood was spilled.

Three weeks later the tsar's uncle Grand Duke Sergei was assassinated in Moscow. He had just said good-bye to his wife, Alix's sister Grand Duchess Elizabeth Fyodorovna, at the Kremlin, and as he traveled through the gate in his horse-drawn carriage, a bomb was thrown directly into his lap, killing him instantly. Ella heard the explosion from the apartment and came running. After first comforting the dying coachman, she then proceeded to crawl around in the snow, trying to find as many pieces of her husband as she could, so as much of him as possible could be buried together. She collected small fragments of his skull, his arm, his torso, but his fingers, still wearing his rings, weren't found until a week later on a rooftop nearby.

Alix was distraught for her sister, and Ella never really recovered. She wasn't allowed to go to the funeral because it was perceived as too dangerous and, announcing fairly quickly after the assassination that she wanted to take holy orders, she proceeded to sell all her jewelry.

It was all so very traumatic. But as Militza pointed out to

Stana, Spirit himself had predicted the assassination that night at Countess Ignatiev's salon. "Why else had he repeated the name Sergei over and over again?" she said.

OVER THAT SUMMER THEY WERE FORCED TO CONVERT PART, OR all, of their palaces in the Crimea into makeshift convalescent hospitals for soldiers coming home from the front. Militza quickly realized they had to move with the times or look out of place. The Russo-Japanese War was lost, the naval fleet destroyed; there were strikes in schools and factories and murders of policemen and Cossacks as well as riots in all corners of the land. There was a mutiny of sailors in nearby Odessa on the battleship *Potemkin*. They had apparently thrown the officers over the side—along with the rotten meat they'd been served—and then trained their guns on the city. They were only stopped from ransacking other towns up and down the Black Sea coast when the ship ran out of fuel.

There was distinctly more than a whiff of revolution in the air. It was a stench. Like the smell of smoke before a fire, people could sense it coming.

Tensions had been running so high at Znamenka that they'd spilled over into a stand-up argument between Nikolasha and Nicky. Dinner had been a little protracted and some wine had been drunk, but that was not to say that the sentiments weren't heartfelt. Militza was shuffling her cards of Marseilles, preparing for a little after-dinner tarot, as it had been a few weeks since Nicky had dined with them. He'd come on his own as Alix was once again bedridden, this time with her bad heart.

They were discussing the plans drawn up by Sergei Witte, an older adviser of Nicky's father, to quell the tides of discontent. Witte had suggested there was a plain and simple choice between a military dictatorship and a constitution, and Nicky was debating between the two with Nikolasha, who had recently been given charge of the St. Petersburg Military District. The discussion became progressively more heated. And while Peter kept his counsel and made sure their glasses were full, Militza kept them in fresh supplies of cigarettes as they argued into the night about the increased hostility, the widespread terror—so much so that when they took their own train back from the Crimea they were advised to travel without the lights on in case they were mobbed.

Then suddenly, Militza remembered, Nikolasha leapt off the divan in the red salon, where they'd gathered after dinner, took his pistol out of his holster, and declared dramatically, "If the emperor doesn't accept the Witte program, if he wants to force me to become a dictator, I shall kill myself in his presence with this revolver. We must support Witte at all costs. It is necessary for the good of Russia!"

"WHAT IS IT?" ASKED STANA, GRATEFUL TO PUT DOWN HER embroidery.

"The boy is bleeding again, from the navel—it's a hemorrhage. The doctor has been called to the palace forty-two times in two months."

"Forty-two?" Stana's face blanched a little.

"Alix has been crying on the telephone this morning, saying the child is crawling, trying to learn to walk, and he's had a bang. But what can you do? It is only going to get worse."

"Much worse," agreed Stana.

"The blood can't be blamed on Gunst and her bandages forever. We need to find a solution, for if that boy dies, what will happen to us?"

"Us?" Stana frowned.

"Our power will disappear overnight." Militza walked across the salon, plucked a cigarette from a silver box, and lit it. A long gray plume of smoke curled out from between her lips. "Perhaps we need to find someone new, as Philippe predicted?"

"New?"

"Someone to restore her faith?"

"What about John of Kronstadt? He has the power to heal through prayer?"

"He is tied up with helping the poor and the needy. He would not come for a bump or a tumble down the stairs. No. We need someone else. Brana has been on the lookout. She's looked over St. Petersburg, trawled the monasteries outside. If only . . ."

"If only Philippe were still alive?" Stana said. "If only . . ." She looked a little wistful. "It's been two months since he died, and I miss him terribly. Remember him predicting his own death? Do you remember? He said 1905. And it happened just as he said. Everything happened just as he said. I miss him so. I miss his counsel, his wise words. The letters were never enough. I can't believe we didn't manage to see him again before he died. I shall always regret that. He was such a dear friend to us all."

"He said someone new would come," said Militza. "But this time we need someone of our own making, someone whom we can control. Someone who is entirely ours, who answers to us and only to us, who has no past to haunt us. We have Father to think of, our country to think of—and we are not going to let all that we have worked for trickle through our fingers like grains of sand."

"And how do you propose to do that?" Stana demanded, looking at her sister with more than a little irritation. She picked up her sewing and started to stitch. Whatever her sister had in mind, she wanted none of it. She was becoming increasingly bored with Militza's lust for power. They had been at the heart of court life for the past five years, and frankly, now that she had fallen into the arms of Nikolasha, she had become a lot less interested.

Not that their relationship had been allowed beyond the walls of Znamenka, which was where Nikolasha was now living and where Stana was a persistent visitor. Unable to stem the growing love between them, Militza had decided it was safer and easier to allow them the confines of the red salon. However, she was amazed how a glimpse of happiness had diminished her sister's ambitions. When Stana was with Nikolasha, little else mattered, least of all the politics of empire. The Montenegrin army had fought alongside the Russians in the Russo-Japanese War—surely that was enough to cement their countries together? Granted, the outcome had been neither quick nor victorious, and it had only acerbated Russia's internal problems rather than solving them. But Russia and Montenegro had fought shoulder to shoulder: they were brothers in arms, and no new guru was going to improve on that.

"I have told her we've found someone already," Militza said. "So now we have to . . ."

"Don't bring me into this. The boy needs a doctor, not a guru."

"The doctors don't know anything. They treat his hemophilia with endless amounts of aspirin. They think it is the new drug to cure all ills. But no one knows what it actually does. What is aspirin? And is it good for weak blood? Weak blood that doesn't clot?"

"How do you know it is hemophilia?"

Militza stared at her sister, her dark eyes narrowed. "Even the pharaohs had the good sense to ban women from having any more children if their firstborn died from a small wound that never healed. How else can you explain what is happening to Alexei? Alix is Victoria's granddaughter. He has the 'royal disease,' that much is sure. Her brother Frittie died of it—she told us how he fell and they couldn't stop the bleeding. We have both seen it spread through the royal families of Europe, taking princes whenever its caprice fancies." She shook her head. "I can't help but think Empress Maria Fyodorovna made a terrible, appalling mistake with Alix. Of all the brides to choose. It was stark neglect, by her and by the Russian court, in finding a wife for Nicky!"

"You know Alexei won't live beyond the age of five?" said Stana.

"He must."

"And how do you propose to make that happen?"

"We'll manifest someone." Stana put down her sewing and looked at her sister. "And tonight is the most auspicious of nights."

"Tonight?" Stana was looking nervous.

"All Hallows' Eve." Militza took a long drag on her cigarette. "The best night of the year to raise someone."

"Or *something . . .*" Stana paused. "Do you have any idea what you are doing?"

Militza nodded slowly as she exhaled steadily. "Perfectly. We'll use the price."

Stana shook her head. "Militza, you can't consort with the dead and expect to be left alone."

"Says who?"

"Do you think you're the only person who can dance with the devil and expect him to listen when you ask to stop?"

"I have looked the devil in the eye." Militza raised her eyebrows, sounding pleased with herself. "All those séances, all those times we have used the Ouija board, where do you think I went?"

"You are scaring me now."

"Don't be so weak. You have known about our power all your life; it goes back centuries. Now is the time to use it."

"But you will open Pandora's box!"

"And then . . ." said Militza, stubbing her cigarette in a silver ashtray, "I shall close it."

THAT NIGHT, THE THREE OF THEM GATHERED IN THE LIBRARY.

Stana had spent the rest of the day begging her sister not to perform the manifestation, but her pleas fell on deaf ears. Militza had promised the tsarina that she should have someone "new," and she, Militza, would provide him. Her logic was that if she manifested him, if she asked Spirit to provide him, then he would forever be in her thrall. She wanted someone truly powerful, who had control over life and death, and as she would provide him, she would be the one to control him. He would be her little monster. And she would keep him to heel.

So that fateful All Hallows' Eve in 1905, while Peter and Nikolasha went into St. Petersburg to see Chekhov's play *Three Sisters*, the two sisters and Brana took out the ancient bowl from the trunk Militza had brought with her from Cetinje and filled it with herbs, henbane, and hashish. As the bowl began to crackle and smoke, Brana brought out a large carpetbag, which she placed in the center of the room.

Militza stood in the far corner of the library and peeled back her eyelids. Staring into the small hand mirror she had brought with her, she administered the belladonna drops, each squeeze of the pipette causing her to wince at the stinging pain. Then she began to chant, swaying from side to side with her eyes closed, inhaling the smoke, repeating her mantra, calling for her spirit guide. Her nostrils flared and her breath grew deeper, her bosom heaving as she felt him enter the room. The candles flickered and the curtains billowed and her chanting grew more frantic; over and over she said the words, biting her bottom lip, trying to control herself. Her shoulders quivered and her back arched as she let out a small, ecstatic sigh, gripping the table with her slim white hands when he did finally enter her. She exhaled at last and opened her eyes. Her mouth open, her lips engorged, she kept hold of the table to steady herself.

"He is here," she said softly, smiling, caressing her own soft cheek with her warm hand. "And he's excited." She paused. "Brana," she said, as if trying to gather her thoughts. She exhaled deeply. "Gosh," she said, her eyes rolling in her head as she slowly circled her hips. "I am not sure I have ever felt him this strongly before . . . Brana?" She exhaled again, her eyelids fluttering. "Is it nearly midnight?"

"Almost," the crone said.

"Then we have no time to waste."

Brana delved into her bag and brought out a glass bowl, a square of pink wax, a pot of dust; then, out of a net amulet around her neck, she produced a small wooden cross. Militza placed on the table the icon that Philippe had given her of St. John the Baptist.

"You can't use that!" said Stana, looking horrified.

"Why not?"

"It's against God, against Nature."

"To hell with that!" Militza replied.

"But it is sacred."

"All the more reason to use it." Militza smiled. "Quick, you fill the bowl with water; Brana, you warm the wax."

The women worked quickly, and soon the bowl was full, the wax soft and malleable in Militza's hand. Her fingers were dexterous as she pulled and teased, and the figure of a man slowly began to emerge from the wax. It was a simple effigy; she didn't have time to make individual legs.

"He can wear robes," said Militza as she fashioned his feet. "Oh!" She smiled. "We must not forget this." She pulled at the wax between his legs. "Every man must have a member!"

"But so big!" said Stana.

Militza giggled. "Don't be so prudish!" And she made it a little longer, just for fun. The hashish must have been stronger than usual. "There!" she said as she dropped it into the bowl. The little wax doll bobbed around in the water, the candlelight dancing with him. He looked part baby, part monk, part holy satyr. "Now," she continued, "the dust from a poor man's grave." Brana handed her the small pot. "Collected at dawn this morning?"

Brana nodded. "From a grave in the village, an old horse rustler, I think."

Militza took a pinch of the dust and sprinkled it into the bowl. As she did so, she began to chant.

"*Koldun, koldun,* come to me, *koldun, koldun,* come to me. *Koldun, koldun,* come to me, and together we can set the tsarina free."

The little figure continued to float and bob around in the water.

"Next, the cross. The icon. And the mirror—the invention of the devil himself!" she laughed.

In one swift movement she slammed the icon facedown on the table. Stana closed her eyes. She could not bear to look. Next Militza dropped the wooden cross on the floor, and she began to grind it underfoot. As she did so, she placed the mirror next to the bowl so that it reflected the candlelight and intensified it, like a bright moonbeam, onto the bouncing figure.

"*Koldun, koldun,* come to me," she began again as she stamped her foot up and down on the cross, pulverizing it under her heel. "*Koldun, koldun,* come to me. *Koldun, koldun,* come to me, and together we can make the tsarevich better be."

Still the small pink figure bounced up and down in the water.

"And now the price!" Militza turned and smiled at Brana.

Brana nodded, and she bent down, opened up her carpetbag once more, and brought out a large, leather-bound Bible. She opened it and gently pulled apart the pages to reveal what looked like a blackened, crisp, oddly shaped piece of paper. Stana inhaled in horror.

"The price!" Militza's eyes shone. "What better way to summon a magician, a sorcerer, a *koldun?* What better way than to use the unshriven, unblemished soul of a dead baby? It doesn't get more perfect than that. To create life, you must take it—and here is a life taken."

"Are you sure?" asked Stana, her hands shaking, her mouth twitching.

"I have never been surer of anything!" her sister said as she plunged what remained of Grand Duchess Vladimir's miscarried fetus into the water.

"*Koldun, koldun,* come to me . . ." She swirled the water around the bowl. "*Koldun, koldun,* come to me." The water gradually began to turn red, blood red, as the fetus slowly began to disintegrate and finally dissolve. "*Koldun, koldun,* come to me, and together we can all powerful be."

The curtains at the window began to sway and the table started to vibrate. Eventually, the whole room was shaking, as if hit by an earthquake. The noise was intense. The three women held on to the table so as not to be thrown over. Militza laughed, hugely, loudly, her mouth wide-open, her larynx vibrating. It sounded diabolic. Stana screamed, but Brana merely stood her ground. And then, as quickly as it had arrived, it was gone. All that remained was an empty bowl of bloodied water.

"Where's it gone?" asked Stana, staring into the empty bowl, her heart pounding.

"Don't worry." Militza smiled. "It will be back."

CHAPTER 19

NOVEMBER 2, 1905,
ZNAMENKA, PETERHOF

MILITZA AND STANA WERE SITTING IN THE RED SALON, staring at the clock on the fireplace, glancing occasionally towards the door. It was approaching three o'clock in the afternoon, and Bishop Theofan was late. He'd been asked to come at two o'clock to hear their confessions. It was All Souls' Day, the day to remember the dead, and they had spent the morning in their chapel next door to the house, saying prayers for their sister Zorka, who had died in childbirth fifteen years before, and, of course, for Militza's own daughter Sofia, the twin sister of Nadezhda, who had arrived innocently into this world, never to draw breath.

It was very unlike Bishop Theofan to be late. A small bird of a man, with a gentle demeanor and a soft, whispering voice, he was the confessor of choice for the tsar and tsarina and therefore everyone else at court.

"Perhaps he's forgotten?" suggested Militza. "But he is usually so reliable."

"Maybe Bishop Hermogenes has asked him to do something?" said Stana, getting out of her seat. "Anyway, I am not hanging around much longer. I have better things to do than confess my sins and take bread and wine; besides, one of Nikolasha's dogs is very ill. I need to tend to her."

"I don't like Hermogenes," Militza said. "He's such a great big beast of a fellow who takes up too much space and is far too much of a traditional thinker—fancy demanding the excommunication of Tolstoy, of all people."

"Yes," agreed Stana, letting out a long sigh, followed by an even lengthier yawn. "Terrible . . ."

A loud knock at the door made them both jump, and in walked the bustling, genuflecting, obsequious Bishop Theofan. Head down, his black robes flowing, his thin hands mincing together as he approached, he spouted a lengthy litany of apologies and excuses. But neither of the sisters was listening, for behind the bishop stood someone else. Someone tall, broad, with a narrow face and a large irregular nose, thick sensual lips, a long beard, his smooth dark hair parted down the middle—this, Militza was later to learn, was to conceal a little bump, a protrusion, reminiscent of a horn.

"Your Imperial Highnesses, please may I introduce to you a very dear friend of mine, even though we have only just met?" He smiled before proffering up a small white hand. "Grigory Yefimovich Rasputin. A holy man from Siberia."

"From Tobolsk, Tyumen Province," Rasputin elaborated.

His voice was thick and deep, and as he walked towards them, striding across the salon, unfazed by the art, the wallpaper, the gilt furniture, and the opulent rugs, he held up a large, workworn hand and placed three fingers together, in the manner of an Old Believer, crossing the air in front of him. Militza and Stana were transfixed.

"Mamma," he said as he kissed Militza three times on each cheek and shook her left hand. "At last we meet."

Militza was shocked by his intimate approach, his pagan left handshake, his kissing her cheek, but it was his eyes she found the most fascinating and could not stop herself from staring. Pale blue like the Siberian dawn: if eyes were the windows to the soul, then what a soul this man must have!

Stana was equally beguiled. Her cheeks pinked the moment he turned his gaze on her.

"Mamma," he repeated, also kissing her cheeks three times. "At last we meet."

Stana giggled despite herself, positively overcome. Rasputin bent down and kissed the back of her left hand, squeezing it as he lowered his head.

"Grigory Yefimovich!" she said. "Do sit down."

As he turned his back to find somewhere to sit on the numerous chairs and divans, Militza glanced, smiling, at her sister, who smiled in return. This was the one.

Over tea, the animated bishop recounted how he had come across the muzhik from Siberia at the Academy of Theology and how this religious pilgrim had spoken to the students and won them over with his knowledge and his incredible humility.

"It is as if the voice of the Russian soul speaks through him," he enthused, rapidly stirring his jam into his tea. "I then introduced him to Bishop Hermogenes and the monk Iliodor, who were equally impressed! He has traveled throughout our great land and seen so many things, haven't you, Grisha?"

Rasputin nodded and stared without blinking at the two sisters.

"Tell us about where you are from, Grigory Yefimovich," said Militza.

"Grisha," he replied, and talked to them of the Siberian steppes and his small village, Pokrovskoye, by the river Tura in Tobolsk, the river where his sister had drowned and his brother had died of pneumonia, having fallen into its depths. He spoke of his leaving his village and taking up a pilgrimage that had led him to walk the length of the land, sleeping under the stars, going from monastery to monastery, living on the charity of others. And now his wanderings had brought him here, to St. Petersburg, where he was looking for funds to help build a church in his village, back on the Siberian steppes.

The language he used, simple and evocative, in the thick Siberian accent of a true peasant, charmed Militza and Stana with its simplicity and its veracity and held them in thrall. Accustomed to the arch, acerbic, overly intellectualized conversations of the rarefied circles they moved in, they found his guilelessness and his ability to paint broad, vital pictures of where he'd been and what he'd seen so delightfully refreshing it verged on the hypnotic.

It wasn't until Grisha had finished speaking that Militza realized her tea was cold.

"There you are!" declared Nikolasha, bursting into the room. "Gentlemen," he acknowledged, brought to a stop by the surprise guests. "It's Luna!" he said to Stana. "She is breathing very heavily. The vet said she has a few months to live, but I fear death is upon her."

"Oh, no!" Stana leapt out of her seat. "Will you excuse me, please?"

"May I help?" asked Rasputin, putting down his cup.

"You?" Nikolasha did not conceal his disdain. "Who are you?"

"Grigory Yefimovich Rasputin," pronounced Bishop Theofan, as if the man's reputation preceded him.

Nikolasha frowned. What could this peasant dressed in a long black tunic with his wild beard and smoothed-down hair possibly do to help his ailing borzoi?

"Come," said Militza standing up. "We'll all go."

They left the house for the magnificent stable block and carriage house. It was built of red brick, with white pillars and impressive towers at either end, and above the double doors stood a large Nikolayevich crest. Once inside, past the rows of some one hundred horses, the party approached a stable, where, lying on a bed of straw, was a beautiful cream-and-white borzoi bitch. Luna was on her side, her long tongue hanging out as she panted, her ribs easy to see through her damp coat, her flanks rising and falling in rapid succession.

"My darling!" said Nikolasha, bending down to stroke the dog. "Look how much pain and suffering she is in." His face was dreadfully distressed when he looked up, and it appeared he was on the verge of tears.

"Move aside," said Rasputin, nodding over his shoulder at the grand duke.

Nikolasha glanced at Stana and Militza. He clearly did not like the man's tone, but as neither sister reacted, he did what he was told. Meanwhile, the bearded Siberian knelt in the straw and placed his hand on the dog's head; then, closing his eyes, he began to pray. Quite what prayer he was saying neither of the sisters could ascertain, for although he moved his lips, the words were inaudible.

Some fifteen minutes later the dog ceased to pant, simply relaxed her strained head back down on the ground. What had he done? The dog lay quite still in the straw. The grand duke moved as if to step forward, but Rasputin raised his hand, stopping Nikolasha in his tracks. "Back!" he commanded, and the grand duke, after a moment's hesitation, complied.

The party watched in silence for another fifteen minutes, after which the dog raised her head, licked Rasputin's weathered hand, and, to gasps from the assembled, got up and trotted out of the stable.

"She will live for some years," the holy man pronounced as he stood and dusted the straw off his robes.

"What joy! What a miracle!" Nikolasha declared, a broad grin on his face. "I can't thank you enough, thank you very much indeed."

TWO DAYS LATER MILITZA INVITED RASPUTIN TO THE COUNTESS Ignatiev's salon. When she, Stana, and Nikolasha collected him from Bishop Theofan's apartment, they were surprised to see him dressed not in the black robes of a priest but in a handsome, loose-fitting cream silk shirt with baggy red trousers and the knee-high boots of a peasant. But not a real peasant—it was more a costume, something that could have been worn at one of the Grand Duchess Vladimir's glamorous parties.

"Good evening," he said, getting into the car. He smelled very heavily of violets. "Your Imperial Highness," he acknowledged Nikolasha with a curt nod.

"What a charming cologne," said Stana.

"I have been to the bathhouse," came his reply. He paused. "Your husbands are with you?"

"Mine?" Stana laughed despite herself.

"Moscow," added Militza. "He had some business to attend to. And Stana's . . ."

". . . is always in Biarritz."

The Countess Ignatiev was so delighted that Militza and Stana should once more be gracing her salon, and that they'd brought a new protégé with them, that she immediately had someone open a bottle of champagne.

"Welcome," she gushed as she handed Rasputin a glass. "We are so terribly excited to receive you here. Your reputation comes before you."

"My reputation, Madame?" asked Rasputin as he drained the

glass in one. "I was not aware I had one." He looked at the glass and, with a revolted face, returned it to the salver. "Do you have any Madeira wine?"

"Madeira? Of course." The countess nodded at a liveried servant, who immediately departed to find a bottle. "Now how is the empress?" she asked, linking arms with Militza as she led them into the room. "And the little boy? They are so ensconced in Tsarskoye Selo, especially since all the troubles, that no one sees them anymore. What does the boy look like? I went to London during the summer and you can't move for photographs of the royal family—at the races, taking a ride out in a carriage, cutting ribbons here, opening other things there. They are forever in the newspapers. But here? We never so much as glimpse ours. Is he a handsome child? You and Stana are the only ones who ever see them!"

"Oh, he is a beauty," said Stana. "Blond curls, big blue eyes, and such a robust, fat thing. He gives his parents so much joy."

"How wonderful." The countess smiled. "And do you think the empress will be doing the season? She cannot remain locked up in the Alexander Palace forever! The last time we saw her was at the Medieval Ball."

"What a night that was." Stana smiled, glancing across at Nikolasha, who was helping himself to a cigarette at the other side of the room.

"What a night indeed," confirmed Militza.

"Now, Grigory Yefimovich—"

"Grisha," he interrupted.

"Grisha," she repeated, smiling. "There are so many people I would like you to meet. Do you know Dr. Badmaev?"

"I am not fond of doctors."

"He's not that sort of doctor, more of an apothecary. And he's terribly well connected. Let me introduce you. Peter!" she said as she approached the table where Dr. Badmaev was sitting, smoking his small clay pipe. "This"—she paused, waving her fan—"is Grigory Yefimovich Rasputin, the man I was telling you about. The man who cured Grand Duke Nikolai Nikolayevich's dog! Apparently, he laid his hands on the dog and she rose again, like Lazarus!" recounted the countess.

"Not like Jesus?" Dr. Badmaev smirked.

"No," replied Rasputin. "I raised the dog, not the Holy Spirit of the dog."

"I'm sure you could manage that too, old boy!" He chuckled and slapped Rasputin on the back while he shook his hand. "A dog indeed! A dog!"

Rasputin stared at Dr. Badmaev, his pale eyes narrowed with irritation. He withdrew his hand and was on the point of saying something, for where he came from such mocking would not pass without some sort of a fight, but the countess merely laughed.

"A dog," she confirmed. "But a miracle all the same. Come, Grisha." She pushed the small of his back to move on. She was looking for a more appreciative audience for her Siberian. Militza was on the point of following.

"I am not sure your friend likes my jokes," remarked Badmaev, a little entertained.

"I am not sure he likes you," replied Militza. "You should really try a little harder, Peter. Everyone needs friends, no matter how powerful they think they are."

He looked at her, a little put out, and changed the subject. "How is the tsarina?" he asked. "I only see the tsar these days, and only when he wants more elixir, which he seems to need more and more. And every time I go, the empress is always in her quarters."

"She is not well," said Militza, her voice quieting. "It is her back, or heart, or both."

"They should leave that palace more, see some people, be seen by people. I know it is a security risk, but—"

"His uncle has just been blown up in the street," she hissed.

"I know that, but even so . . . He's paranoid . . ."

"I think, when you've seen your grandfather blown up in front of you when you're twelve years old, and watched them carry his legless body, his intestines spewing out, to the Winter Palace for the rest of the family to mourn, that might be enough to scare a man." Militza stared at Dr. Badmaev.

"If that's all you think it is," he said.

"I thought you, of all people, would understand."

"I just worry—"

"The tsarevich is fine," she interrupted.

Dr. Badmaev looked puzzled. "It is just that the quantities of hashish and cocaine I've been supplying can sometimes make you a little . . . um, anxious."

By the time Militza had found Rasputin over on the other side of the party, he was ensconced at a table surrounded by a coterie of enthusiastic women, most notably an actress who'd drunk at least a bottle of champagne. She had wrapped her elegant calf around his and seemed to be hanging on his every word.

"Did you know," she said to Militza, her gown slipping slowly off her right shoulder, "he was in Sarov when they canonized that saint?"

"Oh?"

"And he predicted the empress would have a son after that, and she did!"

"Incredible."

"Isn't he!" She grabbed hold of his leg and Rasputin smiled.

"Come!" said Militza to her protégé, pulling him by the hand away from the actress. "Why don't we go and have our fortunes told; there is a woman in the corner scrying with a crystal ball."

Leaving the tactile actress, a somewhat reluctant Rasputin crossed the room to the fortune-teller's table. Dressed in a fringed head scarf, with dark eyes and an even darker complexion, she professed to be a gypsy from Novaya Derevnaya. As he sat down, she stared at him.

"Have I met you before?" she asked. "Do you ever come to see the gypsies on the Islands? To hear us sing?"

"I am new to the city."

She raised her eyebrows for a second, expecting him to say more, then bent down below the table and brought out a smooth, shining black ball. "Obsidian," she said. "It is the hardest but most accurate ball to read. It has taken a lifetime to learn."

"I have never seen one that black," said Militza, leaning in closer.

"Do you scry?" asked the gypsy.

"A little."

"This ball is very rare."

"Get on with it, woman!" yawned Rasputin, looking across the room at the drunken actress.

"Right," replied the gypsy, closing her eyes and breathing slowly as if entering a deep meditation. Suddenly she opened them. "You have journeyed far," she said, looking into the ball. "I see bare feet walking through the snow and the ice and the mud. I see faraway lands and I see churches, statues. Now I see crowns and crosses and tears. I see a baby. I see wealth and power and gold." She sat back and looked at him. "Do you want wealth and power and gold?"

Rasputin shook his head. "I am a man of God, Madame, what would I want with wealth and power and gold?"

"One day," she whispered, "you will be the most powerful man in Russia."

Rasputin roared with laughter. "You gypsies are all the same!

Power and gold! What rubbish! I want no such thing," he said, getting out from his seat. "What I need is more wine."

IT WAS THREE O'CLOCK IN THE MORNING BY THE TIME MILITZA and Rasputin left the salon. Stana and Nikolasha had gone on ahead, leaving them to take the car alone. Rasputin had probably consumed more than three bottles of Madeira wine, and Militza had not had an abstemious evening herself. He sat next to her on the back seat, so close that she could smell his heady violet cologne and feel the strength of his thigh as he placed his leg alongside hers, pushing himself hard up against her. She felt a frisson run the length of her body.

"Did you find that exciting?" she asked, holding her head coquettishly to one side.

She was flirting and he knew it, but she couldn't help herself. He was her creation, she thought, hers to do with as she pleased, and if it pleased her to flirt with him, then flirt she would. It was the wine, his close proximity, and the fact he'd spread his favors so liberally around the room without a thought to her and her feelings. She had bought him to the party; he should have paid her more attention.

"Exciting?" He snorted. "I am not sure you know what excitement is, Mamma."

"I have lived a life!" She laughed. "I have had much more excitement than you'll ever have."

She ran her hands through her dark hair as she turned to look at him. She had certainly drunk far too much wine, but this man owed her. She was an attractive woman, a beauty, or so she'd been told many times. He'd been flirting with other women all night long and now it was her turn.

"Let me tell you what excitement is, Mother." He leaned in

closer to her. She could feel his breath on her lips. And it thrilled her. "Excitement, real excitement . . . is a meeting of the Khlysty."

"That's illegal," she whispered as she stared into his eyes.

"There is nothing illegal about finding God."

"Through sin?"

"It starts with a dance," he began, taking her hand and starting to draw circles with his index finger on her palm. "When the red sun has set, they gather in a small hut." His voice was soft and the circles he drew were softer still. "They are dressed in normal clothes as the singing begins. It starts with psalms and folk songs about longing for the advent of the kingdom of God, for God becoming Man and the outpouring of the Holy Spirit. And gradually, slowly but surely, the music gets more and more jubilant and they start to take off their clothes, put on shirts made of white muslin to commemorate the resurrection of Christ. It is a symbol that they have exchanged their earthly life for a spiritual one, and then they dance. Slowly at first, swaying together, moving as one, to the light of twelve candles." His finger went back and forth across her hand. Militza held her breath. "Then the group splits into couples, and they dance, up and down the room, up and down, as the room gets hotter and hotter, and they start to chant, 'The Holy Ghost is amongst us, the Holy Ghost is amongst us,' over and over and over until their tongues are thick and stiff and paralyzed. Then the preacher speaks of God and Man and the Holy Spirit, while the rest of us shiver and shake like little children. The dancing begins again. This time we remove our tops; women are bare-breasted, their hair flying around their faces like snakes. Out come the whips, made of thin strips of leather, that sting like acid as they hit your skin. We self-flagellate; we thrash and whip until there are cuts and slices all over our backs, until finally we sink to the floor, covered in blood and sweat, exhausted by the dance and the song, but ecstatic, higher than the clouds in the sky. And then, at last, we copulate.

Regardless of age or relationship, you copulate with whoever is next to you, behind you—it bears no relevance. And when you finally, both men and women, reach a shuddering climax of fluid and flesh, there is no more earthly ego, no more I or you, nothing but an indivisible spirit. The Holy Spirit. Ecstasy." He smiled and then sniffed. "That, Mamma, is excitement."

She leaned towards him in the back of the car, felt his large member, the member she herself had fashioned, tumescent against her thigh; she felt a sudden rush of urgent excitement and she swiftly placed her hand on top of his groin, then wrapped her fingers around its wide girth and squeezed. His mouth opened in pleasure and he moaned. Militza was completely aroused as she parted her legs under her silk skirts, awaiting the rough, bracing touch of his hand. How she longed to ride this man! How she longed to feel the thrust of his large shaft inside her, longed to dance naked and covered in sweat, to copulate with him over and over again.

He leaned over. "It is not you but your sister who puts fire into my loins," he whispered, firing droplets of spittle into her ear. "She is the sort of warm whore we dream of on a cold, Siberian night. She is already fucking another other than her husband; what is another cock to service?"

CHAPTER 20

NOVEMBER 11, 1905,
SERGIEVKA PALACE, PETERHOF

THE TEA WAS LAID EXACTLY AS ALIX LIKED IT. AN ENGLISH tea with milk and sandwiches and delicate small cakes, it was to put her at ease, to remind her of her childhood. Militza had telephoned a couple of days before mentioning that both she and Stana had found someone new, someone so exciting, just as Philippe had predicted, someone who was so powerful and whose ability to heal through prayer certainly rivaled John of Kronstadt's. Then the garrulous Theofan had been dispatched to Tsarskoye Selo to tell of his meeting with the muzhik, to recount how he'd met him at the Academy of Theology, how he'd spoken to the students and so beguiled them with his knowledge and charm. He'd been told to mention the Tolstoyan theory that peasants were closer to God, although obviously not the name of Tolstoy himself, due to his recent excommunication from the Russian Orthodox Church.

The sisters had chosen Stana's palace over Znamenka to

remove any association with the séances and Ouija and table-tipping. Rasputin was a man of God, pure and simple. And they wanted to keep it that way.

It was just past four in the afternoon when the royal couple arrived. Militza and Stana were waiting nervously in the hall. As Nicky and Alix walked up the steps to the palace, it was shocking to see how much they had both aged in the last few months, cowed by the riots and the talk of revolution. The signing of the new constitution should have been a weight lifted off Nicky's shoulders, but the opposite was true. No man, Militza surmised, ever wants to give away power, but his gray face and exhausted demeanor were surprising nonetheless. However, it was Alix who had more than aged—she had an air of weary melancholy about her that she was unable to cast off. She managed to smile briefly when she saw Stana's children, Sergei and Elena, asked the rudimentary questions about life and what books they were reading, remarking on how much they had grown. But her warmth, her zest for life, her curiosity, her ability to engage, had completely disappeared. She was no longer present; she was anxious, preoccupied with problems elsewhere.

"How wonderful to see you!" exclaimed Militza, taking Alix by both hands, then escorting her into the yellow salon. "How are the girls?"

"Well," she replied. "I have taken on a tutor for them, John Epps. They need a little help with their English, although I have to admit he is, in fact, Scottish, so I do hope he doesn't pass on his accent. They have already picked up Irish from Miss Eagar—it's a wonder they can be understood at all."

"And . . ." Militza almost didn't want to ask.

The topic of the "Hesse disease" or the "curse of the Coburgs" had not been broached by either of the women since Militza had tidied up the bloody rags from Alix's bed the day Alexei was born. Militza had discussed it with Nicky over the telephone a few times, urging him to tell the doctors at Tsarskoye Selo, so at least they knew what they were dealing with. But all her pleas had fallen on deaf ears. Alexei's illness was to be kept a secret. In precarious times like these, the monarchy had to appear strong and any weakness was to be denied. Neither of the tsar's sisters even knew how ill their little nephew was.

"Alexei?" asked Alix, her voice straining with levity. "He is so well, so very well. He has a new rocking horse that he bounces back and forth on far too vigorously! But he is such a healthy big boy—he doesn't stop eating and his sisters adore him. Don't they, Nicky?" He turned and looked at her blankly. "Don't Alexei's sisters simply adore him?"

"Yes, my darling, they do."

A footman served the tea while they took up position and waited for Rasputin to arrive. Nicholas and Alexandra were sitting next to each other on the yellow silk divan, while Stana and Militza perched on two smaller chairs. Another chair was placed between them.

"Bishop Theofan has been most effusive in his descriptions of Rasputin," said Nicky. "He keeps insisting that he is the voice of the Russian soul and its people."

"I think you'll find him inspiring," said Stana.

"Yes," agreed Militza. "Don't be put off by the way he greets people. He is not used to the ways of the city and is unfettered by manners. He is a free spirit. An honest soul."

The man has no idea about protocol, she thought. She had not spoken to him or seen him since the night of the party. She'd been overcome with humiliation the following morning. The images of her flirting and his rejection had haunted her for days afterwards. They'd returned in vivid flashbacks, each more appalling than the last. But she'd decided it was far better never to mention the car journey. They had both drunk a little too much—he was most certainly very drunk. Far better, she concluded, to pretend it had never happened. Militza was nothing if not determined. She was determined to sit firmly on the moral high ground, determined to concentrate on the matter in hand. She had a favorite to promote, and promote him she would.

"He's from Siberia," said Stana.

"But he is truly a holy man. He is well traveled and has lived amongst holy men and has learned much along the way," added Militza. "Philippe's words have come to pass, as I knew they would. He predicted someone new."

"Philippe taught us much," replied Alix, taking a small sip of tea.

They sat in silence then, looking at the sandwiches, listening to the mantel clock.

"Where is Peter?" asked Nicky eventually.

"He's having luncheon at the Yacht Club," replied Militza.

"On his own?"

"No, Nikolasha is with him," said Stana. "Those brothers never seem to run out of conversation!"

Alix coughed a little and shifted in her chair. "Nicky was out rowing on the lake this morning," she said. "Can you believe the weather? Sun in November—it is virtually unheard of."

"I almost went out without a shawl," agreed Stana. "Although I didn't."

"No," Alix said. "But all the same . . . sun . . ."

Just then the double doors opened and Rasputin burst into the salon. Dressed in a long black tunic, a large brass crucifix around his neck, he looked a little unkempt. He immediately went over to kiss Militza three times, embracing her forcefully as he did so. He clearly had no compunction about the other night. Or maybe he simply couldn't remember it . . . Turning immediately to Stana, he cupped her chin in his hand. "Mamma!" he exclaimed and kissed her with equal vigor. Alix stood up, still holding her teacup.

"Little Mother!" he said turning towards her. "We meet at last!" He walked over and fell to his knees in front of her, clutching her around the calves. "I kneel before you and all of Russia!" Alix was rigid. She had no idea what to do.

"Please stand," she said quietly. "There really is no need."

Rasputin moved on to the tsar. "Little Father," he declared, throwing himself once more to the floor. "I kneel before you and all of Russia."

"Please sit, Grigory Yefimovich," said Nicky, placing his hand on the top of Rasputin's head. "Sit, sir. We have heard so very much about you."

But Rasputin did not sit. Instead he paced around the room, explaining how excited he was that God had seen fit to send him here, how his journey had been so long and arduous, and how now he'd been filled by the Holy Spirit by the very fact that he was standing before them. He went on to say how very much the people loved their "Little Mother" and "Little Father," how they were the soul and spirit of the true Russia and the absolute opposite to these new government officials inhabiting the Duma.

"*They* are the true charlatans, *they* are the leeches on the soul of the true Russia. You were put there by God, you rule by the will of God!" he said, walking up and down in front of the fireplace. "There is a Chukchi saying," he added. "'A brother is not only he whose face and form are like ours. A brother's he who knows our joy and pain and understands.'"

He finished by fixing Alix with his pale eyes. She slowly lowered her gaze, uncomfortable under the scrutiny.

IT WAS A TOUR DE FORCE: THE PACING AND THE PROCLAIMING, the sheer vitality of the man bursting into their quiet, introspective world. Nicholas and Alexandra could not take their eyes off him. By the time he finally sat down to drink a cup of tea with a teaspoon heaped with the jam, Alix was a convert. She sat up, her back straight, her eyes shining. Militza had not seen her this alive and alert since she and Stana had introduced her to Philippe, all those years ago.

"Tell them about your impressions of St. Petersburg," enthused Stana.

"Little Father and Little Mother don't want to hear about that," he replied, licking his spoon. "Why don't I tell them about their own land, the land that stretches as far as the eye can see?" He smiled, pointing out of the window with his spoon. "Where the horizons are wide and the sky touches the earth; the coldest inhabited place on earth, where a mound of snow can change into a girl hiding from the moon and a young boy can change into a whale, his spear into a fin. Where trees have souls and the woods whisper with the sounds of the spirits?"

"I have been to Siberia," said Alix. Nicky looked at her, a little surprised. "Sarov."

"It is nearly there, Little Mother. Not quite. But close."

"The canonization."

"I was there!"

"You were?"

"I was walking barefoot with the pilgrims. I touched the coffin of the holy saint before he was placed into the giant marble-and-granite sarcophagus, and while you bathed in the river at midnight I announced to the congregation in the church that the long-awaited heir to the throne would be born within a year!"

"And he was!"

"He was." Rasputin paused. "And he is well?"

"Quite well, thank you," said Alix. "In fact," she added, "you must come and visit us at Selo." Nicky looked across at his wife, but she ignored him. "I would love for you to meet him. He is a very dear, beautiful boy, with great big cheeks and huge blue eyes. Everyone loves him."

They sat and talked for another twenty minutes before Alix announced they must leave. She wanted to find out how the girls had coped with their new tutor, and she didn't like to leave her boy for too long.

"I am always worried about him," she said, allowing Rasputin to kiss her good-bye. "He is so very precious to all of us, you see."

"And upon him rest the hopes of all of us," agreed Rasputin.

As soon as they left, Rasputin demanded a bottle of Madeira wine, which he proceeded to drink one whole glass at a time.

"I think they liked me," he said, draining a glass. "She is a nervous, skittish thing who appears to have the worries of the world on her shoulders. She needs to relax a little more, have some amusement in her life. She has a sadness that I can't quite yet put my finger on." He sniffed and wiped his nose on the back of his hand and then chuckled. "And His Imperial Majesty is so small! Nothing like your stallion, Mamma!" He grinned at Stana. "Now that is a man! I bet he is an enthusiastic ride."

"Do you mean the Grand Duke Nikolai Nikolayevich? Commander of the St. Petersburg district?" she asked. "My very dear, close friend?"

"A very close friend, Mamma. But when your husband lives abroad, what are you to do except make close friends?"

"If you'll excuse me," said Stana, a little riled. "I must check on the children."

Rasputin laughed as he watched her go, then helped himself to some more Madeira.

"Tell me . . ." He paused to drink from his glass. "I hear you have an icon of St. John the Baptist? Given to you by a Maître Philippe."

"How do you know about that?" asked Militza.

"Bishop Theofan likes to talk."

"Well, he shouldn't."

"He couldn't help himself. It is famous," he said. "It protects whosoever owns it."

"From what?"

"Evil. Death. Assassination." He smiled. "I'd like to have a look at it."

"It is not here."

"Another time," he said, taking another large sip of Madeira. "We have plenty of time, you and I, plenty of time. Don't we, Mamma?" He paused. "I have an icon I want to give the tsar and tsarina—Righteous St. Simeon of Verkhoturye. It's not quite like yours, but it is also one of the most powerful icons I know." He looked at the floor and belched through the back of his teeth. He was lost in his own world for a second. "I can't help but feel they might need it. There is a rocky and difficult path ahead for them. I see it."

He looked morose for a second, as if what he had just witnessed disturbed him.

"But tonight," he announced, getting out of his seat, "tonight, I dine with the gypsies!"

"You do?" Militza was a little surprised.

"That lovely little actress with the milky shoulders, from the other night, has suggested we dine at the Cubat."

"I am not sure that is sensible for a man in your position," said Militza.

"What position?"

"You're a priest."

"I am a man of God, Mamma, not a priest."

"All the same."

"Are you jealous, Mamma?"

"Of course not!" snapped Militza, feeling her cheeks flush a little. "Don't be ridiculous."

"As you wish," he said, taking another large gulp of wine.

"But there is one thing you have to promise me."

He looked at her, his eyes narrowing. "I don't like making promises."

"You must not—and I repeat, must not—go and visit the tsar and tsarina alone. You must only go with Stana or me." She paused, then said, "It's for your own good. We need to be there to help, you understand. I don't want you to make a mistake. I don't want you to overstep the mark, do something wrong."

"Are you saying that a peasant doesn't deserve to dine at the court of the king?"

"No, no. Of course he does. But there are many enemies out there. Take it from someone who knows the pitfalls and traps of the court. You have to be smart and you have to play clever."

"We'll see," he said, turning to walk away.

"We will not see!" Militza raised her voice. "You will do as I say."

"Do as you say? Or what?"

"Or I will destroy you!"

"Destroy me? You barely know me."

"I made you and I can just as easily destroy you!" she pronounced dramatically, then immediately felt a little foolish.

He looked at her quizzically. "You did not make me, Mamma, and neither can you destroy me," he whispered as he stared at her, his eyes unblinking. "I'm a strannik, a wanderer from the steppes of Siberia. I am at no one's beck and call." He started to walk out of the door. Then he stopped and turned. "Have you not heard the story of the fisherman who makes a man out of clay?" She shook her head. "Well, let me tell you." He smiled and he walked slowly back towards her. "So the fisherman fashions a man out of clay and leaves him outside to dry, and when the clay man is finally dry, he sits outside the house and then he tap-tap-taps on the windowpane. At first they ignore him, hoping he'll go away. But he won't stop tapping. Tap. Tap. Tap. On and on. Until eventually the fisherman's wife lets him in."

"And then?"

"And then—he swallows them both up whole: arms, legs, even the fishing nets, all in one go." He clapped his hands together. "The end."

"Actually," interrupted Stana, appearing right behind him, "I am not sure that *is* the end of the story."

"Really?" said Rasputin.

"Doesn't the clay man get too greedy? Doesn't the clay man eat half the village, the milkmaids with their yokes and their pails, the old women with their baskets of berries, only to try and eat the beautiful elk? But the beautiful elk charges into the clay man's open, greedy, expectant mouth, making him explode into a hundred little tiny clay pieces, never to be seen again . . . ?"

There was a pause.

"Well, Mamma," he replied eventually, with a nod of his head. "I commend you on your knowledge of Siberian folktales."

CHAPTER 21

MARCH 12, 1906, TSARSKOYE SELO

IT WASN'T LONG BEFORE TRAGEDY STRUCK.

Out playing with his sailor bodyguard, Derevenko, and Derevenko's own son, the Tsarevich Alexei had fallen in the garden. Everyone had been watching, everyone had been paying attention, but still the child had managed to trip over and land hard on his knee. He'd stood up quickly enough, only to fall backwards, pale as death, into the arms of Derevenko.

Alix had been at his side for three days and three nights, nursing him. She had not slept, or washed, or eaten. She would not, could not, leave her son. There were blue swellings, a sign of an internal hemorrhage, as the boy lay crumpled in agony, clutching at his knee, his small white face poking out above the covers like a corpse in the morgue. Doctors came and went, and Dr. Badmaev arrived with brown packets of herbs and potions, elixirs and an herbal poultice to ease the pain. Nothing made a difference.

It was as if God had abandoned both the tsarina and her son.

Day followed night and there was no respite. The boy cried and moaned constantly, gradually becoming more exhausted by the pain, gradually moving one step closer to death. But still his mother didn't move. No one dared enter the sickroom for fear of what they might see. There was one moment when the tsar himself approached his son's bedside, only for the child to say:

"Papa, it hurts."

Nicky left the room and was soon heard weeping farther down the corridor.

It was Nicky who telephoned Militza.

"You have to come," he'd explained very quietly down the line. "She can't be on her own any longer. For if it is God's will that Alexei dies tonight, she will need her friends."

It was Peter who suggested that Militza take Rasputin along.

"If the situation is as grave as you say, then at least he might prove to be something of a distraction," concluded Peter as Militza was rushing out of the door.

"But can we trust him?"

"He might be able to help."

It was midnight, on the third night, when Militza, Stana, and the muzhik arrived. They left Rasputin in the carriage outside, fearing his presence might spook Alix, and entered the palace through the back entrance, not wanting to go through the numerous guards who would spend too long entering them into official registers. Every step the royal couple was taking these days was recorded, and there were spies and informants everywhere. After walking up the back stairs, they entered the private apartments, where they knocked three times on Alix's door. There was no response, so Militza knocked once more and entered the room, leaving Stana in the corridor. Inside, she found Alexandra prone on her bed. Exhausted, she had long since given up on God and was staring, unseeing, at the ceiling, waiting for the dawn and the inevitable death of her son.

Militza bent down and, placing her face close to Alix's on the pillow, she started to whisper in her ear. She told her help was at hand, that they had brought Rasputin with them. She reminded Alix that he'd cured a dog and had recently saved a child in the village, said that they had so much more evidence of his powers, that the stories were coming thick and fast from Siberia all the time.

"He is a true miracle worker," she hushed. "Let him see Alexei—I know he can help. He's outside, waiting in a carriage, and has a message for you: 'Just tell the empress not to weep. I will make her youngster well. Once he is a soldier, he will have red cheeks again!'"

Alix lay still as she listened; at the mention of Alexei's cheeks turning red, she smiled. "Red cheeks," she whispered, and a single tear snaked down her cheek.

"Remember, my darling, remember what Philippe said," Militza continued to whisper. "That someone will come, someone who is more powerful than he, someone who is a friend. He will make your son well. He will save Russia. God has sent him to you."

Nicky finally entered the room with a lamp. His wife turned to look at him; her eyes appeared glassy.

"My darling," she said slowly, "let the muzhik in, bring in Rasputin. He has been sent by God. By Philippe. Only he can help us now."

Nicky hesitated. Few but this intimate circle even knew his son was ill. Could he trust this man? This man they hardly knew? They'd met him once and now he was about to become privy to their innermost secret. But his son's life was slipping away from him, faster than the melting snow. He had very little choice.

RASPUTIN WAS ESCORTED UP THE BACK STAIRS AND LED ALONG darkened corridors so as not to alert the guards. Finally he appeared at the door to the boy's bedroom. Dressed in a black tunic, his hair unbrushed, he immediately embraced Stana and Militza, and then, turning towards the tsar and tsarina, he kissed them both three times on the cheek. The nurse attending to Alexei stopped mopping the boy's brow and opened her mouth in shock. She had never seen such familiarity. Who was this man who entered the tsarevich's room in the middle of the night?

Rasputin immediately fell to his knees in front of the wall of icons above the boy's bed and began to pray. He then approached the bed, made a sign of the cross over the boy's forehead, and said:

"Don't be afraid, Alyosha, everything is all right again."

The boy opened his eyes and stared at the strange figure above his bed. Rasputin proceeded to stroke the child, moving his hands slowly and gently over his arms, down his body and legs. They were little brushing movements, light as feathers, as if he were clearing crumbs off a table. At the very tips of Alexei's toes, he appeared to flick and brush whatever it was he'd collected off his fingers and into the ether. And all the while he mumbled, all the while he muttered—and all the while everyone else in the room looked on in silence.

"There," he said. "I have driven all your horrid pains away. Nothing will hurt you anymore. Nothing. Tomorrow you will be well and then see what games we can play!"

Instead of being scared by the large figure in black, Alexei was intrigued.

"Who are you?" he asked.

"A holy pilgrim," replied Alix. "A holy man who will make you well again. God himself has sent him to your mama and your papa."

Rasputin sat down on the bed. "I am from Siberia," he said. "A land so vast and wide no one has ever seen the end of it. It is a land where bears roam, where the tigers are white; in the winter months even the sky dances at night."

"Where is this strange land?" Alexei's fever already seemed to have abated. He was so mesmerized by the extraordinary character at the end of his bed that he sat up. And then he smiled. At which point Alix let out an odd whimper and left the room.

"Shall I tell you a story?" began Rasputin.

"Yes, please."

"It begins like this . . . The Sun has many children—"

"Like Mama," said Alexei.

"Just like your mother." He smiled. "The Sun's eldest son is Peivalke, then the Four Winds, the Storm Cloud twins, Lightning, Thunder, and Tempest. But most of all the Sun loves his three daughters: Golden Sunshine, Misty Shadow, and the youngest, Bright Sunbeam. The Sun's daughters live fearless and free, chasing the wild reindeer over the tundra, dancing in woodland glades, darting like silvery fish in Lake Seityavr and reposing on its broad banks. One day . . ."

MILITZA AND STANA LEFT THE ROOM, CLOSING THE DOOR gently behind them. They walked down the corridor in silence, neither exactly sure what they had witnessed; all they knew was that a child on the verge of death had miraculously been brought back to life before their eyes. Had Rasputin hypnotized him? Was he a faith healer? A magician? A trickster? Had he brushed away the tsarevich's pain like a shaman? Who was this man? Militza turned to her sister.

"Thank you!" came a quiet voice from the darkness. It was Alix, sitting slumped in a chair in the corner of the landing, her weary head in her hands. "He is saved," she said simply, looking up, her eyes full of tears.

"Yes!" said Stana, crouching down next to Alix and taking hold of her shaking hands. "I know! We have witnessed a miracle! A powerful miracle! Here, in this palace, in the depths of the night, something happened. Something that we shall never forget."

"Did God not forsake me after all?" asked Alix.

"He did not," confirmed Militza. "Your prayers were answered."

Alix laughed. "What are they doing now? What is my son doing now? My son, who I thought would never see the dawn again, what is he doing?"

"Rasputin is telling him stories about Siberia," said Stana. "About wolves and bears and bubbling rivers and vast open steppes."

"He'd like that," Alix said, her voice weak as if she were in a dream. "He likes stories very much. But he must rest now," she added, looking from one sister to another. "What time is it?"

"It is past three in the morning," said Stana.

"Oh, my goodness!" said Alix, leaping out of her chair. "It is long past Alexei's bedtime. The girlies will be up soon, wanting to play with him. I must stop that from happening. He needs his rest. He must rest. The boy has been through a lot, poor thing. He must rest."

All three returned to the boy's bedroom to find him still sitting up in bed, entranced by Rasputin's stories.

"And then the bear—" said Rasputin, rounding his shoulders, pretending to look fierce.

"And then the bear went to bed!" interrupted Alix.

"Oh, please, Mama!" begged Alexei, pulling his sheets towards him.

"Another time, my darling," she replied. "You must rest."

"No!"

"Do as your mother tells you, little one," said Rasputin, getting off the bed.

"How can I thank you!" said Alix, embracing Rasputin and kissing his cheek. "How can I ever thank you!" She took hold of his hands and kissed them.

Rasputin made the sign of the cross over her head. "Believe in the power of my prayers and your son will live."

She kissed his hands again.

"Come tomorrow! Please, Little Father, come tomorrow," Alexei demanded from his bed. "I will not go to sleep until you come."

"Will you come tomorrow?" asked Alix.

Militza could see him, feel him, staring at her from the corner in the dark.

"Of course he'll come tomorrow," she replied brightly. "We all will. All three of us, together."

CHAPTER 22

SEPTEMBER 23, 1906, ST. PETERSBURG

OVER THE NEXT FEW MONTHS MILITZA AND STANA kept their eye on Rasputin. The three of them were quite inseparable, and as his reputation as a healer grew, they made absolutely sure that everyone knew they were his champions. Somehow the fact that Bishop Theofan had discovered him first, or that he'd been seen around the seminary and had already been spoken about by some of the faithful in church, was all lost in Militza and Stana's version of the story. Rasputin was their muzhik, the faith healer they had conjured from the dying sighs of the night—and as they already had a reputation for rather an esoteric approach to Christianity, everyone believed them.

Soon Militza was claiming that she had met Rasputin years ago in Kiev. She told a story of visiting the Ukraine to see her mother-in-law, Grand Duchess Alexandra Petrovna, who was living as a nun after her husband, Grand Duke Nikolai Nikolayevich the elder, had fathered five illegitimate children with the ballerina Catherine Chislova. The bastard children and her reason for being a nun were not mentioned in the story, of course; neither was Militza's real reason for going, to visit the grave of her dear daughter Sofia, who was born and had died on the same day. She dwelt comprehensively on her meeting with Rasputin, out in the countryside, where he was chopping wood. She embellished the story every time she told it, describing how, despite his abruptness, she'd spotted a miracle worker. His rudeness was part of his integrity, she said. The more offensive and boorish the man, the more genuine were his feelings and emotions. Rasputin represented the true Russian soul; he was not affected or arch or pretentious. In a world when no one ever meant what they said, you could rely on him to speak the truth, no matter how difficult or painful it was.

And he went everywhere with them, regularly attending dinner at Znamenka. He'd also take tea at Sergievka and was often seen accompanying Militza and Stana with Peter and, more recently, Nikolasha to some of the most fashionable drawing rooms in town. He even summered with them for a few weeks in Crimea, only to return, via his family in Siberia, to St. Petersburg at the beginning of September.

His return to St. Petersburg saw his reputation flourish even more as his fame became more widespread. Stories of his greatness traveled back with him from the steppes. How he healed the sick, cured the lame, and calmed the minds of the insane. Countess Ignatiev insisted he attend her Black Salon any Monday he was in town. So stratospheric was Rasputin's rise through the social ranks of St. Petersburg, it was inevitable that he would end up having dinner in the Imperial Yacht Club on the Morskaya.

There were many clubs in St. Petersburg—the English Club, the New Club, the Arts Club—but the Yacht Club, as it was informally known, with only 150 members, was considered the most aristocratic in the capital, frequented by grand dukes, by the highest dignitaries in the court and well-connected diplomats. The waiting list for membership was almost always closed. It was said that those who walked past would stare enviously at this bastion of the establishment and wonder what intrigue, what plot, what career was being made or, indeed, broken, whose luck was in or out within its hallowed walls. It was also said that even the meekest and most mild-mannered of fellows could have their heads turned by gaining membership to the club. Pumped up on self-importance, they couldn't let a sentence past their lips without mention of the Yacht Club. "The Yacht Club thinks this . . . The Yacht Club thinks that . . ."

Where it would normally take a young man a lifetime to infiltrate the club, Rasputin had managed to penetrate it in little under a year.

IT WAS A CLEAR, COLD NIGHT WHEN MILITZA, STANA, PETER, and Nikolasha arrived at the Yacht Club; the frosts were early this year and everyone was feeling the chill. Wrapped up in their furs, with pretty plumes in their hair, both Militza and Stana were covered in an impressive collection of diamonds, rubies, and pearls. They were both wearing new dresses. Militza's was of dark gray chiffon with a square neck and simple, tight sleeves to the elbow, and it was trimmed with crystals and fine Chantilly lace. Stana wore a pale green chiffon dress with a low neck, large sleeves that puffed to the elbow, and a thick lace sash. Unlike the gentlemen's clubs of London, where ladies were not permitted, the Yacht Club was a place to be seen, where dresses were scrutinized and fashion statements made. One didn't simply turn up at the Yacht Club; one dressed for it.

Despite its high baroque ceilings with turquoise-and-white moldings and stunning crystal chandeliers, the dining room still managed to feel intimate. There were heavy gilt-framed paintings on the walls, small piles of leather-bound books lined the alcoves, and round linen-covered tables were surrounded by comfortable, padded chairs. It felt more like a private salon than a restaurant.

It was just after ten when the party arrived, and although it was early, the club was already full. Peter and Nikolasha immediately went to have a glass of champagne at the table while the sisters deposited their furs. As they came into the dining room, they stood for a second behind a silk screen, surveying the tables, waiting to be seated.

"The full expression of his personality is expressed in his eyes," came a distinctly French-sounding voice from behind the screen that shielded one table from the entrance. "They are pale blue, of exceptional brilliance, depth, and attraction." Militza glanced across at her sister to see if she was listening. She most certainly was. "His gaze is at once piercing and caressing, naive and cunning, far off and intent." The man paused. Perhaps to drink from his glass of wine or make sure he had the full attention of those he was addressing? "When he is in earnest conversation, his pupils seem to radiate magnetism. He carries with him a strong animal smell, like the smell of a goat."

"Goat!" said a female voice. "How terribly apt, bearing in mind his—"

"What a good evening!" pronounced Militza poking her head around the screen. "Zinaida! I'd recognize that voice anywhere!"

The startled Princess Yusupova blinked repeatedly in embarrassment, her large black pearl earrings swinging with the shock. She even had the good grace to blush.

"My dear!" she said, nervously fiddling with her long black pearl necklace. "What a surprise! What a pleasant surprise." She gathered her wits. "How are you?"

"Quite well." Militza smiled and nodded, looking swiftly around the table to see with whom Zinaida was dining.

Sitting to her right was Sandro, Grand Duke Alexander, with

his thin hair and thick beard, and opposite was his pretty blue-eyed wife, Xenia, the tsar's sister. She appeared frozen; her slim hand was holding a wineglass in the air, her lips fractionally apart, as she stared at Militza. Next to her was Count Yusupov, his stomach straining at his waistcoat, his thick mustache sweeping across his face. To her left was the man who'd been talking, bald, with a round head, a short white mustache, and a monocle. Militza had not seen him before.

"Anastasia Nikolayevna!" declared Zinaida on seeing her also appear from behind the screen. "You as well!"

"Good evening, everyone," Stana said, smiling.

"Anastasia Nikolayevna." Xenia nodded, seemingly now more capable of putting down her glass of wine. "We are endlessly bumping into your husband in Biarritz."

"I hear it is quite the place these days," added Zinaida.

"Quite the place," Xenia agreed. "The Hôtel du Palais, the Hôtel des Ambassadeurs, and the Continental are packed. The Oldenburgs, the Orlovs—everyone's there. Mama came this summer on her train and had a fabulous time. Parties, the casinos . . . Honestly, Ambassador"—she leaned over and touched the bald man's knee—"it is one of the most wonderful cities in your country."

The bald man nodded his head. "It is very beautiful and the climate is very forgiving."

"And of course everyone speaks French, so there's no language barrier at all! We are so very happy at our little Villa Espoir."

"Do you know the French ambassador, His Excellency Maurice Paléologue?" asked Zinaida.

"Not yet," replied Militza.

"Your Excellency, this is Grand Duchess Militza Nikolayevna."

"And this is my sister Anastasia."

"I have heard a lot about you," he said, nodding. "Mainly through Rasputin—Brother Grisha—whom you know."

"Know?" said Xenia. "Militza and Stana are Rasputin's closest friends! He goes everywhere with them. It is only through them that any of us have heard of him. It was they who introduced him to my brother! In fact, I am surprised the muzhik is not here tonight!" she added, drinking a large sip of her wine.

"He is a little late." Stana smiled.

"He's dining at the Yacht Club?"

Count Yusupov's face said it all. He was shocked and appalled; he was not a man adept at hiding his feelings.

Militza smiled and offered her hand as Rasputin walked out from behind the screen. Dressed in his traditional red silk peasant trousers and silk shirt, he appeared more kempt than usual; clearly the grandeur of the club had affected even him.

"Ladies," he said and smiled wolfishly. He went around the table and kissed each of the women in turn, either on the cheek or deliberately clipping their lips with his soft mouth. Each stiffened and blushed in turn, furious at such an invasion but too polite to do anything about it. "I trust you are having a pleasant evening?"

"Yes, thank you," Zinaida said slowly, her back rigid, her lips pursed, her cheek still damp from his kiss.

"How are you, Brother Grisha?" The French ambassador leapt out of his seat and attempted to embrace Rasputin across the end of the table. Rasputin remained impassive. "Maurice Paléologue," he said quickly, his lips pouting slightly under his short mustache.

"*Monsieur l'Ambassadeur de France,*" added Xenia.

"Ah, Maurice," said Rasputin, raising his eyebrows. "I didn't see you there. I was distracted by the ladies, and my eye must have missed you amid all that treasure."

Maurice chortled with relief. He had spent the last fifteen minutes regaling the present company with stories of his close personal friendship with Rasputin, and to have it denied in front of this illustrious crowd would have been a situation too mortifying for even such an oleaginous old diplomat.

"Well, I must add you look quite unrecognizable yourself," he said ebulliently. "With your smart clothes! Your blue silk shirt!"

"How is your friend with syphilis?" asked Rasputin, his cold eyes locking on to the ambassador.

"Oh!" Maurice did not know whether to deny all knowledge of such a friend or whether the present company might wrongly assume that it was he. "H-he is well, much better," he stammered. "Ever since your visit."

"He paid me in French wines. I found them a little weak."

"Shall we?" asked Militza, taking Rasputin by the arm. "Peter and Nikolasha are waiting."

"Nikolasha?" asked Xenia, her eyes flickering from her husband to Zinaida and then up at Anastasia. "I did not notice him. I thought he was on his estate, looking after those dogs of his."

"No," said Zinaida, with a small, tight smile. "He seems to be spending more and more time in St. Petersburg. He can't seem to stay away."

"And we are fortunate that he is able to join us this evening," declared Militza.

"Is it not every evening?" asked Count Yusupov.

It was true. It was becoming increasingly difficult to keep Stana and Nikolasha's relationship a secret. However, with the tsarina so occupied at Tsarskoye Selo, discretion seemed pointless. And as Stana pointed out in her defense, George's lifelong interest in Biarritz was known even to the pot washers in the restaurants on Nevsky Prospekt. So as Militza and her sister escorted Rasputin through the room towards the table where Peter and Nikolasha were sitting, she could feel the heat of their stares and sense their tongues were desperate to clack. It must have taken immense will-power, she concluded as she sat down and glanced back at the table, for them not to start yapping immediately.

"You took a while!" said Peter, standing up as soon as his wife arrived at the table, kissing her gently on the cheek. "We are already on our second glass of champagne!"

"My darling," replied Militza, stroking her husband on the shoulder, "we were sidetracked by the Yusupovs and Xenia, Sandro, and the French ambassador."

"Yes," added Stana. "They are all having dinner over there."

Nikolasha turned and nodded across the room with a wide smile. "I am not a fan of Maurice. He has the appearance of a busy little man."

"He's a gossip," declared Rasputin, sitting down. "Not to be trusted. But then again, he is French." He picked up his glass and helped himself to a large glass of champagne. He knocked it back and winced. "Like this," he coughed. "I can't stand the stuff."

THE FOOD WAS DELICIOUS. PIKE QUENELLES AND CRAYFISH sauce were followed by sturgeon with peaches and a delightfully light tarte tatin. There were pickles and caviar and shots of vodka as well as glass after glass of fine wines from Burgundy. By the time the slices of pineapple, walnuts in honey, and small glasses of brandy were sipped and sampled, the conversation was indiscreet and unguarded.

"Little Mother and Little Father must leave their palace," opined Rasputin, slouching in his chair and picking a large walnut out from between his teeth. "The people never so much as glimpse them these days. Little children need to see their parents, and they haven't left the palace in months."

"You can hardly blame them," said Peter, taking a large sip of his brandy. "Sergei murdered outside the Kremlin and Ella so shocked she has taken holy orders—Nicky feels under threat."

"Also, never forget, he saw his grandfather assassinated in front of him as a child," added Militza. "For him, death's cold breath is never far away."

"Death stalks us all," whispered Rasputin, taking hold of Militza's hand under the table and slowly stroking the soft white skin on the inside of Militza's wrist. "It waits in the wings, sharpening its scythe."

Militza vividly remembered his touch, the roughness of his skin against the smoothness of her own, the quiver of excitement that shot through her body, right to the pit of her stomach. She knew she should pull her hand away, but she couldn't. It felt too delightful, too sensual; combined with the wine and the brandy, it was hypnotic. There was something about him that made her feel careless, reckless. She shifted a little in her seat.

"He is right," replied Nikolasha. "Our cousin should be more dynamic. He signed the manifesto, and now he should get out amongst his people and gather their support. Indecision will be the death of him."

"The atrophy of power!" declared Peter, with a shrug. "What is to be done?" He sat back in his chair and sighed. "I must say the food here has much improved."

"They have brought in a little man from France," said Stana.

"And while you sup on your caviar and your sturgeon, the people in the streets are starving," replied Rasputin, moving his index finger a little farther up Militza's arm.

"I note where you are eating tonight!" said Peter. "You are such a contradiction!"

"Contradictions! What of them? For you, they are contradictions, but I am Grigory Rasputin and that's what matters. Look at me!" He threw his hands in the air. "See what I have become."

It was true; soigné and clad in silk, he certainly looked different from the wild man of the steppes they had first encountered less than a year ago, although his manners and manner had changed little.

"Brother Grisha!" came an enthusiastic voice.

Rasputin turned. Militza placed her hands back in her lap.

"Frenchman," he said.

"*Monsieur l'Ambassadeur*," corrected a rather attractive young woman standing behind.

"Madame?" Rasputin nodded.

"May I present a close friend of mine," said Maurice. "Madame Ekaterina Ostrogorsky."

Rasputin bowed his head, still staring at the girl. "Are you married?" he asked.

"Yes," she giggled; her pretty cheeks shone in the candlelight.

"Do you have children?" he continued.

"Only one," she replied.

"Why so few?"

"I have not been married long."

"How long?"

She giggled again. "Three years."

"More than enough time to breed," he said, taking up his glass and swigging his brandy. "Do you believe in God?"

"Yes, she does," came the reply. "Dr. Serge Ostrogorsky," the man introduced himself.

He was a small, earnest-looking fellow of little consequence, thought Militza, looking him swiftly up and down. His wife, on the other hand, was a ripe peach, pink and perfect and ready for plucking.

"A doctor?" Rasputin flared his nostrils. "I have no time for doctors."

"I am honorary physician to the court," Ostrogorsky retorted.

"The court?" Rasputin snorted. "Tell me, Madame . . ."

"Yes?" she asked, her pale eyes gleaming as she anxiously licked her lips. "I have been so desperate to meet you." She spoke quickly. "I have heard so much about you. You are a great man," she added. "A very great man. I am honored to be in your company."

"You are kind, your soul is kind. I can see you have a kind soul."

"A soul! I have never heard anything so foolish," the doctor scoffed. "In all my autopsies I have never found a soul."

"Tell me, how many emotions, memories, or imaginations have you found after you have sliced and diced, dear doctor?" asked Rasputin. The man opened his mouth to reply, but Rasputin turned and looked at the pretty girl. "If you need to come and see me in my apartment, I will be happy to help."

"Thank you." Ostrogorsky bowed his head, grabbed hold of his wife, and they both disappeared.

"What a funny little couple," said Stana, picking up a little candied fruit from the silver basket in front of her. "I wonder how they came to be here?"

Maurice was still standing there, a little awkwardly, on his own.

"I hear you have been visiting the palace?" he ventured.

"You do?" replied Rasputin.

"I hear you are a regular," the ambassador continued.

"Don't believe all you hear, dear friend," said Rasputin, pouring himself more brandy.

"I hear you go to give them spiritual counsel." The Frenchman smiled. "Which must be very gratefully received in these dark times. One can only imagine how it must feel, being the only beacon of hope in such a storm."

"I have been there to pray and to help, to offer guidance, succor to their souls," Rasputin finally conceded, flattered by the ambassador's suggestion. "A few times," he added for good measure.

"I knew it." The ambassador nodded rapidly, his little eyes shining.

"But never on his own," chipped in Militza.

"Oh, no." Rasputin smiled in agreement. "Never on my own."

CHAPTER 23

OCTOBER 7, 1906, ST. PETERSBURG

IT WAS RARE FOR MILITZA TO RECEIVE AN INVITATION TO call at the Vladimir Palace on the Palace Embankment. She'd attended parties there, of course, but an invitation to call was different. It was intimate, private, and suggested friendship. Militza could not help wondering what Maria Pavlovna's motive might have been.

"Perhaps it is some form of rapprochement?" suggested Peter over breakfast, pouring himself coffee, dressed in his navy silk dressing gown.

"I wouldn't have thought so—you know how much she has always disliked me."

Militza looked at her husband; at forty-two he was still neat and dapper with his broad shoulders and slim figure, his hair swept off his face, his gray eyes alert and mischievous.

"Perhaps, after all these years, Maria is keen to bury the hatchet," he continued over his newspaper. "Nikolasha says she is desperate to get back into favor. Now that the succession has been secured, she can't afford to be so grand, he says. And these days you—let's face it—are significantly more important than she is."

But Militza was not so naive. Women like Maria never really changed, and no matter how powerful she and her sister had become, to Maria, they would always be daughters of a goatherd smelling of goat. A fact she continually liked to remind them of. However, her barbs were a little subtler these days. A small question as to whether there were any roads yet in Montenegro, or if their father's desire to open a few schools had come off yet. How was the new currency going? Had they recently been home to their dear little country?

So it was with a certain amount of trepidation that Militza stood in front of the giant gray granite palace, staring at the absurd griffin door-knockers, waiting for someone to open the door. She glanced across the Neva at the Peter and Paul Fortress glistening in the late-afternoon sun. The Vladimirs, with their 360-room palace, their extensive river frontage and Venetian gondola, really did have one of the best spots in the city. A footman, dressed in their signature green-and-gold livery, eventually opened the door, and Militza managed a smile as she walked into the hall towards the gilt-and-marble French Renaissance–style staircase. Her plan was to play her cards close to her chest and get in and out of the afternoon tea party, giving away as little information as possible.

"How charming to see you!" exclaimed Maria as she entered the private drawing room on the second floor at the western end.

Unlike the less-imitate Raspberry Parlor, where she was the only grand duchess to entertain divorcées, her private drawing room was decorated in the Louis XVI style. The walls were covered in blue and white silk, with a matching blue carpet, and the room had amazing views over the river.

"It is very kind of you to invite me," replied Militza, walking over to the window. "Delightful."

"Isn't it? I never tire of looking at those boats or the fortress," Maria said, smiling. "It has to be one of the more sublime views in St. Petersburg." She exhaled, as if overcome by her appreciation of her own vista, before pausing and then adding, "Have you met Anna Alexandrovna Taneyeva?"

Militza had not noticed the young, round woman sitting on the sofa. She had fleshy cheeks, simple eyes, and plump little fingers that clutched her handbag tightly.

"She's one of tsarina's new ladies-in-waiting," added Maria.

"I have actually been at the palace a few months now," replied Anna, with a small smile.

"Yes, I think I have seen you." Militza looked her up and down. The woman looked benign enough, but Militza wasn't someone to rely on appearances alone. "Although I don't think we have actually been introduced."

"No," said Anna.

"Anna's father is a composer of some note," said Maria. "And her family are friends of the Yusupovs."

"The young Felix, Nikolai, and I are childhood friends. Although I don't see very much of them anymore. They are often abroad."

"I hear Felix might be going to Oxford University," said Maria.

"I wouldn't know anything about that," Anna said. "Although I do remember dressing up with him a lot. He was such a pretty boy."

Maria laughed lightly. "Zinaida was so desperate for a girl she used to dress him up in girl's clothes!" She laughed again. "Tea?"

"Thank you," Militza replied.

Maria rang a little bell, and the three of them sat and waited.

"So, how are you?" Maria eventually asked Militza. "And how are your children?"

"Marina is fifteen now and at the Smolny Institute, and Nadezhda, who is eight, is to start next year. Roman is a handful, but then he is ten."

"Wasn't he unwell recently? A fit, I heard?" inquired Maria, her head cocked to one side with overt concern.

"He's fine," Militza said lightly.

"No doubt cured by your friend? Rasputin," Maria mused. "Such a strange name for a man of God."

"Grigory Yefimovich was very helpful."

"Little Alexei adores him!" added Anna, beaming. "He only has to lay eyes on him and he starts to smile and clap his hands and say: 'Novy, Novy, Novy.' He's the new one and Alexei can't wait for him to come and see him."

"When Stana and I are there, we can see the little tsarevich just adores him," agreed Militza, looking at the woman, trying to work out her agenda.

"But he is amazing, isn't he?" Anna continued enthusiastically. "Only the other day Rasputin was talking to the tsarina and then he suddenly interrupted himself saying, 'He's in the blue room,' and they both rushed to the blue billiard room, where they found Alexei standing on the table. Rasputin grabbed him off the table only seconds before a huge chandelier fell from the ceiling, crashing on the exact spot where Alexei had been standing! It was extraordinary." Her eyes grew still rounder. "If he hadn't been there, honestly, the boy would be dead! Rasputin quite literally saved his life. The tsarina was so grateful—we are all so, so grateful. The whole of Russia is grateful."

"Very grateful," agreed Maria.

"What a story!" exclaimed Militza.

"Isn't it?"

A pair of butlers arrived with a couple of heavy salvers loaded with fine bone china, a hot teapot, slices of lemon, lumps of sugar, and two tiered platters groaning with delicate cakes. Maria acknowledged them with a nod and dismissed them with a wave of her hand.

"Tea *à l'anglaise*," she said, picking up a gilt-handled pot. "Shall I pour?"

The three women sat in silence as the grand duchess served the steaming-hot tea and, with a rattle of fine porcelain, handed them each a cup.

"I wonder why my sister didn't tell me?" Militza looked at Anna. "The story?"

"She wasn't there," replied Anna, eyeing the plate of cakes in front of her.

"Rasputin was on his own?" Militza inquired as lightly as she could.

"Oh, yes," replied Anna, picking the largest of the cakes. "He does that quite often, particularly at bedtime. He comes to see the girlies, says good night to them in their bedroom, and then he talks to the tsarina and the tsar, looking in on the tsarevich."

Maria could hardly contain her delight as she glanced across at Militza. Had this been the purpose of her tea? Militza was dying to ask more questions. How? When? How dare he! What was he talking to the royal couple about? Without her!

"He is very fond of the children," concurred Militza.

"Yes," agreed Anna, nodding away. "Or so I have heard. I haven't actually met the man myself."

"You haven't?" asked Maria.

"None of us have."

"But you just said—" queried Militza.

"Not that it stops us from talking about him!" Anna giggled, again.

"Tell me," inquired Maria, leaning forward a little conspiratorially and changing tack. "Now I am sure you'd know this, Militza, but is Nikolasha terribly like his father? One can't help but wonder. Does he suffer from the same needs? Does he have the same proclivities? His father was famously keen on the ladies," she said, nodding towards Anna, who was slowly working her way through her cake. "In fact, he was rather well-known for loving *all* women except for his wife!" Anna's mouth moved slowly as she looked from one woman to the other, her small eyes glowing with interest. "Poor woman went mad. Ran away to Kiev and locked herself in a nunnery!" Maria took a sip of fortifying tea before she went on. "So"—she turned to Militza—"is he the same?"

"Is who the same?"

"Nikolasha?"

"I am not sure if I know what you mean?"

"He's inherited his father's height, that's for sure. But does he have a keen eye for the ladies?"

"Nikolasha is not married."

"Yes, I know. But we are amongst friends, close friends . . ." Militza, still reeling from the previous conversation, didn't quite understand what the grand duchess was getting at. "Is he serious, or is he the sort of man who likes to go to the 'gypsies'?"

"The gypsies?" Militza looked confused. "I don't think he is a man who enjoys dancing."

"He is very well acquainted with your sister, is he not?" asked Anna with the direct manner of the guileless. "They are always mentioned together when people speak about them in court. When I first arrived—you won't believe this—I thought they were actually married." She laughed.

Maria took a sip of her tea. "Anastasia is, in fact, married to George Maximilianovich, Duke of Leuchtenberg."

"Oh, I am not sure if I have seen him at court?"

"He spends most of his time in Biarritz."

"So they are just friends? I can't believe I was so foolish! But they are quite a couple, aren't they? Him heading up the army and she—and indeed you—so close to the tsarina." Anna giggled. "What a fool I am! But you know, when you don't know who everyone is and you are trying to work out who is who and what is what . . ."

"It is an easy mistake to make," said Maria. "But I also think it is so wonderful that two brothers and two sisters get on so ter-ribly well together." She paused. "Don't you, Militza?"

Militza looked up. "Yes, it is a very deep friendship." She smiled, using a line she had used many times before.

"That's just what I told Xenia the other day. She was com-plaining of a 'disgusting nonsense' she heard that was going on. She said she didn't believe it until she saw it with her own eyes at the Yacht Club. We were shopping with her daughter, Irina, on Morskaya, seeing if there was anything interesting in Fabergé, and I informed her that, quite apart from the fact that is it against the law for brothers and sisters to have relationships, they were merely just friends and that Stana is indeed still married to George. But she was quite insistent she'd seen and heard otherwise."

"Well, we all know Xenia's situation is hardly whiter than white," Militza said, rallying.

"Yes, well, *she* is the tsar's sister." Maria smiled. "And appar-ently she'd heard her mother complaining that Nikolasha was suffering from a 'sick and incurable disease'?"

"Indeed," replied Militza, immediately understanding the reason for the invitation to tea: confirmation or denial of some silly gossip. "I can assure the Dowager Empress and Xenia that Nikolasha is quite well and suffers no fever whatsoever."

She simply didn't have time for this, although, had Militza paused for a second and thought, the freedom with which this was being discussed was certainly worrisome. If the tsar's own mother and sister were in conversation about Stana and Nikolasha, then it was certainly worse than the worst-kept secret at court. It was now being discussed as if it were a plain fact that no one felt any need to be discreet about anymore. But she was deaf to how gossip had been spun, deaf to people fearing how powerful they had become, deaf to how people didn't like their closeness to the tsar. All she heard was the proof of Rasputin's betrayal.

"It's as if the tsar and tsarina are all part of the same Nikolayevich family," enthused Anna, warming to her theme. "A little exclusive group of six."

"I wouldn't go quite that far." Maria's smile was tense. "The tsar is very close to all the members of his family. For example, to us—we are all excellent friends."

They all sat and sipped their tea.

"I am terribly sorry," announced Militza suddenly, getting out of her chair and draining her cup. "I am afraid I need to leave."

"Leave?" Maria looked stunned.

"So soon?" asked Anna.

"Yes, I am very sorry, do please forgive me, I had forgotten something terribly urgent. Terribly urgent indeed."

And with that Militza ran out of the house, her head swimming, her pulse pounding. He had completely disobeyed her! She had trusted him and now he had turned against her. What was he doing? All those years of work, of maneuvering by her and Stana, were they all for nothing? She looked up and down the street, trying to find her car. Where was her chauffeur? She had asked him to come and collect her at six. It was five thirty. What was he doing? Where was he?

It was dusk; the weak sun had disappeared, and a bitter wind was blowing off the river. She shivered. She was alone on the street and she needed to find Rasputin immediately. The Judas! She needed to put her protégé in his place. What was he thinking? Should she walk? His flat was not far—12 Kirochnaya Street, about ten minutes at the most. She could not wait for her driver. She looked up and down the embankment for a droshky for hire but could not see anything, so she pulled up the ermine collar on her coat, put her head down, and started to walk, her thoughts churning. How could he be so disloyal? After all she had done for him. Also, all the money she had given him. It was all because of her he'd moved out of that stinking hovel he used to have into a two-story wooden house in his village in Siberia.

She'd paid for the house; she'd furnished it and paid for a piano. An Offenbach! He couldn't even play the wretched thing. It was for his daughters, he said, to teach them to become ladies. Oh, how the humble had risen! How quickly he'd escaped the dust! He had flower boxes at the front of his house now, a tin roof and a gramophone, all of which she'd paid for. She was furious.

She strode along, pounding the pavement in her anger. How dare he! She'd made him promise, so what was he doing, cutting her out? Making a move? Excluding her and Stana from the inner circle? The injustice of it all made her walk faster.

But as she turned right off the embankment, she realized the silk shoes she was wearing were useless in the damp streets of St. Petersburg. She'd been driven to the door, she was to be collected from the door, and she had dressed accordingly. Now her feet were wet, as were her stockings. It was dark, the street lanterns were not yet lit, and she was becoming increasingly cold. She looked up and realized she had no idea where she was.

She knew his flat was down a side road, on the other side of the Fontanka. But which one? And where? The dark streets began to fill up a little more. The workers from a nearby factory had been let out and were walking home, trudging off the grinding monotony of their day. They glanced at her from beneath their caps, at her fur-lined coat, the glimmer of her jewelry; she was not the sort of woman to be walking alone.

As she approached the gates of the factory, the pavement was suddenly packed. A stream of workers with their heads down, their hands in their pockets, their elbows out, marched past her. One of them deliberately knocked her as he passed with a sharp jab to the ribs. It was painful, but Militza stifled her cry, forcing her gloved hand into her mouth and biting her own finger, instantly aware of how vulnerable she was. Then came another jab, harder this time, like a burning-hot poker to the ribs. And then another. A crowd of men surrounded her, jostling and jabbing with their thin fingers and sharp bones. Her heart was pounding, her mouth dry as she looked around in panic. This was dangerous. She was scared. She could sense their hostility, feel their anger; she could smell the vodka on their breath and the fury in their souls. Then she saw an alley, just alongside the factory, and without thinking, she ran. She ran without a care for her shoes, her clothes, the rope of pearls she had around her neck. The men didn't follow her; they'd had their fun. Militza didn't look back.

Once through the alley she stopped, fighting for breath in her corseted afternoon dress. Her lungs were burning as she huffed and puffed, her nose running and her heart thumping in her chest. Leaning against a wall, she saw the road was wide, the pavements busy; she frantically looked around. Suddenly she realized that she was standing right outside 12 Kirochnaya Street. How she'd got there, how she'd found it, she would never know. She rang the bell and the doorman answered. Was Grigory Yefimovich at home?

"Mamma!" he exclaimed, leaping out of his seat as she burst into his sitting room, her heart beating wildly, her faced flushed, and her feet soaked through. He strode over and embraced her, kissing her intimately three times on the cheek. "Sit," he ordered, indicating to a low shabby chair opposite him. "You look as if you've just seen a ghost."

Militza stood in the middle of the room and looked around. She had expected to find him alone, but instead he was sitting at a table surrounded by at least five or six women. Militza was too taken aback to count properly. Who were they? What were they doing here? The plan that she should arrive all indignant and high and mighty, exuding a justified fury at his betrayal, had completely fallen by the wayside. Her hands were shaking, her feet were freezing, and the only indignity she could describe was how she had been treated by some workers in the street.

"You must have some tea, Your Imperial Highness Militza Nikolayevna, please sit here." Rasputin indicated the grubby brown chair once more. The other women bristled at the mere mention of her name, which, of course, was his reason for using it. A show-off by nature, he could not resist announcing her lofty presence to the room, and he smiled softly at its effect. The women shifted in their seats, sat up a little straighter to take in Militza's pale white skin, her ruby red lips, and her large, dark, oblong-shaped eyes. Her dark green dress was obviously expensive, as was her ermine-edged cloak.

"What can I do for you, my child?" asked Rasputin, his arms outstretched magnanimously, playing to the gallery.

"Do?" Militza shot him a look as she sat down. "Tea is what you can do."

"Dunia! Tea!" Rasputin shouted, throwing his right hand in the air. "And some of our finest cakes."

"Cakes?"

Dunia came shuffling out from the small, hot, airless kitchen to the right of the salon. She was clearly of peasant stock, with a broad waist, thick wrists, ruddy cheeks, and a large bosom that must have suckled at least eight children, not all of them her own.

"I am not sure what cakes you might mean, sir?" she said, staring at him with her simple gray eyes.

"Cakes!" he repeated, smacking her behind so hard and so swiftly that she stumbled. He rested this hand on her large buttocks as he continued to speak. "If we have none in the house, we must send out for some. The grand duchess has come to see us, she is our guest, and we must entertain her."

Militza glanced around the room. Instead of being shocked by Rasputin's bawdy behavior, his entirely female audience looked a little envious. One, a rather pretty young girl dressed in pale blue silk, bit her bottom lip as she watched. Militza recognized her. Was she the girl from the Yacht Club? The doctor's wife, with the kind soul? She wasn't sure. But her presence was disconcerting. What was she doing here? Whatever all these women were doing here, it was obviously not to discuss the intricacies of the Old Testament scriptures.

"Go!" he said, hitting Dunia firmly on the backside once more. "Go and find some cakes!"

Despite her fifty-something years, Dunia yelped like a schoolgirl as she left the table, collecting her shawl before she closed the apartment door.

"While we wait for cakes, my grand duchess," continued Rasputin as he leaned across to the table to grab a white tin painted with simple red, yellow, and green flowers, "we have some eggs. Who would like one?"

"Oh, yes please," said the pretty girl in the blue dress. "I'm desperate."

"Desperate?" asked Rasputin, meeting her eye.

"I haven't eaten an egg in weeks," she replied, returning the stare. "Perhaps months."

Rasputin took five white eggs from the pot and proceeded to peel one on the table. He pierced the shell with his blackened fingernails, tearing it roughly. As soon as he'd finished, he laid the egg in the palm of his hand and looked around. Each of the ladies stretched out their hands.

"An egg please, Brother Grigory," said one.

"Yes please, an egg," added another.

"Who's first?" He smiled, looking at the circle of hands.

The pretty girl in blue smiled. "I think I am, Brother."

"I think you are, my dear."

He nodded, and he placed the egg in her hand. She ate it straight out of her own palm. She did not use her fingers or bite into it delicately, as manners dictated. Instead, she munched at it, wolfing it down in big chunks, like a horse might eat an apple out of its master's hand. The whole effect was so revolting that Militza had to look away.

"Tea?" he asked Militza, wiping his hand on the tablecloth.

He picked up a small pot of strong cold tea, poured it into a glass, and pushed a smeared jar of cherry jam towards her. "The hot water is in the samovar," he continued, nodding towards the fireplace. He picked another egg. "Who's next?" he asked, tapping the white shell hard on the table. "Grand Duchess?"

"No, thank you," she replied, taking her glass and walking towards the samovar. "I have just been to see Her Imperial Highness Grand Duchess Vladimir, and she had plenty of cakes."

All the women stared at her, genuinely affronted. How could she refuse an egg peeled and served by Brother Grigory's own hand?

Militza poured hot water into her tea. All she really wanted to do was leave, take a taxicab home; she didn't know any of these women, and what she saw perturbed her.

"How is the Grand Duchess Vladimir? Old Miechen?"

She turned around and he leered. He was deliberately teasing her, using the familiar nickname in public.

"Well," said Militza, smiling, refusing to rise to the bait. The other women sat incredibly still, listening. "We had a delightful tea."

"Did she mention she'd seen me?" he asked.

"Seen you?"

"Yes. At the theatre."

"You were at the theatre?"

"She invited me into her box."

"What was the play?"

"The play?" he laughed. "Who goes to the theatre to watch the play! Wouldn't you agree, ladies? Who cares about the play!" A few of them tittered in agreement.

Militza put down her tea, untouched, and walked towards the door. "I am afraid I am late for another appointment," she said. "Do forgive me . . . ladies." She smiled.

"But you have only just arrived," he said, quickly getting out of his chair and following her into the little corridor that led to the hall.

Militza's hands were unsteady as she fumbled her way in the darkness along a row of pegs, looking for her coat.

"There is no need for you to go," he said.

"I must," she said, struggling to put her coat on. She really didn't want to stay here a moment longer.

"Here," he said, helping her in the narrow confines, holding up the coat so she could put her arms in the sleeves. "You came to see me." With both hands, he slowly raised the fur-lined hood about her face. His touch was surprisingly delicate. "What did you want? Did you need help? You only have to ask me, you know, and I will always help you."

They were standing so close she could feel his warm breath on her face. His clear blue eyes stared into hers and she watched his pupils dilate in the darkness. He leaned over, and his lips brushed against hers. With one swift movement he pushed her against the coats, his rough tongue probing into her mouth. It was thick and coated and tasted of gherkins and black bread. His right hand grabbed at her bosom and the left pulled her body towards him. Militza squirmed and shoved—there were people in the other room; she did not want a scene—and pushed him away.

The latch on the front door opened and Dunia appeared in the doorway with a bag; she stood blinking into the darkness, not quite sure what she could see.

"I have your cakes, Brother," she said.

"Cakes!" declared Rasputin, stepping away. "Sadly, the grand duchess is leaving us."

"Oh?" said Dunia, looking from one to the other.

"Don't worry, little woman. She won't be able to resist us for long."

CHAPTER 24

OCTOBER 20, 1906, ST. PETERSBURG

H E WAS RIGHT OF COURSE, ALTHOUGH THE NEXT TIME
they met, it was *he* who was not able to resist and *she*
who had planned his total, inexorable seduction.

"George has finally agreed!" exclaimed Stana as she burst
through the double doors to her sister's private salon to find her
horizontal on her divan, taking tea, while leafing through *Nightmare Tales*, by Helena Blavatsky.

"What has that boring little man finally agreed to now?"
asked Militza, putting down her book and slowly sitting up as she
rearranged her robe. Despite it being after midday, she was still
not dressed. "Death?" she yawned.

"Divorce!"

Stana triumphantly sat down on the divan, her black eyes
glowing, her thin white hands quivering with excitement as she
turned and looked at her sister.

"After all these years, after all this time!" Stana was shaking her head with astonishment. "Can you believe it!" Her eyes welled up. "Can you?"

"Why now? Why after all this time?"

"I don't know! Maybe he wants to marry the whore? Maybe he just wants to be rid of me! Maybe he wants to run into the deep blue Mediterranean and drown himself!" She laughed. "I don't care. Perhaps he has at last engaged his very mediocre brain and realized that life is short and he doesn't want to be unhappy."

"Or maybe the whore is pregnant? And he doesn't want a bastard?"

"Perhaps. I don't mind, I don't care; I never want to have to see the man again." Stana was speaking quickly. "I am just glad, so glad, so very glad, he has come to his senses. I have endlessly asked him, endlessly pleaded with him." She looked up at her sister. "Begged."

Stana did, in fact, look a little shocked. This was almost too much for her to take in. Years of pain, years of misery and years of embarrassment at her situation were about to come to an end.

"Oh, thank God!" she said, throwing her arms around her sister and hugging her. "Thank God! At last."

"Thank God," agreed Militza. "It is over."

Stana sighed deeply, closing her eyes. Could this really, truly be happening after all this time?

"You will have to get the permission of the tsar and tsarina," added Militza.

"She'll grant it."

"I know," confirmed Militza, tucking her sister's hair behind her ear and kissing her on the cheek. "Of course she will. When they say brothers and sisters are not allowed to marry, it means just that and not brothers- and sisters-in-law."

Stana smiled. "The relief . . ." she whispered as she brushed a tear off her cheek. "It is only now I realize quite how terribly unhappy I have been."

"How about Elena and Sergei?"

"The children will be fine. Sergei is sixteen, practically a man himself, and Elena is only two years younger. Besides," she said, shaking her head, "they are very fond of Nikolasha." She looked at her sister. "I know," Stana said, nodding her head and clasping her hands in front of her. "I know, I love that man with all my heart."

IT WAS A COUPLE OF DAYS BEFORE THE TSARINA AGREED TO SEE them. She was ill, again. She had been visiting wounded soldiers, with the girls, at the nearby hospital and had strained her back, picking up a tray of medical equipment. The pain was so bad that when they did finally meet, Alix was pushed into the Maple Drawing Room in a wheelchair.

"Oh, my goodness!" declared Militza, leaping off the curved polished bamboo sofa. "How are you?"

"It is really nothing to worry about," said Alix with a weak smile as she was wheeled around one of the many bearskin rugs that lay on the floor. "I only need to rest; rest and relaxation is what the doctor ordered, only, sadly, these days one gets very little of either. I have been given aspirin, so all should be well soon."

"Well, just so long as you are not in pain," added Stana.

"I am always in pain," Alix sighed. "There is always pain. Some days are more painful than others. But let us not dwell on that."

The three women looked at each other. The reason for their requesting such an urgent audience hung like a question mark in the air.

"Every time I come here, I think Meltzer has done such a fine job in this room," said Stana brightly as she walked around admiring the new decorations. "Look," she declared, peering through a glass-fronted cabinet at an extensive collection of Fabergé eggs. "How darling! What does this pink egg do?"

"You press a button and there's a sweet little crown inside." Alix smiled. "Dear Nicky . . ."

"How charming!" said Stana.

"I think the mezzanine is charming myself," Militza enthused.

"So do the children," said Alix, smiling. "They keep suggesting it might be a wonderful place to put on a play."

Militza couldn't help noticing how frail Alix looked. Her face was strained, and all the life had disappeared from her pale blue eyes. Her skin and hair were gray, and she exuded a sort of sorrowful lassitude. How ironic, she thought, that Alix—who should be the happiest woman alive, with her four beautiful daughters, a husband who loved her, and a much-wished-for son—was living in a permanent state of anxiety, was almost a recluse. She rarely left the palace, and her daughters' freedom was being increasingly curtailed.

"Have you seen all the photographs?" Alix indicated lethargically towards the window, where there was a large display of silver-framed photos, mainly of the four sisters dressed in matching white dresses with picture hats, fooling around somewhere on the estate. "Nicky is obsessed with that Brownie of his . . . Also, have you seen? Someone's drawn on the new window already. They've tried to scratch something using a diamond. So irritating . . . I am sure it is one of the children, or Nicky, only the handwriting is so bad I can't tell who it is . . ."

It was difficult for Militza and Stana to know when to pick their moment. After all these years they had never asked for a direct favor for themselves. For Montenegro and their father their demands had been endless, but on the subject of their own personal happiness they had remained silent.

They had decided the tsarina would be easier to approach for permission than the tsar. Nicky was not known to be terribly sympathetic to affairs of the heart—they only had to recall the terrible business of Nicky's younger brother Michael to realize they'd get short shrift from him. Nicky had refused him permission to marry Princess Beatrice of Saxe-Coburg and Gotha, his cousin known to the family as Baby Bee. And Michael was now, seemingly deliberately, irritating his older brother with his new choice of lover, Natalia Sheremetyevskaya, the married ballet dancer and former lover of Nicky himself. So the best way to get approval would be through Alix; Nicky, as everyone knew, always did what Alix asked him.

"But the children are well?" asked Militza, trying to think of an easy way to bring up her sister's divorce.

Alix grew a little more animated. She discussed the girls, their visit to the hospital, and particularly how the "bigs" were growing into their roles and their responsibilities so very well. She would make nurses of them yet. The "littles" still had a lot to learn, but they were making her terribly proud, as was Alexei, who was so very splendidly talented at playing with his new train set.

"That is good news," began Stana rather tentatively. "I also have some good news . . ." Alix looked at her expectantly. "Um, George has decided to grant me a divorce." She smiled a little hesitantly.

"Isn't that wonderful news?" Militza enthused immediately.

It was not how she would have introduced the subject, but she had to back her sister. Alix looked from one sister to the other; the appalled look on her face said it all.

"I am so thrilled," continued Stana, for she had no choice. "All these years. All these lonely years . . . and at last . . ."

She looked across at the tsarina for a whiff of empathy, but there was none. Alix was stone-faced; her thin mouth had hardened, and her pale hands gripped the wheel of her chair. Had she the strength to wheel herself out of the room, she would have undoubtedly done so.

"And all I need now is your—"

"No."

The tsarina's response was barely audible. The two sisters strained forward.

"No," she repeated a little louder. "Absolutely not."

"But . . ." said Stana.

"He's had a lover in Biarritz for years," said Militza, trying not to sound shrill. "The marriage has been over for a long time. He's an adulterer."

"I know. We all know. But that is no excuse, no reason for divorce. Marriage is for life. It is a promise made before God. And promises made before God must be kept."

"But you have the power to grant a divorce," said Stana. "You are my friend. My dear, close friend."

"I am your *sovereign*. The country is in chaos at the moment, you have no idea, I have no idea what is going to happen next," continued Alix, staring at the floor, unable to look Stana in the eye. "There is terror everywhere. Poor Prime Minister Stolypin! A bomb? Thrown at his dacha right here in St. Petersburg. How he survived I shall never know. But that bomb not only injured his children, it killed thirty other people. Thirty." She shook her head. "That is why I keep my girls under lock and key."

"How is Natalya?" Militza asked, endeavoring to empathize. "How is she progressing?"

"His daughter? Well, I took Grisha to see her in hospital four days ago, and he was so very helpful. He stood at the end of the bed and held up the icon of St. Simeon of Verkhoturye and he prayed."

"You took Grisha to the hospital? With you?" Militza glanced across at her sister.

"Yes," continued Alix. "And after he prayed, he told the doctors, 'Don't worry, everything will be all right.' And"—she smiled gently—"it is. They think Natalya will walk again and walk quite soon. So," she added abruptly, looking up, "what the court needs is stability, and we don't get stability with a divorce, now do we? We don't need scandals; we don't need to give the impression that, while the whole of Russia is in turmoil, all we think of is our own amusement. Grisha explained it to me just the other day when we were discussing this very issue. 'Little Mother,' he said, 'the Russian people find the goings-on in court too debauched, too decadent.' And there is nothing that talks of decadence and debauchery more than a divorce, is there?"

She looked at the sisters. Her tone was patronizing; her face exuded superiority. It was as if she were admonishing her children.

Stana couldn't help herself. Had she heard the tsarina correctly? She stood up, her hands on her hips, glaring at Alix.

"After all we have done for you?" she said.

Her voice was surprisingly steady. Militza was waiting for her to shout and spit, like the explosive little cobra she remembered from childhood.

"Don't be silly!" Alix blushed slightly as she fiddled with the long rope of pearls around her neck. "That business is all in the past."

"I am not sure every business can be buried in the past," retorted Stana. "Stories always come out."

She started to pace the room. The heels of her shoes brusquely tapped along the wooden floor. She stopped at the edge of a bearskin rug and turned.

"Suzanna, for example? How long can she remain buried in the past?"

Militza held her breath. Did her heart just stop? What was Stana playing at? They had not discussed this. This was not their plan. They were supposed to charm the woman, make her see sense and cajole her into giving her permission. It was a simple plan for what should have been a simple favor; neither of them had ever thought for one second the woman would say no. But this, this was an extremely dangerous game to play. The tsarina was not the sort of woman to respond well to blackmail.

"I think you have said enough," said Alix very quietly, clutching her heart. "My back hurts, my breath is short, and the doctors say my heart is most certainly enlarged. I am not well." She leaned across the arm of the wheelchair and picked up a little bell. "I think you'd better leave."

"After all we did for you," said Stana, shaking her head and walking slowly towards the door. "In your hour of need, we were there. In your darkest moments, we were there. When you had no one . . ."

The tsarina simply stared at them; her eyes were dead with cold and denial. "Good-bye," she said in a voice that dripped rage. She rang her little golden bell.

STANA WAS HYSTERICAL IN THE CAR ON THE WAY HOME. Militza had never seen her so distraught, so angry, so completely out of control of her emotions. Tears poured down her cheeks, her teeth were chattering, her breath was snatched and panicked, her hands were shaking, her nose was running, her whole body was shaking with the trauma of the tsarina's response. The small ray of light that she'd so briefly glimpsed at the end of the long, miserable tunnel had been extinguished. Her life was in ruins, her reputation destroyed—she would be permanently known as a wronged woman turned adulteress, and she and her husband were to be trapped in this hideous partnership forever.

Militza wanted to shout at her sister; she wanted to slap her face and berate her for being so damned selfish and foolish. It was just like her to throw all caution to the wind and ruin what had been a careful plan. Why was she still naive enough to think that her prince would come and she would be happy?

But Militza didn't shout. She was too worried. For by the time they reached Sergievka, Stana had made herself quite unwell. She was white and sweating, and by the time they pulled up to the house and the footmen came to greet them, she was almost incapable of walking. She staggered across the gravel drive and fell against one of the Doric columns by the main entrance. She steadied herself with her right hand, only to retch violently on her own doorstep.

"No one's here," comforted Militza as she struggled to keep her sister upright. "Don't worry."

"Of course no one's here!" Stana wailed; her eyes were wide with terror, her face dank with sweat, and her breath reeking of vomit. "He is never here! I am always alone! Quite alone! FOR-EVER ALONE!" She screamed so loudly as she held on to the pillar that her whole body shook and her face turned crimson. It was as if decades of agony were pouring out of her. She shivered and panted, sobbing and struggling to breathe. An increasingly large pool seeped out below the hem of her skirts. She'd relieved herself all over her pale leather boots.

Horrified, she flung herself through the door and straight into the arms of Pierre Gilliard, her children's French tutor, who was dressed immaculately in a black coat, his mustache waxed into two sharp points just above his mouth. Appalled at her sudden closeness, he swiftly attempted to disentangle himself from her.

"Madame," he said, bowing and shuffling a step backwards.

"Where are you going?" demanded Stana, turning her puffed pink face towards him.

"It is 4 P.M. I am off to teach the grand duchesses," he replied with a nod, clicking his heels together. "Olga, Tatiana—"

"I am well aware of their names," snapped Stana.

"You were the person who suggested it, *Duchesse*. Sharing French lessons with the tsar's children," he added, stepping around her, departing as quickly as he could.

MILITZA MANAGED TO GET HER SISTER UP THE STAIRS AND into her bedchamber, where she stripped off Stana's vomit-stained dress and urine-soaked underwear and rang for Brana to bring something to relax her and take her mind off the terrible last few hours.

"Have some laudanum," said Militza, offering her sister the warm glass of brandy-laced tea, administering a few drops from her blue glass pipette. "Laudanum is always a good solution to any problem."

Stana grabbed her sister's hand. "Rasputin!" she hissed as the tea splattered on the bed. "Get Rasputin! He is the only person who can persuade her to change her mind."

"I don't think so." Militza's tone was mollifying, as she added some more drops to the half-spilled drink. "I think her mind is set."

"You're wrong," replied Stana. "She will do whatever he says. She thinks he's wise, she thinks he's a miracle worker. You'll have to persuade him to help." She stared at her sister. Her long hair lay in Medusa-like strands across her shoulders, and her dark eyes were exhausted; she looked broken. "You have to help me. You have to persuade him."

"I don't think he will listen to me."

"But he is your creation!"

"Maybe. But I am not sure I can make him listen."

"Of course you can make him! You *have* to make him." Stana's white face was imploring. "Do it for me!" She drank some of the tea.

"How?"

"Seduce him." Her black eyes stared.

"Don't be ridiculous! He much prefers you, anyway!"

Stana looked confused. "But you're his mistress. You made him. You're in charge of him. He's yours."

"What would Peter say?"

"He doesn't need to know. You seduce Rasputin and then you ask him to change her mind." Stana was undeterred. "You seduce

him and he will do what you say. A man is always at his most
malleable after sex. They're like dogs after a hunt—at their most
obedient when they're spent."

"I can't."

"You have to! You promised me once you'd look after me.
You sealed it with a kiss, all those years ago. You can't break that
promise. You simply can't."

"I can."

"You've done worse things. It is all your fault for manifesting
him in the first place." She tugged at her sister's hand. "If not for
me, then for both our sakes and for the sake of Montenegro. For
if I go down, so shall you!"

AND SO A FEW WEEKS LATER MILITZA RETURNED TO RASPUTIN'S
filthy flat on Kirochnaya Street. She stepped out of her car and
immediately pulled her fur-trimmed hood around her face, for
there were spies and informers everywhere, selling other people's
secrets to the police. She could not be too careful, even on this
unremarkable street.

"Goodness, Mother," he said as she took off her cloak. "You
look very beautiful."

She had made an effort, it was true. It was the first time
she'd set out to seduce anyone, but she'd concluded that dressing the part, wearing a costume, might help. So, despite it being late afternoon, she was wearing an evening dress of dark
ruby red; it revealed her smooth white shoulders and the line of
her neck. She'd piled her hair up with a few diamond-studded
pins and was wearing a Bolin diamond-and-pearl *collier de chien*.
She'd also swallowed half a bottle of Dr. Badmaev's cocaine
elixir, which always made her feel a little better.

"I am on my way to the opera," she explained, which was
true. Although she had certainly made an extra effort with her

toilette, judging by the heavy smell of violets that permeated in the apartment, so indeed had Rasputin. His normally matted hair was clean and combed, and his open-necked peasant shirt and baggy trousers looked as if they had recently been washed.

"Oh." He sounded a little disappointed. "I had rather hoped we might drink some Madeira." He looked down at two polished glasses he had placed on the table.

"I am happy to have a glass of wine," replied Militza, sitting down opposite him, with a swish of silk. She was more than happy to have a glass of wine; she was sick to her core with trepidation and was desperate for anything to calm her nerves. "No friends here today?" she asked breezily, looking around the room.

He even appeared to have put a small vase of dark roses on the table. Their perfume was trying—and failing—to compete with the heady notes of his cologne.

"None of my little women are here today," he said, looking across at her as he poured the wine. "I dismissed them as soon as I knew you were coming." He handed her the glass, and Militza had to admit she was a little flattered. "None of them compares to you."

He raised his glass to her and took a large sip of sweet, heavy wine. There was something about the man's directness, coupled with his disarming eyes and his coarse peasant hands, that made him very attractive to an aristocratic woman. He was not bound by convention, and he exuded a physicality, a sensuality—and a sexuality that most of the fine young men of St. Petersburg had mislaid decades ago on the way to the salon.

"I know why you are here," he continued.

"Really?" Militza was a little taken aback. Were the dress and the jewels too obvious?

"You are annoyed with me," he said. "I can see the anger in your soul."

"You can see my soul?" She drank a sip of her wine.

"I can see all souls," he said, pouring himself more Madeira. "They glow like halos around the head. The happier the person, the brighter it shines. Spirituality awakens the soul. Today, I can feel your anger and your soul is diminished, it doesn't shine; it hangs around you like a gray, sad cloud. You are much like when you were last in my flat, when you were agitated and angry."

"Well, you are right," she conceded, taking another large sip of wine.

"I am always right," he replied.

"Only a fool thinks he is always right."

"I am no fool, my lady. I can tell at a glance whether someone is ill and if I concentrate a little longer I find out what ails them and how to cure their illness."

"Pure hypnotism and witch-doctoring, you're no better than any of those dozens of shamans you find in the Altai." She smiled. "You're not the only one to be able to dilate their pupils at will."

"Yes, but some of us, Mamma, make use of drops. And now you are angry because I am curing the young boy without you. What do you care about more? Yourself? The young boy? Or the future of Russia? Don't tell me you don't care about the future of Russia?"

"I am not angry about you helping the tsarevich. I have children and I would hate to see any of them in pain," she countered. The man was certainly no fool, but then neither was she. "What you are doing is so helpful to the tsarina and indeed the tsar."

"They would be broken without me," he said, draining his glass and banging it down on the table. "Broken! You should see their pitiful, grateful eyes every time they look at me. Their souls lie in tatters and I am sewing them back together again, one stitch at a time. How can that make you angry?"

"I am not angry."

"You are lying. You have the dark soul of a liar."

"I want you to help the tsar and tsarina, that is why I took you there, that is why I introduced you to them. I am so happy you can help the poor boy," she said, taking another small sip of wine and then looking up at him. "I am only worried for *you*, Brother Grigory."

"Me?"

"Yes, Grisha, you. I am worried about the gossip, about the sharp tongues that surround the court, about what the cabal of harpies would say about you visiting at night."

"You should hear what they say about you, my dear," he said, staring at her as his hand slowly moved across the table to stroke the soft skin between her thumb and forefinger.

His touch was so unnerving that Militza could not respond. She felt panicked. *She* was supposed to seduce *him*. She needed to gather herself. She thought of her sister and the position she was losing, the position they would both be losing. She closed her eyes. She must concentrate.

"Do you want to hear what they say about you?" he asked, his voice soft, his caresses even softer.

"What do they say, Grisha?" she asked, her gaze meeting his. "What awful, terrible things do they say?"

"That you're a witch!"

"A witch?" She laughed gently and moved a little closer. "Is that all?"

"A witch who casts spells and can see dead people."

"Dead people?"

"And that you smell of goat."

Militza flinched. Would this insult never go away? She was sitting right next to him now on the velvet banquette, all the more determined to see it through. Smell of goat? She would show them. Let them see quite how powerful she could be. With her sister married to Grand Duke Nikolai Nikolayevich and she to Grand Duke Peter Nikolayevich, the pair of them would be an incomparable force. All she needed, all they needed, was for the tsarina to grant the divorce.

"Is that all they can come up with?" she said, taking a large sip of Madeira. She raised her eyebrows and then ran her index finger the length of her soft lips.

Rasputin watched her, his mouth ajar as he breathed a little more heavily.

"You are certainly a witch," he said. "A bewitching witch. Who is casting a spell right now."

Militza leaned over and kissed him. She felt his stiff whiskers on her face; she tasted his rotten breath as his rough-coated tongue probed its way into her mouth. It was all she could do to continue. And yet, as she put her hand on his muscular thigh and felt a vigorous energy ignite within him, she was thrilled.

"Come here, Mamma," he said, getting up off the banquette and leading her towards the low, shabby brown chair he'd offered her during her previous visit. Instead, it was he who sat down. Then, opening his legs, he put his hands down the front of his loose-fitting baggy trousers and pulled out his member. It was huge. Already pumped up with blood and excitement, it curved back towards his stomach. "Come and take a ride."

Militza stared at his cock as she undid the buttons down the front of her dress. Her hands shook as she wondered: Could she really have fashioned this out of wax? Was its size and the odd-looking wart on the end something she had actually constructed? Or was this all some sort of coincidence? Was the spirit world teasing her for her arrogance at thinking she could manifest someone, something, or was this all part of some very complicated fantasy she and her sister had dreamt up?

She hesitated, her heart pounding. Then her red silk dress dropped to the floor, leaving her in her corset, her stockings, her cotton knickers, and a fine lace-trimmed chemise. Could she?

"Don't tease me," he said, stroking his length. "You have seduced me, you little minx, so do your worst. I am wax in your hands, mold me how you will."

Militza thought of the tears and the endless miserable years ahead for her and Stana if they were rejected from the fold now. They'd be Goat Girls forever. Slowly, she walked towards him.

"Come here!" he barked, grabbing her by the wrist with one hand and using the other to loosen her drawers. He tugged at her stockings and ripped at anything that got in his way as he pulled her now naked buttocks towards him. He parted her white, soft thighs with his rough hands and pushed his mouth between her legs. Militza nearly lost her balance as she grabbed hold of the arms of the chair and tentatively thrust her splayed legs towards him. His long, leathered tongue began to lick her; it poked around the pink folds of her flesh, and she found herself beginning to quiver with excitement as she stood on her tiptoes and opened herself up more, pushing her legs wider. The more he licked her and sucked her, the more she arched her back and the wider she forced her legs, opening up like a rose before him. He leaned back in the chair to admire her. "What a pretty cunt," he said, smiling as he played with its curled, unfurled edges with his fingers. Then suddenly he pushed two fingers inside her. In and out, in and out, in and out they went. He was vigorous and thorough, and the wetter she became, the harder he pushed. His rough skin and the hard lumps on the sides of his fingers only gave her greater pleasure. She was now completely straddling the chair, her bosom spilling over the top of her corset, her cunt sodden as she moaned and shook and writhed on the end of his hand.

"Come, Little Mother," he said.

He grabbed hold of her naked buttocks, and slowly, slowly he lowered her on top of his huge, hard shaft. Militza cried out in glorious pain as he entered her. Never before had she encountered a feeling like it. His cock was so thick and long and large she felt as if she'd been eviscerated—and yet she'd never experienced pleasure like it before. As he thrust into her, she found herself thrusting back; the harder he rode her, the harder she rode him back. The sound of flesh on flesh, her buttocks rippling, her bosom jigging . . . she had never fucked with such joyful abandon in her life. She wanted more; she wanted him deep, deep inside her, wanted to feel him high up in the pit of her stomach. Harder, faster. Deeper, deeper . . . Finally, eventually, at last, they came together. Rasputin bellowed like an ox as he ejaculated, his head falling slowly backwards against the chair. She, on the other hand, quietly quivered on top of him, then collapsed with her arms around his neck, her bosom pressing against his face, his cock still inside her.

"Naughty girl," he whispered in her ear.

CHAPTER 25

DECEMBER 12, 1906, ST. PETERSBURG

IT WASN'T ENOUGH THAT MILITZA ARRIVED LATE AT THE Mariinsky that night, smelling of intercourse. Not only did she have to tiptoe in through the dark shadows of the box to take up her seat next to her husband, having already missed the opening scene of Tchaikovsky's opera *Eugene Onegin*, set on the Larin estate, but she was also required to remain seated throughout the whole of the interval as she'd lost both her silk stockings.

"Darling," said Peter, appearing at the entrance to the box, a flute of champagne in hand, "are you coming out for blini and caviar?"

"I'd rather not," replied Militza.

"Are you sure?" He looked a little surprised. After all, half the reason for going to the theatre was to catch up on the gossip during the interval. There were some who'd happily miss the second half if the conversation was revealing enough.

"I am not feeling terribly well," she explained, shifting a little in her seat, carefully pulling her skirts over her bare ankles. "I can feel a slight fever coming on."

"A fever? Would you like to leave?" His concern was touching.

"Certainly not," she insisted. "You've been looking forward to this for a long while. I am perfectly happy to sit here."

"If you are sure?"

"Absolutely."

DURING THE SECOND HALF, IT WAS ALL SHE COULD DO TO STARE blankly at the stage, letting the music wash over her. Her mind was whirring, febrile, wondering what she had done, what terrible sin she had committed. Her stomach churned, and yet she still quivered with excitement; it was as if she'd slept with the devil himself. How she wished the opera would finish. She wanted to scream, run wild, take her clothes off, writhe naked, fuck him again and again. The longing, the tightness, the tingling of erotic expectation was unbearable. What had he done? What lustful fire had he ignited? But all she could do was sit still and feel his warm wetness slowly seep between her thighs.

AS SOON AS SHE GOT HOME, MILITZA, STILL PLEADING A SLIGHT fever, rushed upstairs.

She dismissed her lady's maid, and alone in her bedroom, her hands shook and her body shivered as she frantically removed her clothes. The smell of him was all over her: his sweat, his saliva, and the strong, high scent of his semen both revolted and delighted her. Her skin felt different. It was smooth and tingled with desire. Her breath was short, her stomach felt tight, and there was a dizzy, throbbing yearning that pulsed between her thighs. She pulled off her drawers, undid her chemise, and stood naked, looking at herself in the mirror. Was she different? What had he done to her? Where were the cuts? The bruises? Her white skin and black hair appeared to gleam in the light, and the only signs of him were the two large, dark, damp circles between her legs. She smiled and slowly stroked her fingers up and down her thighs, rubbing them against the wet surface of her skin. She then placed her fingers, three of them, in her mouth at the same time. She let out an involuntary moan. The taste of him, the sweet sticky texture of him . . . She sat down on the stool in front of her mirror and spread her legs.

There was a tap at the door, which made Militza start.

"Darling?" It was Peter. "Darling . . . ?"

"Just a minute," she said, quickly grabbing and putting on her long white lace nightdress and picking up her silver hairbrush. "Just a minute . . . I am brushing my hair."

"Can I come in?"

"Um . . . Of course, my darling."

She held her breath and he opened the door. Would he notice? Could he sense the change? Could he smell the sweet smell of sex that seemed to permeate the whole room?

"Are you all right?" he asked. "Should I send for Brana or a doctor?"

"I am fine," she said, sitting at her dressing table, brushing her long black hair.

"Only it's so very unlike you not to have a nightcap or a glass of champagne at the theatre." He walked towards the dressing table and stood behind her, looking at her in the mirror.

"Darling, really, I am fine. I am much better now."

"You don't look your normal self." He smiled at her reflection.

"Really?" A bolt of nerves shot through her.

"Well . . ." He paused and looked down the top of her white

shoulder that nestled in the lace of her nightdress. "I think . . ." He leaned down and slowly kissed it. "You . . ." He kissed her again. "Might . . ." And again. "Be . . ." He looked at her in the mirror, his lips still on her shoulders. "More beautiful than normal . . ."

Militza smiled at him sweetly, all the time trying to ride the terrible wave of panic. If she gave in to Peter's conjugal demands— something, frankly, she was wont to do—he would surely know. He would surely notice she had already been ridden.

He leaned forward and cupped her right breast from behind as he kissed the side of her neck. He had done this many times before, and Militza usually felt nothing more than delight at being touched by her husband. But this time the fear and the panic were overwhelming.

"Peter, Peter, Peter," she said, pushing his hands off and spinning around in her seat. "My darling . . ."

"Yes?" he said, reaching for the buttons down the front of his trousers.

"I really don't feel well enough."

He paused. "But you just said you felt much better?"

"It comes in waves. The headaches, the nausea . . ."

"The fever?"

"And the fever." She smiled stiffly.

"Oh." His arms hung limply by his sides. "Very well then," he replied, clearly a little hurt. "I shall see you in the morning"—he turned towards the door—"when hopefully you will feel better."

"I shall," replied Militza. "And I really am sorry, my darling."

"Of course," said Peter, standing by the door. "I don't know what I was thinking. You are not well. Very selfish of me. It was just something about the way you looked . . . Irresistible," he said, closing the door.

Militza slowly put her head in her shaking hands and sighed with relief.

꒰ᵔ

RASPUTIN HAD DRIVEN A HARD BARGAIN, MILITZA LATER EX-
plained to her sister. Not only had he ridden her rough, like a
Cossack herding stallions across the steppes, he had also demanded the icon of St. John the Baptist as payment for the favor.
Her flesh apparently had not been enough for him. He wanted
Philippe's icon as well; otherwise the deal was off, he'd explained
after he sucked her nipples raw. He would not deign to approach
the tsarina without it. She'd had little choice.

So the icon was delivered to 12 Kirochnaya Street the very
next day, and Rasputin duly went to speak to Alix.

"The marriage of the brother and the sister will be the salvation
of Russia," he told her. He was a clever man. He didn't say which
brother and which sister; he was far too astute for that. What he
did do was make a simple prophesy—and any form of salvation
for Russia during this period was obviously extremely welcome, so
Alix could not ignore it. Not to embrace Brother Grisha's prediction was unthinkable for her. Her faith in God and her blind faith
in him meant to demur would be impossible. It would have caused
her such unnecessary worry and heartache. And yet to grant Stana
her wish was to go against all that she, Alix, held dear: loyalty, hon-
esty, fidelity, and the sanctity of marriage before God. Yet she was
prepared to give this all up for Rasputin . . .

And so on November 15 the divorce of Princess Anastasia of
Montenegro and George Maximilianovich, 6th Duke of Leuchtenberg, was finally granted.

THE DOWAGER EMPRESS WAS FURIOUS. THERE WAS NOTHING
now to prevent Stana from marrying Nikolasha, and she continued to tell whoever would listen of Nikolasha's "sick and incurable" disease. She suggested he might have succumbed to some

sort of "spell." He'd been enchanted. The Black Peril, the Sibyl Sisters, had got to him. The man was a fool. A sick fool. An embarrassing sick fool. And she was appalled. But what galled her most was not only had Nicholas forbidden his own brother Michael from marrying his cousin Baby Bee, but now he was about to allow both Goat Girls to be married to two of the most important men in Russia. It was too much for her to cope with. How could Nicky have let this happen? How weak-willed was her son? How easily led? How influenced by his wretched wife? She was beside herself.

And she wasn't the only one who felt that way.

"It is the work of Satan himself," said the Grand Duchess Vladimir to Baroness Sophie Buxhoeveden as they prepared the lace stall for the Christmas bazaar. The baroness did not comment. She was not a woman who shared her opinion freely. Free opinions were dangerous, especially during these times. "Satan," continued the grand duchess as she riffled through the lace, putting it in piles. "In fact, that whole household is an axis of evil."

It was only a few minutes past two in the afternoon, and the four-day Christmas bazaar had just opened. The cream of St. Petersburg society was about to fill the Noble Assembly Hall on Mikhailovsky Square, although since the doors stayed open until midnight, plenty of them were taking their time.

"Is not Satan better than a large part of the human race we are trying to save from him?" came a voice.

They both looked up from the lace.

"Brother Grisha." Maria Pavlovna smiled. "What a delightful surprise! I didn't expect a little trifle like this would interest you."

"On the contrary, Madame, trifles and any work for the poor are always welcome." He smiled and nodded his head. He had changed so much from the simple peasant who'd arrived so recently.

"Have you been introduced to Baroness Sophie Buxhoeveden?" Sophie smiled. "Good day to you."

"This is Grigory Yefimovich Rasputin."

"Grisha," he said. He took hold of her hand, which she had somewhat reluctantly offered to him, and he kissed it. It took all of Sophie's willpower not to pull it away from him. She found him utterly repellent. "What pretty little hands," he said, continuing to hold them. "So small," he added, turning them over. "So delicate . . . so soft."

"Thank you," she replied, snatching them back.

"Do you know what they say about a woman with small, soft hands?" he asked, staring into her eyes.

"No?" Sophie was intrigued, despite herself.

"She has never toiled in her life."

He smiled. Maria Pavlovna laughed. "Good God, Grisha!" she said. "You terrible thing! Who on earth thinks a hard day's toil is good? Far better to have never toiled at all than to have ruined one's pretty hands in the earth! Everyone knows that. Look at mine." She thrust her little pink fingers forward. "Just like a child."

He looked down. "It is easier for a camel to go through the eye of a needle than for a rich man to enter into the kingdom of God." He paused. "It is the peasants who are closer to God, my lady."

"Really, Grisha! Who on earth wants to be close to God?"

Maria laughed again, although her mirth failed to reach her eyes. How dare he? The man was really beyond the pale. How Alix and Nicky tolerated him, she could not comprehend. Spouting his dull little platitudes. It was like conversing with a clairvoyant at a fair! Thankfully he walked off over to another stall, where a collection of delightful young ladies vied for his attention as they laid out some homemade biscuits on pretty little plates.

The two women watched as he flirted and chatted and eventually helped himself to a tray of biscuits, handing over not so much as a kopek in return.

Maria glanced around the room to see if anyone else had noticed, but they had not. Everyone in the vast atrium was busy. All along the horseshoe-shaped line of stalls, grand duchesses, princesses, and their ladies-in-waiting were arranging and rearranging their collections of decorated boxes, cloved oranges, knitted mittens, and embroidered samplers, as well as a veritable treasure trove of other knickknacks and objets d'art. Although the majority of stalls were selling homemade crafts and fare, there were other stalls, such as Fabergé, ready to take advantage of the illustrious clientele.

To the melancholy tunes of the guards' band, whose music filled the hall all afternoon, the flower of St. Petersburg society mingled, trading gossip and intrigue, while helping the poor.

"That man really is too much," announced Maria Pavlovna, looking down at her small hand.

"Yes," muttered Sophie. "And look who he is talking to now."

They both stared across the room as Militza, Stana, Peter, and now, of course, Nikolasha entered the hall.

"The Black Peril," said Maria, raising her eyebrows. "I was wondering if they would come. Given the circumstances."

"Unbearable," mumbled Sophie.

"They are now." Maria observed them all gathered together at the other side of the room as they presented a united and indomitable front. "Now that the divorce has come through and she will marry Nikolai Nikolayevich . . ."

"Are you sure?"

"That's what everyone says. Apparently, there is a ceremony planned."

"But they are brother and sister!" exclaimed Sophie.

"Not in the eyes of the tsar."

"But in the eyes of God."

"It depends which God." Maria shook her head. "And anyway, those Black Princesses don't deal in God; they are Satan's handmaidens, and now they are the most powerful family in Russia."

The two women continued to stare as Rasputin approached the group.

"And with him," sighed Maria, "they are untouchable."

"AND HOW ARE YOU, MY CHILDREN?" ASKED RASPUTIN AS HE kissed the sisters with overt familiarity, running his thumb down each one's cheek in turn.

"So well," beamed Stana, who since the announcement of her divorce had bloomed remarkably.

"You are blushing like a new flower," he replied. He leaned forward and whispered in her ear, "No need to thank me."

Stana smiled and patted his arm, before graciously looking around the room. She knew all eyes were on her and him, so she continued to smile, but how she disliked being in thrall to this man. How many more times was he going to take credit for her happiness? How many more times would he take liberties? How she wished that both she and her sister had not stirred up the Fates that desperate dark night of All Hallows' Eve. How she wished she'd refused her sister, begged her to change her mind. But Militza was impossible to refuse when she put her mind to something. And even now, when she felt at her most happy and fulfilled, Stana could not help but feel anxious.

"You are so kind, Grisha," she continued, bowing her head slightly. "And how are you enjoying the bazaar?"

"It amuses," he said. "And you, my dear?" He turned and kissed Militza on the corner of her mouth. Peter bristled with irritation. He'd noticed Rasputin's fondness for kissing all the ladies on the mouth, but even so, to kiss another man's wife in front of her husband was very poor form indeed. "Are you here for the biscuits or the Fabergé?"

Militza's dark eyes narrowed while her heart beat wildly in her chest. His teasing was unbearable. It was almost as unpleasant as the smell of his hair and the heavy scent of garlic and gherkins on his breath—and yet all she could think about as she stood so very close to him was the thickness of his shaft and the way he'd ridden her so hard astride his filthy armchair . . . She felt her pulse quicken and her breath grow shallow as she tried to control herself.

He referred to the episode as a "healing" and had suggested she come to his flat for several more. It was part of the teachings of God, he'd assured her quietly, whispering in her ear as they conversed at Countess Ignatiev's salon. God was there to help the sinner. "Go out and sin so that you don't think yourself so holy," he'd said, pulling her closer to him. "The Lord abaseth him that is exalted and exalteth him that is abased," he'd added as he'd rubbed his cock up against her thighs, and she'd felt its urgent excitement even through the silk of her skirts.

So far she had resisted another visit to his apartment, although in private she'd thought of little else and longed for nothing more than to be "healed" once more.

"I am here to help the poor," she said quietly.

"The poor?" he asked as he moved a little closer. "Now what would you know about them, Mamma?"

"Brother Grisha!" came a call from across the room. "Do come and try my biscuits!"

Militza looked across the room, and there, behind a stall, was the pretty blond girl who had been at the Yacht Club.

"Ah!" He waved before turning briefly to face Militza. "Madame Ekaterina Ostrogorsky, the little doctor's wife." He smirked before he leaned over and whispered, "The only woman I have met who is wetter than you." He laughed silently, his hot breath whistling in her ear, before he walked across the room, his first three fingers raised, ready to make the sign of the cross at whoever he felt needed it.

"My darling," said Peter, exhaling boredom through flared nostrils as he surveyed the scene. "Shall we at least take a look at the Fabergé? I am afraid I can't bear to feign interest in another little piece of stitching." Militza looked up at him in a state of confusion. "Fabergé?" he repeated.

"Oh, yes, yes," she stammered, trying to gather herself as her head swam and her heart palpated. "Fabergé, why ever not?" She snatched at her husband's arm.

"Are you all right, dear?" he asked giving her the briefest of glances.

"I am quite all right," she replied. "It is just very hot."

"It is always ghastly here," he concurred. "There are far too many people. Frankly, I have never seen the appeal of it myself. It always feels like one large vanity trip for the Vladimirs—and as far as I can see they need no encouragement in that department."

They began to walk through the crowd, past a stall of shawls and another covered in cloved oranges tied up with purple ribbons.

"I see the Dowager Empress has deigned to join us," muttered Peter, smoothing down his mustache. "With Cousin Xenia."

Militza felt him move in the opposite direction. Normally she would chastise him. Why should they give way? After all, they were the more powerful couple these days. But this time she felt too weak to say anything. She didn't have the strength for a fight. Instead, she faltered along at his side, holding his arm tightly as they wove their way towards the other end of the hall.

Peter didn't seem to notice his wife's uncharacteristic unsteadiness. Had he heard Rasputin? she wondered. No, he admired

Rasputin, thought him a man of God despite his little dalliances with the gypsies; he couldn't suspect anything. She shivered. There would be no telling how he would react if he found out. Militza tried to steel herself. She was a good liar, she knew that; however, this was going to be a test even for her.

Peter chatted away to the stiff-looking gentleman manning the Fabergé stall as he riffled through the stunning collection of bejeweled trinkets, which included silver photograph frames, cigarette boxes, and necklace chains: portable knickknacks to make charming Christmas presents.

Meanwhile, despite her best efforts, Militza couldn't take her eyes off Rasputin as he drifted from stall to stall, helping himself to whatever amuse-bouche he fancied. He alternately embraced or blessed any of the twittering females who crossed his path—and there were many. Cheeks flushed, heads cocked to one side, hands clasped in front of them, they giggled and smiled and touched the backs of their heads, patting their pinned hair as they flirted with him.

Militza found it hard to contain her emotion. She wasn't sure if she was simply jealous or plain annoyed. But the confidence he exuded and the aura of physical power emanating from him was something to behold. His presence was magnetic, and it was obvious that most of the women in the hall thought so too.

"How is your Friend?" asked the Dowager Empress, standing right next to Militza and following her gaze.

"Oh!" Militza started. "Your Imperial Majesty, I did not see you there!"

"No." She gave a half smile. "You appeared lost in your own little world. And what a world!" she continued. "You must be congratulated." She nodded, her lips tight. "Who would have thought two women from such a ghastly little backwater, with so little breeding and so few connections, could rise so high. It's as if you were made of wisteria. It climbs as high and as quickly as it can. Like a weed. Suffocating all in its wake. Funny plant," she added. "I have never seen the appeal of it myself. It has to be trained and cut back, taught how to behave. It does flower, very beautifully, once, and then leaves such a terrible mess afterwards. Tell me"—she paused—"have you found a church in all of Russia where a brother can actually marry his own sister?"

"You make it sound like a sin," said Militza, her heart beating. Even after all these years the Dowager Empress could still manage to make her feel as if she had just arrived in the city with thick black mud under her fingernails. All those insecurities, all the misery, came flooding back. She could feel herself flushing like a virgin at her first ball.

"It is, my dear. Incest." She shivered. "It's a hideous sin."

"Well, as a matter of fact we have found a church. In Livadia," Militza replied, despite herself. "In April. Such a pretty time of year."

The Dowager Empress looked horrified, but only for a second and then she shrugged. "Sadly, I think I shall be in Biarritz, or Spala. Or somewhere far, far away."

"I don't think it will be a big wedding," added Militza.

"No," Maria Fyodorovna said, raising an eyebrow, "I imagine you'll be struggling for witnesses."

"Your Imperial Majesty." Peter turned around from the Fabergé table and kissed the Dowager Empress's hand. "Have you been buying Christmas trinkets in aid of the poor?"

"Just a few little biscuits," the Dowager Empress replied. "Xenia and I are off to Cartier."

"Excellent," he said, turning back to the table.

"Cartier?" Militza asked.

"It's a private invitation," replied the Dowager Empress, looking her up and down. "Didn't you receive one?"

There was something about the triumphant look on the old woman's face, the hardness behind her pale eyes, that was depressingly familiar. Militza couldn't stop herself from imagining what it would take to get rid of the woman. Just some sleeping water drawn after dark. Some dust from a dead man's grave, worn as an amulet. It would be so simple. So quick. So final . . .

"I am not sure I need any more bibelots," Militza replied eventually. "Sometimes a woman has enough sparkles. There are other ways to occupy one's mind."

"Very wise," replied Maria Fyodorovna. "I imagine yours is quite occupied at the moment. The idea of your dear Friend coming to the palace after dark, filling the little boy's head with stories of Siberia, bringing an icon with him that he says is all-powerful and then afterwards retiring for an evening tea with *her*. The German." She paused, her dislike for Alix so profound, she was unable to pronounce her name. "That would occupy my mind. Actually. That, and his increasingly well-known fondness for carousing with actresses."

"But he is a man of God!"

"Is he?" the Dowager Empress whispered before adding loudly, "Oh, look, there is my daughter. Cartier beckons!" And with a rustle of silk, she walked away.

"Has she gone?" asked Peter, joining his wife.

"I really hope your brother knows what he is doing," said Militza.

"And your sister," agreed Peter. "I don't think I have ever seen the Dowager Empress so out of sorts."

"Out of sorts?" Militza looked at her husband. "She is furious."

"No. The day Nicky married Alix, *then* she was furious." Peter nodded, watching the Dowager Empress make her way through the hall. "She disguised it as grief, copious weeping for the death of the tsar. But in retrospect, I am convinced it was because her beautiful Nicky, her favorite son, was marrying a provincial with no apparent sophistication at all."

"She could have made an effort to like her daughter-in-law," suggested Militza.

Peter turned and looked at her and laughed. "You really don't know dear old Minny at all, do you?"

"Or maybe she simply hates her because she was the one who chose her?"

"Possibly," agreed Peter. "What do you mean?"

"Nicky married Alix at her behest—so dear old Minny introduced the 'curse of the Coburgs' into her own family!"

"What entertains you so?"

Rasputin was standing next to them. Beside him was the doctor's wife, her little hand hooked through the crook of his arm.

"Nothing," replied Peter, waving away the question, his mind spinning at Militza's suggestion.

"I like jokes," persisted Rasputin. "I like to be entertained."

"There was no joke," said Peter.

"What a shame."

Rasputin smiled as he slowly stroked the back of the doctor's wife's hand. She smiled, and the ringlets at the back of her head quivered as she slowly turned her somewhat glassy gaze this way and that.

"Grisha is very fond of being entertained," she said sweetly.

Peter nodded. "I hear the gypsies think all their Christmases have come at once when you arrive, you order so much champagne!"

"Champagne!" Rasputin looked shocked. "I thought you knew me well, brother! There is nothing I dislike more than those weak French bubbles!"

"And there was me thinking you'd shed your peasant's coat!" replied Peter. "For those are fine silks you are wearing."

Both men looked down at Rasputin's crimson silk trousers, gathered loosely at the waist.

"Another present from an admirer!" Rasputin laughed, shaking his right leg a little to show them off. "The shirt was embroidered by the empress herself!" He flung his arms wide-open for it to be admired. "But the trousers were a little present after a healing."

"A healing?" Militza's mouth was dry.

"The empress embroidered you a shirt?" asked Peter.

"Yes." He nodded.

"Grisha heals so many women," interjected the doctor's wife. "Hysteria, sadness, woes—they all come to him for help. Some are so desperate, they are on their knees, praying; sometimes there is a queue. And he heals them all."

Militza's dark eyes darted back and forth between Rasputin and Ekaterina Ostrogorsky. Was the woman aware of what she was saying?

"Those whom he can't cure by laying his hands on them come into the back room for a more in-depth healing," she continued. "And they leave with their cheeks flushed and a light in their eye. It's amazing!" She turned slowly to look at him, gently stroking his hand. "He really is a man of God."

"Yes," concurred Militza, her eyes narrowing. "A man of God, indeed."

CHAPTER 26

APRIL 10, 1907, ST. PETERSBURG

Rumors of Rasputin's spectacular "healing" powers swept through the city, tormenting Militza at every turn. He'd ignited a fire within her that she could not control. Every meeting she had with him, every party they spoke at, every time they prayed together in the freezing chapel at Znamenka, all she could think of was the long, lapping length of his tongue, the rough thickness of his powerful fingers, and the pleasurable enormity of his shaft. She could not bear it. The slightest giggle from a general's wife, the warm smiles of a compliant debutante, the high-pitched squeal from a countess sent her heart pounding with jealousy and her blood coursing with rage. And the worst was Anna Alexandrovna Taneyeva.

That plump little nobody, whom she'd met the year before sitting on the sofa in the Grand Duchess Vladimir's salon, had managed to ingratiate herself with the tsarina to such an extent that Alix herself had asked Militza to introduce Anna to Rasputin.

It was not the easiest of carriage rides. The fallout from
that afternoon in the Maple Drawing Room had carried on for
months. Despite the intervention of Rasputin and the agreement
of the tsar, the atmosphere hanging between Militza and Alix
was as cold and dank as a crypt. As the horses took their well-
worn route around the park at the Alexander Palace, Alix defiantly did not bring up the subject of Stana's wedding plans. She'd
never been the sort of woman to back down in an argument or
to knowingly change her mind, so she preferred to remain silent
on such unpleasantries. And Militza studiously followed suit.
Children and the weather were topics that filled the afternoon
affably enough, so when Alix did eventually ask Militza to make
the introductions between Anna and Rasputin, she agreed with
alacrity. Apparently, it had been Anna's abilities as a nurse that
had impressed Alix. One of her older ladies-in-waiting had been
taken ill, and Anna had made herself absolutely indispensable
at the bedside. And there was no quicker way to Alix's heart,
according to Alix, than devout and devoted selflessness. Plus, the
little woman was all atwitter about her impending marriage to
Alexander Vasilievich Vyrubova, and it was all she could talk
about. Should she marry the naval officer, decorated in the
Russo-Japanese War? Or should she not? Militza would watch
her plain moon face looking for answers around the Mauve
Boudoir. She and Stana found her a dreary irritation and were
more than a little annoyed that Alix had taken her so easily into
her confidence.

However, with Stana's marriage just over two weeks away,
any straw was to be grabbed with both hands.

Militza, therefore, reluctantly shared "Our Friend" with the
foolish little woman, inviting her to tea at her mansion on the English Embankment. Rasputin was late. It was an hour before he
arrived. An hour during which time Militza had discussed God
and Anna's unswerving faith since she'd escaped the jaws of death

and been blessed by John of Kronstadt, no less, who'd cured her from a mortal typhus by sprinkling her with holy water. Apparently, she'd seen him in a dream and begged her father to call for Father John, and he'd come and cured her the very next day with a blessing and a splash of water.

"The Lord is indeed kind," said Militza, nodding her jaded head.

"Very kind," agreed Anna, adding another spoon of jam to her tea.

They sat in silence save for the scraping of Anna's spoon round and round the bottom of her glass cup.

"Her Imperial Majesty says that Rasputin is a man of God," she ventured, eventually.

"He is," sighed Militza, despite herself. "Now," she said, turning towards Anna, "don't be shocked if I kiss him three or more times when he arrives. It is customary for him to greet those he knows well in a familiar fashion. It's his way. He is a man of the people, a true man—a real man whose being is closest to the Russian soul."

"Of course," replied Anna, her small eyes widening. "Are you feeling well?"

"Yes." Militza's tone was irritated.

"Only your cheeks are a little red?"

"It's the fire; I have no idea why the servants insist on a fire in April, when it is perfectly clement outside."

Before she needed to explain any further, the door to the salon burst open and Rasputin strode in wearing a short black caftan, accompanied by a cloud of violet cologne.

"Mamma!" he exclaimed, his three fingers raised in a blessing. "How are you?" He turned briefly to glimpse Anna before planting a kiss very firmly on Militza's mouth. "Bless you," he said, holding her face in his hands before kissing her hard again on the lips.

Anna simply stood and stared. She had never seen anything like it before. Thankfully, Militza had warned her; otherwise she might have run from the room in indignation and shock.

"How are you, my child?" he asked, kissing Militza for a third time.

"Well," Militza replied, before dabbing her lips with a handkerchief. The man was showing off; she knew he was. He had a new audience, and there was nothing he liked more than that. Torn between slapping him and demanding he take her now on her lilac buttoned divan, she inhaled and exhaled rapidly, trying to take control of her emotions. She knew she had to stop feeling like this. She'd been "healed" once, and she was not going to offer herself again, even if she wanted to. Desperately.

"May I introduce you to Anna Alexandrovna Taneyeva?"

"You may." He turned to look at the lady-in-waiting.

"This is Grigory Yefimovich Rasputin."

"Grisha," he replied.

"I have heard a lot about you!"

Anna smiled, and Rasputin did what he always did when he did not know what to say; he stared. His piercing blue gaze had already unnerved so many at court, and Anna was not immune. She simply stood and smiled back at him, saying nothing more.

"Ask him to pray for you," suggested Militza.

"Oh, yes," said Anna.

"Shall I pray for you?"

"Yes," she declared, more than a little flustered.

"What shall I pray for?"

"Pray, pray . . . um . . . that I may spend my whole life in the service of Their Majesties!"

"So it shall be," he declared, before he turned immediately on his heel and left.

"Is that it?" asked Anna, her head twitching from side to side.

"Yes," replied Militza with mild amusement. The poor woman

had only garnered his attention for a few minutes. "Grisha has no need of incantations and incense. If he says it is done, then it is done."

"But I wanted to ask about my marriage! About marrying Alexander Vasilievich."

"Another time," Militza said, smiling, placing her teacup down on the small occasional table in front of her. A signal for the woman to leave. Which she did. Eventually. A full forty-five minutes later.

A LITTLE OVER TWO WEEKS LATER, ON APRIL 29, THE SUN shone and the flowers bloomed for the wedding of Stana and Nikolasha. A small and intimate affair, it was the antithesis of the ruinous day she had walked down the aisle to marry George in a haze of heat and hatred, the cream of St. Petersburg looking on with their tight mouths and heavy jewels. There was no need for drops or little pick-me-ups; in fact, all she and Militza had before the ceremony itself was a glass of chilled champagne.

Stana was light and full of life; her dark eyes shone and a smile played on her lips. "Oh, Militza," she declared, adjusting her Bolin diamond tiara, her hair piled graciously up on her head, "thank you!" She smiled, leaning over to kiss her sister. "Thank you for all you've done. I know it's been difficult and I know you have sacrificed much for me, but I can't tell you how much I am in your debt. When anyone has been as unhappy as I, she is glad to have a home with a kind husband and to be quiet."

"Quiet?" laughed Militza. "I am not sure your life will ever be quiet."

"But that is all I want."

Militza looked at her sister. "But you're only thirty-nine years old—there is much ahead of you."

"Nikolasha is fifty."

"And still playing politics and soldiers," said Militza.

"He wants nothing to do with politics, and he says he wants to retire from the army and hunt wolf with his borzois."

"Of course!" laughed Militza. "So what was last summer about?"

"What do you mean?"

"Me persuading Nicky to replace Prime Minister Goremykin with Stolypin? Who do you think was behind all of that?"

"Peter?"

"Nikolasha! Nikolasha and his friend General Rauch. They begged me to ask Nicky and Alix. They were desperate for Stolypin to be prime minister. So I asked. And it happened. You don't get more political than that."

"Well, he's not interested anymore," she said, taking a small sip of champagne. "Quiet. That's what we want. Nice and quiet."

"This coming from a man who sliced his borzoi in half at the dinner table just to demonstrate how sharp his sword was?"

"That was years ago and no one remembers that," mumbled Stana. "Anyway, he's happy now."

That much was certainly true. Nikolasha was unrecognizable from the fractious giant he once was. Famed for his quick temper and rash actions, he had become a much more jovial, affable fellow since he'd been with Stana. Militza had once joked it was the power of regular intercourse that had changed the man, much to her sister's annoyance. Stana put it down to the far more cerebral meeting of souls. She even credited Philippe, posthumously, with granting her fulfillment at last. Nikolasha himself, when talking of happiness, told Militza, "For a long time I sought it, and when I had lost all hope of finding it, unexpectedly I received it."

THE WEDDING WAS SIMPLE. DESPITE PETER'S OFFERING, STANA chose to walk down the aisle alone because none of her brothers, nor indeed her father, was able to attend. Her brother-in-law had been terribly charming to offer, but she preferred to stand firm. Meanwhile, Nikolasha was flanked by a guard of honor led by Colonel Dundadze, commandant of the Yalta garrison. There were representatives from Montenegro and Italy, as well as various members of the army present, but the most notable absence was the royal family. They all stayed away; their excuses, Militza remembered, were too numerous to recount. An illness. Urgent travel. Business abroad. Nicky and Alix sent the charming Prince Vasily Dolgorukov in their place, but the others were not so diplomatic. Xenia was so horrified she told everyone who'd listen she couldn't believe they'd found a church that would actually marry them! Her husband, Sandro, refused even to send a telegram of congratulations, and the Dowager Empress was said to have been so appalled when she'd heard the news that the wedding had actually taken place she'd had to retire to her chamber and be administered with tranquilizing drops.

Stana and Nikolasha smiled broadly as they left the church, apparently oblivious to the outrage they had unleashed. After the ceremony, the luncheon that followed the service was a subdued, abstemious, but nonetheless joyful affair. Plates of smoked sturgeon were followed by spring lamb, pheasant in aspic, fresh asparagus, forced rhubarb and sweet fruits in wine, and ice cream, plus plenty of toasts. There was a gypsy band playing, but they did not kidnap the bride as usual; instead, Nikolasha insisted on paying them beforehand: the idea that anyone might relive or be reminded of that hideous night—of Grand Duchess Vladimir's bloodied skirts and the scarlet trail she left across the ballroom—was more than anyone could bear. So the guests retired into the balmy southern spring evening with memories of a pleasant afternoon that was neither ostentatious nor inappropriate.

LATER THAT WEEK, STANA AND NIKOLASHA WENT ON A HONEY-
moon tour of his many country estates, where the groom hunted
wolf and fox with his hounds while his new wife read and walked
his expansive grounds, delighting in her own company, her pain,
loneliness, and humiliation a thing of the past.

Meanwhile, Militza returned to St. Petersburg, alone.

Still engulfed in the last gusts of winter, the city felt cold. Perhaps it was simply the inclement weather, after the longer, milder
days spent in the Crimea, or maybe it was her reception that was
enough to chill the blood. Either way, Militza felt a certain froideur
every time she entered a room. Before her sister's wedding, all eyes
had naturally turned towards the two of them, even at a discreet dinner at the Yacht Club. But now, suddenly on her own, with her sister
enjoying the first flush of marriage, Militza found herself isolated.

And Peter was no help. The fact that he had helped persuade her father and thereby Montenegro to back Nicky in the
failed war against Japan was enough for him to want to maintain
a low profile. He'd believed, like the late Minister of the Inte-
rior Vyacheslav von Plehve, that "a short victorious war would
save Russia from all its internal problems." The war had not been
short, or remotely victorious: it was catastrophic, with appalling
loss of life, and it had gone a long way to exacerbate Russia's internal problems, with strikes, insurrections, and insubordination
on the rise all over the country—so much so that no one who
held office was safe; death in the form of ardent revolutionaries
stalked the streets, ready to strike at any moment. Even Plehve,
who'd survived at least two assassination attempts, had finally
succumbed to a bomb back in July 1904.

So Peter had suddenly, rapidly, become very interested in the
running of his estates. His conversion was practically Tolstoyan; he
developed an all-encompassing fascination with land management

and the welfare of his workers. He was happy to spend the occasional evening with the tsar at Tsarskoye Selo, as well as give little dinners for twenty or thirty or so at Znamenka in the countryside. But that's where he wanted to stay, at Znamenka; therefore he was much less inclined to come into town to attend the Grand Duchess Vladimir's parties or any of the court balls. He left Militza to go on her own.

Towards the end of May, she accepted an invitation to a *soirée chinoise* at the Vladimirs' on the Palace Embankment. Given the recent defeat at the hands of the Japanese, some would have thought any Oriental theme tasteless, but such nuances had never bothered the grand duchess, and with Alix always detained in the countryside, so prone to ailments and aches and so terribly, terribly frail, there was a vacuum at the heart of St. Petersburg society that Maria Pavlovna thought it her duty to fill. "One ought to know one's job," she would say. And her job was to make up for the darkened windows of the Winter Palace, where not one glass of fizz was served, nor a note played.

As Militza entered the Raspberry Parlor in the second floor of the palace, Maria greeted her with unusual enthusiasm. A symphony of golden thread and diamonds, the Grand Duchess Vladimir shimmered with delight.

"How are you?" she inquired, thrice kissing the air on either side of Militza's white cheeks. "And how was the little wedding? Do tell all!"

"Intimate wedding," corrected Militza.

"Very intimate. I hear poor Alix's sciatica prevented her from attending?" Maria's face was positively contorted with delight. "Anyone else make it?"

"Is she unwell again tonight?" asked Militza, pretending to look around the room in search of the empress.

"Poor Alix." Maria nodded, looking over Militza's shoulder. "To be so afflicted."

"Poor Alix." They paused to agree. "What a stunning dress," added Militza. "Gold."

"Isn't it charming? I was inspired by my recent trip to Vienna. We took our little train, and I met this very interesting artist, Gustav Klimt. I'm thinking of ordering a few works. He's not terribly expensive."

"Is the tsar coming?"

"Why wouldn't he?" She looked around the room. "*Ma chère!*" she called to a friend, waved, and walked off. "Have I told you about my trip to Vienna?"

Militza smiled stiffly and took a sip of her champagne. It had been a long time since she'd felt this out of sorts. Surely her sister's marriage could not have such dramatic repercussions? Was she imagining this feeling? They were four of the most powerful, connected people in the whole of Russia; everyone knew they had the ear of the tsar and the tsarina and control over Rasputin. There was no one more powerful than they were. Nikolasha was president of the Council of State Defense, in charge of rearming the troops and the navy; he was popular with his soldiers, well loved. They were all well loved, she concluded, walking towards the ballroom and the sound of the orchestra. Then why didn't she feel it?

She paused by the impressive dining table that ran the length of the banqueting hall. It was groaning with curls of smoked salmon, silver bowls brimming with caviar, and a mountain of exotic-looking fruits—pineapples, cherries, oranges, apricots, and grapes—that, on closer inspection, turned out to be made entirely of marzipan.

"Well, if it isn't one of the Black Crows," came the familiar voice of Count Yusupov.

Militza turned around. How dare he call her that! She'd heard that some referred to her and her sister as Crows, or Spiders, or

Black Crows or Black Spiders, but never to her face. He was deliberately riling her, and she needed to calm down. Why on earth was she feeling so vulnerable?

"Good evening." She smiled briefly. "I was on my way to the ballroom. I've heard there's a performance."

"Anna Pavlova and the rest of the corps did a little Chinese thing organized by Diaghilev," he replied, popping a small marzipan apricot into his mouth. "You missed it." He chewed. "How were the heinous nuptials? Did the Lord strike with a thunderbolt? Did the heavens weep at such a union?" He chuckled to himself, wiping the length of his thick mustache with the back of his hand. In fact, such was his mirth that his small eyes watered.

"The wedding passed without incident," replied Militza. "How very kind of you to ask."

"And without witnesses?"

"There were plenty who came."

"No one of significance. Poor Nikolasha, a man of his standing and not a royal cousin to be seen; he has indeed fallen under some spell."

"I can assure you, the man is of sound mind," replied Militza.

"Not that your little tricks are much good," he declared. "'Look after your son!' you said to me once in that silly salon of yours. 'Look after him.' Pah! As if you knew what you were talking about. What rubbish! Both my sons are alive and well. Felix is here tonight."

"Not singing in the Aquarium Café?" The count stared at her, his florid cheeks pulsating with anger. He slowly opened his mouth as if to speak, but words failed him. "This is a small city," continued Militza. "And stories travel like head lice in a workhouse. Particularly the ones about naughty boys who like to dress up as pretty girls and sing cabaret songs for a living, despite being from the richest family in all of Russia." She smiled. "It's going to take more than those daily icy showers to cure such flamboyance, I'm afraid. Now, if you will excuse me . . . ?"

MILITZA WALKED THROUGH THE LARGE, OAK-PANELED BANQUET-ing hall with its polished red copper chandeliers and walls decorated with traditional Russian fairy tales, painted to look like tapestries. It was an odd room that felt dark and solid and was in great contrast to the large, open, gilt and pale gray ballroom, with its elaborate ceiling of pert-breasted caryatids and well-nourished cherubs.

Inside the ballroom, the music was loud and the air was heady with the smell of cigarettes and champagne. Many of the guests had arrived in splendid Oriental outfits, many borrowed from the Mariinsky Theatre but others speedily made in the ateliers around Nevsky Prospekt. Some—the Grand Duchess Vladimir's, most certainly—had surely come from Madame Auguste Brissac's studio on Moika. The overall effect was of effortless decadence as the shimmer of silk and the rustle of taffeta accompanied the glorious music. A green-liveried footman arrived with a silver tray heavy with champagne coupes. He bowed his head while Militza helped herself. As she sipped from the chilled glass, she watched the tsar drift around the room. He looked well, nodding his head, smiling at the guests; it even looked for a moment that he might be about to dance. Alexei must be doing better, thought Militza. The tsar's health and happiness were now so inextricably linked to the welfare of his son and Alix that his humors were like some sort of medical weather vane.

She smiled as he approached. She could feel the eyes of the room looking sidelong at her. Would the tsar still be irritated by the wedding? Would he hold a grudge? Would he punish her for her sister's happiness?

"So, it is done!" he said as he came over to embrace her. "Stana and Nikolasha are at last united!"

"They are." Militza smiled, trying not to appear too relieved.

"My mother is furious," he whispered in her ear, "and my sisters are horrified. But they're only upset because I refused Michael and Baby Bee."

"They were first cousins."

"Yes, and Nikolasha and Stana are brother and sister."

"Not really."

"I know." He paused. "You must come and tell us all about it. We miss you. It has been two months at least. And you missed Anna's wedding."

"Anna?"

"Taneyeva, now Vyrubova. Our Friend warned her a few days before that it would be an unhappy liaison, but she went ahead regardless." He shrugged his large golden epaulets. Militza stared at him. How on earth could the tsar be talking about the marriage of the plump, dull Anna? As if it would be of any interest to anyone! "She has a little cottage now, just by Tsarskoye Selo."

"Who has? Anna?"

"Alix much prefers to meet people there these days," he declared. "Far fewer guards." Nicky patted her upper arm and turned to move on. "Oh, by the way, your father isn't worried about being left out of the peace treaty with Japan, is he? It's not like the Montenegrins did that much fighting or committed many troops. You lot don't really have that much of an army or navy to speak of!" He laughed a little. "Your father's support was more symbolic, I feel."

"Of course," replied Militza.

"Jolly good," said Nicky.

THREE DAYS LATER, MILITZA'S CAR PULLED UP OUTSIDE A SMALL yellow-and-white villa just two hundred feet from the gates of the Alexander Palace. It was a low two-story building, more of a summerhouse, really—absolutely not the sort of house Militza would have ever noticed before. There was no garden to speak of, but the surrounding trees were in bud and blossom, making the approach to the house a little more charming. As Militza walked up the short path, she stopped. She could hear the sound of piano music drifting out of the open window, and there were two people singing. One was a high soprano voice; the other was low and unmistakable—the tsarina. Militza had heard Alix sing before, a few times, but never outside her Mauve Boudoir.

A footman showed her into the small, cluttered drawing room. The flock-paper walls were full of paintings, and nearly every table, sideboard, or dresser was covered in little knick-knacks, bits of china or porcelain—cups, jugs, dogs, cats, and little cherubs. There were newspapers and magazines piled high on various tables, and plates of nuts and sweetmeats at every turn. Alix and Anna had their backs to the door as they sat at the piano, squeezed onto one chair, only one buttock each firmly on the seat. They were laughing and bickering slightly over what piece of music to duet next. Militza cleared her throat. They both turned.

"Your Imperial Highness!" said Anna, immediately leaping out of the seat. "I am afraid I did not hear you enter!"

"Militza," Alix said, smiling. "I am afraid you have discovered our terrible secret!" She laughed a little.

"Secret?"

"Our awful piano and our even more terrible singing!"

"On the contrary, I thought it very jovial," said Militza.

"As did I."

Militza turned around. There he was, sitting in the shadows, watching them.

"Grisha!" Her voice was unexpectedly high with surprise.

He nodded. "How was the wedding?"

"Well—" began Militza.

"Don't let's speak of it," interrupted Alix, her thin white hand in the air. "I never want it spoken of again."

Militza was about to say that Rasputin had himself blessed the union and that she herself had persuaded the tsar to give his permission, but there was something about the adamant little hand in the air that made her realize some things were best left unsaid.

There was a pause. Militza remained standing, while Rasputin looked from one to the other. This was the sort of uneasy situation that amused him.

"I met a very pretty young lady yesterday." He watched as all three women turned to look at him. He had their attention. "Very pretty," he added. "And so very young," he embellished, his pale eyes darting around the room, reading all their facial expressions. "Munia Golovina."

"Princess Paley's niece?" asked Alix.

"Perhaps." Rasputin was not entirely sure.

"She is a close friend of the Yusupov family," added Anna, nodding knowledgeably. "Some say she might marry Nikolai Felixovich one day. They are practically betrothed." Rasputin looked at her, his eyebrows raised with interest. "Although he perhaps has his eyes on another, someone who is already taken?"

"Married?" Militza asked.

"I couldn't possibly say," replied Anna, her round face shining with innocence. "I am not a woman who likes to gossip."

"Quite right," said Alix brusquely. "I can't abide idle chatter. It's the devil's work."

"She was most ardent in her questions," continued Rasputin.

"Not as ardent as I, surely?" asked Anna.

"No one is more ardent than you," replied Rasputin. "No one believes quite like you, my child."

"Mama! Mama!" The two eldest grand duchesses, with long blond hair around their shoulders and large picture hats, came dashing into the room. "Please say yes," they began, their young hands clasped together in prayer. "Oh, please do, please say yes."

"What are you two up to now?" asked Rasputin.

"Oh, Grisha!" they exclaimed, not at all surprised to see him sitting there. "Do help us with Mama."

"Tatiana, Olga! Calm down!" said Alix. "What on earth is going on?"

"Just say yes!" began Olga. "I am nearly twelve."

"And I'm nearly ten," added Tatiana.

"What are you asking?"

"Mr. Epps has to go into town and he was wondering if we would like to go with him?" asked Olga, extremely tentatively.

"Whatever for?" asked Alix, visibly thrown.

"To buy buttons and ribbons?" suggested Tatiana.

"No." Alix shook her head. "Town? Don't be so ridiculous!"

"But we've been before," said Olga.

"When?"

"Yalta."

"That was different," said Alix.

Militza remembered that day so very well. They'd all, on a whim, decided to walk the few miles from Livadia to go shopping. The girls had been terribly excited; they'd skipped all the way, accompanying Alix in her large wheelchair. It was one of those very brief moments of freedom when no one knew who they were. The empress had been told off for resting her wet umbrella against some display in one of the shops, and the girls had been shocked to pay for their buttons and ribbons with rubles, only to receive change! They had no idea what money really meant. Unfortunately, their anonymity did not last long, and as soon as they had left the shop, they were surrounded by well-wishers, keen to gawp at the tsarina and the grand duchesses. They had to call for a motorcar to come and collect them.

"Please?" they now begged together.

"No." Alix shook her head. "And if you carry on asking, you will make my heart painful, and you don't want me to have to lie down with a pain of two?"

"No, Mama," replied Olga.

"I hate pain of two," said Tatiana.

"It means we can't see you," added Olga.

"Exactly," said Alix. "Now leave us."

"They should go," said Rasputin.

"Yes," agreed Alix. "Leave us."

"Into town," he continued. Alix looked at him in astonishment. But she said nothing. "What harm could it do? A little trip to buy some frivolities? I see no harm in that at all."

"But . . ." began Alix.

"God does not take against the enjoyment of children," he said simply. "In fact, He delights in it. They should go. In the fresh air."

The two grand duchesses looked stunned and stared at their mother, awaiting her response.

"Well . . . Very well then," she said tentatively. "Very well. If *you* think so, Grisha."

"I do." He nodded slowly.

"Thank you! Thank you!" The girls could not believe their luck. "Thank you, Brother Grigory!"

"Only for a short time," instructed Alix.

"Of course, Mama!" they promised.

"Back by five."

"Five!"

They rushed out of the villa as quickly as they'd arrived.

"How lovely! A trip," mused Alix, with a little laugh to herself.

"Tea?" offered Anna, picking up a large silver pot that had been brought into the drawing room.

"Shall I be Mother?" offered Rasputin, getting out of his chair.

THAT EVENING, AS THE MAID KATYA ATTENDED TO MILITZA'S toilette, brushing and piling up her long black hair with diamond pins, Militza stared at her reflection, running over and over again in her mind the scene she'd witnessed at the little yellow villa. Alix had let Rasputin overrule her. And there was something about Grigory's manner as he sat in the chair, something about the way he'd looked at Militza, the way he challenged Alix, that she found disconcerting. He appeared powerful—worse, comfortable with those in power. Her mind wandered to the icon he'd taken from her. Was that the difference? Now that he had Philippe's St. John the Baptist, the angel of the desert, was he truly as untouchable as Philippe had foretold? But what was worrying her most was that he appeared not to need her, Militza, anymore. She knew he visited Tsarskoye Selo without her, despite her protestations. But how often? And Brana had told her that he'd even turned up to the palace once or twice completely uninvited. He passed by whenever he liked. If she really pulled rank, reminded him exactly who he was and where he'd come from, could she grasp back control? He was hers. Entirely hers. She'd made him. Perhaps she needed to remind him of that.

She sighed. While Katya finished heating and placing the last few curls around her face, Militza called Brana to her room. Her little collection from Badmaev was growing on her dressing table, but what she really needed was a little cocaine elixir. A couple of drops should do the trick before she went out. If it had not been a soirée at the Countess Ignatiev's, she would surely have sent her excuses. A few minutes later and there was a knock at the door and the crone arrived with a small red bottle on a tray. She drank the entire contents of the bottle and felt significantly better: her thoughts were clear; her brain was focused. She thanked Brana and then picked up her Marseilles cards from out of the top drawer of her dresser.

Should she? Why not? Just three cards before she went out. She normally didn't turn cards for herself. In her early teens, she'd turn cards every day and live her life exactly according to them. But her mother had warned her against it and she'd broken the habit. But now, having drunk Badmaev's elixir, she felt her self-control weakening.

"Are you sure?" asked Brana, tray in hand, as she watched Militza shuffle the cards.

"It's fine," snapped Militza. Sometimes the woman really was too much. She closed her eyes and held the pack close to her chest. She inhaled deeply before she chose three from the deck. "*Le Diable,*" she said, staring straight at the devil. "Chaos, anarchy . . . *Le Pendu,* the Hanged Man, suspended from one leg, unable to do anything . . . helpless . . ." Her heart was racing; she felt a little sick. The cocaine was surely a bit strong. She paused before she turned the final card. She'd asked about the future. This was not what she had anticipated.

"What's the last one?" asked Brana.

"*Le Judgement,*" said Militza, looking down as the black eyes on the card stared directly back at her. "So the dead shall rise and we shall all be judged, not by our words, but by our actions and our deeds."

"The cards are never wrong," said Brana. "Maybe the question you asked was incorrect?"

It was late by the time she arrived at Countess Ignatiev's apartment on the French Embankment. Even the stairs outside were littered with people: some were talking; others were smoking; all were in quite an intoxicated state. Inside, the air was thick with conversation and the smell of cigarette smoke and hashish; the low light was crepuscular, and it was almost impossible to see the faces of the guests or to distinguish one person from another.

"Goodness," exclaimed Sophia Ignatiev when Militza finally discovered her seated at a small card table in the corner. "There are so many people! I swear half the clergy are here." She puffed her face as she exhaled and waved a pretty peacock-and-ivory fan. "But I am so glad you are here. I have been having these dreams, proclamations really." She inhaled heavily on a small pipe. "Father Seraphim keeps appearing to me, and we discuss the fact that there is a prophet here amongst us whose purpose is to reveal the will of Providence to the tsar and lead him on the path of glory." She exhaled a small curl of blue smoke. "And that person," she whispered, leaning forward. "And that person is . . . Rasputin. Absolutely it's him. I am sure of it."

"Right," said Militza.

"My dreams are actually prophetic. I have told everyone." She waved her hand about her to indicate she had told the whole room. "Everyone." She smiled. "He's here, you know, Rasputin. In the other room. Talking to some journalists."

"Journalists?" Militza looked towards the door.

"Yes," she said, nodding vigorously. "You should see them! Eating out of the palm of his hand."

Sure enough, as she walked into the next-door room, there was Rasputin surrounded by an attentive group of acolytes. There was the actress with the plunging décolletage; there was the weak-willed general and the British journalist with the bad breath who always insisted on pinning you in a corner and asking the most impertinent of questions. Tonight, he was right next to Rasputin, asking him all sorts of things that didn't seem remotely polite, but Grigory was loving the attention and gorging himself on red wine. He glanced over at Militza as she walked into the room, and a smile briefly floated across his lips before the actress thrust herself a little closer to him and took his attention.

How different he is outside of the company of the tsarina, thought Militza, staring at him as he leaned over and kissed the actress's plump bosom. I wonder what Alix would think if she knew exactly how her dear Friend behaved without her? Perhaps someone should tell her?

She turned and walked back into the slightly quieter room, encountering Dr. Badmaev as she did so.

"I was hoping you'd be here!" she exclaimed, moving to kiss him on the cheek.

"Will you sit and have a glass of wine with me?" he asked, indicating two chairs.

"Of course." She smiled. "Do you have any of your elixir with you?"

"The cocaine?" She nodded. "Here," he said, pulling a small red bottle from out of the pocket of his loose trousers. "The tsar goes through about three of those a week," he said, handing over the bottle.

"It's a good way to start the day," said Militza. "Poured into sweet tea to take away the taste. Thank you," she added, immediately pouring some into her wine. "It's so crowded in here these days." She looked around the room before taking a sip.

"I remember when it was simply Stana, you, and me and the countess, plus a few divorcées!" chuckled Badmaev.

"What's happened?"

"It's the boredom, I suppose. In these gilded drawing rooms, life becomes weary much faster. When money can get you whatever life offers, even the most fantastic possibilities fail to satisfy." He paused to take in the crowded room before him. "Everyone is tired, everyone is jaded, and in such times people gravitate to what lies beyond human comprehension. Talking to Spirit. Table tipping. Tarot. Even your Martinism." Militza raised her eyebrows. "People tell me everything." He smiled. "Even Rasputin."

"What of him?"

"The tsarina talks of little else. When I am summoned to prescribe herbs for her heart or her sciatica, she always talks of him. The man of God who is no priest, the miracle worker from Siberia."

"She says that?"

"But both you and I know there are no miracles, only science."

"And faith."

"But where will your faith get you when your son is bleeding to death?" he asked.

"Hush!" She shot him a look. "Maybe that is all she has?"

"And what of all of *my* medicines and *my* expertise and all that I have done?" he replied sharply, placing another bottle of cocaine elixir down on the table. "For you," he said, standing up as if to leave. "Don't take it all at once!"

"Well, well, if it isn't my old friend from Tibet!" Rasputin placed a large hand on Badmaev's shoulder. "Don't trust him!" he said to Militza. "He'd sooner betray you and sell your soul for a kopek!" He roared with laughter, rocking back and forth as he slapped the doctor hard on the back. "What?" he declared. "Have you lost your sense of humor? Come on, friend!"

"Go to hell," hissed Badmaev.

"Me?" said Rasputin, taking a step back and flinging his arms open as he laughed even louder. "I'm already there! Come," he added with a chuckle, putting his arm around Militza. "What on earth is wrong with him?" He yawned. "Must be terribly upsetting, losing one's position at court! Take me home!"

AS THE CHAUFFEUR DROVE THROUGH THE CHILLY STREETS OF St. Petersburg, Militza listened to Rasputin ramble on about his dealings with the tsarina and his afternoons at Anna's little yellow house. He was obviously drunk—and with her he did not feel the need to hold back.

"That fat little Anna," he laughed. "She just repeats everything I say; it's as if she does not have a mind, or will, of her own! She is the emptiest of vessels. Like a great big bell. If she weren't so plain, like a poorly cooked suet pudding, I might bend her over a table and show her the way of the Lord! As for the other one, Little Mama, squeaking through the gardens in that wheelchair of hers, she is so scared and isolated from her own people. I don't think she's left her quarters for months. She claims ill health, but I am not so sure." He snorted. "But she listens to me, and me alone. She'll do anything I say, anything to keep that little boy of hers alive. It would be sweet if it weren't so pathetic." He leaned over towards Militza, his eyes staring into hers, the pupils slowly dilating. "See this," he said, waving his hand in her face. "Between these fingers I hold the Russian Empire! Its future is in my hands." He laughed as he thrust his fingers between her thighs.

CHAPTER 27

NOVEMBER 20, 1907, ST. PETERSBURG

I T TOOK MILITZA THE SUMMER TO BETRAY HIM.

She was not a woman to react rashly, so she went over and over what she had seen and heard during the last few months, and just before the tsar went on maneuvers with the navy, she, together with Peter, invited Rasputin to dinner at Znamenka. It was far enough away from the city, they concluded, that he couldn't arrive and then disappear off on another appointment. They also invited Nicky and Alix—and were somewhat surprised when they both accepted.

What passed was an extraordinary evening, where the true extent of Rasputin's influence became frighteningly apparent. They learned he visited the palace two or three times a week, turning up unannounced, arriving at any time he pleased, and that Alix was calling him frequently on the telephone. It wasn't daily (not yet, anyway), but she spoke to him three or four times a week, about many subjects, but mainly for advice on the Little One.

"He is always so reassuring," she said, playing with her food.

"It makes Alix happy," Nicky added, patting his wife on the back of her hand.

Rasputin simply sat there, smiling, soaking it up, drinking more wine, eating more sweetmeats, appearing more and more benevolent.

"Just so long as I am near, the young boy will be well," he declared, his knife and fork in the air.

"So reassuring." Alix nodded.

"Very reassuring," agreed Nicky.

"I don't know what we'd do without him." Alix smiled.

Fortunately, Alix and Nicky left early because Alix had a slight chill. As soon as the door was closed, Peter and Militza turned on Rasputin. They accused him of betraying them, of ignoring their wishes, their express wishes, for him not to visit Tsarskoye Selo without them. They told him he was disloyal, unfaithful, treacherous, untrue. He was trying to undermine them. He was trying to edge them out, pushing himself forward at their expense. Somewhat embarrassingly, they ended up shouting at him. Both of them raised their voices in fury.

"You are a charlatan! And a traitor!" Militza yelled.

"We trusted you!" added Peter.

"We made you!" Militza continued.

"You couldn't make a simple borscht!" sneered Rasputin before starting to laugh. "You can't make anything! You, Mamma, are nowhere near as powerful as you think. I could destroy you—like this!" He clicked his fingers. "I have Philippe's icon, John the Baptist . . ." He smiled wolfishly and then laughed louder.

"What's he talking about?" asked Peter, looking bemused and certainly the worse for wine.

Her husband could wait. She could explain away the icon and the wolfish stare. It was the laughter that really unsettled Militza.

She hated the sound of laughter. It reminded her of the night when George—Stana's George—had laughed in her face, showering her with spittle and humiliation. How she hated the sound of laughter. And Rasputin would not stop. He laughed as he walked down the steps of Znamenka and laughed as he stepped into the car to take him to the station. Militza imagined he laughed all the way back to St. Petersburg.

If she'd doubted her plan, or hesitated for a moment, then it was Brana who strengthened her resolve. The stories the old crone had discovered after ferreting about in the filth of St. Petersburg beggared belief.

"Sex," she said as she shuffled along the path to the walled herb garden, her stooped shoulders covered in a dark cape despite the sunshine.

"Oh?" Militza feigned surprise.

"In the banya . . ." This was news. The banya? "In the afternoons. Two, three—as many as four at a time. Women. Girls. Sometimes it is hard to see through the steam and the writhing flesh. But he's there, all right, surrounded by a harem. It's like an orgy, sometimes they're whipping each other with birch. You can hear the screams—"

"Of pain?"

"No. Pleasure," replied Brana. "They scream for more, apparently. They drink vodka, loads of it. Beer, sometimes. And not all the girls are young. Some are married. Wives whose husbands are hoping that if they manage to satisfy the beast, he might put a word in, write a letter, get them a job or a promotion."

"So the women are prostitutes?" Her mind was whirring with confusion.

"No, Madame. Aristocrats. He is said to have bedded half the court."

"Not half, surely?" Her hand quivered as she gripped her parasol.

"His member is reported to be the size of a horse," Brana continued, with a wide toothless grin. "It has a wart on the end, which apparently makes it more pleasurable."

"Really?" Militza swallowed.

"A healing—that's what he calls it."

"That'll be all, thank you, Brana," she snapped. How much more detail could she bear?

IN THE END IT WAS EASY TO DENOUNCE RASPUTIN AS A MEMBER of the Khlysty. If he was going to offer himself so freely around town, with his favors and his healings, and not acknowledge her as his mistress, if her charge would not behave, then she would see him hounded out of the city herself.

It was not difficult to convince the police that Rasputin was some sort of permanently priapic holy satyr. His behavior in the city was enough. Plus, there were the rumors beginning to surface out of Siberia, where as many as eight women were cited as living in his house in Pokrovskoye. The house that she, Militza, had paid for! She had also donated five thousand rubles to build a new church in his village. Where had that money gone? Blackmail? Prostitution? Corruption? There was talk of meetings below his floorboards, of secret dancing and whipping. Plenty of whipping. There were also several young girls who came forward and spoke of being stroked and caressed, so the Tobolsk Ecclesiastical Consistory was alerted and an investigation was launched.

All Militza had to do was to put her considerable weight, rank, connections, and credibility behind these allegations, sitting there dressed in black, a heavy veil over her face, as she convinced them the dreadful sectarian should be banished back to Siberia with his substantial tail between his legs.

Did she feel guilty while she was whispering, playing with her handkerchief, sharing her accusations? Not in the slightest. He'd betrayed her confidence and been totally duplicitous. Even Stana was inclined to agree that Rasputin had overstepped the mark. Not that she was prepared to put her name to anything. The man had been so instrumental to her current happiness she could not turn against him. And besides, she was still such a firm follower of Philippe (who'd foretold of Grisha) and a colleague of his, the eminent Papus, who had come to visit over the summer and shared his knowledge and his Martinist beliefs, that she found it hard to speak ill of Rasputin. In fact, truth be told, she was a little scared. She'd seen him read minds, look into souls. What if he could read hers? See into hers? What if he knew she'd betrayed him? What then? She knew how powerful he was. She'd been there, at the beginning, knew how powerful the magic had been to create him. So she was glad when he disappeared, glad he'd been warned about the investigation, glad he'd decided to go back to Siberia, to lie low, hoping the thing would blow over.

Life was a little more relaxing and predictable when he was not around.

However, the void Rasputin left behind at Tsarskoye Selo took both Stana and Militza by surprise. They'd presumed, in his absence, it would be like old times, that they could pick up where they'd left off, spend their afternoons together talking, reading books to one another, playing the piano, bezique, sharing their thoughts. But every time either of them went to take tea with Alix, inevitably with the rotund Anna, and occasionally with the grand duchesses and the little Alexei, it seemed as if the whole palace was in mourning. They were dull, listless, depressed, devoid of conversation; they had no news to tell. But then, none of them ventured beyond the park these days. The tsarina had not been into St. Petersburg itself now for over a year.

"Mama is so quiet these days," Olga confided in Militza one afternoon. "She stays in her room eating biscuits in bed and rarely comes out. She dresses to see Papa in the evening, but hardly sees the rest of us at all. She will sometimes come and take the air with us. She might watch Alexei on his toy horse. But Anna is her only comfort."

WITH RASPUTIN GONE, THE TSAREVICH'S BODYGUARD, ANDREI Derevenko, barely let the heir's feet touch the ground. He was carried everywhere, at the tsarina's insistence, although he was now three years old and perfectly capable of walking without endangering himself. But Alix was terrified should anything happen to him. The result was that the boy was becoming increasingly spoiled. He'd cry if things didn't go his way and refused to do as he was told. His sisters ("OTMA"—as Alix referred to them as a group, using their initials) had been brought up to share bedrooms, sleep on camp beds with no pillows, make their own beds, take cold showers every day, and had received few presents save for a diamond and a pearl for every birthday. However, Alexei's room was infinitely more luxurious, lined with icons and full of toys, including a giant train set that he'd play with for hours, his Cossack guard always at his side.

But Militza persisted in her visits, despite their dullness— she had her father's interests to think of; he had ideas to expand his circle of influence in the Balkans, and Nicky owed him and Montenegro a sense of loyalty. Needless to say, her father also wanted money. He always wanted money. The perper, his new currency, was not doing so well, and he'd had to relinquish some power, like most leaders at the time, to his increasingly demanding populace. But he had his eye on the future and his jubilee celebrations next year, which he'd certainly need some assistance in financing.

Stana also was very much at her side. Returning from her honeymoon, she'd seen enough of the reaction to her wedding to know that good relations with Nicky and Alix would be her lifeline back into society. While Militza's diary was full to capacity for the social season—some twenty-two balls in almost as many days—hers was more sparsely filled, and this worried her. She was married to one of the most powerful men in Russia; she should be right at the top of everyone's list.

"Isn't there something you can do?" asked Stana one cold February afternoon as she and Militza traveled in the carriage together for tea with the tsarina. Though swathed in fur and blankets, both were still shivering.

"I think in time it will be fine," replied Militza. "They don't like change, it's that simple."

"The truth is it was much easier to invite me when I was on my own. They could patronize me, feel sorry for me. I made everyone feel happier about their own lives. 'At least I am not Stana,' they could say. 'At least my husband isn't openly fucking whores in Biarritz.'" She sighed.

"One whore."

"One whore," agreed Stana. "Which is worse."

"That's true," said Militza, staring out of the window at the flat gray light and the thin, cold layer of snow that barely covered the ground. "Mostly I am sure they do it just to keep warm!"

Stana laughed. "Do you know, I barely think about him now? Nearly twenty years of marriage and I can't think of a single thing I miss. I pity that poor whore, actually. He was a terrible lover and, worse, a boring conversationalist. She's welcome to his soft cock and dreary anecdotes! And don't tell anyone I said that!"

"Of course not!" Militza smiled, patting her sister on the knee.

"They can all go to hell. I don't care about the court and their opinion of me!"

"You sound like the tsarina."

"For her it's different. The more she stays away, the more stories they tell to fill the vacuum."

"Rumors are more dangerous than the truth." Militza nodded. "You and I know that."

"I hear terrible things. That the tsarevich suffers convulsions, that he has tuberculosis . . ."

"He was born missing a layer of skin . . . I know," agreed Militza. "But also, the more isolated she is, the more difficult it is for her to talk when she does come to something. She doesn't know half the people's names anymore, she doesn't know any of the stories, she can't ask them about their children as she hasn't ever met them—and those girls," she added, shaking her head. "They know nothing, they have seen nothing. She's isolated them too, and they don't know what to make of the world. At least before, they used to be able to look out of train windows when they traveled to the Crimea—now, since that incident with the madman who tried to blow himself up on the train, they travel in secret and put curtains on the train so they can't even see out anymore. I can't help but think that's bad," she said. "In England they keep their royal family visible, they meet their subjects, but ours? They hide away. No one knows what they look like. I see things. Terrible visions, visions about the future that are so frightening . . ."

"Like what?"

"You don't want to know," whispered Militza; she rested her forehead against the cold windowpane, her breath fogged against the glass. "Not even the devil himself could conceive of such misery." She looked back at her sister. "Even he might have to turn his face away in shame."

As they drove through the frosted park towards the palace, they saw Nicky out walking with his dogs. Eleven long-haired border collies ran in circles around him, wagging their tails and barking. He was shouting at them, white clouds of his breath hanging in the air. His arms gesticulated, telling them to heel or pointing out terrified squirrels for them to chase. He looked around as he heard the car and waved happily as it passed.

"I often think Nicky would have found more joy in his life if he weren't on the throne," mused Militza as she watched him striding through the long grass in the fading afternoon light.

"The mantle of government weighs heavy on those narrow shoulders," agreed Stana, also looking out of the window towards the frozen ornamental lake and the upturned boats on the grass.

ARRIVING AT THE PALACE, THEY WERE ESCORTED TO THE Mauve Boudoir, where they found Jim Hercules standing guard outside the door. Dressed in his scarlet-and-black uniform, with golden tassels and golden epaulets, a red turban on his head, he was the only black American servant to work in the palace. As tall as the Abyssinian doormen, the erstwhile boxer hailed from the South of the United States and famously brought pots of delicious guava jelly back for the children whenever he went home on leave. His job, like his fellows', was simply to open the door, but his appearance in the room would indicate either that the tsar or tsarina or both were about to arrive or, more usefully, given the dreariness of many a garrulous official, that they were about to leave. The children adored him, as did the tsar and indeed anyone else who regularly frequented the palace. Normally, he would stand immobile as a statue, but he was permitted to respond if spoken to.

"Good afternoon, Jim." Militza smiled, speaking in English. "Is Her Imperial Majesty in her boudoir?"

"She is indeed, Your Imperial Highness." He bowed and Militza smiled; she found the way he spoke enchanting.

"Going home soon?" asked Stana.

"Not for a while yet, Your Imperial Highness," he replied, moving to open the door.

"When you do, please bring back some preserves," implored Stana.

"Sure thing, Your Imperial Highness," he said, opening the door.

The sisters entered the boudoir to find Anna sitting in one of the pale purple upright chairs, a cup of tea in one hand, an egg sandwich in the other, while Alix lay prone on a divan, dressed in a pale high-necked day dress, her legs covered in a fine cream-colored blanket, her head propped up with the lace pillows.

"Ah!" She managed a little wave in the direction of an attentive footman. "More tea."

"How are you?" began Militza, bending down to kiss her on the cheek. "Is it your heart? Or your back?"

"Have you heard from him?" asked Alix, grabbing hold of Militza's hands. "Our Friend?" She shifted around in her divan. "When's Our Friend coming back? Anna had a letter last week."

"I did," the lady-in-waiting said, nodding, taking the corner off her sandwich.

"He talks of building his church and of praying with his family," said Alix. "He says he's busy, says he's neglected his duties. But he doesn't say when he is coming back."

"I think it may be better for him to stay away at the moment," suggested Militza.

"Better for whom?" Alix sounded a little agitated.

"Him," added Stana. "He needs to be with his family. He has not seen them in a while. His wife, Praskovya; his three children."

"But we're his family," Alix replied.

"I am sure he feels that," agreed Militza, patting the back of the tsarina's hand, "but I think he's missing them."

"Let's bring them all to St. Petersburg!"

"I'm sure he'd love that," replied Stana, smiling as she glanced out of the window.

Something had caught her eye, and she laughed and gestured for Militza to turn around. Through the large, almost floor-length window, the girls were playing on the terrace, sliding sideways, skidding on the thin ice over the frosted paving stones, their arms extended, pulling faces through the window. First Olga, then Maria, followed by Anastasia and Tatiana—each more ridiculous and hilarious. Maria's was perhaps the most amusing, with her tongue out and her eyes crossed; she was by far the naughtiest of the girls. Their laughter was contagious. By the time they slid past for the second time, their gloved hands in the air, their faces contorted, everyone in the room was giggling. Then suddenly little Alexei joined in. Arms open wide, he slid past the glass pane, grinning like a fool.

"He shouldn't be doing that!" Alix said, yet laughed despite herself. "But look at him. He is so silly!"

"Derevenko is outside," said Anna.

"There he goes again!" Alix smiled, pointing at her son. "So funny!"

"I didn't know he was such a comedian," laughed Stana.

"No," agreed Militza.

Then it was back to Olga, who was perhaps a little too old to be fooling around on the ice. And then suddenly it was Alexei again. He skidded, grinned, threw his arms in the air, and then slipped, crashing down on the terrace, landing on his forehead. Alix screamed and leapt off the divan, running towards the window.

"Alexei!" she yelled, pounding on the glass with her fists. "Alexei! Alexei!"

Militza ran after her, Stana right behind. They stared through the window as Derevenko ran towards the boy and snatched him off the ground. Immediately, blood poured out of the gash on his head.

"Oh, my God! Oh, my God!" Alix was hysterical, banging harder and harder on the window. "Alexei! Alexei!" she shouted. The boy turned to look at his mother, too shocked to cry, too bewildered to do anything as the blood poured down his face.

"Do something!" implored Alix, turning to look at Militza. "Do something! He's going to die!"

For the next ten minutes there was total chaos as servants ran, Alix wailed, and Jim Hercules rushed outside, bringing the girls in. By the time Derevenko carried the boy into the Mauve Boudoir, Alexei's face was so swollen and covered in blood that he was no longer able to open his eyes.

"My darling, my darling," wept Alix, placing her son on her divan. "What have you done to yourself?" Covering him in her blanket, she immediately set about trying to stem the dreadful flow of blood with her handkerchief. "Get me warm water," she shouted. "Towels!"

By now the room was full of people, running to and fro, trying to help.

"The blood!" exclaimed Anna. "I have never seen so much blood!" Her round face blanched as she collapsed into a chair.

Stana glanced over at Militza. The blood would not stop. The boy was now screaming in agony. They had to do something.

"Is he all right, Mama?" asked Olga tentatively, her hands twisted with concern.

"Of course he's not—and I blame you all. You know he is not allowed to play around outside! He is to be carried at all times!"

Olga withdrew, as did the other girls; this was clearly not the first time they'd been blamed.

"Has Botkin been called?" Alix asked, looking around the room with her haunted, pale eyes.

"Yes, Your Imperial Majesty," confirmed a footman.

"Where is Our Friend?" She started to sob. "Where is he!" The tears poured down her cheeks as she started to rock back and forth on the edge of the divan, hugging herself.

"Hush, Mama," Alexei whispered through his dry, swollen, bloodied lips.

"You hush, you hush," she said, sniffing, gently patting his arm. "It'll be all right, you'll be all right." She dabbed tentatively at the blood that continued to seep from the cut on his face. "You're strong and God will look after you."

Militza indicated to Stana that she should follow her out of the room.

"What are we going to do?" Militza hissed as soon as they were out of earshot. "He looks terrible. And the blood is unceasing."

"I know." Stana's eyes were wide. It was the first time either of them had witnessed "an incident" at close quarters.

"It's my fault," whispered Militza, her hand shaking a little.

"No, it's not."

"I sent him away."

"You didn't!" Stana took hold of her sister by the shoulders and stared into her eyes. "You reported your well-founded concerns to the authorities and they are investigating him. You have *not* sent him away. He has chosen to leave town while the authorities look into his actions. That is all. You did not do anything or say anything. You have not sent anyone anywhere, he went of his own accord."

"As I knew he would!"

"No one knows it was you who reported him, and no one ever will."

"But what if they look at the records?"

"There will be no records, Nikolasha will see to that." She nodded firmly at her sister. "Do you understand? There will be no record that you were involved at all. And the tsarina knows nothing. She doesn't know why he left. She doesn't suspect a thing."

Dr. Eugene Botkin rushed past the sisters, clutching his leather bag. "Is it bad?" he asked, a look of deep concern on his kind face.

"Not good," replied Stana.

"Poor soul," said the doctor, pausing to gather himself a little before the footman opened the door. He smoothed down his thinning hair and took a breath, crossed himself, and placed a smile on his face. "Hello," he said, taking a step forward. "Now what have we here . . . ?"

"A spell?" suggested Stana. "We could call on the Virgin to sew up the wound?"

"I haven't used that spell in a long while," replied Militza, shaking her head, her shoulders slumping.

"What's wrong with you?"

"I feel responsible." The color drained from Militza's already pale cheeks.

"But you are not. You're not responsible for him falling. You're not responsible for him having the Hesse disease. You are—"

"But I am the reason Rasputin is not here!"

"To hell with him!"

"He's the only one who can help."

"You don't really believe that! You're much more powerful than him. You made him!"

"I am not more powerful now that he has Philippe's icon."

"Just do the spell! Go to the garden, the park, find somewhere and call up your guide." Militza looked at her sister. "Now! Go!"

MILITZA FOUND HERSELF IN THE PARK IN HER SILK SHOES, shivering in her satin dress; she'd had no time to find her felt boots or put on her furs, for Stana had pushed her through the French doors with some force. In the crisp, cold dark, she looked around for a rowan tree that might help her spell, but the sky was black and there were no leaves on the trees, let alone any red berries to help guide her.

"Come on," she said to herself, rubbing her hands together in the freezing damp air. Her whole body was beginning to shake, and her nose was dripping with the cold. "Come on." She scoured the silhouettes in the darkness, stumbling and tripping in her thin, soft-soled shoes. "Concentrate. You can find it, use your second sight." The wind blew through the trees; the loose thin powdering of snow swirled and whirled, as the branches began to talk.

"Militza!"

"Militza!"

"Look out!"

"Take care!"

She looked left, right, her breath catching in her throat, fear mounting. It was as if *he* were there. Rasputin. Stalking her. Tracking her through the trees, like a wolf playing with a deer. She could hear him breathing, panting down her neck. She could hear him pawing the ground. She ran faster, deeper, deeper into the woods.

"Militza!" cried the trees.

"Liar," rustled the leaves.

"Turncoat!" mumbled the frost as she crunched it underfoot.

"Bitch!" cried the moon.

"Whore!" cried the wind.

She could see his eyes. Those haunting, horrible eyes, pale as glass. Behind her. In front. Her heart was pounding, her hands were shaking, her body was shivering. Still she ran. She ran from what? From whom? From herself? She no longer knew. Branches tore at her clothes; brambles scratched at her ankles. BANG! God help her! She screamed. There *he* was! She felt his arms, his rough hands, his tight, tight grip. She shut her eyes.

"Militza?" said Nicky, slapping her gently around the face. "What are you doing out here?"

THAT NIGHT, WHILE ALIX SLEPT, THANKS TO A LARGE DOSE OF laudanum administered by the traumatized Dr. Botkin, Militza and Stana prayed.

On discovering her running through the woods, Nicky had immediately removed his thick fur-lined coat, wrapped it over her shoulders, and escorted the disorientated Militza back to the palace, where he'd immediately placed her in the capable hands of his valet, instructing him to draw her a hot bath, feed her warm brandied milk, and give her a change of clothes. Meanwhile he hurried, his face blanched white with worry, to his son's bedside. There, the vision of a bleeding Alexei, blinded by bruising, attended to by his hysterical, wailing wife, was enough to chill his soul.

"Nicky!" she screeched, throwing herself towards her husband as soon as he walked through the door of the boudoir. "Help him! Get Rasputin!" At which point Alix promptly fainted.

After that, although she was determined to tend to her critically ill son, Dr. Botkin forbade Alix to leave her own chamber.

"You need your strength," he told her firmly as he placed the drops on her tongue. "Alexei needs you, and you are no use to him if you don't rest."

So, fortified by her bath and brandy-soaked milk, Militza joined Stana and sat up with Alexei, tending to him along with the old nurse Gunst, who had been at the boy's side ever since he was born. The amount of blood pouring from the wound was slowly easing; Botkin had cauterized the edges in an attempt to stem the flow, but the boy's face was so swollen, his eyelids so red and inflamed, that he was still unable to open his eyes. He barely spoke as he lay there, only emitting the occasional agonized moan. Gunst went back and forth during the night, bringing fresh bandages, water, compresses—anything that the sisters asked for. And all the while Militza and Stana chanted, prayed, whispered, and lit heavily scented herbs—sage to clear the air of bad spirits, rosemary to sterilize—and rubbed henbane on his feet to induce sleep. And as he slept, they called on the Virgin to heal him.

"In the sea, in the ocean, sits the most holy Virgin," mumbled Militza, her eyes closed as she fingered Alix's jet rosary.

"We call on her," whispered Stana. "We call on her now."

"She holds a golden needle in her hand, she threads a silk thread, she sews up the bloody wound. You wound, do not hurt, you blood, do not flow . . ."

"You wound, do not hurt, you blood, do not flow . . ."

"You wound, do not hurt, you blood, do not flow . . ."

"You wound, do not hurt, you blood, do not flow . . ."

Again and again they repeated it, over and over they chanted, the words slowly slipping and merging together, the room beginning to hum as the meditation reverberated. It was hypnotic and strangely relaxing. Soon the tsarevich began to snore.

COME THE FIRST RAYS OF DAWN, THE WOUND WAS NO LONGER bleeding, but the child was shivering and shaking with a fever.

"This is how it happens every time," said Dr. Botkin as he stood, slowly shaking his head, in the doorway to Alexei's room.

"Every time?" asked Stana, rubbing her tired eyes. Both she and Militza had been at the boy's bedside the entire night. The doctor nodded. "But he will live?" she whispered.

"The worst is over, I think," he replied. "But the illness can carry on for weeks. No wonder the mother is so exhausted." He glanced up the corridor towards Alix's room. "She spends her whole life fearing the worst—and when the worst does happen, it's agony. And the agony lasts for weeks. It never stops and it will never stop . . ." He sighed. "And the only person she seems to listen to, or who can do anything to help her, is that filthy Siberian peasant."

Militza walked out of the room, closing the door quietly behind her. "Brother Grigory?"

"He's no man of God," the doctor snorted. "But she's sent

word to him already, in whatever dark corner he resides. Some-one is standing by for a telegram lest he bother to reply! As if that appalling man is going to make any difference!"

"How is he?" came a voice from behind them.

"Your Imperial Majesty!" said Dr. Botkin, with a deep bow. His cheeks flushed a little and his mustache moved nervously. How much had she heard?

"Any better?" she asked, reaching for the door handle. "Nicky keeps telling me he's fine. But then, Nicky always tells me he's fine."

"He's well, though feverish." Botkin smoothed his hair.

"Feverish? How we hate fever." Her voice was weak. She appeared drained of all emotion. She slowly lifted her eyes to look at Militza. They were flat and dull, all joy and life long since extinguished. "Has any news come from Our Friend?"

CHAPTER 28

MAY 1908,
POKROVSKOYE, TYUMEN, SIBERIA

IT WAS EARLY MAY BY THE TIME MILITZA DEPARTED FOR Siberia. Rasputin had sent a telegram that stated that the bleeding would stop at eight in the evening, which it had, and that the fever would go after three days, which it did. The boy was better now, but for how long?

Stana had begged her sister not to go. She repeated over and over that it was an admission of guilt if she stepped on the train. Quite apart from how dangerous such a journey might be for a woman in her position, there were spies and revolutionaries everywhere; even the tsar, she reminded her, with all his soldiers and guards, now traveled in a blacked-out train. And besides, as soon as Rasputin saw her, he'd realize she'd been the one to denounce him as a member of the Khlysty. Peter was equally anxious. There was something about the way Rasputin had looked at his wife on the night they'd confronted him that made his blood run cold. The man should be left to rot in the Siberian permafrost.

"Darling, don't go," he urged over breakfast. Dressed in breeches, a loose-fitting white shirt, and highly polished riding boots, he stood up from the table.

"Where?" asked Marina, looking across the table with her large dark eyes, stirring cherry jam into her hot black tea. "Where's Mama going?"

"I am going on a trip." Militza smiled, giving her husband a brittle look.

"A trip?" Roman was straight-backed at the table, his dark hair parted and smoothed flat on his head; his large square chin displayed the odd whisker.

"Where to?" queried little Nadezhda, who at the age of ten always preferred everyone to stay just where they were.

"The east." Militza smiled.

"To see Rasputin," added Peter, pacing up and down. "Is that really wise?"

"Are you going to forbid me?" Militza put down her teacup, her eyes narrowed.

"After nearly twenty years of marriage I know that would only encourage you," replied Peter, leaning on the table. "I know you will do as you wish. But the man is deceitful and disloyal, and you do not have my blessing."

Militza went anyway. Somehow, she concluded, if she managed to persuade him to return, she would feel less guilty about denouncing him—and just think how terribly grateful the tsarina would be.

So she pulled her fur-lined cape up tightly around her face and spoke to no one. For four days she watched the vast Russia steppes roll out before her, gray and flat, just shedding the cold coat of winter but yet to burst into spring. She spent her time dozing, reading, and dining alone in the restaurant car. She needed to travel as incognito as possible. It was imperative that no one notice her.

After four days, she arrived in the bustling market town Tyumen, whose businesses and commerce were booming due to the Trans-Siberian Railway. She booked herself in the unremarkable Sofia Hotel, where her presence raised an eyebrow. What was a woman doing here on her own, without even a lady's maid for company? She ordered hot soup in her cold room and remained there until early the following morning.

She'd often thought about where Rasputin might have come from. Where the Four Winds traveled, where Spirit searched, where the unshriven soul had alighted: where they might all have found him. He was always talking of Pokrovskoye, particularly after a few glasses of Madeira, when he'd get poetic and sentimental. He'd describe the beauty of the steppes, the enormity of the endless sky, the freedom of the wide seas of swaying grass; it was where man and God met, melded and lived in perfect harmony, or so he said.

However, descending slowly out of her carriage after nearly two hours of being shaken and bumped on the rough post road from Tyumen, Militza could not believe how desolate the village felt. How could anyone live here? It wasn't the poverty of the place. She'd seen that before, back home in Montenegro and in Russia. She'd picked her way through the slums in St. Petersburg a few times, a handkerchief clutched to her nose and mouth, when she and Brana had been searching for miracles for the tsarina, and she was not silly enough to think all the world lived in fine houses with gilt ceilings. Even so, she had not been prepared for the endless mud, the squawking, scratching chickens, the grunting filthy little pigs, and the lack of people. It was silent, save for the sound of the livestock, and deserted—a one-road town where the road led precisely nowhere. Unless you were a convict, of course. For Pokrovskoye was on the convict trail, where unfortunate souls would be dragged along, their irons clinking, farther and deeper east to their fate. On either side of the narrow road was a collection of wooden houses. They were mostly the same size, single-storied shacks, with wooden roofs and wooden shutters, but at the far end of the village there was one substantially larger house of two stories, with a balcony, empty flower boxes, large wooden gates, and a tin roof. Militza smiled to herself. She knew immediately where all her money had gone.

Pulling at the hood of her cape, she sidestepped a large puddle and walked on towards this house. She had no need to ask where Rasputin lived, which was fortunate as there was no one to ask. And yet she sensed eyes, many eyes, boring into her back.

She paused at the wooden gates to gather herself, calling to her guide to help her, muttering under her breath, asking for assistance and protection. Standing there, she could hear music, clapping, and the sound of shrill laughing voices. There was clearly some sort of party going on. When she'd planned this, she had imagined him at prayer when she knocked; it would certainly be quiet, nobody else around. Should she leave? She turned to look back at the carriage waiting for her. She could just get back in it and return to Tyumen . . . No, that would be ridiculous, she told herself. She pushed on the gate, which swung open easily. The courtyard was thick with mud, cluttered and unkempt. There were piles of wood, broken cart wheels, and empty sacks strewn all over the place; a plow and a yoke were propped up against each other in the corner of the yard, and next to them was a small blue cart pitched at an angle, half full of fetid rainwater and rotten leaves. As she walked towards the wooden door, long-legged chickens squawked and scattered in her wake. She had one foot on the porch step when the front door burst open and out came a screaming woman dressed in a long white nightdress; her dark hair hung loose around her shoulders, and her eyes were shining ecstatically as she tugged at something with her hands.

"You're a god!" she yelled as she spun around, her hair flying and flicking everywhere. "A god!"

In the doorway, standing directly behind her, was Rasputin, his red baggy trousers around his knees; in his hand he held a whip, which he cracked sharply across the woman's backside. She called out.

"More!" she yelled, her back arching in pleasure as she fell to her knees. "More! You *god!*"

Rasputin cracked the whip one more time across the woman's back as she shuffled on her knees towards his groin. Militza could not believe what she was witnessing. The woman, who had been tugging at Rasputin's member while he whipped her, now placed his shaft in her mouth. And while Rasputin stood in the doorway, his eyes half closed, she gorged on his cock like a half-starved peasant who had not seen flesh for months.

"Olga?" said Militza, shocked to realize that she recognized the middle-aged woman. "Wife of Vladimir Lokhtin! What are you doing here?"

Rasputin opened his eyes suddenly at the sound of her voice.

"Mamma!" he said, pushing Olga's head out of the way as he pulled up his trousers. "You catch me a little busy."

"You are my GOD and I am your LAMB!" yelled Olga, clinging to his leg as he buckled up his trousers and tried to walk away.

"Olga! My child," he said, looking down at Olga still crouched on the floor. "You are saved!" He placed his hand on the top of her head in a form of a blessing. "Now go inside with the others and get back into the bath."

"Bath?" Militza questioned.

"Akilina, Khionia, and Olga were bathing," he declared. "I have been helping, Mamma." He smiled.

As he talked, Olga gathered up her nightgown and crawled away from him. Militza slowly shook her head as she remembered first meeting Olga, the beautiful, if dull, wife of an engineer named Vladimir Lokhtin, a few years before. Rasputin followed Militza's gaze.

"I have been curing her of hysteria," he said.

"It seems you have been very successful," replied Militza.

"Would you care for some tea?" he asked, opening the door.

How Militza maintained her composure that morning, she couldn't quite recall. But the memory of the lunatic woman hanging on to his member and the leery pleasure etched on his face as he thrust himself into her open mouth was something that would haunt her dreams. Why she didn't turn and leave immediately, she didn't know. Why she wasn't horrified or totally revolted, she could not explain. Or more importantly, why she didn't put a stop to him and his behavior by screaming loudly and calling for witnesses, denouncing him as a member of the Khlysty, again, was something she would ask herself over and over again. But perhaps she was intrigued? Fascinated? What on earth could induce a woman of that class to let herself go like that?

Militza spent the rest of the morning sitting next to a steaming-hot samovar drinking strong, jam-sweetened tea.

Inside, his house was considerably grander than the outside suggested. She looked around, taking in all the luxuries that she had paid for. There were comfortable chairs, a thick carpet on the floor, icons on the walls, as well as mirrors, a chandelier, and other finery. There was a large floor-standing clock and, of course, the Offenbach piano. It was absolutely not the usual home of a man of God.

The three bathers dressed and took their seats by the fire, where they proceeded to conduct themselves as veritable visions of piety and decorum. They inquired after Militza's journey, asked how inclement the weather was, how things were in St. Petersburg, and all the while, the party was waited on by Rasputin's wife, the diminutive and sturdy Praskovya, who scurried back and forth with small bowls of conserved fruits, or pickled cucumbers and tomatoes.

Rasputin barely acknowledged her presence, let alone thanked her, while he dug into the bowls with his large hands, helping himself to everything, eating ravenously, pausing only to turn for a moment towards Olga.

"Humble yourself," he said, offering up his filthy fingers, which she proceeded to slowly and sensuously suck clean.

Militza was transfixed. Revolted. Repulsed. Horrified. And yet she was suddenly engulfed by a terrible wave of jealousy. How much would she too like to lick his fingers? Or feel the strength of his shaft? Hear his bellowing orgasm in her ear? How much did she want to straddle that filthy chair once more?

"So, Brother Grisha," she asked, banishing such thoughts from her head, "when will you be returning to St. Petersburg?"

"When Mamma apologizes," he replied.

"Me?"

"Last time we spoke, you were not very kind," he said. "You raised your voice."

"For which I apologize," said Militza, watching Olga slide her tongue up and down the side of his index finger.

"Also when the charges have been dropped," he said and shrugged.

"I would not worry about those." She smiled briefly. "And anyway, it is only an investigation; no charges have been brought, and the ecclesiastical court in Tobolsk has not accused you of anything."

"They could just as easily denounce me as a Skopets!" he laughed. "It would have as little meaning! But I am fortunate enough to have too much use for my cock to want to cut it off in the name of the Lord!" He laughed with such gusto that his chair shook. "Don't you think?" He stared at her. "Who would want to castrate themselves for God?"

"Ridiculous accusations," she agreed enthusiastically. "I think you should show how unafraid you are of them, how foolish they actually are, and come back to the city."

"What use have I of the city when I have all I need around me here?" He removed his hand from Olga's lips. "God has seen fit to reward me well."

"You are his humble servant," said Militza. "But I wonder if the rewards aren't greater in St. Petersburg."

"Why do I have need of more rewards?" He appeared a little entertained at such a suggestion.

"No one *needs* rewards," replied Militza. "But they can make life a little more pleasurable, can't they? Fine wine? Madeira? The beauty of the ballet and gypsy song?"

"You reap what you sow."

"And you have sown, Brother Grigory," she said sweetly and smiled.

OVER THE COURSE OF THE DAY GRISHA'S HOUSE BEGAN TO FILL with people. A long line of acolytes gathered, forming an orderly queue in the courtyard outside. Some were mad, some were ill, some just wanted reassurance that something they feared would never happen—the death of a cow, the failure of a crop, a well turning sour. There were mewling children and sniffing adults and a laborer whose arm had been scythed off at the last harvest. Where they'd come from, how they knew he was there or what time they should arrive, Militza was never told. But they queued up, shuffling in, dressed in their peasant garb. The combination of the heat of the room, the boiling-hot samovar, the fire, and their unwashed clothes made for an intense, heady smell, a cocktail of sweat, vodka, and pickled garlic. The poor light and the continuous low mumble of prayer, combined with incense and the intoxicating bodily perfumes, made Militza feel quite sick and faint.

She stumbled out on the porch. In comparison to the fetid, febrile atmosphere inside the house, the sharp Siberian afternoon air was something of a shock. It burnt the back of her throat as she inhaled. Holding on to a wooden railing for support, she breathed deeply. The oxygen made her feel better—anything to be out of the heat and the smell. She should be getting back to Tyumen. It was an arduous journey and much more dangerous in the dark. Who knew who'd be out there in the pitch-black wilderness? How many escaped convicts on the road? The rules were changing and respect for the aristocracy was ebbing. She was a woman on her own, and she did not want to be out after dark. Anyway, she'd got what she'd come for. He had no idea she was behind the allegations. But what she really wanted was to be able to announce his return to St. Petersburg to the tsarina. She'd surely done enough to tempt him back, reminding him of the riches he enjoyed there. After all, there was nothing Rasputin liked more than temptation.

"Leaving so soon?"

"Grisha?" She was a little startled when he appeared at the other end of the porch. "I thought you were inside."

"I have been asking myself all day, why have you come?" He stared at her, his eyes narrow. "Why would my mamma come all this way to see me, Grisha, out here?" He gestured slowly around his courtyard with an outstretched hand. "Curiosity?" He paused. "Self-interest? Contrition? Or guilt?"

"Guilt?" Militza smiled. "Why would I possibly feel guilty?"

"I have been wondering who could have denounced Grisha to the police, who knows Grisha well enough to do that." He took a step forward, his head moving slowly from side to side like a cobra about to strike. "Do you know?"

"Me?"

"Your sister?" He came closer.

"Stana? Why would she do that?" Militza laughed a little.

"Nikolasha?"

"You cured his dog, helped his marriage . . ."

"Not the tsarina!" He smiled. "She likes Grisha."

"Yes," agreed Militza. "As does the tsar."

"The tsarina likes Grisha so much she makes clothes for him, embroiders his shirts." He smiled again. "So that leaves you."

"Grisha . . ." She smiled and walked towards him. "I could never do that." She stood in front of him and stroked the side of his face with her hand. "We are one and the same, you and me. We are made of the same things, of the same Four Winds, the earth and the fire beneath it." Her heart was beating fast, but she maintained the light, playful note in her voice.

"It can only be you," he said, grabbing her wrist.

"Grisha!" she exclaimed quickly. "I came here to be healed!"

"Healed?" He was a little taken aback.

"Yes!" she lied. "I have thought of nothing else. Nothing else at all, over the days and nights on the train across Siberia."

"A healing?"

"I want to be healed like Olga. Heal me!" she shouted. "Heal me!"

"My dear, my mamma, if you don't sin, you don't repent. If you don't repent, you cannot be saved . . ."

CHAPTER 29

JUNE 1908, ZNAMENKA, PETERHOF

MILITZA LEFT SIBERIA NEITHER REPENTANT NOR SAVED. Her driver, upon hearing her shout the words "Heal me!" loudly and repeatedly, had, as instructed, come running into the courtyard to suggest she immediately leave for Tyumen. So with Rasputin still grappling with his belt buckle, she was taken back to her carriage, lamenting her lack of healing and begging him to return to the city.

THE TSARINA WAS NATURALLY ECSTATIC WHEN MILITZA GAVE her the news in the Rose Drawing Room at the Lower Dacha.

"At last!" she declared.

"I thought I'd come and tell you as soon as I heard."

"You did well." Alix paused, as if debating whether to say something else. She took hold of Militza's hands, and her own were cold to the touch. "You must never speak of what I am about to tell you," she whispered. "Never."

"Of course."

"And I am only telling you because I know you will find it as outrageous and unfounded as I," she continued, still holding Militza's hand. She nodded. "I've heard some terrible rumors that . . ." The tsarina paused and lowered her voice even more. "That . . . Our Friend . . . has been investigated for improper behavior—for being in a sect!" Her voice was barely audible. "A sectarian! A member of the Khlysty."

"But that's illegal."

"I know!"

"And was he?"

"In a sect?"

"I don't know. And I don't care! I put a stop to it as soon as I heard." She looked horrified. "Can you imagine such a thing?"

"Rasputin being a Khlyst?"

"Anyone wanting to investigate Our Friend! I was so angry. Dear, gentle Grisha who has never hurt a fly. Don't they know how important he is to me? To the imperial family? It's treasonous! They have no regard for us. It is like they are deliberately trying to cause me pain. Me! Their tsarina!"

"Awful." Militza shook her head. "Do you think he knows?"

"I should imagine so. They searched his house for two whole days!"

"Who launched the investigation?"

"I asked," Alix said, her voice raised and quivering with anger. "And guess what?" She touched her nostrils with her lace handkerchief. "The file is missing. Typical!" She shook her head. "Only in this country can the tsar's closest friends be investigated and the tsar not be able to find out who did it! This country is not Europe." She shivered. "It is savage!"

"Awful," agreed Militza again, thanking Nikolasha in her prayers. "But anyway at least now he is coming back."

"Yes," the tsarina said, sitting down in the sofa. "What a relief for us all."

The conversation changed to the happenings of the last few months. Instead of talking about Stolypin and Nicky's endless problems with the Duma, which wanted to take more and more of the tsar's power, Alix wanted to know about the children and their plans for the summer. For the imperial family, there was a trip planned on the Gulf of Finland in the *Standart*. Work was starting on Livadia, which they were hoping might be ready in time for Olga's sixteenth birthday, in just over three years' time. Just as she was expressing her surprise that her eldest was getting so old, there was a knock at the door and Anna walked in. Militza smiled through her irritation. She'd been alone with the tsarina for only half an hour. Half an hour. And she was being interrupted by that bovine little woman, who persisted in talking about the breakup of her marriage and how Rasputin had predicted it all along! And what a good Friend he was. And how often she saw him and how terribly close they were. And . . .

"Have you heard?" she said, her head cocked to one side, her hands clasped in front of her. "Prince Yusupov is dead."

"The count?" asked Alix.

"The son," both Militza and Anna replied at the same time.

"You knew?" asked Anna, looking surprised and disappointed at the same time.

"Which one?" asked Militza.

"The oldest. Nikolai. The good son."

"Nikolai? Oh, how awful! How awful to lose a son," said Alix, grabbing hold of her handkerchief and covering her mouth in horror. "How totally, terribly awful. Poor Zinaida. Poor, poor Zinaida . . . How?" she whispered.

"A duel," replied Anna.

Militza shook her head. Her mouth went dry and the breath left her lungs. She'd known something terrible was going to happen to one of those boys. That night, long ago, when she'd seen the cards: The Ten of Swords. Death. The King of Swords. She had never forgotten it. In those quiet moments before dawn, when she'd lie in bed and think things through, those three cards always appeared before her. But a duel? What a waste. What a terrible, useless waste of a young man's life. A duel? She closed her eyes, and then, all of a sudden, she could see it. The early-morning sunshine, the dappled ground under the beautiful poplar trees. It was positively bucolic, flowers, birds, the noise of the wind in the trees . . . The young men were giddy with adrenaline, their fine clothes rumpled by the breeze. There was the smell of wine, the sound of their friends shouting, telling them not to do it, urging them to put down their weapons, to desist. And then the shots, the echo around the woods. What recklessness this was! Not a care for anyone, even themselves. Why didn't they stop it? Why?

"First time they both missed," said Anna. "So they did it again and Count Arvid Manteuffel shot Nikolai straight in the chest, while Prince Yusupov, he fired—"

"Up in the air," said Militza, opening her eyes.

"So you did know?" asked Anna.

"No," replied Militza with a shake of her head.

"Up in the air?" asked Alix. "So he deliberately missed?"

"It appears so," replied Anna.

"And why did this duel take place? What foolish thing made this madness happen?" asked Alix.

"Why do they ever?" said Militza.

"An affair. Between Arvid's wife, Countess Marina Heiden, and Nikolai," added Anna, shooting Militza a look. "It had been going on awhile and the husband had asked them to stop. Many times. So there was nothing else to be done . . ."

"But it was all so very avoidable," said Militza.

"Quite," agreed Alix, nodding her head slowly. "How appalling."

IT WAS A FEW WEEKS LATER THAT MILITZA CAME ACROSS THE ashen face of Count Felix Yusupov. They were at the Vladimirs' for a soirée in Yalta, and despite the golden light of the dipping sun and the joyful, glamorous crowd, the man looked broken, standing by a tree, staring out to sea. It was a beautiful party. Some one hundred or so people floated across the lawns, serenaded by musicians, entertained by dancers, as they flitted from group to group, chatting about the summer, the picnics they planned, the fun they were organizing and who exactly had been to visit the tsar and tsarina since they arrived in the Crimea ten days ago.

"Have you been?" asked Militza, running her long string of pearls through her hands as she spoke to her hostess.

"I can't stand the German," said Maria Pavlovna, conveniently forgetting her own heritage. "She is the reason my beautiful Kirill lives in exile, and for that I shall never forgive her."

"Of course," said Militza, taking a sip from her glass.

"While they were very happily letting your sister marry her brother, they were banishing my son for marrying his cousin! I don't see the fairness in that."

"No, well—"

"And it was all *her* fault, *her* idea, but then it always is, isn't it? Tell me, does *he* have any opinions anymore? Or is he guided entirely by his wife?" She sighed loudly, looking down the beautiful terraced lawns, lined by cypress trees, lit by flickering flares that dropped all the way down the Black Sea below. "He hangs on to that shit Stolypin, who is nipping away at our power and gives in to Duma after Duma. The man has no judgment at all. And in the meantime, his prudish old wife prattles on about the sanctity of marriage. Just because Victoria divorced the tsarina's brother to marry my son. I don't see *that* as a good enough reason for them both to be stripped of all their titles and banished from Russia!"

"I am so sorry," said Militza, suddenly realizing quite how upset the poor woman must be.

"So am I." Maria Pavlovna sniffed a little. "It's just seeing your sister and Nikolasha so happy, laughing at my party." She nodded over at the pair as they walked down towards the sea, holding hands. "And I can't help but wish my son was here too."

"You could ask Rasputin, I suppose." Militza felt her cheeks flush a little with embarrassment. She was sure she wasn't telling the grand duchess anything she didn't already know.

"Him?" she snorted. "Rasputin-Novy as that is what we are supposed to call him these days! I thought those sorts of double-barreled names were reserved for aristocrats, not peasants from Siberia." She shook her head. "I don't think I need his help. I'm sorry . . ." she said before walking off.

"Upset someone else, have you?" asked the count, leaning against the trunk of a tree. "You and your little cabal of necro-mancers?"

"I am sorry to hear about your son," she said quickly, for the man's face was almost unrecognizable with grief.

His normally ruddy complexion looked pale and waxy; his eyes were blank and rheumy. His ebullient mustache that had been so aggressively thick and determined appeared thinned and limp, as if no amount of wax could stiffen its resolve. He also looked unsteady on his feet, as though he would struggle to climb the stairs. Sorrow drains the blood quicker than the sun dries a sponge.

"Well, you were the one who knew," he said. "You saw it in the cards . . ." He raised his eyebrows as his voice trailed off.

"I am sorry I couldn't tell you more . . ."

"More!" He turned to smile at her. "If you think I believe you knew anything about the death of my son, Madame, then you are mistaken." He drained his glass of vodka. "You were simply taking a chance, like the charlatan you are. You *guessed*. You were lucky."

"I lost a child . . ."

"Dear lady, we have all lost children. Babies. Not sons. There is a large and profound difference. My wife wept for her babies— but for her son, my wife is mute. She does not laugh, she does not smile, she does not move, such is her grief, such is her pain, such is the misery that has torn at her soul. So don't talk to me of loss and how you empathize. You don't. You're a sibyl. A witch. An odious little soothsayer with some trick cards up your sleeve. Some around here think you have a gift, with your prophecies and your gurus and your séances. But I think you are nothing. I despise you as I despise your black cabal of lechers and lepers— and I despise that man who you introduced to our tsar."

"Good evening, Count Yusupov, I am so sorry to hear about Nikolai," said Stana as she approached, smelling a little of champagne and the roses she'd picked from the garden.

"Go to hell!" he said as he slowly walked away, back up the stone pathway leading towards the house.

Stana was shocked at Count Yusupov's outburst. A rose fell from the small bunch that she'd picked. Militza reached into the pocket of her cream silk dress for the small red bottle of Badmaev's tincture. Her hands were shaking a little as she opened it and knocked the solution straight back in one. She shivered as she swallowed.

"The man's upset," she said to her sister. "He's grieving. I am sure he didn't mean to be so rude."

"I know. It's just I am tired of all the enmity, tired of being the focus of so much hatred. I was trying to be kind. That is all." She sighed. "Have you seen Nikolasha?"

"Is that the other son?" asked Militza, ignoring her sister, her eyes half closed as she tried to focus on a slight, eccentrically dressed young man striding towards her.

Clean-shaven, his blond hair parted and smoothed flat, he was very handsome; he smiled, and his white silk, open-necked shirt ballooned as he walked. He was wearing a pair of loose-fitting crimson trousers with a sash that was held in place around the waist by what looked like a heavily diamond-encrusted clasp.

"Grand Duchess Militza? Grand Duchess Anastasia?" He bowed and his heels clicked together. "At last I make your acquaintance!"

"Prince Yusupov." Stana smiled.

"Felix Felixovich," replied Militza.

"I believe we have a mutual Friend." His smile was conspiratorial as he glanced around the party.

"We do?" asked Militza.

"His name is not allowed to be mentioned in our house—come to that, neither is yours," he laughed. "But I have a friend, Munia Golovina, who is an ardent follower. Ardent," he repeated. "And so is her mother. My friend Munia even collects his hair to bring her good fortune. She has a stunning little box of his strands that she swears can cure most things." He paused and leaned in, putting his hand up so he could whisper behind it. "I know a little of what you can do! I myself have seen a clairvoyant in Paris, Madame Freya. Do you know her? You probably do. She's very good. She told me many things! Some are hard to believe—but fascinating. I have also visited the Isis-Urania Temple in St. James's Street, London, *and* I have even been to Blythe Road."

"Blythe Road?" asked Stana.

"The battle of Blythe Road, Madame," he said, his eyes twinkling with amusement. "Where Mr. Crowley, dressed in the black mask of Osiris, god of the dead and the underworld, attacked Mr. W. B. Yeats and shouted spells and wished the man burn in hell!" The prince laughed. "It was a fantastic place!" Militza stared at him. The young man was clearly a flamboyant, spoiled sort who knew little of what he was talking about. "I have premonitions, you know," he continued, smoothing down the front of his shirt. "I see things. Everyone says I am gifted, that I am special. The other day"—he lowered his voice—"when in Oxford, I was having dinner with a friend of my parents and a great dark cloud descended. No one else could see it but me. But I knew, right then and there, it was a bad omen. Terribly bad. And do you know what?" He paused, his bright eyes dancing from one sister to the other. "The man died. He died! The very next day. Well, almost. And I knew he would! I knew it. Amazing, don't you think? I saw that!"

"Yes," said Militza. "What did he die of?"

"Who? The man? I don't know. Opium, I think. But I knew you'd be fascinated." He threw his head back and ran his hand through his blond hair. "Anyway, Munia keeps insisting that I meet Rasputin. She thinks we might have a lot in common. Apart from our backgrounds, of course."

"No one has your background," agreed Stana.

"No." He smiled. "Totally unique, isn't it? There's no one in Russia who can claim to be related to the Prophet Muhammad *and* the kings of Egypt."

And with that he walked back into the party.

"That boy is trouble," said Militza as she watched him go.

"He's just vain," said Stana.

"He's powerful, rich, *and* vain," corrected Militza. "Which is much more dangerous."

BACK IN ST. PETERSBURG, EMBOLDENED BY THE CASE AGAINST him being dropped, Rasputin enjoyed an ever-widening circle of influence.

In little over a year he went from a name mumbled quietly in the hushed corners of the court to a feature at all sorts of parties and soirées and eventually in articles in newspapers such as the *Moscow Gazette*. There were pages and pages devoted to his flagrant boasting of his access to the tsar and tsarina, and the fact that he went back and forth to the palace, up and down the back stairs, in and out of the young grand duchesses' bedrooms did not sound good.

The truth of the matter was that most of his boasts were true. He was visiting the palace at all hours of the day or night, without an invitation, whenever he was so inclined, quite often sitting up, alone, late into the night with Alix. He did go and see the grand duchesses at bedtime and would spend hours, unsupervised, in their bedrooms. And he endlessly talked about it and them and waved about the letters they'd written to him. Just a bottle or two of Madeira was enough to loosen his already garrulous tongue.

Even his flat, once frequented only by an inner circle of ardent egg-eaters, was now a gathering point for up to two hundred Rasputinki a day who would collect and sell everything the man touched or blessed. They'd sew his toenails into their dresses for protection from evil, believing also that human fingernails—especially his—would be useful to claw their way out of the grave. The divan in the back room was subjected to so many "healings" that, apparently, the arms eventually gave way.

"Your Friend is certainly making a lot of noise," said Badmaev one afternoon as he arrived at Znamenka, carrying his soft leather case of supplies.

"I thought he was your Friend too?" replied Militza as she counted the number of phials he was placing on the marble-topped table.

"No." The Tibetan shook his head. "He drinks too much and screws too much for my liking, and he can't control his lusts—he's a liar and a satyr. The reason for that recent trip to the Holy Land?" He sniffed. "Fucking a Finnish ballet dancer, Lisa Tansin."

"I heard."

"There are photographs, plenty of them. Him, naked with her and a harem of prostitutes."

"Mercifully, I have been spared those."

"And do you know what the empress does while he is away? Mourns his absence and writes down her thoughts in the notebook he gave her . . . Nineteen? . . . Twenty?"

"Twenty-five, don't you think?"

"If you're sure?" he asked, taking another five bottles of elixir out of his bag.

"I find it helpful."

"So is the opium," he replied. "And the veronal. Barbiturates are helpful in inducing sleep, but . . ."

"I'd prefer not to sleep," she said. "Sleep is for the weak." She smiled, taking a small bottle and pouring its contents slowly across her tongue. She closed her eyes and felt its bitterness trickle down her throat. "I have become accustomed to its taste these days."

"Do you see much of him, then? Rasputin?" asked Badmaev, packing up his things. "He now only contacts me when the child is ill—has a headache, has fallen over, that sort of thing—and he's after medicine. I have to say I give it grudgingly. If it weren't for Alexei, I would not do it . . ."

"I see him often." Militza swallowed hard and inhaled deeply, riding the sudden wave of adrenaline that hit her.

"That is good," he said. "I'm very glad. You need to be there. Because I heard the other day that he who controls the mystic controls the tsar—and therefore Russia."

"I control the mystic, I assure you." She smiled. "I introduced him to the tsar."

"I know you did."

"I made him," she said, laughing suddenly. Badmaev looked at her strangely. What was she saying? "I manifested him," she continued. "I summoned him. Don't you worry, I'll look after him. The mystic is mine."

CHAPTER 30

DECEMBER 31, 1910, ST. PETERSBURG

IT WAS PAST MIDDAY, AND MILITZA WAS LYING IN BED WHEN the telephone rang and the footman knocked on her door.

She was a little tired from the night before. She had been to dinner and a ball and hadn't arrived home until 3 A.M. And this was the third time she'd been out this week, not including the ballet. She had also visited fifteen people the day before, handing out her visiting card and drinking endless cups of tea, making polite conversation, inquiring after everyone's health, hearing the same stories over and over again. Normally she was more abstemious, choosing her parties and refusing invitations, but with her daughter, Marina, already eighteen, it was her duty as a mother to escort her to as many parties, teas, and occasions as there were hours in the day. Poor Marina was finding it all a little unbearable. An intelligent young woman with dark eyes and pale skin, just like her mother, she enjoyed her own company more than that of others and would have much preferred to spend her evenings sketching or painting, a passion for which she was particularly talented. But Militza's early years in the city still haunted her, those lonely days at the Smolny Institute and those dreadful parties where she and her sister would sit around, waiting for someone to write his name down on their dance cards. Marina was not going to have the same experience.

"They know!" came the voice down the receiver.

Militza was now standing in her dressing gown in the hall.

"Stana?" She could feel her heart beginning to race. "What? Who?"

"I can't talk on the telephone," continued her sister. "You never know who is listening."

Militza dressed quickly. Her maid Katya was taken aback. Normally, when she would be out visiting most of the afternoon, the grand duchess would spend a good hour on her toilette, choosing the latest in fashionable day dresses, ironing her hair, picking out the perfect shoes with just the correct amount of heel, coming home to change again before going out to dinner and a dance and maybe on to one of the more fashionable restaurants late into the night, but today she simply pinned her hair and chose a high-necked white shirt and a dark blue skirt that stopped just short of the floor.

Stana was already in the drawing room when Militza came down the stairs. They sat in silence while the footman served tea and small slices of plain cake.

"Anna Vyrubova told me," said Stana as soon as the footman closed the door. She leapt off her seat, and in a rustle of maroon silk, she came to sit next to her sister on the divan, taking hold of her hand. "She was in Donon's last night . . ."

"What was she doing in a French restaurant?" asked Militza, a little surprised.

"She'd been to the theatre and she had drunk a glass of champagne," continued Stana. "I'd come fresh from the Vladimirs' dance. Anyway, there she was—a look of delight on that face of hers. Apparently Alix knows it was you . . ."

"Me?"

"Who reported Rasputin as a member of the Khlysty." Stana licked her lips nervously.

"How?" Militza was horrified.

"Olga Lokhtina."

"Olga?"

"Olga told her, and then Anna told Rasputin and the tsarina . . ."

"Both of them?"

"Apparently. Militza, they *all* know. Only Rasputin doesn't believe it. He says you would never do anything to hurt him, but the tsarina . . ."

"She believes Olga?"

Stana nodded.

"But how? Everyone knows that Olga is a deluded fool who suffers from nerves. I have seen her with Grisha, her mouth in his trousers."

"People believe what they want to believe. The more you tell them otherwise, the stauncher their beliefs become," said Stana. "Olga says that's why you went all that way to see him in Siberia."

"But the woman's mad."

"Mad—and an old friend of Anna's. They have known each other since childhood."

"Who doesn't Anna know! Who hasn't she played with since she was a child?"

Militza took a sip of her tea. Her hand was shaking, and she was terrified; she needed some elixir. Just to think straight. She reached into her pocket and, pulling out a small red bottle, she poured its contents into her tea. Stana watched her.

"What shall I do? I can't think, I can't think!"

"No wonder," Stana said, looking at the fortified tea.

"The tsar takes twice as much as I do, and anyway, it is good for the blood," snapped Militza. "You are not being helpful."

"Ignore it," said Stana simply. "It's Olga's word against yours and, most importantly, Grisha believes you."

"But for how long?"

"You must remain above suspicion."

"How?"

"By being more ardent than ever."

Militza's heart sank. Surely it could not have come to this. Surely her close relationship with the tsarina—the favors, the secrets, the things she knew—would hold her in good stead. Surely they had been through enough together before Rasputin. And after he'd arrived. Even the problem of Stana's marriage had faded a little into the background. There were so many other problems, so many other storms brewing on the horizon; their love match was no longer a bone of contention, except with the Grand Duchess Vladimir, who was still furious at her own son's exile. But now, just as the seas and the sands were beginning to settle, this. How on earth could the monster she herself had created be her last and only resort?

But that very evening she realized just how precarious her position was. What should have been an entertaining New Year's Eve at Prince and Princess Orlov's stunning Marble Palace—one of the city's first and finest neoclassical buildings—turned very sour indeed. She and Peter arrived with two of their children in tow. Marina, dressed in pale yellow, nervously stood by her mother, while Roman, who was by now fourteen years old and studying in Kiev, exuded the tentative confidence of a youth who was just beginning to discover wine and pretty girls. (Poor Nadezhda, their youngest, being only twelve, was forced to stay at home.)

The party was in full swing, romances were beginning to unfurl between the younger members of the soirée, and everyone was looking forward to the end of what they frankly acknowledged had been a difficult decade. It was going to be a good evening. Prince Vladimir and Princess Olga were renowned for their well-judged, delightful parties, where the food and Veuve Clicquot champagne were overly abundant. So abundant was their hospitality that the old prince had, over the years, become notably larger than his extremely thin wife. He was so fat that when he sat down he was unable to see his own knees, so fat that there was not a horse in the army that could carry him, so fat that on parades the poor man was reduced to panting alongside the tsar so he could keep up with the retinue. She, on the other hand, was so exceptionally tall and thin that she was positively brittle in appearance. She was one of the tsarina's esteemed ladies-in-waiting, while he was a lieutenant general in the army; they were an odd couple and when they appeared together at court, it was once remarked: "Behold the Prince and Princess Orlov, in flesh and bone." Forever after they were known as Flesh and Bone. Everyone loved them and their generous parties, as indeed did the tsar and tsarina, who were both expected that night—out in society for the first time in months.

"Are they here yet?" Militza asked Peter as they stood together alongside Marina in the corner of the ballroom.

"Why on earth are you interested in the whereabouts of Nicky and Alix?" asked Peter, taking a lengthy drag on his cigarette. Were it not for his son's and daughter's social life, he would not have been standing there; much as he loved Flesh and Bone and their generosity, balls and parties increasingly bored him.

"I just heard they were coming and it would be nice to see them," lied Militza.

"Nice?" Peter looked at her quizzically. "I could think of infinitely more joyful company." Peter looked at his daughter. "And you, my darling, why are you standing here?"

"I'm just a-a little—" Marina stammered.

"Your dress is beautiful, *you* are beautiful; now go and talk to some people." Peter nodded towards a group of pretty young girls standing near the door. "Those girls over there." He glanced across at a group of handsome young officers dressed in smart red uniforms. "But those young men should be avoided!"

Inevitably, the tsar and tsarina were announced late. They came without any of the children, not even Olga, who at fifteen should certainly have been allowed out to celebrate the New Year. And within minutes of the tsarina arriving, she was under duress. She was uncomfortable in her gown and she kept pulling at the tight silver-embroidered sleeves, tugging at the high neckline because of the heat; her heavy sapphire earrings seemed to pain her, so she took them off within five minutes of her arrival, placing them carefully in her small evening bag. But it was the expression on her face that warded off any small talk. She was tight-lipped, and large red patches across her cheeks seeped down the back of her neck. Poor Nicky, it was obvious he wanted to leave his wife's side, but Alix clung grimly to his arm as they made their way around the room. Eventually they ended up standing in one corner of the ballroom, she like a statue, staring mournfully ahead of her, while he twitched and itched, his pale gaze darting around the room, trying to catch someone's eye.

Finally Fat Orlov went over to converse with his old friend, full of jovial bonhomie, and after a few minutes Nicky managed to loosen his wife's grip and move to the other side of the ballroom, to be introduced to some of the blushing young debutantes out for their first season.

Seeing Alix on her own, Militza went over, taking the shy Marina with her.

"Happy New Year!" she began. "Well, almost . . ." Alix looked at her and said nothing. Militza carried on, "And are you looking forward to Orthodox Christmas?" She smiled, but the tsarina appeared to look through her. Militza felt color pouring into her own cheeks. The woman was ignoring her completely, and those around were beginning to notice. "Doesn't Marina look lovely?"

"No," came Alix's tart reply as she looked the girl up and down. "The gown," she remarked, taking in the pretty yellow sleeves and the low neckline, "is not suitable for a girl so young."

"It—"

"It suggests loose morals." The tsarina placed her glass of untouched champagne down on the table. "And a girl of low class. Or a tradesman's daughter. It is not at all becoming."

As the tsarina walked away and was swallowed up by the crowd of glittering silks and jewelry, Marina burst into tears.

"Keep quiet," said Militza, tugging her daughter by the arm. "Don't make a scene." But Marina was inconsolable. She was not a girl who brimmed with confidence; she did not look like the other debutantes with their pink cheeks and fair curls. She was pale, with black pools for eyes; Militza often wondered if she'd inherited more than just her looks.

"Why did she say that? Why?" she sobbed.

Militza looked around the ballroom; they were beginning to attract attention. "Come outside." She pulled her weeping daughter through the crowded ballroom, weaving and elbowing her way through the throng to the library next to the giant entrance hall. "What is wrong with you!"

"What is wrong with her!" wept the girl, tugging at her dress in disgust. "She is unkind and evil. The woman's a witch!"

"I don't think you are allowed to say that of the tsarina without ending up in the Peter and Paul Fortress," said a voice.

Mother and daughter turned to see Anna Vyrubova standing in the doorway, her plump figure pulled into a tight pink ball gown, her large bosom covered in a modest voile. Her top lip might have been glistening with sweat from the heat of the ballroom, but there was a look of triumph in her eyes.

"She's upset," spat Militza.

"But those sorts of comments are treasonous," declared Anna.

"Just leave us," said Militza.

"Or what? Or you'll try and send me away too?"

"I have no idea what you are talking about," snapped Militza, hugging her daughter close.

"The tsarina's upset with you." Anna smiled, her hands on her hips. "She doesn't like it when someone tries to take her Friend away."

"I introduced her to Grisha—why would I want to take him away?"

As soon as she said it, Militza realized it was a mistake. To enter into conversation with this woman was an error because there was no telling what she might say, what conversations she might repeat, what bons mots she might decide to share. Militza had been a fool to underestimate this woman. A fool to write her off so easily. Appearances were deceptive, and she of all people should know that. Just because the woman looked bovine didn't mean she was. In that moment she realized that she and her sister were in a lethal fight. A fight for influence, position, power—a fight they could not afford to lose.

Leaving word with her husband to stay at the party, Militza left the ball with her weeping daughter. Their early arrival home shocked the footman as he had been dozing in the chair in the hall; equally disconcerting to him was the fact that the grand duchess and Marina arrived alone, leaving the grand duke and his son at the ball.

"Wake Brana!" barked Militza as she ushered her daughter up the stairs. "And tell her to find the black votive candles immediately and meet me in my private salon."

"The black, Your Imperial Highness?" The footman bowed.

"Yes! Black! And get on with it!"

꙳

A VERY BASIC SPELL CALLING ON SANTA MUERTE SHOULD DO the trick. Easy, thought Militza, as she counseled her distressed daughter—easy, strong, and powerful. It was far beneath her and she knew it: this was crude magic, the same spell she'd once berated her sister for. Santa Muerte and black votive candles might not be terribly sophisticated, but Anna could suddenly discover she was not in such rude health after all.

So as Marina lay in her bedroom, staring at the ceiling quietly, seething with humiliation, Militza lit her candles in front of the gruesome image of Santa Muerte, the dancing spirit of death whose magic she began to call upon.

> *Come, Santa Muerte, dance with me,*
> *Help make Anna Vyrubova no longer be,*
> *Come, Santa Muerte, come to me,*
> *Help make Anna cease to be,*
> *Come, dancing death, come and dance with me,*
> *Kill Vyrubova, one, two, three . . .*

Round and round the room Militza spun, mumbling, muttering her zagovor as the black candles burnt in front of the grinning skull. Her heart beat faster as she felt Anna's heart beat faster. Up and down the ballroom, the tubby little woman galloped. She'd never been asked to dance by so many young men before. So many lovely young men! It must be her proximity to the tsarina, she concluded, that was making her so attractive. Everyone loves power, and she, Anna—yes, Anna—was right at the center of it. What fun!

Round and round Militza spun, fashioning a small fat poppet of black wax in her dexterous, well-practiced hands. She would see to it that Anna, the little gossip, the eyes and ears of the tsarina, the smuggest of all confidantes, would see and hear no more. Olga Lokhtina might have started the rumor about Militza denouncing Rasputin, but it was Anna, Anna who'd spread it, Anna who'd fanned the flames, Anna who was the toxic cancer at the heart of the court.

Up and down Anna trotted, her pink dress pinching her waist, the heat and her dress's high neck beginning to suffocate her. If only Militza had wax from a "dead" candle, she thought, for candles made from the fat of the dead are much more efficient at dispatching the living, but they were increasingly hard to get hold of these days. Fewer peasants were inclined to exhume the dead to make tallow candles, especially when an old church candle was almost as useful. But not quite useful enough. So Militza spun faster, manipulating the wax from her votive candle and chanting louder, and all the while plump little Anna Vyrubova struggled for breath as she was swung around, forced up and down, under the arm, holding hands, whooping along. And the faster she danced, the tighter the dress became, the shorter her breath. Militza stuck the pins into the short fat poppet she'd made. One, she jabbed the stomach. Two, she pierced the leg. Three, she slowly pushed the needle into the doll's silent, open mouth.

ANNA VYRUBOVA DIDN'T SEEM ABLE TO SCREAM AS SHE FELL TO the ground in agonizing pain. Her stomach hurt, her headache was excruciating, and for a good few minutes her mouth opened and shut, but not a word could come out.

"She looked like a giant codfish," said Roman the next morning as he drank his coffee at breakfast. "She was like this . . ." He opened and closed his mouth. "And her face was scarlet and there were blotches all over her skin."

"Nothing more?" asked Militza.

"It was quite a scene," said Peter, an amused curl to his lips. "She was rolling around on the ground, holding that expansive waist of hers. I have never seen anything like it."

"And nothing else?"

Roman shook his head. "The tsarina took her home."

"She probably needed an excuse to leave the party," said Peter, taking a sip of his coffee. "I have never seen anyone drink champagne with such reluctance in my life!"

"Maybe I should go and visit poor Anna . . ." suggested Militza.

"I shouldn't bother," said Roman. "They took her back to Tsarskoye Selo."

"The tsarina refused to stay the night in town, again," confirmed Peter. "It is far too dangerous for her in the city. Or so she maintains."

MILITZA NEVER DID MAKE IT TO SEE IF ANNA WAS RECOVERING from her "sudden turn" at the ball. Not that she felt remotely guilty. She'd acted in haste—she knew that. It was fortunate that there had been no "dead" candles to hand; otherwise Anna's "turn" might have been something else. But she needed to think about what she might do to neutralize her, bring the fat woman down, make sure that whatever she said in the future would not be taken seriously again.

In the meantime, she had an afternoon tea with the Grand Duchess Elizabeth (or Mavra, as she was more usually known) at the Yacht Club, followed by an evening at the ballet to think about. Militza was very fond of Mavra and her husband, the flamboyant Grand Duke Konstantin Konstantinovich, whose penchant for poetry, the theatre, and late-night trips to obscure banyas made him more entertaining than most of the other dreary souls at court. Also, the two women were attempting to encourage the small flame of romance that was kindling between the charming, talented, poetic Prince Oleg (the fifth of their eight surviving children) and little Nadezhda, still aged only twelve.

"Did you hear the tsarina called for Rasputin last night?" declared Mavra, playing with a small piece of buttered bread and red caviar.

"In front of everyone?" asked Militza.

"No, I gather a car was sent to collect him. Apparently, they trawled the city until they found him in a private room at the Villa Rhode."

"What was he doing at the Villa Rhode?" asked Militza, already knowing the reply.

"I heard he was so drunk that he swore and yelled, screaming he didn't want to leave his nice warm whore!" She grinned. "But the driver was having none of it and they forced him to leave; they dragged him kicking and screaming down the stairs, and eventually he slept in the car and managed to sober up by the time he arrived at the palace!"

"Really?"

"It gets worse. Last night, Fat Orlov told Nicky he wasn't fond of Rasputin! Only for Alix to overhear. Her face was thunderous, to say the least. Apparently, the Orlovs are now *personae non gratae*, to the tsarina at any rate. That woman's not well!" Mavra shook her head. "I also hear she wasn't nice to Marina?" She raised a fine eyebrow.

"She was charming," said Militza quickly. "I think Marina was a little overawed by the ball."

"Indeed." Mavra smiled, biting the most delicate corner off her piece of bread. She paused. "Are you going to the ballet tonight?"

"We are invited to the Imperial Box."

THAT NIGHT WAS ONE THAT MILITZA WOULD TRY IN VAIN TO forget. What ballet she and Peter went to see, she could not afterwards recall, perhaps because she never actually saw the performance.

She and Peter arrived early at the Mariinsky Theatre, Peter dressed in white tie while she wore her favorite ruby silk dress with diamonds, sapphires, and long white evening gloves. There was nothing out of the ordinary. In the crimson bar with the red velvet banquettes and the gilt ceiling, just behind the Imperial Box, the cream of St. Petersburg sipped champagne and waited for the first strains of the orchestra to strike up before taking up their places in the golden auditorium. The conversation was as usual: Who was in? Who was out? And what on earth had happened at the Orlovs' the night before? Poor Anna's crisis was much discussed. But the festering, fermenting swill of revolution in the countryside and the slums of the cities were not topics that bothered anyone.

Still, Militza was nervous as she sipped her champagne; her sixth sense was making her feel twitchy, anxious, paranoid.

The orchestra struck up a few chords, and the glittering crowd drained their last few bubbles from their flutes and moved, en masse, towards the door. With a surge of entitlement they pushed at each other with discreetly pointed elbows, for the seating in the Imperial Box was something of a free-for-all. The tsar and tsarina were, naturally, on their thrones in the middle of the box, where they could see and be seen, but the other chairs were not allocated. The tsarina might pat one close to her to indicate where a favorite might sit, but other than that, tickets were not issued. With Anna still prone in her bed, fighting what Rasputin had declared was little more than a slight fever, Militza jostled her way forward with confidence. Her eyes were firmly on the prize, a seat to the right of Alix. The tsarina looked directly at her. The trumpets sounded, the blue velvet curtain began to part, and Militza smiled and prepared to move forward, but instead Alix turned suddenly around and gently tapped the shoulder of her lady-in-waiting Sophie Buxhoeve-den. And that was it. Militza had no seat. There was surely a seat for her somewhere, in among the shadows and tucked away in the pleats of velvet, but she couldn't see it. Peter had been swept up over to the other side of the box and was chatting away to Uncle Bimbo; he had no care for his wife. Why would he? She had always been seated close to the tsarina in the past, so why would tonight be any different? Militza's head swam. She turned around and around, and the lights in the auditorium dimmed. She could not see anything.

The orchestra began the overture, and Militza realized she must get out before the lights on the stage went up and it was noticed she was standing on her own, without a chair. With seconds to spare, she stumbled swiftly out of the box.

"Madame?" queried a voice as she made her way into the private bar, flushed and blinking. "Are you all right?"

Militza looked around, confused. Furious indignation coursed through her veins. After all she'd done for that woman! That disloyal, half-brained idiot!

"Prime Minster," declared Militza, cauterizing her feelings as quickly as she could. She offered up a gloved hand for him to kiss.

"Your Imperial Highness." Peter Stolypin kissed her hand. "Are you not watching the ballet?"

"I don't feel the inclination," she replied with a wave of her fan.

"Oh?" He looked at her quizzically.

"I felt like a glass of champagne." She nodded towards the bar and the large silver bucket, full of ice, where there lay a bottle of the tsar's favorite champagne, Louis Roederer Cristal. "And you?"

"A meeting at the Duma. It went on for hours."

"Well, I won't keep you, sir, have a good evening," she said brusquely. She wanted to get outside into the street, to breathe in some of the ice-cold St. Petersburg air, to steady herself, her brain, and her emotions. Whatever was going to happen next, the tsarina would pay.

"Is the Friend in the box?" he asked, looking at her directly. "Rasputin. Or Rasputin-Novy, as we are now supposed to call him?"

"Him? No." She shook her head.

"I can't stand the man," he said, running his hand through his thick beard. He scrutinized her expression as he slowly turned up the corners of his curled and pointed mustache. Militza revealed nothing. "I cannot stand him at all."

"But didn't he help your daughter?"

"It is what he is doing to Russia that I can't abide."

"Then you'll be pleased to know he is not in the theatre to-night." Militza smiled.

"I believe you and he are well acquainted?"

"I know Rasputin," she confirmed.

"Well?"

"Quite well."

"Well enough to go to Siberia, if I am not mistaken?" Militza was taken by surprise. How did he know?

"It was a brief visit." She smiled charmingly. "And now, if you will excuse me, I simply must go."

"Was that before or after you went to the police?" he asked.

Militza glanced around the room. Had anyone heard him? How did he know so much?

"If you will excuse me, Prime Minister, I really must leave."

Stolypin slowly sat down on the banquette, rubbing the top of his shining pate. "Unfortunately the tsarina herself called an end to that little investigation?"

"I am afraid I don't understand quite what you are saying, sir?"

"Khlysty charges?"

"I think you are mistaken, sir."

"The man is bad news," he continued, quietly, careful not to be overheard. "He is a tragedy for this country. I love this country and that man is ruinous for all of us. He has letters from the grand duchesses, intimate letters that he is bandying around town. He reads them aloud when he is drunk." Stolypin's tones were hushed, but the importance of what he was saying was clear. "They only need to fall into the wrong hands. The press are on to him already, the endless profiles, the cartoons—the man is more famous than any courtesan. If they find the letters . . ." He shook his head. "He needs to go. And he needs to go far, far away."

"Well then, Prime Minister . . ." Militza leaned over, her pendant sapphires shining in the candlelight. "Ban him from the city," she whispered. He stared into her black eyes. "You have the power to do that, sir. Ban him so he can never set foot in St. Petersburg, or indeed Tsarskoye Selo, ever again."

CHAPTER 31

FEBRUARY 10, 1911, PETERHOF

AND SO IT WAS THAT HE CAME CAREERING THROUGH the woods, barefoot and breathless, throwing himself at her mercy, begging her to let him in.

Quite who'd tipped him off that there were guards waiting to arrest him and serve him with his citywide ban and arrest warrant he would not say, but he was incandescent with rage and fury that they would be after him. Him! Of all people! But he had just enough time to throw himself out of the train and run through the snow. He'd managed to commandeer a car at some point that took him to the forest outside Peterhof, where he'd leapt out and gone straight to Znamenka. He was like a lost dog who'd managed to run all the way home, only to arrive panting, starving, and shivering with the authorities not far behind.

❧

IT WAS STANA'S IDEA TO HARVEST HIS TOENAILS, MUCH LIKE they'd harvested the Grand Duchess Vladimir's dead baby all those years ago. They needed something, anything, to work with. Rasputin's power was strong, and his influence was all-encompassing, seeming to grow by the day. The more the newspapers wrote about how appalling he was, the more determined his followers became and the more the tsarina cleaved to him. "People believe what they want to believe," Stana used to say. But Alix was more than a believer. It was almost as if he were her own spoiled child and she were the only one who could control him. It was, of course, like so many things with Grisha, entirely the other way around, for it was he who controlled her. Not that the tsarina noticed. By this stage she rarely left the palace and never sought counsel of anyone outside her trusted circle—Anna, Rasputin, Nicky, and the children. Very occasionally the tutor Mr. Charles Gibbes, an Englishman, was allowed to have an opinion or an idea, but mostly everyone's job in the circle of trust was to agree with Alix.

And no one agreed more vociferously than Anna. Anna, who recovered rather too quickly, agreed with anything Alix said. She lived on her doorstep, loved the tsarina with all her naive heart, and became Rasputin's most ardent supporter.

Stana and Militza had often idly wondered quite how ardent a supporter she was. Was she being "healed," or was her pink, plump flesh not to the Siberian's taste? They knew they themselves were not to *her* taste; Anna's feelings for the sisters were abundantly clear. Over a relatively short period and in mirrored sympathy with the tsarina, she had managed to become the daily supporter of Rasputin and the daily detractor of Militza and Stana. She refused ever to refer to them by name and insisted on calling them either "the Black Women" or "the Crows." Within a matter of weeks, it was as if a war, a war of rumors and of gossip, had broken out between the palaces.

So when Rasputin chose to knock on Militza's door in the middle of the night and ask for sanctuary, not only was Militza shocked, she was also most accommodating. She could have thrown him to the lions, which was what she wanted to do. Stolypin had done exactly what she'd suggested. But yet . . . if she could lure Rasputin back into her thrall, then perhaps he might open the doors to the palace for her once more. After that night at the ballet, the invitations had most certainly dried up, and what little love there was left between the tsarina and Militza and Stana, the bustling, busy Anna was doing her best to destroy.

Yes, he was worth more to her alive. If not, at the very least, she could harvest him and get her beloved icon back.

As he snored on the divan with the soldiers circling the palace like a pack of wolves, Militza went through his leather bag. Even for a strannik, he traveled light. Inside was the hand-embroidered shirt the tsarina had given him along with a few other items of fetid clothing, a well-worn leather Bible with the pages beginning to fall out, and a collection of letters, all of which were addressed to "Sir." They were sealed and written in Rasputin's scrawling uncontrolled hand. Sitting back on her haunches, Militza examined one. She'd heard that, for a small fortune, Rasputin would and could recommend you or someone you nominated for a job or a helping hand. Apparently, he carried the letters around with him, which he'd sell. This one read:

Dear Sir,
　　Give whosoever is standing in front of you in possession of this letter whatever they ask for.
　　　　　　　　　　　　　　Sincerely, Rasputin-Novy

This, so they said, was how business was being done in the city now. She'd always presumed it was a rumor, put about by his increasing number of enemies, but the large bundle of cash at the bottom of the bag seemed to confirm the stories. But Militza had enough money; what she wanted was her icon.

"It protects all who own it. No harm will ever come to you while you have it in your possession," Philippe had told her as he'd given it to her.

But then the monster had stolen it from her. Her monster. The one she'd fashioned in wax and baptized with the soul of an unborn child. And he didn't deserve protection.

Her hands were shaking as she rifled through his bag. His large belly was rising and falling as he snored like a drunk in the snow, but his breathing was irregular and every time he stopped, snorted, or coughed, she held her breath. Finally, at the bottom of the bag, she saw it, but as she pulled it out she lost her grip and it clattered across the floor.

Rasputin woke with a start. He leapt off the divan, his eyes wide-open as if he had never been asleep. "What are you doing?" he barked. "Why is my bag undone? What's the noise!"

"Grisha! Grisha!" she whispered in a loud panic. "You must go!" She glanced across at the icon that lay glittering half under the divan. She moved a little closer, hoping to cover it with the skirts of her long velvet robe.

"Go?" He looked confused.

"The solders, they are banging at the door!"

"But I hear nothing."

"They have just smashed some windows; my doormen are holding them, but they won't be able to contain them for long. Please! While you can, Grisha, my love." She smiled and ran her hand over his lumpy forehead. "Go!" She gathered up his bag and pulled on the leather strings to tighten it before handing it to him. "Go!" she urged. "Hurry! Before it's too late!"

She hustled him down the back stairs and watched the footman help him with his boots.

"Where shall you go to?" she asked.

"Far," he said, glancing over his shoulder. "Far from the city, back to the steppes and the land I know. Good-bye," he said, kissing her briefly.

He must be afraid, thought Militza as she felt the touch of his wet lips clip the corners of her mouth; normally he would have slipped his tongue into her mouth or rubbed his rough hand up her skirt and between her legs, not always for the pleasure of the experience but mainly because he could. Tonight he didn't.

"I will look after the police," she said.

"I am in your debt," he said as he flung open the back door. A blast of icy wind whistled in straight off the Gulf of Finland. "Thank you!" he said, throwing the small leather satchel over his shoulder, and he was gone in a flurry of frost and snow.

MILITZA WAS AS GOOD AS HER WORD AND OCCUPIED THE POLICE who remained camped outside the palace watching everyone's movements for the next three weeks. Their vigil was brought to an end by a telegram received from the governor of Tyumen Province announcing Rasputin's safe arrival at his house in Pokrovskoye. Apparently, the feather-mustachioed young officer in charge had been so incensed by Militza's apparent sorcery and Rasputin's miraculous escape that he'd knocked on the office of Stolypin himself and begged to be allowed to travel to Siberia personally to serve Rasputin with the papers that banned him from the city. But Stolypin simply batted the man away. He was tired of the fight, and anyway, now that the tsarina knew exactly what the prime minister thought of her sage and guru, he knew his days were numbered.

Although quite how short in number was a shock to all but Rasputin.

The initial snub was obvious. Stolypin did not receive an invitation to ride on the imperial train from St. Petersburg to Kiev; instead, he had to make the three-day journey on his own. When he arrived, he was not included in the imperial entourage, having to make his own way through the crowds for the inauguration of the local government in southwest Russia in a small carriage, all alone. In fact, his treatment by the imperial family was so cold it was enough to make the man ill, so much so that Rasputin, who had naturally been invited, remarked as he saw Stolypin waving at the crowd, "Death is stalking him. It rides behind him."

Death was indeed close. Very close. Stolypin was shot that night, September 14, at the opera, while attending Rimsky-Korsakov's *The Tale of the Tsar Saltan*. Fortunately, Militza recalled, the Grand Duchesses Olga and Tatiana had gone to find some tea in the foyer when the gunman struck, shooting Stolypin square in the chest, his own bodyguard having conveniently disappeared off for a cigarette. And as the orchestra struck up "God Save the Tsar," the imperial family left the box while Stolypin staggered out of the theatre to a waiting stretcher. It took the man four days to die. The tsar visited twice and was eventually banned from the bedside by Stolypin's grief-stricken wife. Alix, however, never called to pay her respects at all.

"Do you know what she said?" asked Stana, taking a sip of wine as the sisters and their husbands sat on the terrace, admiring the sunset over the Black Sea.

"What?" asked Militza.

"'Those who have offended Our Friend can no longer count on divine protection.'" Stana nodded.

"So she believes Stolypin's assassination was divine retribution?" asked Peter, a curl of cigarette smoke leaving his lips.

Stana nodded. "For banning Rasputin from the capital."

"A ban that was never even enforced," added Nikolasha. "That creature left for Siberia and came right back again, in a bloody heartbeat. He spent the summer with acolytes in the country, only to turn up again in Kiev. All that happened was that poor Stolypin was left with a black mark by his name while Rasputin continues to roam free." He sighed. "That woman is losing her mind."

"I am not sure she ever had one," said Peter.

"Do you know what I heard the other day," continued Nikolasha. "And I am not one to gossip . . ."

"But?" Stana smiled.

"Apparently when Alix has a headache—"

"Which is often," chipped in Peter.

"That's true," agreed Nikolasha. "In order to cure the pain, she writes down Grisha's little sayings to help clear her head."

"She does that every time he leaves the city," said Militza.

"What sayings?" asked Stana.

"Banalities," said Nikolasha. He cleared his throat theatrically. "For example, on marriage . . . he says: 'A good graft revives an old tree.'"

Peter laughed. "I bet he did."

"On making a journey . . . 'Before crossing the river, see that the ferry is in its place.'"

"Very profound," said Peter.

"And apparently he said to Prince Yusupov, 'You could feed five villages with what's hanging on your walls.'"

"Well, at least the last one is true," said Peter, stubbing out his cigarette. "Although five seems rather a small number."

"What was he doing talking to Yusupov?" asked Militza. "I thought the family disliked Grisha?"

"They do," replied Nikolasha. "But you know Felix, he'll do anything to annoy his father!"

WHEN GRISHA RETURNED TO THE CITY IN THE AUTUMN OF 1912, his salon of Rasputinki was so popular that even the corridor outside his second-floor apartment was full of followers, all bearing tributes and requests for his help and assistance. Such was his fame and notoriety there was not one person from St. Petersburg to Sakhalin who did not know who he was. His name was on everyone's lips, and stories of his powers and reputation were traded over glasses of watered-down beer in every traktir across eleven time zones. Not least since the supposed "Miracle at Spala," where Alexei had been taken so ill that his imminent death had been announced in the newspapers, only for him to be saved by a telegram sent by Rasputin from his ever-more-luxurious house in Siberia.

"God has seen your tears," he'd told the tsarina, "and heard your prayers. Don't be sad. The little boy will not die. Do not let the doctors torment him too much."

AS THE WINTER SET IN, THE QUEUES OF THOSE DESPERATE TO meet the holiest man in all of Russia were so immense that many would sleep outside on the freezing street, waiting for him to return from any one of his plentiful nights out.

If her father had not demanded she help him, Militza would never have gone anywhere near Rasputin's apartment. He'd obviously realized by now that he'd lost the icon of St. John the Baptist, but still she did not want to answer any of his questions. However, there was conflict in the air. The Balkans were in crisis, and her father had declared war on the Ottoman Empire and needed Russia's help. It was her duty to use her connections and all the influence she had to get Nicky to agree to send his troops south. So, with Stana at her side, they set off in the car in the hope of persuading Grisha to help them.

"Whatever we do, we don't talk about the icon, or even mention the icon," said Militza. "And if he asks, we deny all knowledge."

"Surely he'll think he lost it in the woods while he was running from Stolypin's wolves."

"I'm sure. And perhaps he feels a little foolish for losing it."

"Absolutely," Stana sighed.

They sat in silence as they drove through the city.

"Nothing infuriates me more than having to go on bended knee to him," said Militza suddenly as she stared out the window.

"It is Father's will," replied Stana. "And we all know about Father's will," she laughed wryly. "What he asks, we do."

"What he *demands*."

"Yes, what he demands, no matter how badly it turns out for us."

"I have no idea why he decided to declare war on the Ottoman Empire in the first place," said Militza. "It's foolish to enter into a war you aren't sure you can win."

It was a cold, blustery afternoon, and the gray St. Petersburg streets were full of crepuscular characters bent against the vile wind as they walked, and the normally calm waters of the Fontanka were being whipped into wild white horses as they crossed over the bridge. There was a storm on its way. A brigade of soldiers was marching along the center of the road, past a meeting of factory workers on one corner, where a young man was standing on a box, his arms gesticulating as he shouted slogans at the receptive crowd.

"What are they talking about?" mused Stana as they drove past.

"Defending our Slavic brethren over the Ottoman infidels?" suggested Militza.

"Or the cost of bread?" Stana turned to her sister. "Nikolasha says it is quite bad out there in the countryside."

"It is always bad in the countryside," replied Militza. "That's why the towns are so full."

As they drew up outside Rasputin's apartment, the true extent of his popularity became clear. There were at least two hundred people waiting patiently in an orderly line on the pavement; meanwhile there was another group of men standing across the road. They were dressed in thick coats and warm fur hats, their hands firmly in their pockets as they walked around, scuffing their shoes in the mud, with apparently little else to do.

"Is that . . . ?" Stana peered through the window.

"The Okhrana."

"They don't look terribly secret for secret police."

"They monitor his every move."

"Why?"

"Everyone wants to know everything, I suppose."

"Look at the queue," sighed Stana. "Does he know we are coming?"

"I'm told so," said Militza. "I am glad you are with me—I am not sure I could face this on my own."

The sisters made their way up the back stairs, as instructed, bypassing the slumbering queue of women who squatted on the main steps. The back stairs were reserved for Rasputin's private visitors: aristocrats or certain ladies who'd taken his fancy the night before. They were steep and narrow and smelled strongly of spilled vodka and stray cats. It was not the sort of place anyone would want to spend any time in, and yet, as the sisters came to the top of the stairs and the door into his apartment, there were three women waiting on the small landing.

"Excuse me," announced Militza, holding her skirts up with both hands for fear of them dragging along the filthy floor.

"Ssshhhh," replied one of the women. "He's praying."

They all stood, ears cocked against the closed door, listening intently to the noises emanating from the other side. First there was the scraping sound of furniture being moved around, and then a woman shrieked, only once, before she laughed and there was silence. And then after a minute there came the rhythmical shunting, grunting sound of sex. It started slowly, like a train leaving the station, then gathered pace as it rattled along the track. It went quicker and quicker and was accompanied by the sound of a hand slapping against the wall. Finally there was a loud groan—from her or him, it was impossible to say. And then it stopped as suddenly as it had started.

"He is finished." The woman nodded, her tone and expression entirely matter-of-fact. "You may enter."

WALKING INTO HIS APARTMENT, MILITZA WAS IMMEDIATELY struck by how little it had changed since she'd last been there. The corridor with the coat pegs and the sitting room with the round table were just as they were. What was surprising, though, given the sounds they had just heard from the back room, was that the seats around the table were full of women, waiting, about fifteen in total. Some were drinking tea; others were knitting, or sewing, or reading religious texts, or sitting on their hands, their backs straight, their eyes focused on the closed door.

"Militza Nikolayevna? Anastasia Nikolayevna?"

The sisters looked around the room. There in one corner, eating boiled eggs dipped in salt, was Anna Vyrubova—and sitting next to her was another of the tsarina's closest confidantes, Lily Dehn. Lily Dehn was new to the Rasputinki, but she was one of his more fervent supporters. She had recently very publicly taken against the governess to the imperial family, who'd also, very publicly, complained about Grisha's unsupervised, late-night visits to the grand duchesses in their rooms. And while most of Moscow and St. Petersburg was up in arms at such a transgression of protocol, Lily let it be known that the governess was simply mad with jealousy and was constantly throwing herself like some lovelorn schoolgirl at Grisha herself. The poor governess was relieved of her post, while Lily Dehn continued to destroy her reputation.

"Have you come to join our little club?" she asked, eyeing the sisters up and down with deep suspicion. What on earth did the "Montenegrin sibyls" want with their man?

"Your club?" questioned Stana, looking around the room at the eclectic collection of women. Granted, some were young, and some were young and beautiful, while some were clearly with their mothers, but the majority were middle-aged and matronly or, like Anna, blessed neither with looks, nor charm, nor any figure to speak of.

"Yes," said a large woman who had a thicker mustache than the young officer who'd hammered at Militza's door in the dead of night all those months ago. "We're the ten o'clock club. We meet here every morning at ten and wait for a meeting with Our Father."

"Your father?" Militza frowned.

"Our Father Grisha. We wait to speak to him, hear his words, be blessed by him. Sometimes he is pleased with us and sometimes he is not."

"And what happens when he is not pleased with you?" asked Stana.

"Grisha strikes whoever doesn't please him," she replied.

"And the harder he strikes, the closer we become to God," added another.

"For it is only through punishment that you can reach salvation," said a third.

Stana looked across at her sister.

"Sometimes we come and ask to be beaten," said the large woman, smiling. "Our Father always says, 'If you mean to do wrong, first come and tell me.' And if he can, he will beat the wrong out of you." She nodded and picked up an egg, dipping it into the small saucer of salt in front of her before popping it into her mouth.

"Shall I tell him you are here?" suggested Anna, her round

eyes constantly moving between the two sisters. "I am normally the person who does the introductions. I supervise who goes in and out . . ."

"Mamma!" declared Rasputin as he strode out of the back room, his shirt hanging loose over his trousers. He held his left hand across his stomach, his right hand aloft as if blessing the sisters. "I heard you were here!" He made the sign of the cross. "Bless you, for coming! Tea? Or wine?"

His arrival sent a current of electricity through the group. The women sat up, tweaked their white shirts, adjusted their plumed hats, straightened their silk skirts—and they all smiled. It was as if they were debutantes at a ball, all trying to catch a suitor's eye. His warm embrace of the two sisters sent a frisson of jealousy around the room.

"Come," he said, ignoring the expectant, upturned faces. "Come through here so we can talk."

"Shall I come and help?" asked Anna, getting authoritatively out of her chair.

"No," replied Rasputin, waving his hand, without a backwards glance.

Militza and Stana followed him through to the back room, which, even in the dying light of the day, appeared to be in terrible disarray. The sheets on the divan were crumpled, there were half-drunk glasses of wine and Madeira on the table, and the stuffy air reeked of sweat and sex. Militza glanced at the divan, expecting to see some exhausted well-ridden woman gathering up her skirts, but the room was empty. The healed acolyte must have fled down the back stairs.

"Now," he said, patting the still-warm patch on the divan. "Sit and tell me why it has taken you both so long to come and see me?"

His question surprised them. There was no mention of the icon, no mention of the last time Militza had seen him, when he'd begged for her help. They came out with their excuses, pretended that they had tried many times to see him; many times they'd drawn up their cars or their carriages, but there had simply been so many people, or they had not wanted to disturb him. They'd glanced at him at court, but he was always so occupied.

"Everyone wants me," he confirmed, nodding magnanimously. "And I just can't help them all."

He poured himself a large glass of Madeira. Militza leaned forward, her father's request on the tip of her tongue. Rasputin raised his hand and immediately began to recount his visits to the palace, his close and intimate conversations with the tsar and tsarina, as well as the numerous times he'd been called up to help the Little One. On and on he went, describing each crisis, each episode, and how terribly grateful the weeping tsarina always was, how much she relied on him. And eventually how only his telegram to Spala had saved the heir to the throne and indeed Russia and the empire itself.

"Extraordinary," agreed Stana.

"I wonder . . ." began Militza. "I have a note here from my father." Up went the hand again. "I'll leave it here." She pushed the envelope, with its thick red royal wax seal, across the table towards him.

He glanced down at it briefly before he continued on. The more he drank, the more his chest expanded and the more pompous his attitude became. It became increasingly obvious that he was no longer talking to them, but was recounting some well-rehearsed stories and anecdotes that he told to everyone, anyone. The two sisters had ceased to exist; they were simply his audience. And all that was left was Rasputin himself.

CHAPTER 32

FEBRUARY 22, 1914, ST. PETERSBURG

I T WAS NOT UNTIL SOME MONTHS LATER THAT THE SISTERS realized quite how duplicitous Rasputin had been.

A few days after listening to his drunken, boastful ramblings in the overheated, sex-soaked room, Stana and Nikolasha had managed to speak to the tsar in private. As Nikolasha was commander in chief of the army, his opinions, ideas, and advice were important to the tsar, no matter what minor tribulations went on between both their wives, so they were invited to a meeting in his office in Tsarskoye Selo, where they fervently pleaded with the tsar that Russia should commit to helping Montenegro in the Balkan War.

Their argument was quite simple: since Montenegro had backed Russia during the ill-fated Russo-Japanese War, it was now time for the tsar to honor their alliance and stick up for his staunchest ally, Stana's father. They were family, after all. They left the meeting buoyed by Nicky's response, safe in the knowledge that

Rasputin would meet with the emperor later that day to shore up the plan. After all, they'd left him the letter and had sat, listening attentively, while he'd drained a couple of bottles of Madeira and talked endlessly about himself for over two hours.

Except that was not what happened.

IN FEBRUARY, WHILE THE POOR STALKED THE SNOW-COVERED streets looking for food and the threat of war hung ominously in the air, the court celebrated the wedding not of the decade but perhaps the entire century.

The union of Princess Irina Alexandrovna, the only daughter of the tsar's sister Xenia and Grand Duke Alexander, with Prince Felix Yusupov, the richest and most eligible prince in all of Russia, was quite some match. The beautiful, aristocratic, educated Irina, the emperor's only niece, was regarded as the finest catch in the empire, and for her to marry the empire's richest prince made the ceremony and the party afterwards the ultimate social occasion.

The wedding was held in the private chapel at the Anichkov Palace, and the bride arrived in a state coach pulled by eight white horses. She eschewed tradition, and instead of wearing the usual court dress with a kokoshnik, she wore a silk satin gown of the latest fashion, stitched with silver thread, with a rock crystal tiara from Cartier holding in place Marie Antoinette's lace wedding veil. The groom, as he had no rank in the army or official military roll, wore a dark frock coat embroidered with gold-and-white broadcloth trousers. She was led down the aisle by the tsar himself, who gave her twenty-one uncut diamonds as a wedding present; he also bequeathed Prince Yusupov unlimited access to the Imperial Box at the theatre in lieu of his original gift—a position at court—which the young prince had turned down.

It was indeed a splendid occasion, a glitter of expensive jewels, rich silks, and dashing uniforms, with the receiving line into the reception over two hours long. And while the happy couple stood there, along with their parents, accepting congratulations from the guests, everyone else sipped champagne, ate spoonfuls of caviar, and talked about the terrible increase in hostilities both at home and abroad, while occasionally glancing out of the windows at the canal and the gray streets below.

"What did you think of the dress?" asked the Grand Duchess Vladimir, her Bolin diamond-pearl tiara quivering.

"I thought it was beautiful," replied Stana, taking a sip of her champagne.

"I thought it quite dull in comparison to the usual court dress; quite why Xenia let her wear that I have no idea." She smiled, before proffering up her small plump hand. "Do you like my little Christmas present to myself?" On her index finger glinted a large cabochon ruby ring, the size of an emperor beetle. "Cartier." Since her husband's death almost five years before, Maria Pavlovna had been in receipt of one million rubles a year as a pension, which she had mostly spent on jewelry.

"It is beautiful," said Militza, for it was indeed stunning.

"I hear your Friend is opposed to going to war," Maria said, retracting her hand and taking a large swig from her glass. "Don't look so surprised!" she continued. "I thought you knew? Only the other day he was asking the tsar not to engage with the Ottomans."

"When was this?" asked Nikolasha.

"Not long ago," said Maria. "I heard he was actually lying on the floor, begging him not to support your lot."

"Begging?" asked Nikolasha.

"That's what I heard." She smiled.

"Begging?" he repeated, a look of horror on his face. "That man will stop at nothing. Can you believe it?" He turned to look at Stana. "After all that?"

"He's moving apartments too," continued Maria.

"Where?" asked Militza.

"Gorokhovaya Street—number sixty-four, fourth-floor flat, apparently. A grubby street," she said. "The tsar's paying his rent—one hundred twenty-one rubles a month. But it is very close to the train station, with a direct line to Tsarskoye Selo."

"You seem very well-informed, Maria," declared Nikolasha.

"Of course I am," she laughed. "I had tea the other day with that weasel Anna Vyrubova—that woman knows more than the Okhrana and is stupid enough to answer any question you ask!"

"Who knows more than the Okhrana?" quizzed a small, neat man with a wide face and brown, thinning hair. "Oswald," he said, introducing himself. "Oswald Rayner, I am a friend of Prince Yusupov's from Oxford University."

"Good evening," responded Militza, nodding. There was something about the fellow she found appealing. His face was intelligent and his manner charming; it was easy to see why the prince had befriended him. "We were just talking about an acquaintance of ours."

"Who is a dear, close friend of Rasputin," added Maria. "If you know who he is?"

"I have learned not to mention him by name," laughed Mr. Rayner. "Talk of Rasputin is more dangerous than Rasputin himself."

Nikolasha and Stana were too furious to stay any longer at the wedding. Nikolasha was more humiliated than annoyed; he'd trusted the Siberian to speak to the tsar, he had believed he would help them—and to have been outplayed by a peasant wounded him greatly. This was not a trifle, a little game. This was war.

THE NEXT MORNING STANA TELEPHONED HER SISTER.

"I don't know what to do," she said. "Father is furious. He was relying on Nicky to back him and Nikolasha said it was simple enough, but now Rasputin's changed everything. That man is totally out of control. He is conducting the orchestra while the rest of us just sit in the stalls. We have to do something."

"We need to think, Stana. Let's not be rash."

"Rash!"

"We need to come up with a plan."

"No, dear sister, *you* do."

MILITZA BROODED. SHE SPENT HOURS IN HER SALON, CONTEMplating what she should do. It was five days later, at the Countess Marie Kleinmichel's Persian Ball in honor of her three young nieces, that she realized she could wait no longer.

A masked ball? For three hundred guests? For which Léon Bakst, the celebrated costumier for Sergei Diaghilev's Ballets Russes, designed the majority of the costumes? The countess had been besieged by so many people wanting to watch the proceedings, there had been talk of allowing them to view from the balconies above. But in the end, the countess put her foot down and decided she wanted to seat every guest for a midnight supper and a total of three hundred was all her kitchen could manage. The ball opened with an Oriental quadrille, followed by an Egyptian dance, a Cossack dance, a traditional folk dance, and a Hungarian folk dance. The costumes were stunning—caftans of golden thread, capes trimmed with sable, blue silk pantaloons, crimson jackets, silver lamé turbans; the champagne flowed, the caviar circled the room, and everyone was quite breathless with excitement.

It was billed as the ball to end all balls and it certainly was. It was the last great ball in Imperial Russia before the outbreak of the First World War, the last time the court was to dance in all its finery. Not that anyone knew that that evening. Indeed, the opulence and profligacy, the purchase of such extravagant costumes for one night only, was not questioned by any of the guests. They were used to dancing while the rest of St. Petersburg starved and shivered—why would it not continue forever?

Stana danced most of the night, watched by Nikolasha, who, although reputedly a fine dancer, preferred a spectator's view. Peter asked each of the Kleinmichel daughters for a quadrille, hoping that others would be as generous with his own daughter, while Militza was deep in conversation with Mr. Rayner. Prince Yusupov's Oxford University friend, although wearing a red turban, had decided against the remainder of his costume, preferring a simple white tie in lieu of the loose blue silk trousers that he'd been offered earlier that evening.

"What is it with the Russians and dressing up?" he asked an amused Militza. "Why can't they have a normal evening? With normal food. In normal clothes. It's exhausting!"

"I suppose there are so many parties it's the only way to differentiate one from the other," she replied.

"Yes," he said. "The season here is like no other I have ever witnessed. The relentless hedonism is something else. And quite why anyone would want to go to a party dressed as a Hun is beyond me." He drank his shot of vodka and pushed an irritating feather out of his face. "Particularly during this time—and for you it must be very galling indeed." He nodded.

"Me?"

"Being from Montenegro and your father not securing help from the Russians," he replied. "It's almost as if someone's rubbing salt into wounds."

"Yes." Militza laughed lightly—the man seemed remarkably *au courant*. "And what are you doing here?"

"Nothing much," he replied. "Seeing friends. I'm thinking of renting a little flat on Moika."

"So you will be staying with us long?"

He nodded. "I think things might be getting a little interesting here."

"Interesting? I think you flatter us, Mr. Rayner," declared Militza, taking a large sip of her drink and walking towards the other side of the ballroom.

"So do you like my friend?" asked a rather inebriated voice in the crowd.

"Prince Yusupov," declared Militza. "I didn't recognize you with all the feathers and the turban. Are you not on honeymoon?"

"I leave tomorrow," he said, with a wave of his slim hand. "Paris, where we know far too many people. So I am sure we shall have to slip off somewhere else if we are to find any peace; I'm quite fond of Egypt, what do you think?"

"Good," agreed Militza. The man was very obviously drunk; his pale eyes were staring at her, one slowly closing independently from the other, and he was clearly in a combative mood. She made as if to walk away.

"So, do you like my friend?" he asked again, taking hold of her upper arm.

"He's charming," she replied, looking furiously at his grip. Like father, like son. He loosened it.

"Well, I don't like *your* Friend," he said. "Rasputin!" He practically spat his name as he staggered back a step or two.

"I thought you were friends—or at least your friend Munia Golovina and her mother are most certainly close to him."

"What a charlatan he is! The man tried to hypnotize me the other day. To cure me, he said. What an utter fraud!"

"I think you might have drunk a little too much." She smiled gently. "It might have warped your judgment."

"You're the one with warped judgment. You're the one who brought this evil charlatan into all our lives."

"That is not true."

"Who found him? You. Who introduced him to the court? You. Who championed him? You. Who helped him infiltrate the imperial household? You. Who paraded him around St. Petersburg?

You. Your house, your palace, Znamenka . . ." He paused, his lips curling with hatred. "That palace is the axis of all that is evil in this world, and you are the personification of all that is evil. You have opened Pandora's box, my dear, and . . ." He paused again, staring at her. "And you have no idea how to close it." He turned as if to leave, and then he stopped, swaying a little as he spoke. "I pity you. You think you are so very clever. But you are not. Your monster is out of control, Madame! It's gorging itself on power, girls, and alcohol. While you? You think it will be fine, but it won't. You suffer from hubris, dear lady, hubris. And it will defeat you in the end!"

THAT NIGHT MILITZA FOUND IT IMPOSSIBLE TO SLEEP. SHE was haunted by images that kept whirling and swirling round in her head. Felix Yusupov's furious, drunken, plumed head berated and hectored her all night, as did vibrant images of Rasputin— his blessings, his healings, his filthy fingers being licked clean, his laughing, his dancing, the smell of his fetid breath and the rough touch of his hands, as well as his haunting voice in her ear: "Naughty girl . . . Naughty girl . . . Naughty girl."

As dawn broke, Militza lay covered in a cold sweat, staring at the gilt ceiling; her mouth was dry, her brain was exhausted, but her jaw was set, her mind made up. She must exorcise the beast: she must kill him.

Later that morning she called Stana and demanded they meet in a quiet corner of the Yacht Club—to discuss such a thing on the telephone would be unthinkable—although a discussion was not what actually took place.

"No," SAID STANA SIMPLY, HER DARK EYES WIDE WITH HORROR. "Are you insane? Have you been taking too much elixir? You don't look like you've slept at all." Her hand shook as she poured herself tea, spilling a little on the white linen tablecloth. How could it have possibly come to this? "Murder Rasputin?"

"Keep your voice down!" Militza's furtive eyes glanced around the club. "The walls have eyes and ears. The Okhrana know everything."

"I don't care who hears because I will not entertain such a thing."

"But he is out of control!"

"I know!"

"He's now so powerful, the other day the tsar sent him to look Stolypin's replacement in the eye to see if he was a 'good man.' And guess what?"

"What?"

"He wasn't. And guess what?" She paused and leaned across the table. "He's not the prime minister."

"That doesn't justify killing him," said Stana, stirring her tea.

"Doesn't it?" Militza felt her heart beat rapidly in her chest. "I don't know if you have noticed between quadrilles and appointments with your dressmaker, but you and I are not welcome at the palace anymore."

"No one is welcome at the palace; they don't see anyone."

"But instead of us advising, guiding, smoothing the ruffled feathers, it's them."

"Well, Nikolasha's heard that Anna thinks we only introduced Rasputin to the tsarina so that we might later use him as a tool to further our own goals." Stana took a sip of her tea. "It seems the tool no longer needs its master."

"When was the last time Alix was at Znamenka?"

"I can't remember."

"When was the last time Nicky spoke to Nikolasha, the cousin he loves so much?"

"I can't remember."

Militza sighed. "Felix Yusupov called our house the axis of evil."

"Well, his family have always hated Grisha."

"But I thought Felix didn't?"

"That was before Grisha tried to cure him"—Stana lowered her voice to just above a whisper—"of his lusts."

"Lusts?"

"Boys."

"Homosexuality."

"Yes." Stana nodded.

"Well, that's hardly a secret; the man has been dressing up as a woman ever since he could walk. And he'll tell anyone that he was so convincing as a girl he once caught the eye of King Edward VII!"

"Well, Grisha suggested he go to the gypsies in Novaya Derevnaya. He said they would soon coax it out of him!"

"The gypsies are his answer to every question."

Stana nodded. "Since when is murdering him the answer to yours?"

The argument went back and forth. The more Stana refused to discuss the idea or even entertain such a concept, the more Militza believed herself to be correct. Every time she pondered the future with him still in it, she was overcome with nausea and paranoia.

"I'm anxious, I'm worried," she whispered to her sister as the waiter came to clear away the tea.

"I think you need to speak to Dr. Badmaev about all the elixir you are taking," said Stana. "It's affecting your nerves."

"Are you scared of Rasputin?"

"No," Stana replied defiantly. "I just hate him. According to Nicky, 'Better ten Rasputins than a hysterical Alix.' Whatever Rasputin does, however duplicitous he is, he makes life more bearable at Tsarskoye Selo. He keeps Alix calm and so Nicky gives him what he wants. His prayers coincide with the recovery of Alexei, and now, after Spala . . ."

"That child of many prayers," said Militza, shaking her head.

"I could not take that away," said Stana. "Despite what he's done to our country and the war."

"The truth is you think he made all the difference to your wedding. You think it was all down to Rasputin that you and Nikolasha got married in the first place. Well, it wasn't. And the person who made the ultimate sacrifice for you was not him but me!" Militza stood up from the table. "So I don't need your help, I don't need your approval. I shall do this with or without you!" She looked at her sister. "Without you it is!"

And so she waited, as she knew she had to, although she was desperate not to. But she would only have one chance, so she bided her time and prepared. On her own, her magic would not be strong enough against him, for he was a formidable force. Quite what the Four Winds had found when they'd scoured the land looking for a *koldun*, she could not tell. But his magic was strong and his will was even stronger. Perhaps he had been born with a small tail? He certainly had two budding horns on the top of his head. Maybe he had been born with teeth? Or was he the product of three generations of illegitimacy? All she knew was that he had certainly signed a pact with the devil, using the blood of his left little finger. And it would take all of her powers to stand up to him. She would have to call on the magic of all the ancient sisters who'd gone before her to rid Russia of his evil soul. For days, she disappeared into her salon in Znamenka. She pored over her books while she played with the toenails she'd so painstakingly harvested from him and kept in a beautiful handcrafted box that had been given to her by Papus himself, inlaid with a large Martinist star, the symbol of the order. Rasputin had come willingly to her house, she reminded herself, a fact that would make the spell more powerful. She had not taken her trophies using force.

But the spells of the past seemed weak. What use was an old

spell and graveyard dust in his drink or food? "As the dead no longer stand up, may the body of Rasputin no longer stand, as the bodies of the dead have disappeared, may the body of Rasputin also disappear"—it all seemed so ineffectual. Brana could certainly find the graveyard dust and she might be able to sprinkle it on his food, but the idea he would suddenly keel over did not seem plausible at all.

She must think, she must plan—and all the while she kept reminding herself that she was the one who had the St. John the Baptist icon. She was the one who was protected and he was not.

So she waited for June 23, for midsummer's night and the feast of St. John's Eve; then, stepping out into the forest, her cape tied tightly around her, she could not help but think how much she missed her sister, of the summers they'd spent gathering herbs wet with morning dew. The last time they'd gone out together was years ago, when they'd tried to help Alix. The woman was so disloyal not to remember that, remember how they had helped her, how Militza and Philippe had come to her rescue when the fifth daughter was born. Funny how the poor child was not mentioned now, funny what people remember, funny what they choose to forget . . .

It was a beautiful night as she wove her way through the forest. The sky was clear and the sun low in the pale blue sky, trying in vain to set. She loved these white nights, where the days lasted forever and the city was not allowed to sleep. There was always a sort of madness in the air that made malefic spells trip more freely off the tongue. She was looking in the forest for foxgloves, known as dead man's bells, so Rasputin might hear them ringing in his ears; for hemlock grown in full sunshine so it would be more virulently poisonous—and, of course, for henbane. Brana had already secured a mandrake. She'd been dispatched two nights before with a sword and one of Nikolasha's borzois. Under strict instructions, she'd traced a circle, three times, around the plant and had tied the plant to the dog; then, while she covered her ears, she'd placed a plate of meat outside the circle so that the dog pulled up the plant as he lunged forward for the food.

While Militza wandered alone through the forest, Brana busied herself melting down a cross, fashioning the molten metal into a bullet. The only way to kill a *koldun* as powerful as Rasputin was to force a metal bullet through his heart.

It was about 6 A.M. by the time Militza came back to the palace with her foxgloves, hemlock, and henbane, all glistening with St. John's Eve dew; then the two women set to work. Militza fashioned a doll in the shape of Rasputin, just as she'd done all those years before, taking care to reproduce the large member that she and Stana had added out of foolishness. What an appalling act of folly that had turned out to be. She warmed the wax from a fresh corpse in her hands; it was a much softer, whiter fat than the wax she was used to, and there was something deeply unpleasant about the way it melted and slid all over her hands, covering them with the grease. The smell was acrid and made her eyes water, and she needed to be quick, for the poppet of fat would not keep its shape for long. She placed it in a small metal dish.

"Quick," she said to Brana. "Pass me the mandrake." Brana sprinkled the powdered mandrake into a glass of wine, dark and red, the color of blood for her drink.

"Kulla! Kulla!" she began, draining the glass in one. "Kulla! Kulla!" she repeated, her eyes flickering and her body swaying as she worked herself into a meditative trance. "Kulla! Kulla!" She picked up the small bullet made from the molten cross. "Kulla! Kulla!..." She pushed the bullet slowly into the chest of the poppet made of fat. "Kulla! Kulla! Blind Rasputin, black, blue, brown, white, red eyes. Blow up his belly larger than a charcoal pit, dry up his body thinner than the meadow grass, kill him quicker than a viper." She reached into her box and pulled out three of his toenails. "Kulla! Kulla!" she continued as she squashed them into the fat. "See these nail clippings, may he never be able to clamber out of his dead man's grave, may he never climb to heaven, may he always be in hell!" She looked up. "Brana, the window!"

Brana rushed to open the window as Militza sprinkled the foxgloves, the hemlock, and the henbane over the small metal dish, then lit the candle underneath it. Soon the little poppet began to sizzle in the dish. The doll melted, and suddenly the liquid and herbs all caught fire.

"I call upon the winds!" Militza had her eyes closed and her arms outstretched. "I call upon the winds to take this zagovor with all its maleficence and take it on the wind, find Rasputin, wherever he is." She opened her eyes a little; there was nothing but a light breeze coming through the window. "I call upon the winds! The Four Winds! I call upon them to take this zagovor, take it! Take it and find Rasputin!"

Suddenly the curtains billowed and there was a loud whistling as a huge gust of wind came charging through the window like a whirling dervish. Books and papers flew everywhere; glass and china smashed on the floor as the wind tore around the room, howling, moaning, weeping in Militza's ears. It wrenched at her clothes, lifted tables and chairs, flew paintings off the wall; it was so strong that she could not manage to open her eyes. And then suddenly it left. The curtains lay flat against the wall and the room was silent. Militza looked down. The metal dish with the bullet, the herbs, and the pool of melted human fat had disappeared. The spell had flown.

NOT LONG AFTER, MILITZA WAS WOKEN BY A TELEPHONE CALL in the middle of the night. Rasputin had been stabbed in the stomach by a noseless whore just outside his own house.

Militza smiled softly and went back to sleep.

CHAPTER 33

AUGUST 17, 1915,
ZNAMENKA, PETERHOF

THE CRYING, THE HAND-WRINGING, THE HYSTERICAL weeping lasted for days.

"Grisha is no more! Grisha is no more!"

The crowds chanted like a Greek chorus as they bore his semiconscious body off a steamer in Tyumen. The tsarina was prostrate with grief, unable to get out of bed, calling for all the elixirs Dr. Badmaev had in his little leather bag; she was more upset at the attempt on Grisha's life than the assassination of Archduke Franz Ferdinand and Austria-Hungary's declaration of war on Serbia, Russia's ally, a month later. The tsar was sleepless with anxiety; if the mystic died, who would help calm Alix's nerves and her painful heart? He was exhausted by the hysterics; he'd never prayed so forcefully for another man's life.

Meanwhile, the rest of the court held its breath. When could they celebrate?

For the first few days, his life was in the balance. The

noseless whore ravaged by syphilis, Khionia Guseva, had yelled, "I have killed the Antichrist!" as she dug the knife into his belly—and had managed to slice through his stomach so deeply his entrails had fallen out. The doctor stitched his gut back together—as well as his soul, apparently—on the dining room table by candlelight. But his pain and agony were so profound that the icon of the Virgin of Kazan hanging in the corner of Rasputin's house in Pokrovskoye was said to have wept tears of sympathy.

But he survived. He survived well enough that by the fourth day of his ordeal he was photographed sitting up in bed, looking sad, clutching his chest as he always did, exuding tremendous piety and religious fervor, all the while declaring that any nurses on the ward with him should be relieved of their corsets. It was, thus, a little easier for him to put his hand up their skirts.

Militza was furious; instead of freeing Russia from the clutches of this monster, she'd only succeeded in creating some sort of living saint—a saint with a newfound fondness for opium, to dull the pain of his assault, but a saint all the same, whose Lazarus-like recovery from a whore's knifing made him more remarkable than ever. The fact that the whore was an ex-lover of his was rarely, if at all, mentioned.

His return to St. Petersburg—now more patriotically named Petrograd—was a return to his old ways. Except this time with impunity. The queues outside 64 Gorokhovaya laced all the way down the street; the moaning from the back room divan was constant; the ten o'clock club was superseded by daily 10 A.M. telephone calls from Tsarskoye Selo on his new telephone, Petrograd 64646 (the number of 6s was not lost on Militza); and the Okhrana were no longer following him around as he walked the streets of Petrograd but chauffeuring him in his new private car.

With Nicholas away at the front, Rasputin's visits to see Alix, Anna, and the children became as regular as his visits to the banya and the nearby brothel. By now, dislike for the man had spread through every corner of the empire, and even previously loyal acquaintances of the imperial family and indeed other members of the imperial family could no longer hold their tongues. The Dowager Empress declared dramatically that unless Rasputin was removed from the court, she would move to Kiev . . . She moved to Kiev. Xenia and Sandro were equally vociferous in their distaste; they too were ignored.

And still Stana would not change her position. She simply refused to talk about the man. She even purchased one of the "Rasputin Is Not Discussed Here" signs on sale in the market around Nevsky and placed it very firmly on her mantelpiece in the salon. For many, this was a standing joke in the fine sitting rooms of Petrograd, but for her it was a little different. Her position was untenable. With Nikolasha as commander in chief of the army and Rasputin constantly speaking out against the war, Rasputin's and Stana's were two paths that would never meet.

By the spring of 1915, nearly four million Russians had been killed, wounded, or captured in the war. The situation on the front was becoming increasingly desperate. There was talk of a second round of conscription (commandeering all twenty-one- to forty-three-year-olds). There was panic in the countryside. These men could not go to fight! Who would sow and bring in the next harvest? Who would stop the rest of Russia from starving? There had not been a call-up of the second round since Napoleon's invasion in 1812.

In Petrograd itself the atmosphere was febrile and frightening. Rumor was rife and revolution was in the air; there were meetings and gatherings and speeches—the peasants had had enough, and the government and the imperial family were becoming a laughingstock, tellingly ruled by the Cock. All conversation began and ended with the name Rasputin. As did all verse.

> A sailor tells a soldier,
> Brother, no matter what you say,
> Russia is ruled by the cock today.
> The cock appoints ministers,
> The cock makes policy,
> It confers archbishops
> And presents medals and positions.
> The cock commands the troops,
> It steers the ships
> Having sold our motherland to the Yids.
> The cock has raised all the prices
> So the cock is mighty and powerful
> And rich with talents.
> Clearly this is no ordinary cock,
> They say it's fourteen inches long . . .
> Peasant women enjoyed the cock,
> And those in town as well,
> Once the merchant wives had tried it
> They had to tell the noble ladies too.
> Thus the holy man's cock gained so much power
> It might well have been made a field marshal.
> Soon it reached the tsar's palace
> Where it fucked all the ladies-in-waiting,
> And the tsar's maiden daughter too,
> But it fucked the tsaritsa most of all . . .

"Enough!" declared Militza, taking hold of the piece of paper. "Where did you get that?"

"They are all over the city," said Dr. Badmaev. "You can't move for stories or tales like this." He nodded out of the café window towards the street outside, where the pavements were bustling with soldiers. "I did warn you a long time ago. I said I didn't like him, and now he is not just unlikable, he is dangerous."

"You're talking to me as if it is my fault."

"Well, isn't it?" His dark eyes narrowed. "'Be careful what you wish for,' I think that is the saying."

"I didn't wish for anything," replied Militza indignantly.

"No?" he asked. "I seem to remember a conversation we had once."

"I am sure I can't recall it."

"There is something very unseemly about him, as if he was indeed manifested, or is perhaps a walk-in, when a maleficent soul floats around until he finds a benign host—and what could be a more benign host than a simple peasant from Siberia?"

"I am well aware of what a walk-in is," said Militza. "I have seen many in my time."

"Many?" Badmaev looked puzzled. "I have seen them rarely— and they always appear to be reasonable at first, but slowly the maleficent soul takes over. Like a cancer it eats away at the weaker, benign soul until the other withers, so that there are only flickers of the previous, little sparks that die over time, never to be seen again. I have only seen them a few times over my travels. Perhaps they are more usual in Montenegro?"

"Perhaps." Militza nodded.

She was behaving childishly, she knew it, but there was something about Badmaev's tone that worried her, something about the way he looked at her that chilled her to the bone. It was similar to the look the drunk Prince Yusupov had given her. If he also blamed her for Rasputin's rise from a Siberian backwater to the foot of the throne itself, it was only a matter of time before others followed. Rasputin would be her legacy. It was enough to make her wish she had never been born.

She only had one more card left to play: Stana.

If she could persuade her sister to join forces with her, if they could unite one last time, then together they stood a chance of defeating him. Together, their strength, coupled with the icon of St. John the Baptist, might well be enough to end this. For one thing was certain: after the stabbing and his resurrection in Siberia, she was not capable of ridding Russia of him all on her own.

So, with Peter away in Moscow, she invited both Stana and Rasputin for dinner at Znamenka. It was her last throw of the dice. Little did she know how effective it would be.

As she lit the candles in the dining room that night, her hand shook with nerves. She had not seen Grisha in over a year, not since the attempt on his life, and was more than a little anxious lest he knew it had been her doing. Had he heard her spell on the wind? Did he know how she really felt? The rumors, the testimonies to his "supernatural forces," were so rife; his ability to read thoughts, see souls, and raise the dead was no longer questioned. If you were to lure the devil to your chamber, she thought, with the intent of doing him harm, surely the devil would know? She glanced over at the shelf next to the fireplace; there she could see the glint of the small frame of the icon of St. John the Baptist, hidden behind some books. She prayed it would keep her safe.

"Philippe, Maître, Friend," she muttered under her breath. "I need you now."

Stana arrived fresh from tea and a game of bezique with the Grand Duchess Vladimir, who despite the awfulness of the war was still trying to enjoy her summer as best she could, preferring to stay out of the city as much as possible.

"She says she wants to keep away from the awful proletariat," laughed Stana as she sipped her champagne. "I am not really sure she knows what the word actually means! But the word is *à la mode* and she loves to discuss things *à la mode*, while she happily spends a lifetime's wages on a little bibelot from Cartier!" She stopped and noticed the table was laid for three, not the two she was expecting. "Are we to be joined?" she asked. "Roman? Marina? Nadezhda?"

"Grisha," came Militza's explosive reply.

"Grisha!" Stana put her glass down as her cheeks blanched white. "Well, I am afraid I shall have to leave, I would rather die than spend a second in that man's company."

"Please don't go!"

There was something about Militza's tone that stopped Stana in her tracks. For the first time ever in her life she detected a note of vulnerability in her sister's voice.

"Why?"

"Because we need to change the course of events," she whispered, "and I need your help to do that."

"What do you mean?"

"It's our fault he is here. We asked for him, we called upon the Four Winds, and we created a monster and now . . ."

"And now what?"

". . . we must kill him."

"No, I will not," said Stana adamantly. "I have told you before, I do not want his blood on my hands."

"If not us, then who? When did you last see him?" asked Militza.

"I don't know. I try not to think about him. Nikolasha won't have him in the house; Rasputin offered to come and see the troops the other day at Stavka, saying his arrival might boost morale, but Nikolasha said he'd see him hang if he came anywhere near the front."

"You have no idea how awful he has become?"

"I hear . . . I hear stories . . ."

"Then you know he is now more powerful than ever. And with Nicky at the front, he's been left to run riot. Alix does what he says. Especially after he saved Anna Vyrubova's life after that appalling train crash, he can do no wrong. Everyone thinks it's Badmaev's drugs that are sending the tsarina mad, but it is him. It is just her and him. In charge. With Nicky apparently too stoned or incapacitated to care. He is atrophied by indecision and the war, and so the other two try to rule. It is a disaster. He's unstoppable. Some members of the court offered him money, two hundred thousand rubles plus a house, a monthly allowance, and bodyguards, if he'd go back to Siberia, never to be seen again—and do you know what he said?" Stana slowly shook her head. "'You think Mama and Papa will allow that? I don't need money; any old merchant will give me what I need to hand out to the poor and needy.'"

"What a charlatan," said Stana quietly. "His house is crammed with gold and precious things."

"I know!" Militza nodded. "And it will only get worse. I need you to see him. I need you to see him—*it*—in the flesh. I need you to understand the gravity of the situation. Please, please stay."

Stana nodded and slowly sat back down in silence. She remembered the kiss and how her sister had always stood by her; she remembered the sacrifices, the sordid sacrifices Militza had made for her, and she realized it was time she did something in return. It was time to pay back.

"Ha-ha-ha!" A weird chortling noise came from outside the room. The door opened and in walked Rasputin, his hair dramatically unkempt. His gait was lurching and his gaze swiveled around the room; it was as if he'd been exhumed or pulled out of a party by his legs. "Two . . . little . . . witches . . . in . . . one . . . room!" he sang, trotting around on the spot, holding up the edges of his loose black caftan. "Two little witches in one room." He leered at the sisters, his smile wolfish as he danced towards them. "Two little witches! One!" He pointed at Stana. "Two!" He jabbed his finger at Militza. "In one room!" He laughed loudly, throwing his blackened mouth in the air, before collapsing with a loud sigh onto the divan closest to the unlit fire. "It's cold!" he declared loudly.

"Grisha, it is August, not even the tsarina has a fire in August," replied Militza.

"Grisha, how delightful to see you," began Stana in a singsong voice she reserved for dull society parties or other people's children. "How are you?"

"How am I?" he asked as he rolled around on the divan, attempting to sit up a little straighter. He was clearly in a lot of pain. "Death is near me, she is crawling towards me on her hands and knees like a whore." He gestured loosely towards the door. "And when I die, what no one knows is that Russia will perish along with me." He inhaled and belched loudly. "The country will be tormented, it will tear itself apart, limb from limb, and the river Neva will flow with the blood of grand dukes!"

Stana looked across at Militza; how much had the man drunk to reach this level of morbidity?

He continued on until they sat down for dinner, bemoaning his fate and the fact that his and Russia's demise were inextricably linked. He sat at the head of the table and monopolized bottle after bottle of his favorite Madeira. Rasputin would normally not have eaten any of the meat on offer, but that night, he couldn't avail himself of enough flesh; he gnawed at the bones of his partridge and sliced sliver after sliver off the haunch of venison placed next to him. And all the while he talked about his approaching death. They, the people, were all lining up to kill him, women with guns in their dresses, young men with knives in their breeches—it was not hard to imagine a revolutionary hurling a bomb through his window at any minute.

"And then there's poison!" he said, his knife raised in the air. "But I have protected myself against that."

"How does anyone protect themselves from poisoning?" asked Stana, still using the singsong voice.

"Taking little drops at a time," he said, waving his knife from side to side.

"Mithridatism," said Militza.

"Eat apple pips," he added. "Stones of peaches and apricots. All day, every day. Ground up in water. Cyanide can't touch me!" He coughed. "But it is dangerous out there—and now I no longer have the icon."

"The icon?" asked Militza, suddenly feeling nervous.

"The one you kindly gave." He smiled briefly.

"St. John the Baptist?"

"I lost it long ago," he sighed, wearily, slumping a little at the table. "Long, long ago . . ."

"You lost it?" Militza feigned surprise well.

"I don't know where or when. I was traveling and I mislaid it. I try and see it in my mind, picture it hiding in the long grass by the side of the road. How I feel its loss greatly. How I need it now. Without it, I shall surely die. For death is near me, she crawls towards me . . ."

"Yes, yes." Militza smiled. "Enough!"

He paused, his eyes narrowed. "Maybe it was stolen from me?" He looked wildly around the room.

"Surely not!" exclaimed Stana.

"I have trophy hunters in my house all the time; they steal the hair off my head and the nails off my toes as I sleep." He laughed wryly. "And now She's given me bodyguards because She fears for my safety."

There was no need to ask who She was.

"She needs me, you see." His face changed to one of mocking sympathy. "She ne-e-e-eds me!" He laughed. "She needs her Friend. 'Our Friend.'" He looked down the table at the two sisters. "I'm the only one she's got!" He laughed.

"How about Anna and Lily?" inquired Stana.

"Anna? That old cripple! I am worth a thousand of them," he replied, digging his fork into his venison and eating another slice. "No one can satisfy her like I can!" He laughed again.

"I am not sure I understand you," said Stana.

"You're a woman of the world, little witch!" he replied. "But I am a man of God. And the poor woman has little left but her faith."

"We should all have faith," confirmed Stana.

"I am living a quiet life," he declared. "I visit the Little Mother and the Kazan and St. Isaac's cathedrals each day, that is all."

And the Makaev wine shop on 23 Nevsky, thought Militza, and the Villa Rhode and the Yacht Club and the banya up the road from Gorokhovaya and Madame Sonya's whorehouse not far from the Fontanka. He was a man of God with an exemplary record.

"But I feel the hand of God above me," he continued.

"His hand is above us all," said Militza.

"No." He turned to stare at her, his pale eyes suddenly finding focus. "You will live, my little witch. You will escape. You will breathe the fresh air of freedom. But God will come to gather me!"

He stared mournfully at his glass for a second, swilling its blood-red contents around. It was as if he could see nothing but misery, torment, and writhing pain within the spinning liquid.

"But one must not be sad!" he said suddenly.

"Indeed not," agreed Militza.

"We should have a party! Let's invite some gypsies." He looked around the room as if expecting it to be full of people. "We need music! Parties always need music. Do you have a gramophone?"

The footmen were called; a gramophone was found, as well as some records, and the sisters watched as Rasputin started to dance. They knew of the all-night parties that he hosted in his apartment, where the telephone was always ringing, the door was always open, and the wine never ran out. Munia once told Militza about a party where everyone had stayed over because they were all too drunk to leave, only for two husbands to arrive the next morning, each with a revolver, on the hunt for their wives. The secret police delayed the husbands long enough for the wives to dress and disappear down the back stairs, but Munia had been horrified and said she would never attend one of his parties again.

Rasputin moved slowly; his stomach was still clearly giving him some pain, but the more he drank, the less he cared. He held his arms outstretched and waved his hips from side to side, swaying along with the music.

"Oh, this!" he announced, closing his eyes, listening to the soaring sound of the violins. "This reminds me of Siberia. The space. The skies. And the plump peasant girls!" He laughed again, as if he were transported back there. "Dance with me!" he demanded, looking from one sister to the other. "Dance!"

"No, thank you." Militza smiled, taking a sip of her champagne.

"You!" He pointed at Stana. Stana shook her head. "I am the most powerful man in Russia and I command you to dance."

"Really, Grisha, no," said Stana.

"I *command* it!" he shouted.

"Thank you, but no," said Stana.

"Dance!" he spat. "I have people queuing down the street wanting to give me money, presents, paintings, carpets for five minutes with me, and you, you won't dance with me when I command it!"

"Just dance with him," hissed Militza.

Stana reluctantly rose from the divan. It was a sultry night and the air hung close; Rasputin smelled high and acrid with old sweat. He grabbed her and pulled her towards him as he rocked her from side to side. Stana's heart was beating fast. She was desperate to pull away from him, but his grip was firm, almost as firm as his shaft, which she could feel through the folds of her dress.

"Oh, Stana, Stana, Stana," he whispered in her ear, his spittle spraying the side of her neck as he spoke. "You've come to me at last. All those years, all those years I have watched, all those years I have longed for you . . ." He pulled her tighter towards him. "I knew you'd come in the end. Women can't resist power, my power, the power of Grisha, they bounce up and down on it like whores at an orgy. Come closer, my little whore . . ."

"That's it!" declared Stana, pushing him so hard in the chest that he stumbled back a step. "I am leaving. Good night, sister!" Grabbing her fan and her wrap, she ran out of the room and down the front stairs, bursting through the front door and out into the evening air. She inhaled deeply, looking up at the pale blue sky and the stars. What an odious creature that man was! Truly he was unbearable.

She glanced around the drive. Her car was on the other side of the fountain. She stumbled across past Rasputin's car, which was waiting, complete with Okhrana driver snoozing at the wheel. Stana opened her car door and slipped into the back seat. Where was her driver?

"You should be a little nicer to me," came a voice right next to her in the shadows.

Stana screamed. He covered her mouth with his rough, gnarled hand. How did he get there? How did he leave the palace more quickly than she? He truly was the devil himself! "Shhhhh," he hissed in her ear as he heaved himself on top of her. "I don't know who you think you are, little witch, but I control armies, I control governments, and I control the imperial family. You have not been nice to Grisha, and so Grisha won't be nice to you."

"I am a married woman!" spat Stana. "Leave me alone. I love my husband."

"Your husband?" He stared. "You wouldn't have that husband if it weren't for me. And what I have given, I can also take away."

"No, you can't. He's much more powerful that you, he's head of the army."

"No one is more powerful than Grisha."

"What utter rubbish, I am not afraid of you. I have never been afraid of you!"

"Silly girl." He smiled. "I shall have him sent to the Caucasus!"

He leaned forward and forced his hard tongue in her mouth. He worked his way deep down in her throat, jabbing and rolling it around, making sure he probed every corner, and then he licked her face, her cheek, and her lips as he slowly pushed himself off her. He opened the car door and slammed it behind him without another word. Stana was left, her clothes crumpled, her face covered in saliva, rigid with indignation and fury. Her driver suddenly got into the car, along with a trail of cigarette smoke.

"Sorry, Grand Duchess, I didn't see you leave the palace," he apologized. "Where to?"

"Home," she said quietly.

It took less than thirty-six hours for Nikolasha to learn he was to be relieved of his duties as commander in chief of the Russian forces. He was to be replaced by the tsar himself. He and his wife were told to leave the city, to move south. To the Caucasus.

CHAPTER 34

DECEMBER 16, 1916, PETROGRAD

IT WAS CHANCE. OR WAS IT?

How many things in life happen by chance? How many paths are preordained? How free is our own will? And how much is down to the Fates?

It had been over a year since the sisters had seen each other. With Nikolasha relieved of his post and sent south, Stana had been living in Tchair, their house in the Crimea, while Militza and Peter had been based in Petrograd and, of course, Znamenka. In normal times, the sisters would have managed to see each other, but times were anything but normal. There were riots in the streets, strikes in every province, rebellions in the cities, food shortages and power cuts everywhere; none but essential travel was advised, especially among members of the aristocracy—the stories of those who'd succumbed to banditry were too numerous to mention.

But a year in the Crimea, while lovely and most certainly full of charm, had left Stana desperate to see her sister and her nieces and nephew, so she finally made it to Petrograd in the middle of December, despite the war, the misery, and the constant fear of attack. Militza was beside herself with excitement.

"Are you sure it is open?" asked Stana as they sat, muffled together, holding hands, in the back of the car.

"I heard it was," said Militza. "Although nothing is sure these days."

"If not?"

"If not the Yacht Club, then I am not sure if anything else will be open—all the nice restaurants are shut because there is not much food in the city."

"It looks very different," said Stana, staring out of the window at the gray, intimidating streets.

"Yes—and it is dangerous to go anywhere alone at night," said Militza. "You never know who you might bump into."

They pulled up outside the club and looked up at the windows; a few rays of light seeped hopefully through the tightly shut curtains. There was a smell of boiled cabbage in the street as they picked their way through the salted slush on the pavement. Militza knocked on the door, and it was opened a crack; a pair of eyes looked her up and down.

"Grand Duchess Militza Nikolayevna," she announced, and the footman opened the door.

Upstairs in the dining room the place was packed. In comparison to the gloom and misery outside, here life was joyful; there was laughter—and most importantly of all, there seemed to be a fully functioning kitchen and plenty of wine. The textile workers might be on strike across town due to the shortage of bread, but here there was sturgeon, morels in a cream sauce, pommes dauphinoise and braised cabbage leaves, plus plenty of fine Bordeaux and even a small glass or two of champagne.

"He is unstoppable," said Stana, eating a little fish off her fork. "Nicky came to Kiev, and both Nikolasha and Minny told him to get Rasputin out of the palace." She leaned forward, her eyes glancing left and right. One never knew who was listening. "And Ella went to Tsarskoye Selo to plead with *her*. Her own sister—a nun—and she still didn't listen." Stana shook her head. "Apparently she drove her away like a dog! It is so, so sad."

Little did anyone know that it was the last time the tsarina would ever see her sister Ella again. Both would be brutally murdered, one day after the other, in less than eighteen months' time.

"But there is nothing to be done," continued Stana. "If the tsar persists in being ruled by his wife and his wife persists in being ruled by *him*—"

"Your Imperial Highnesses!"

Militza looked up. "Mr. Rayner?" she asked, a little unsure, for the light was behind him and the man appeared to have slicked back his hair. "Mr. Oswald Rayner?"

"Lieutenant Rayner now," he said with a little nod. "How very charming to see you again."

"Absolutely," agreed Militza.

"And how is your friend Yusupov?" inquired Stana.

"Quite well. Felix is even entertaining tonight, I believe," he said.

"I can't believe people still have the energy to entertain," said Militza, "with all that is going on around us. And fear standing at every street corner."

"Indeed, Madame, it's not quite the city it was, is it?" he replied with another nod.

"No," agreed Militza a little wistfully.

He looked from one grand duchess to the other. There was a pause, and they all three looked at each other. "Well, good evening to you both." He nodded. "I am on my way home."

And that could have been that. A chance meeting in the Yacht Club, a brief conversation, a quick crossing of paths. And nothing. They could have all disappeared into that gray night without consequence. Except Militza said something. Quite why, neither of the sisters ever knew. The Fates? The gods? Spirit? Perhaps it was all preordained . . . She was compelled to speak, she said later, didn't have time to think. The request just came flying out.

"Do join us, Lieutenant Rayner," she said. "It is awfully cold out there and the brandy here is delicious. I demand you stay and have one before you leave!"

Except Lieutenant Rayner did not have one brandy; he had three. And during the process of his drinking, he recounted Prince Felix Yusupov's last few meetings with Rasputin.

"He's been 'curing' him," said Rayner, his eyes shining over the rim of his crystal glass.

"I thought Felix couldn't stand Grisha?" said Militza.

"That much is true. He says Rasputin's eyes are like 'two phosphorescent beams of light, melting into a great luminous ring.'" Rayner smirked. "'They drew him 'nearer and then further away,' apparently he was 'powerless, powerless, in the full beam of his hypnotism!'" Rayner laughed loudly, and the sisters smiled briefly; they liked Lieutenant Rayner. "He is with him at the palace tonight!"

"The palace?" asked Militza.

"On Moika." Rayner nodded, taking another sip of his drink. "Rasputin's gone to meet Irina—apparently he's madly in love with her! As is everyone in Russia, of course. What's not to be in love with?"

"Irina Alexandrovna Yusupova?" asked Stana.

"Yes, that's right. He's desperate to meet her apparently! Weak at the knees! The old dog!" He laughed again.

"But that's impossible," said Stana.

"Why?" Rayner's smile disappeared.

"She is in the Crimea," said Stana. "I dined with her just before I left. And I arrived only today, so she can't possibly be here."

"Oh," he said and then scratched his head.

"Well, that is odd," said Militza. "Why would Prince Yusupov lie?"

Oswald Rayner, of the British Secret Intelligence Service, was remarkably garrulous for a man whose job it was to keep secrets. Maybe, as a British spy, he didn't take the plot seriously. The idea that the effete, spoiled prince he'd met at Oxford, the man he'd befriended at the Bullingdon Club, the man he'd spent wild nights with, drinking and dancing, watching him dress up in women's clothes and flirt outrageously with fellow students, the idea that he—a ponced-up peacock of a prince—could possibly be the perfect candidate to pull off the political assassination of the century was clearly some sort of joke to him. And the method? Some poisoned cakes laced with cyanide. Cakes? Only children dreamt of killing people with poisoned cakes!

"They're all there," he said, checking his watch. "About now!" He drained his glass. "Him and a few cronies, hoping the beast is going to eat a few madeleines and keel over!"

"Well, that won't work," said Militza, picking up the decanter and replenishing Rayner's glass.

"I know, I've told him!" agreed Rayner, taking another rather large slug of brandy. "If you want to kill someone, you really have to shoot them." He tapped his top left-hand pocket. "You need a bloody gun!"

"No, I don't mean that," said Militza. "Rasputin is immune to cyanide. He's been eating apple pips, apricot and peach kernels for years."

"Mithridatism," said Rayner, sitting up straight in his chair, suddenly very serious indeed. "Well . . ." He shrugged and scratched his head again.

Militza looked at her sister. Their time was now, right now, and they both knew it.

"Your gun?" asked Militza quite simply. "Is it loaded?" Rayner nodded. "Then come with me," she said, getting slowly up from the table. "Don't hurry," she said with a wide, generous smile, beaming around the room. "There is no need for any fuss."

Militza led the others straight into the kitchen. If this was to be their one and only opportunity, then there could be no margin for error. It was difficult to explain to the kitchen staff that they wanted herbs. Lots of herbs. Smoking a pistol with a bunch of sage was not a usual request. But the commis chef was Italian and viewed such bizarre Russian behavior as none of his business. Besides, the country was at war—anything was possible. So Rayner looked on as the two sisters burnt the sage over the stove and let the smoke curl around the muzzle of his pistol. They began to chant and mumble and mutter strange words in a language he did not understand; all he knew was something momentous was about to happen and that he, somehow, was going to have a part in it.

They walked out of the club and straight into Militza's waiting car.

It was two in the morning.

"The Yusupov Palace," said Militza to her driver.

"Really?" asked Rayner, sounding more than a little anxious.

"Absolutely," came her firm reply.

They all sat in silence as they drove through the side streets of Petrograd. The moon and stars were hidden, the streets empty save for a few drunks weaving their way home. It was a still night, not a breath of wind to stir the snow-covered pavements.

It was the perfect night for a murder.

"WHAT WERE YOU DOING BACK THERE?" ASKED RAYNER eventually as they edged towards Moika. "In the kitchen?"

"A smoked barrel never misses," said Militza frankly as she stared out of the window. "Here!" she said to the driver. "We don't need to park outside the palace, it is a good night for a walk."

"A walk, Your Imperial Highness?" asked the driver.

"Yes," she stated flatly. "It's an excellent night for a walk."

The three of them headed along the two blocks to the palace at 94 Moika. It was hard going in the thick snow, in silk shoes with leather soles, but neither of the sisters noticed. They were calm, focused on what they were about to do. They slowed just as they reached the railings to the courtyard at 92 Moika, adjacent to the Yusupov palace. They glanced up and down the road and across the canal. There was no one on the street. Militza nodded at Rayner, and he slowly nodded back at her, tapping his top pocket, where he'd placed his gun.

Suddenly they heard a door bang and spun around. Through the darkness they could see a figure staggering away from the side of the palace and running towards them. It lurched left and right, its knees buckling, falling and scrambling up again. It was roaring and yelling, screaming in pain like a mortally wounded animal. Suddenly another two figures burst out of the small door at the side of the palace in hot pursuit. One fired a gun, and a bullet whistled through the air, landing in a puff of snow. The next clipped the arm of the first figure, who screamed again in agony. Bang! came another. And finally the first figure skidded and slipped, only to fall right in front of them.

Rasputin lay flat on his back in the snow, blood seeping from his arm, blood seeping from his chest. His eyes were wide-open.

"Mamma," he whispered as he caught sight of Militza staring down at him. "You came."

"Shoot him!" she said quite calmly to Rayner.

"Me?"

"Yes, you! Now!"

Rayner whipped his British standard-issue Webley .455-caliber pistol out of his pocket and aimed it at the man lying in the snow. There was nowhere for Rasputin to run, nowhere for him to hide; he was cornered like a rat and about to die like a dog. Rayner's hand shook and Rasputin whimpered.

"Shoot!" shouted Militza. "Shoot him! In the name of the tsar and all of Russia—kill him!"

Rayner took aim. He held his breath, closed his eyes. He squeezed the trigger. And then . . . he couldn't. This was cold blood. An assassination. An execution. His shoulder relaxed for a second. Immediately, Militza grabbed the gun. Rasputin's eyes narrowed as he stared at her.

"Naughty girl," he whispered, just as she shot him straight through the forehead.

The screaming was unbearable as it ricocheted about the courtyard. Militza dropped the gun in the snow and covered her ears. The noise in her head and the pain in her heart were unbearable. The crows that had been nestling in the trees behind launched off their branches at the sound of the gun and dived and bombed and screeched around her. She covered her head as she slowly sank into the snow.

It was done.

"Good shot!" shouted Yusupov as he ran over to join them. "You?" He stopped in his tracks, looking stunned. "Militza Nikolayevna, you shot him! You shot Rasputin!" He smiled broadly as he looked down at her in the snow. "Good shot, good shot indeed!" He patted her on the shoulder and then turned to look at the body lying on the ground. "Do you think he's dead? Oswald?" He looked quizzically at his friend. "You're a man of the world, you know about these things."

"He looks dead to me," replied Rayner, his voice quiet.

Felix slowly leaned down and ripped the golden cross from around Rasputin's neck. "He was no man of God. He was the devil himself. The devil incarnate. Harder to kill than a rabid dog.

Twice we tried—and twice he rose again! For you, Madame," said Felix, handing Militza the cross, "a small trophy for your pains."

"Drown him," mumbled Militza.

"But he's dead," said Rayner.

"Drown him!" Militza was still kneeling in the snow. "Drown him."

"There's no need," said Prince Dmitry Pavlovich, who was standing behind Prince Yusupov. He moved forward and kicked the body for good measure, his young, fresh face beaming with delight. "He's dead. The beast is dead, all right! Long live the tsar! Long live Russia!"

"Drown him," said Militza, as slowly and as emphatically as her quivering lips would allow.

"Just to make sure?" queried Rayner.

"No," said Stana, looking down at her sister. "You cannot canonize a drowned man. You can't make a saint out of those who perish in water. A soul drowned in water can never come back. So do as my sister says—drown him."

"Where?" asked Prince Dmitry, looking at Yusupov.

"I don't know," said Felix, who suddenly shivered and retched dramatically. "I can't bear to look at him. He's the devil. Satan himself. Even now, lying there . . ."

In silence they all stared at the corpse, unable to take in what they had done. They were an unlikely group of murderers—two grand duchesses, two princes, a deputy from the Duma, a doctor, and an army officer, accompanied by a British secret agent.

Suddenly, there was a quiet thud and Militza looked to her left to see that Prince Yusupov had passed out cold in the snow. It was all clearly too much for him. It was going to be up to her to think of a way of disposing of the body.

It would be dawn soon. People would start to ask questions, and Rasputin's followers would be knocking on his door. Even the secret police might start searching the drinking dens of Novaya

Derevnaya, looking for their charge. There was no time, no opportunity for depth of deception or any finesse.

"Throw him into the canal," suggested Rayner. "The ice should
hold the body for a few days; that way we can clear our tracks."

"But where?" asked Prince Dmitry, looking from one to the
other.

"Petrovsky Bridge," suggested Militza. "It is not far and the
water is deep."

"We can use my car," offered Vladimir Purishkevich.

So first they bound Rasputin's hands and feet with a
cord they found in the back of Purishkevich's car. Next they took
Rasputin's fur coat out of the basement salon, where, earlier in
the evening, he'd been fed cakes laced with cyanide, and wrapped
him in it. And then, finally, in a panic, they tore a blue velvet curtain off the wall in the Yusupov Palace and rolled him up inside
it. They placed the body into the boot of Vladimir Purishkevich's
car and drove slowly, constantly stalling, with the body bouncing
around, to Bolshoi Petrovsky Bridge. Prince Yusupov, who was
not deemed well enough to come in the car, retired to the palace
in the company of his valet. Militza also insisted that Rayner take
Stana home; her car had been waiting on the corner for some two
hours now and was surely about to attract attention. Frankly, the
fewer involved in the disposal of the body, the better.

It was still dark when they finally arrived at the bridge. The
moon was hiding its face, almost as if it did not want to bear witness to the heinous crime going on below. However, the wind was
up, blowing a dank and bitter cold off the Neva.

Militza and Prince Dmitry watched as Purishkevich, Lieutenant Sergei Mikhailovich Sukhotin, and Dr. Stanislaus de
Lazovert struggled to throw the corpse over the side of the bridge
into the Malaya Nevka below. They removed the blue curtain, but

still they strained and pulled and tugged. Eventually, finally, they raised the body high enough to mount the barrier and they pushed it off the wooden railings into the icy water below. As the body fell through the ice, Sukhotin realized a galosh was missing. He scoured the bridge and, finding it, picked it up, and in his panic, he hurled it in the air. It landed on the bank, missing the river entirely.

The body refused to sink. Prince Dmitry had forgotten to load the corpse with the heavy chains he'd packed into the car. So it floated. The fine fur billowed out in the freezing-cold water, like some sort of sail.

Militza stared. Rasputin looked as if he were sleeping, his eyes closed as he lay on the surface.

"God forgive me," said Militza. "Forgive me, Grisha."

Her hand was shaking over her mouth as she stood, shivering, on the bridge. The relief, the loss, the horror of what she had done was so overwhelming that she ceased to feel anything. It was all too much to take in. She was numb. She looked down into the deep, dark water. Through the ripples, the cord around Rasputin's wrists appeared to loosen; his pale gray eyes gently opened and stared up at her as he sank, finally weighed down by his fur coat; his right hand moving slowly up and down, he made the sign of a cross.

EPILOGUE

Militza, Peter, Stana, and Nikolasha and all their children survived the 1917 revolution. They escaped off the beaches of the Crimea with some of their fortune, rescued by the British on HMS *Marlborough* in April 1919 along with Prince Felix Yusupov, his wife, Princess Irina, plus his parents, Princess Zinaida Yusupova and her husband, Count Felix Yusupov, as well as Grand Duchess Xenia and her mother, the Dowager Empress Maria Fyodorovna.

After a somewhat protracted journey, where they were deposited in Greece while the others continued on to Malta, Militza and Stana and their families ended up living in the South of France, where Grand Duke Nikolai eventually died in 1929, followed by Grand Duke Peter in 1931, and Grand Duchess Anastasia in 1935.

Militza lived on, only to become caught up in the Second World War. She left France for Italy to stay with her sister Queen Elena. But the situation became very unstable, and as the king and queen went into hiding, Militza ended up seeking refuge in a convent close to the Spanish Steps in Rome. A few months later she managed to escape to the Vatican, where she received sanctuary within the walls of Vatican City for three years. Eventually she escaped, along with her sister Elena and the rest of the Italian royal family, to Alexandria, Egypt, where she lived along with a myriad of other deposed royals, including King Zog of Albania, as a guest of King Farouk of Egypt. Grand Duchess Militza died in Alexandria in September 1951, aged eighty-five.

Several days after his murder, the body of Rasputin was found with a gunshot wound to the forehead. It was pulled out of the river from under the ice at Petrovsky Bridge. His lungs were said to be full of water, as if he had, in fact, drowned, and his hands had freed themselves from the cord that tied them and were raised as if he had been scratching at the ice, trying to get out.

ACKNOWLEDGMENTS

ALTHOUGH THIS IS A WORK OF FICTION, THE MAJORITY of the story is true, and I am deeply indebted to my dear friend, the journalist and ridiculously brave war correspondent Nikolai Antonov, who first told me about the "Black Princesses" all those years ago, in 1992, as we sat around his kitchen table in Moscow, drinking strong vodka and eating stronger pickles. His eyes shone as he wove a magical tale about these two beautiful young princesses who arrived from Montenegro, married into the Russian royal family, introduced Rasputin to the tsarina, and brought down an empire. "Power, magic, sex!" he laughed. We charged our glasses, and I promised him I'd write it as soon as I got home.

I didn't, of course, I ended up writing other things, but Nikolai would not give up. He called me often from Moscow, sharing little bits of information he'd discovered. They were hard women to track down. Being neither the victors nor male, they were usually consigned to the footnotes of history. But I do remember one telephone call from Nik, some ten years later and just days, in fact, before he died: he'd just found out the most fantastic fact and he had to tell me right away.

"The reason they were called the Black Princesses," he said and paused for dramatic effect, static cracking down the line, "was not because they had black hair, or because they liked black magic, but because they had black eyes! Black eyes," he repeated.

And I have been haunted by their black eyes ever since. Theirs was a story that would not give up or go away. It gnawed away at my subconscious, a monkey on my back for over twenty years, the sisters with their black eyes, their visions, their powers and what drove them. And the more I read, the more convinced I became of their crucial involvement in this extraordinary part of Russian history. The story of the succession, the tragedy of little Alexei—they were there. They supplied the gurus, the drugs, the spells, the incantations; they were there in the bedchamber; they were there at the parties and the balls. Confidantes, friends, allies, and supporters of a tsarina who must have carried guilt of the Hesse disease around with her like some toxic burden every day. Mother and murderer of her own son? There's nothing to ease that sort of pain. Not even Rasputin.

In the end, Nik was correct. It took me over twenty years, but I did write it. And during this protracted process, the list of people who helped me along the way is lengthy . . .

Firstly, I would like to thank the London College of Psychic Studies for their joyful, fascinating, inclusive, and inquisitive approach to life. Nowhere else can a complete novice learn to scry, read palms, study mediumship, and meet themself in a past life. I am extremely grateful to my teachers for their kindness, knowledge, and patience, most especially Robin Lown, who has put up with me in his palmistry class for the last four years.

I would also like to thank the amazing Katya Galitzine. Her knowledge of all things Russian is unsurpassed, her friendship is boundless, and she is the only person I know who would happily break into Znamenka with me, marching up that daunting tree-lined drive, just as the sun was setting, as if it were the most natural thing in the world. I have bored her with my questions, raided her bookshelves, and sat for hours in the stunning Prince George Galitzine Memorial Library in St. Petersburg, where I researched a lot of this book, taking notes from its volumes of incredible and rare books. Thank you.

There have been many other generous and kind friends who have helped and supported me along the way. The wonderful Daisy Waugh, who kept me going, plying me with wine, pizza, life-affirming good advice, and supportive tarot! The incredible Jessica Adams, writer, astrologer, and very good friend whose wise words, knowledge of the world of magic, mystery, and spirit, and ability to manifest cabs at 2 A.M. are invaluable.

There are many others who listened to me endlessly discuss Militza and Stana and what they did, and what they might have thought, worn, ate, chatted about. For your patience, allowing for my repetitious anecdotes and one-track-mindedness, I thank you: Candace Bushnell, Claudia Winkleman, Sarah Vine, Anne Sijmonsbergen, Sean Langan, Ciara Parkes, James Purefoy, Sebastian Scott, Peter Mikic, Susanna Michaelis, Jennifer Nadal, Rebecca Frayn, Joanne Cash, Eleanor Tattersfield, Bella Pollen, Katie Walker, and, very especially, Tina Cutler and the fabulous Jane Gottschalk. Your wit, wine, and wisdom were gratefully received.

My sister, Leonie, the saint, who read, reread, and re-reread the many versions of the manuscript until 3 A.M., thank you. My stepfather, Colin Campbell—you edit like a dream. My incredible mother, Scarlett, you rock! My wonderful, handsome husband, Kenton—for listening to yet another anecdote or idea like you've never been asked the same question before.

Special mention goes to my agent, Eugenie Furniss, who walked with me every step of the way with this—nearly ten years in the writing as she read and retweaked and reread and edited and advised—thank you! You are a very good friend.

To my wonderful editor, Sara Nelson, who got it. To all at

HarperCollins—you're brilliant and fabulous and a joy to work with—thank you. And to Michael McCoy at Independent—let's do this!

Also to Joth Shakerley, who was there that night at the kitchen table in Moscow and who has been there always. I love you. Your positivity, support, and deft swipe with a salted fish move mountains. You are the best of friends.

And lastly my children, Allegra and Rafe (whose knowledge of Rasputin is now encyclopedic): Thank you for letting me sit, think, and be. Thank you for your love and understanding. I love you both very much—and I promise I am now out of the office!

ABOUT THE AUTHOR

IMOGEN EDWARDS-JONES is an award-winning journalist, novelist, and screenwriter. She is the author of the bestselling Babylon series of industry exposés, which has sold over a million copies worldwide. The first book in the series was adapted into *Hotel Babylon*, the returning prime-time BBC One TV series. She is the editorial consultant on Julian Fellowes's *Belgravia*.

She read Russian at Bristol University. An honorary Cossack, she traveled extensively in the old Soviet Union, writing a travel book, *The Taming of Eagles: Exploring the New Russia*, published by Weidenfeld & Nicolson.

About the book

2 The Story Behind the Story

Read on

7 Further Reading
Other Books on or Around
the Subject

Insights,
Interviews
& More . . .

The Story Behind the Story

The story of *The Witches of St. Petersburg* has haunted me ever since my lovely friend, then war correspondent and documentary producer Nikolai Antonov, sat me down in his tiny kitchen and opened a large bottle of tepid vodka. That was more than twenty-five years ago, back in 1992, when Nik was still alive and I was a reporter for the British press, researching the story of the collapse of communism during the dying days of the Soviet Union.

Sitting around the gray, Formica-topped table in his flat in the outskirts of Moscow, Nik talked into the night and the more vodka we drank and the more pickles we ate, the greater and more magnificent the story became: two princesses who brought down an empire and destroyed a dynasty on the roll of one die. No matter how many other books I wrote, or other stories that engrossed me, those princesses would always be there, lurking in the background. It was almost as if they were biding their time, waiting for the right moment, for the stars to be aligned, in order to tell their story.

And what a story! Sisters, known as the Black Princesses because of their dark hair and pitch-black eyes, who were obsessed with black magic and the occult, who isolated the tsarina and helped her try to produce the son and heir that she so desperately needed. And then, when their power was waning, trickling through their fingers like sand, they introduced Rasputin into the Russian court. And with that, the fate of the sisters and the empire was sealed.

Having read Russian at university, I have long been fascinated by this period in history—the lavish excess, the beauty, the turbulence, and the terrible tragedy of it all. But I also have always thought that because the tsar kept himself so very isolated from his people, that what happened at home within the confines of his various splendid palaces impacted him and his rule more than most of the politics of the day. In short, this was in fact a female story that should be told from a female perspective in the hope that the fresh light might be startling and illuminating.

Researching these amazing women has been a long and arduous process. They were like wisps who danced through the pages of history, their feet so light they barely left a trace. I would find a snippet here, a sentence there, and so very few of the stories ever tallied. But what was certain and what is true was that they were there, at the heart of it all, every step of the way, with their spells and their schemes and their plans.

Their country, Montenegro, was beautiful, yet feudal at the time, with ▶

few roads, no sanitation, and no real army to speak of. Through their efforts, their negotiations, and their incredible determination as they paced the marble halls of St. Petersburg, they managed to launch their homeland forward centuries in mere decades. They secured its future. They brought it onto the world stage, creating the foundation of the modern Montenegro of today.

There have been so many brilliant and delightful moments when foraging for facts and details on the lives of Grand Duchess Militza Nikolayevna and her younger sister Grand Duchess Anastasia Nikolayevna, but none was more shocking than when I visited the basement rooms of the Yusupov Palace, where Rasputin was murdered. For there, on the wall of the palace, near the waxwork models of Rasputin and Prince Felix Yusupov and his other coconspirators was a photograph of the sisters. Their black hair and their black eyes were unmistakable; they stopped me in my tracks. It was the first time I had seen their faces. I stared. It was as if they'd been lurking there in the darkness, waiting to be discovered.

In an effort to understand their way of thinking and the skills they were capable of, I joined the London College of Psychic Studies. Formerly the London Spiritualist Alliance, it was set up at the beginning of the last century as an expression of gratitude from the bereaved of the First World War who were desperate to contact their dead fathers, sons, and lovers. It was chaired at one point by the famous Sherlock Holmes author, Sir Arthur Conan Doyle. There, I was introduced to the world of mediumship, tarot, palmistry, scrying (crystal ball reading), and many other magnificent things. The college also has one of the more fascinating libraries in the world with the most extraordinary books, some of which come from Sir Arthur Conan Doyle's personal collection.

Somewhat overwhelmed by the choice and selection on offer, I asked a friend which books I should choose. She told me simply that I should stand in the middle of the room and the books I needed would make themselves known to me. Which I did. And the first book to "leap" off the shelf was *Witchcraft* by Charles Alva Hoyt, a whole new journey in itself!

As I finished *The Witches of St. Petersburg* and stepped away from the keyboard, I have to say I felt suddenly, incredibly bereft. Militza and Stana have been with me for so long they are practically part of my own family. I have gotten married and had two children while trying to write their story, and it is now extremely hard to let go. I still think about them all the time; I still see them everywhere. Out of the corner of my eye. In the mirror when I wash my face. But ▶

The Story Behind the Story *(continued)*

most of all I hear them in the voices of women who are still struggling to be heard. For they had been painted out of history, glossed over in favor of supposedly more significant figures. But they were there, right at the center of things, they saw and heard everything, and they have an important story to tell.

I hope you enjoy reading it. Thank you. ∿

www.imogenedwardsjones.com

Further Reading
Other Books on or Around the Subject

Nicholas and Alexandra by Robert K. Massie. No one is better than Massie at explaining the grand sweeping scope of the era. I read *Nicholas and Alexandra* on the way to Australia and did not sleep all the way. My boarding pass is still inside the book as a bookmark.

The Bathhouse at Midnight—Magic in Russia by W. F. Ryan. An amazing in-depth study of magic in Russia. It was my go-to bible for all things after dark.

Rasputin—The Holy Devil by Rene Fulop-Miller. By far the juiciest, most salacious, most entertaining biography of Rasputin. First published in 1928.

Rasputin—A Short Life by Frances Welch. Small and perfectly formed, this biography is packed with detail and delight. It even has his telephone number in it—St. Petersburg 64646!

Four Sisters—The Lost Lives of the Romanov Grand Duchesses by Helen Rappaport. A fantastic book that not only humanizes the girls but also tells of their lives in incredible detail.

The Jewels of the Romanovs—Family and Court by Stefano Papi. Incredible photographs with amazing stories and sumptuous page after sumptuous page of glittering diamonds, emeralds, and pearls. Riches that you cannot believe. ▶

Further Reading *(continued)*

St. Petersburg—The Hidden Interiors by Katya Galitzine. There is no better way to orientate yourself through the plush drawing rooms of the city. Beautiful photographs and amazing historical detail. It was invaluable during my research.

Rasputin—His Malignant Influence and His Assassination by Prince Felix Youssoupoff (another way of spelling Yusupov), translated by Oswald Rayner (yes, him!). An extraordinary piece of written history!

Rasputin by Douglas Smith. Huge, thorough, and myth busting. The latest and possibly the best researched biography there is. ❧